DARK PLACES
LIGHT PLACES

Also by Jessie Gresham Zapffe

Reflections of Consciousness
THE ZODIACAL JOURNEY

DARK PLACES
LIGHT PLACES

A novel of love . . . and grace

Jessie Gresham Zapffe

sunfire productions

PO Box 1289, Mt Shasta, Ca 96067

ISBN 0-9624139-1-7
Library of Congress Cat. #90-070327

Cover Design by Mark Peyton, Ft Lauderdale, Fla
Book Design by PanDesign, Mt Shasta, Ca
Typesetting by Kim Solga Artworks, Mt Shasta, Ca
Printing by McNaughton & Gunn, Inc. U.S.A.

For Steven Labensart

June 14, 1951 - March 27, 1989

To the house of Beauty I go
Wherever she takes me, I'll go
Oh my love awaits me
And in the Darkness, she'll embrace me.

And a soft golden light
Will guide my steps through the night.
Oh my joy awakes me
And in that Brightness, I'll embrace thee.

Oct. '88

Acknowledgments

The author wishes to express her deepest gratitude to the following special people, without whose loving assistance, this production could not move forward.

My wonderful friend, Alan Mainwaring, who spent hours at my side offering me his keen insights and editing skills, and who gave me total love and support, especially when my fear began to gnaw at my soul.

Linda Rose, who has, with great poise and diligence, seemingly effortlessly typed and retyped this manuscript, always returning it to me with a smile.

Kim Solga of Kim Solga Artworks, who gave me the opportunity to pull it all together in this sleepy little hamlet, for a fraction of the cost, and twice the professionalism of a larger city.

Pan Brian Paine who took the complete manuscript and formatted everything, who is responsible for the typesetting on the cover, and whose discerning eye and positive encouragement set me at peace.

Mark Peyton for his lovely cover art.

Irene Swain for the love, joy and support she brings to my life.

My sister Carlotta K. Tutor whose loving generosity has helped me time and time again.

jgz
Mt Shasta, Ca

Chapter One

FRANCE 1770

The Port of Marseilles was teaming with activity. Another vessel had arrived from the Far East, and with it came the silks and other delicacies that were so loved by the French. Overhead, the seagulls made frenetic patterns in the blue sky, sporadically dropping down to retrieve anything that resembled food. The winter had been an unusually harsh one for the Mediterranean climate, and the birds had become increasingly aggressive in their attempts to outlive the cold spell.

Beneath their flapping wings, men were preparing the ship for a lengthy stay at port, for she had been through two severe storms which had inexorably damaged the foredeck and the hull. There would be a good month, or longer, in repair before she would set sail again.

All of the goods from the storage area had been moved up to the deck for portage onto the shore. The docks were crowded with hopeful merchants who anxiously awaited news about the arrival of their orders. Soon, their shops would be flooded with wealthy patrons excitedly anticipating the imported gifts brought in from worlds beyond their own limited horizons.

As the ship activity diminished, the seagulls became more frantic, for the garbage would inevitably be thrown overboard into the dirty waters, and their long awaited feast would begin. Their anticipation was eventually rewarded as they spotted two men, coming up from the galleys, carrying with them the meager remains of the food that had been rationed over a period that far exceeded the expectations of all of those who had weathered the voyage.

The men tried in vain to fend off the swooping birds, and eventually they ran for cover beneath the decks. "Let the little bastards have at it, mate!" One of them spat out the words to the other as they quickly descended, once again, into the galley.

As the high energy of the morning surrendered itself to the calm of the early afternoon, two men in long brown robes could be seen approaching the ship. There was nothing unusual about the monks; however, it was not often that men of the cloth came into a market as open as the Port. Since there were only a few men left to work the ship, their appearance went almost unnoticed, save for a deckhand who emerged from the shadows as the monks drew closer.

He walked out to meet them, without signaling, and watched them quietly climb aboard the vessel. The priests and the deckhand looked at one another in silence, and then the elder of the monks spoke.

"Has the package from China arrived?"

"Yes, Father," replied the deckhand. It was awkward for him to be in the presence of holy men, after six months of enduring the crude exchanges with his shipmates. "The package almost did not weather the storms. There was some concern over the food, for milk does not keep, and our two she goats died in a storm off the west coast of Africa."

"Perhaps Divine Providence was on our side." The priest spoke again. "Will you be so kind as to direct us to our merchandise?"

The deckhand turned and motioned the priests to follow him. After the intense sunlight, the inside of the ship seemed extremely dark. The monks paused until their eyes became acclimated, and then they took after the sailor who was already halfway down the narrow passageway.

At the end, there was a narrow staircase which lead them more deeply into the bowels of the vessel. The men did not speak. They stopped in front of a door which was firmly bolted. The deckhand removed a key from his pocket and, slipping it into the lock, he pushed open the door and bade them enter.

The monks were careful to lower their heads as they stepped into the cabin. The space was small and claustrophobic. There were two bunks hanging from the inside wall and a small porthole which allowed only a modicum of light to enter. The cabin itself was hardly large enough for one man, let alone the two who shared it.

[2]

When all three were inside, the deckhand shut the door firmly and faced them.

"Due to the nature of the package, I thought it best to have its quarters close to the chef's galley. There would be more warmth," he said.

"And where is the package?" the elder monk asked.

"On the lower berth."

Both monks turned toward the bunk. "Have you a lantern?" the younger asked.

"Yes, I'll light it for you."

The deckhand pulled an oil lantern from a small wall closet. He was precise in his actions, and eventually a warm glow filled the dark room.

"Bring it here, please," the younger priest spoke.

As the light intensified, the monks were able to discern the outline of a small form on the bed. The younger one took the lantern from the deckhand and brought it close for further inspection. Simultaneously, both monks knelt in front of the bed.

Before them, crudely wrapped in blankets, was a small bundle. A slight aperture at the top revealed a pair of dark almond shaped eyes, that were carefully watching their movements. The elder of the monks reached out to remove the blanket. Without the thick wool as padding, the baby's size became starkly apparent. There was no meat on his frail frame, and his body bore the markings of rough covers. Although he was dirty, one could see that his skin was more yellow than that of the olive skinned French. He lay quietly and submitted himself to the gentle handling of the two men in dark robes.

"How old is he now?" the younger asked.

"About four months," the deckhand replied. "We took him on shortly after his birth."

"How many others know of his presence?" The older monk tried not to show the concern he was feeling.

"Only two besides myself. The others left ship at Lisbon. We rotated watch over him, but none of us is used to babies. Thank God, he made little noise." The man was frankly relieved to have relinquished his care of the child to the two brothers.

[3]

Certainly he had been well paid for his silence, and for his responsibility; however, there was a gnawing feeling of guilt over the circumstances surrounding the child's passage. He also felt a somewhat paternal sorrow for the baby who, in spite of his age, had survived the strenuous voyage with such serenity. Perhaps some innate sense within the tiny being had revealed to him the inevitability of his own death, should he make his presence known to the world.

Accompanying the relief over the discharge of his duty, was an unfamiliar feeling of melancholia, for a certain bonding had taken place between the coarse deckhand and the unusual package he had helped to smuggle aboard, in the dark of the night, prior to setting sail from the Port of Macao, some three and a half months ago.

Not one for introspection, the deckhand regained his sense of duty and went over to the closet where he had found the lantern. Placing his arm inside, he reached behind some extra blankets and pulled out a small bag.

"These were sent along with the child," he said, placing the satchel on the bed.

The younger monk turned and looked at the parcel. Before opening it, he looked back at his partner who nodded his assent. He gracefully untied the knots and lifted the top flap.

Inside were several pieces of clothing and a pair of small shoes for the child. Each item was made of the finest silk and had been embroidered by masterful hands. The clothing gave them an idea of the background their protégé had left behind him. Beneath the clothes, there were several pieces of jade, amber, and a miniature gold Buddha, all worth a veritable fortune in the hungry French marketplace. The last of the contents was an envelope.

The young priest opened the parchment and pulled out a rosary that had been ornately carved in jade, the beads reflecting a rich blue-green in the dim light of the cabin. The cross was pink, with a small figure of Christ done in gold. He gave the rosary to his brother, watching him carefully for a reaction. Seeing there was none, he returned his attention to the envelope and a card which lay inside. Chinese figures extended from one side of the card to the next. Beneath them, written in English, was the name T'ien Li.

The monks looked back at the quiet child, who was unabashedly staring at them. "He certainly doesn't resemble his father," spoke the elder.

He reached over to bundle up the baby, making sure his face was covered, and then in unison, both priests stood. The younger one opened his shoulder bag and emptied it onto the bed. He held it open for the baby to be placed inside.

"Let's pray he maintains his silence," he said, for they did not want nosy officers asking questions. Turning to the deckhand he added, "You may take the contents of the bag and do with them as you will. He won't be needing anything to distinguish him now."

He watched as Brother Ambrose placed the Buddha, the rosary, and the card in the pockets of his robe. The deckhand's eyes lit up. He was aware of the value placed on jade and on silks as fine as these. He hadn't been expecting anything extra in the transfer of his charge, and this pleasant surprise would enhance his leave far more than he could imagine.

Eager to leave the bleak cabin and return to the sunlight, the monks walked toward the door. The deckhand followed them through the corridors and up to the fore deck; however, he remained in the shadows, while they bid him farewell. They walked across the deck to the plank, which led them onto the docks below.

Without looking back, and with heads bowed, the two brothers moved purposefully down the long dock toward the shore. Ahead of them were two French officials, whose curiosity they did not wish to arouse. It was not often that the officials saw priests in the Port, although they were rarely surprised. Years of working the docks had tempered their reaction to almost everything.

As the monks approached, the heavier official instinctively felt an inclination to stop them. Little escaped his attentive eye, and he proudly considered himself an expert in ferreting out smugglers and the like.

However, the morning had been unusually busy, and the Port's activity had all but died. His stomach was reminding him that it longed for a good bowl of bouillabaisse, some thick bread, and a nice bottle of wine at his favorite little café. He knew a waitress

[5]

whose face would light up at the sight of him.

"Forget it, Jacques" he whispered to himself. Aloud, he said, "Last rites for someone?"

Brother Ambrose looked calmly at him. "Yes, my friend. It was a rough voyage."

The official could find no argument. He had seen the damaged vessel and had heard that a good part of the crew had been lost at sea during the storms. But priests being called to administer last rites to a crew member? Oh well, perhaps it was an officer from a wealthy family, and the body would soon follow.

He motioned them through the gates and watched them recede into the distance. There was nothing unusual about their retreat, and his disquiet left him as they disappeared around the corner of Hotel de Ville.

* * *

Brothers Ambrose and Andrew did not alter their pace, once they were obscured from the official's view by the baroque walls of the hotel. Instead, they walked as nonchalantly as possible, until they came to the Rue de Rome where a carriage had been waiting for them.

The driver, a rotund monk, had seen them from a distance and had jumped from his seat to open the door. Without pausing, the monks stepped inside the coach, shutting the door behind them.

When the driver had resumed his seat and coaxed the horses into movement, Andrew removed his shoulder bag and laid it next to him. Inside, the baby had been lulled to sleep. With the sudden start of the coach, and his removal from the bag, he awakened and stared at his handler.

"Ambrose, will you pass me the damp rag and some oil from the basket under your seat?" Andrew asked. "Perhaps he is accustomed to a filthy body, but I feel great discomfort over it."

The elder monk passed his friend the requested items, along with some milk and bread they had brought with them. He sat quietly as Andrew bathed the small child, watching the yellow skin turn a slight shade of pink as the blood began to circulate beneath

[6]

Andrew's deft hands.

"How he survived is beyond me," Ambrose spoke to himself, as he marveled at the size of a baby who, at four months, probably weighed as much as a newborn.

When Andrew finished cleaning the infant, he rubbed olive oil over the tiny body. The almond eyes watched him in silence, goose flesh rising across his skin. He had rarely been out of his blankets, and this makeshift bath was an unpleasant novelty; however, he was also conscious of Andrew's calming gentleness, which alleviated some of the discomfort.

"There now, isn't this a difference?" the monk said, smiling at his friend. "Ambrose, please, his blanket."

Ambrose handed him a thick blanket in which to wrap the child, one which had been made from the finest fleece. Clothes were waiting for him at the monastery, and until then, this would suffice.

Andrew took the baby in his arms and dipped a crust of bread into the cool milk. He held it over the container to allow the excess milk to drip off, and then he placed it against the baby's lips.

"Oh sweet one, how hungry you are," he thought, "as you anxiously take your food. Your eyes never leave my face, as if you don't quite trust your fate in my hands." Aloud, he said, "What shall we call him, Brother?"

Ambrose remained silent. The two men had been together for years, and there was a genuine affection between them, as well as a tolerance for each other's idiosyncrasies. While Andrew acted with a fluid spontaneity, Ambrose thoughtfully calculated each word and action before its execution. This time was no different, for within him was the desire to give a name to the boy that would benefit him in his growth.

His birth name was certainly the most suitable; however, outside the walls of the monastery, it might induce curiosity. With his strongly Oriental features, the child would be an anomaly in a cloister whose inhabitants represented European heritages. It was best to distinguish him as little as possible.

Ambrose was still struggling with his own conflict over the whole situation. What would sixteen men, whose lives were devoted to Christ, do with a small baby? Their sense of family was

[7]

purely adult, and with such a young initiate, their parental awkwardness would be inevitable. He smiled inwardly at the thought.

He knew Andrew would respond well as a surrogate parent, for he had a feminine quality about him that was always nurturing to the other monks. Andrew not only loved Christ, he loved everyone. And yes, it was hard to deny the joyful energy a child would bring to the small community. Their solemnity would be laced with the wonderment of a new life.

"I, most of all, could use the gift of innocence," Ambrose thought. "It's been a while since I have felt joy over anything."

The mother had sent enough money to insure their commitment in raising the child, although Ambrose would have done anything for the boy's father. The financial assistance would keep the monastery flourishing for a number of years, a pleasant addition to the income they earned from their wool and their wines. However, with the growing political unrest in Paris, the relationship between Church and State foreshadowed ominous changes.

"Yes," he thought prophetically, "I have seen that which is to come, and this extra money will be a safeguard against that time."

Ambrose parted the curtain to look at the lush countryside. Inside his heart, a decision was made, and his feeling of sadness was replaced by acceptance. Closing the curtain, he looked back at Andrew and smiled. "We shall name him after his father. He will be called Etienne."

Andrew's face registered a slight surprise, before it was masked by his smile. "Well then, he has a grand name to live up to!" he replied.

Andrew resumed feeding Etienne, until his appetite was sated. His little belly expanded inside the soft blanket, and for the first time in his short life, he felt comfort. His eyes slowly closed as the rhythmic movement of the carriage lulled him back to sleep. The two men settled into the comfortable silence that was natural between them, as they prepared themselves for their return journey north, into the Loire Valley.

Chapter Two

His earliest recollections were of being cold within the grey stone walls of the Abbey. He would not remember arriving late in the afternoon, of the second day of his journey, with Ambrose and Andrew. Nor would he recall the monks, who were gathered at the gate, when the distant sounds of the horses drew closer.

Most of them had eagerly awaited the tiny bundle, and throughout the day, their ears were tuned to noises outside the monastic walls. With sixteen men who lived and worked so closely together, it was hard to withhold any information. Although none knew of the reasons for taking the child, each of the brothers had become aware of his imminent arrival shortly after Ambrose had made the decision.

In this small monastic order outside the town of St. Benoit-Sur-Loire, there was little of a hierarchical system. Each of the brothers had been drawn by his own inner voice to the massive gates and high walls, which cloistered them from the outside world.

The townspeople assumed they were, in some vague way, connected to the St. Benoit Abbey when, in fact, their order was not affiliated with any other church or organization. Its inhabitants freely pursued the study of philosophy through esoteric interpretations, rather than through the usual Christian dogma that was associated with monasteries. Consequently, the brothers' lives went undisturbed, and their isolation, accentuated by the thick forests, prevented all but the most curious from interrupting their routines.

Even the King and his ministers paid them little attention, for they were happy to be the recipients of plump tithes earned from the sale of lamb's wool and wines. As long as money came in, there was no need to question the nature, or the whereabouts, of the order.

Moreover, the Abbot at St. Benoit had known Brother Ambrose and his group for years, and he held them in high esteem. The nature of their order was a little mysterious to him, but he too was given a generous supply of wine and woolens. After all, why create complications that would send the King's ministers down from Paris?

It was as though nature and man were cohesively united to protect the location of the Abbey in the Forest, and those who were meant to pass through the gates would keep the secret until death.

Without the normal hierarchy, each of the monks had an equality with the others. Seniority often meant greater responsibilities, and if a brother demonstrated a particular talent, he was encouraged to use it. There was a genuine love and respect among them, that was often absent in other monasteries.

All were united through their love of Christ; however, the Church would have been shocked to hear of the teachings that were followed and would have condemned each monk as heretical. The desire of the Church to have unquestionable authority held little ground among these men for whom truth, wisdom, and individual integrity were honored. It was not a time, historically, when man had the right to pursue his own path toward self-realization. Thus, the little monastery flourished ahead of its time in a world that was soon to experience a tremendous upheaval brought about by revolution.

Life went on as usual, but on the day of Etienne's arrival the monks' routine was disrupted by their excitement over their intriguing addition to the Abbey. As the carriage pulled up outside the walls, they quietly left their work and went to open the heavy gates, which swung easily on their oiled hinges. Ambrose alighted from the coach and turned to receive Etienne from Andrew. He faced the group and held the tiny baby up for all to see.

"My dear Brothers," he said. "This is T'ien Li; however, as long as he dwells with us, we shall call him by his father's name, Etienne."

Movement, provoked by surprise, spread through the men. Brother Pasqual hurriedly stepped forward holding a small brown robe, a miniature replica of their own.

"This is for our newest initiate," he said, smiling. "We, each one of us, welcome him to his new home."

The sight of the tiny robe broke the ice among the men, who

laughed among themselves over Pasqual's ingenuity. Ambrose came forward and took the garment.

"Pasqual," he said, "you are indeed creative!" Turning to the others, he continued. "Due to the chill in the monastery now, Etienne's bed will be placed in the kitchen near the ovens. He belongs to all of us, as one of us. He was drawn into these circumstances for a special reason, which we can only surmise. Now let us resume our lives as before."

Thus it was that Etienne was carried behind the walls of the Abbey in the Forest to live with the brothers. Etienne of the almond eyes and yellow skin. Etienne, born into a part of the world none of them would ever see.

He was taken into the kitchen and laid in his crib, after a careful change and some food, and then left alone while the monks gathered in the chapel for their evening meditation.

Etienne did not sleep. His eyes took in everything they could see in the dim light, while his psyche tried to absorb the new energy around him. In spite of his warm robe, the chill of the evening settled into his small body. He grew uncomfortable, but he had been tempered by his harrowing life at sea, where his fearful cries went unheard in the fury of the storms. He did not complain, for he had learned that his wailing would go unheeded, and he diverted his attention from the cold to the lengthening shadows which crawled across the room.

* * *

Ambrose was in the library when Tristan found him. The latter knew that Ambrose often spent his hours in contemplation among his beloved books. It was here that he would read the news of the growing turbulence in France, especially in Paris where the poor were becoming increasingly intolerant over their desperate plight. It was here where he would also read his mail. A few letters had arrived sporadically from China, their appearance temporarily lifting Ambrose's spirits.

After Etienne's departure several years ago, Ambrose had been despondent. The monks were aware of the bonding between the two brothers; however, they were surprised at Ambrose's attachment. They never quite knew the reason for Etienne's sudden embarkation on a journey that would take him across Europe and through China into Peking, via the Silk Road. Unknown to them, an unresolved quarrel between the two had precipitated the event.

Ambrose had never shared his feelings of loss. News of Etienne's arrival had come from Peking months after it had been sent, a period that had seemed like an eternity to Ambrose.

Etienne had previously been a Jesuit priest, who had come to the Abbey after a disappointing exclusion from a prestigious position in Rome. He was guided to St. Benoit-Sur-Loire by a succession of dreams, which had mystically instructed him to the gates of the monastery.

Being the scholar that he was, he had been thrilled to find such an extensive library, and one which needed to be supplemented by his erudite knowledge. And so, Etienne had joined the brothers to add his own uniqueness to the order. He and Ambrose immediately became good friends, and they spent hours in the library enjoying the silence of reading, writing, and meditating.

The last news to reach Ambrose from China was that of Etienne's untimely death. There were no explanations given for it. Ambrose was unable to conceal his grief from the other brothers, although he tried to do so. He cloistered himself among his beloved books, until one day the ravaging sorrow lightened itself within his heart, and he was again able to walk among his peers with the peace he had once carried. When the letter had arrived regarding Etienne's child, Ambrose found a renewed sense of purpose. The man, whom he had so dearly loved, had left a living legacy!

For a long moment, Tristan stood in the doorway unnoticed. He was observing his friend. It was good to have the old Ambrose back, for he had long been the pillar of strength among the small community. Ambrose's presence was a soothing balm to them all.

"Ambrose," Tristan spoke quietly, not wanting to disturb his reverie. "Have you plans for the child?"

Ambrose turned and looked at Tristan's inquisitive expression. It never ceased to amaze him how one so young could be so mature and purposeful. His dark eyes shone in his expressive face. Tristan had never regarded the age difference between them, for to him, their physical vehicles housed ageless souls.

Tristan had entered the order when he was a youthful eighteen, and he had spent three years proving his intent, before he was fully accepted into the community. Ambrose, at fifty, regarded him as a son. He knew any father would have been proud to claim the handsome and intelligent young man as his own, although there was some mystery regarding his background.

In the seven years Tristan had been in the monastery, he had never received any correspondence or visitors. Perhaps one day he would reveal his past. What was important was Tristan's solicitous care of the sheep that brought forth such fine wool year after year. Although Pasqual saved some of it for blankets and clothes for the monastery, much of it was sold for a good profit.

"Why, we shall raise him here as one of us." Ambrose's reply was slow in coming.

"Do you think it is in his best interest to be given a childhood among adult men?"

"My dear Tristan," Ambrose smiled at him, "where else can we place him? There is absolutely no choice. He would have been killed in China, and he would never survive outside the monastery. Have you another suggestion?"

"No, I suppose not. I was just concerned about our adequacy in parenting."

"You mean you are concerned about the fact that it's the first time for all of us?" They both smiled at the thought, and Ambrose continued. "Tristan, there are no trial runs with parenting. What is, is. This is to be Etienne's life as he chose it. We are merely guides for him."

"How will we relegate the care?" Tristan had visions of the little child running after his sheep, sending them in all directions. He was fiercely possessive of his animals and treated them like royalty!

"I think everything will work itself out. You know I have the time, as does Andrew, and the child will integrate with all of us."

"Brother, your optimism amazes me!" Tristan exclaimed. "I would hope that one day you will enlighten me on his background."

"We both have things to share with one another, Tristan, when the time is right," Ambrose replied mysteriously. He stood to end the conversation. "And now, I must attend to our new charge."

Together, they left the library, Tristan going to the chapel and Ambrose to the kitchen. It was late afternoon, the day after little Etienne's arrival, and Ambrose had some concern over the baby's adjustment. He had already looked in on him several times.

Etienne had spent the day watching the movements in the kitchen, silently taking in the dynamics at play among the brothers. Each time Ambrose had entered the room, Etienne's gaze had fallen upon him. A certain bonding was already taking place between the two in the etheric worlds, and the wise soul within the diminutive frame recognized this.

Ambrose lifted the baby. "My son," he whispered into his ear, "it is time for you to begin your lessons with me. We shall start by walking through the Abbey to familiarize you with your new home."

The chefs, Brothers François and Charles, watched their friend squeeze the little fellow's legs to check them for warmth, before carrying him from the kitchen, his scrawny yellow face peering back at them from Ambrose's firm shoulder. Together, the man and boy child examined every room, with the exception of the wine cellar. It was too cold to step outside, but tomorrow hinted at the promise of sun, and there was all the time in the world for the two to explore.

Ambrose considered the irony of a child of Oriental birth being raised with a Christian background. "Ah," he mused, "worse fates have befallen others."

Etienne registered the sights and the feel of the Abbey with equanimity. There was comfort for him in Ambrose's heartbeat, which he could feel beneath the robes. His experience had not lent itself to being carried much. For the first time in his life, he welcomed the sensation of warmth. The two of them were quite a pair with the little head and almond shaped eyes bouncing against Ambrose's grey beard and brown shoulder.

The halls were long and dark, with doors that led into individual cells and storage rooms. On the inside wall, there were larger doors, intermittently spaced, which opened onto a spacious courtyard.

The entire monastery was built around this courtyard, and in the spring and summer, the doors would remain open, so that the beauty of its trees and flowers could be seen from the halls. This precious space was a favorite among the monks, and it was here that they would commune with one another under the sun, or under the stars, soaking up the abundant verdure.

From the far side of the monastery, the sound of bells beckoned the monks to their evening meditation. Ambrose carried Etienne swiftly, his robes making a swishing sound in the long hallways. They entered the chapel quietly, and Ambrose took his customary seat near the front. The room was very simple, with the exception of three very beautiful stained glass windows that filtered rays of sunlight through their rich colors. Beneath the windows was a large altar, upon which were placed two candelabras and a cross. Behind the altar and running against the walls, were velvet covered benches. A single candle was lit to represent the monks' unity with all life.

Ambrose sat with Etienne on his lap. The little one's eyes found the light of the candle and fixed their gaze upon it. It would not have been in character for him to fuss, and he remained silent with the others, until the sound of the small bell ended their reverie. One by one, the monks stood and left, leaving Ambrose and Andrew behind with the child.

Astonished, Ambrose asked his friend, "Who is this soul who accepts the tradition of silence so well?"

"He is one to whom God has shown His quality of mercy," Andrew replied wisely.

* * *

Etienne settled into the routine of monastic life with great ease. When the brothers arose at four-thirty in the morning for their meditation, he would be awakened by the rustling of robes moving past the kitchen on their way to the chapel. He would lie peacefully, until François and Charles came in to prepare the hot cereal for

[15]

breakfast. Eventually, either Ambrose or Andrew entered the kitchen to lift Etienne from his makeshift bed and to ready him for his presence among the others.

Each day was different. Sometimes, Pasqual would take Etienne and place him on piles of thick wool. There, Etienne sat and watched the wool being spun into thread and later made into robes and blankets.

Pasqual was from the provincial town of Lourdes, near the Pyrenees, and he sang songs as he worked. Spanish, picked up from his childhood, filtered into Etienne's mind along with the French. Pasqual offered a necessary aspect to the baby's life, in that he lacked the solemnity of the other brothers. Whenever the need for levity arose, it was Pasqual who offered his delightful personality.

Hence, Etienne learned to appreciate the joyful monk, for although Ambrose gave him love, there was also a quiet sorrow about the elder. Pasqual's upturned mouth, and his sing-song voice, mesmerized the little one who, himself, was very serious.

Tristan would tie the baby on his back and take him out to watch the flocks of sheep. Etienne's eyes were often so busy taking in the sights of the stately trees, the birds, and the squirrels, that the sheep were almost of secondary importance. How, in the freshness of spring, he loved the feel of the cool grass against his face!

Ambrose was preparing the extraordinary child to be another scholar. It was he who began the early disciplines, when, at six months, Etienne had learned to sit alone. Ambrose would place him upon the massive oak table and read aloud to him from books of knowledge so rare, their beauty became the timbre of his voice, their truth illuminated his face.

Next to Etienne's plump little legs, Ambrose would place the jade rosary, and the gold Buddha. These signified to Etienne that a different energy was about to fill the room, and that he was to sit quietly and listen. His dark hair stood straight up, framing his yellow face and dark eyes. François had a habit of using olive oil to force the hair down, but eventually, it would revert to its upward position. If anything, Ambrose was overly zealous with his small pupil; however, with Pasqual and the others, a necessary balance was maintained.

[16]

His body lost its emaciated look as he filled up on milk, breads, and fruit. Gradually small dimples showed up on his knees, his cheeks rounded, and his little belly extended itself under his robe. By eight months, he was crawling. To facilitate his movement, and to protect his knees from getting scraped by the stone floors, Pasqual made several small pairs of pants and some short robes.

One evening, as the brothers sat in meditation, Etienne crawled off his bench and began to walk. His intent was to get closer to the candle, which he had been watching for months. The uneven patter of feet ended the meditation well before the tinkling of the bell.

There was a celebration that night in the dining room over Etienne's adventurous accomplishment. Charles slipped him an extra rice cake, which he joyfully shoved into his mouth. At the height of the celebration, when the gaiety was strong enough to provoke him, Etienne laughed aloud for the first time.

That he was fifteen months made no difference at all. The tiny sound of his laughter, brought tears to the eyes of the brothers. Thinking he had done something wrong to induce the sudden silence, Etienne stopped laughing and looked uncertainly at the monks.

Feeling awkward, he lowered his eyes and began to play with the remainder of the rice cake. Sensing his discomfort, Andrew got up and went to hold the small child. The moment of levity had passed, and each man at the long table thought about the joy, and the responsibility, of this living gift. The question of his destiny did not fail to cross anyone's mind.

Chapter Three

When there is a pleasant routine and when one does not hurry from one experience to the next, there is no anxiety over time's passing, and it gently carries on into the future. Thus it was at the Abbey in the Forest. Etienne grew. The others, never noticing their own age, were conscious of each year that passed for him. He had just turned three, and winter was approaching.

The afternoon was lending itself to the chill of evening, and Ambrose was in the library reading while Etienne sat next to him, his feet dangling over the edge of a large chair. He had had a long day with no nap, and his eyelids were growing heavy as he languorously settled more deeply into the chair. Suddenly the peaceful silence was shattered by Andrew and Tristan, who simultaneously pushed open the library doors and walked into the room with purposeful strides.

"Ambrose," Tristan said, "I think you had better come to the front gates!" His face showed a quizzical concern.

"What is it?"

"There's a driver outside the walls with a carriage," Andrew replied. "He has something inside which he insists must be delivered to you and to no one else."

Ambrose moved swiftly out of his chair. He looked over at Etienne who was now fully alert, his dark eyes fixed intensely upon Tristan and Andrew.

"Watch Etienne, Tristan. Andrew, come with me."

The monks walked out of the library and down the halls to the front doors where François and Pasqual were standing. As the two brothers approached, they opened the doors for them and then followed, without closing the doors behind them.

The massive gates were opened to reveal a somewhat impatient driver standing in front of a well worn carriage. He refrained from talking until the monks were standing before him.

"Which one of you is Ambrose?" he asked.

"I am called by that name," Ambrose said, stepping forward.

"Then this is for you!"

The driver turned, opened the door of the carriage, and stepped inside, momentarily out of their sight. A bag was flung out which landed at the monks' feet with a dull thud. The four brothers looked up to see what would be coming next.

From inside, the shuffling of the driver indicated a weightier object. His back came into view, and it was apparent that his arms were wrapped around something. As he laboriously turned, they saw it was a man. Grunting and puffing, more from his own weight than from that of the body he carried, he positioned himself to avoid falling, and then he threw the body out of the coach onto the cold ground.

Ambrose bent down quickly and turned the figure over. "Who is this?" he demanded.

"That's none of my business!" the driver responded, his surly attitude intimating that his role was finished. "I was just paid to do my job." His fat lips rolled up, and he spat upon the ground.

"Do you know where he came from?" Andrew asked.

"Look at his face. That'll tell you." With those words, the driver climbed aboard his seat, grabbed his whip, and without looking around, commanded the horses to move.

The deafening noise of the coach became more muted as it was swallowed by the thick forest. Finally, it was distant enough that the horses hooves were barely audible, and then all was silent again. The four men stood dumbfounded around the small figure.

"We can't see much out here," Ambrose said. "Let's get him inside."

François and Pasqual lifted the body and carried him ahead of Andrew and Ambrose, who closed the outside gates and the front doors. They walked into the light of the kitchen, where the man was placed on a large table.

"My God!" François exclaimed. "Don't tell me he, too, has come from China!"

"Is he still alive?" Pasqual asked, placing his hand on the man's wrist. "Yes," he answered his own question, "there's a faint pulse."

"Good!" Ambrose was fully alert. "Let's wash him up. He

smells half dead. Pasqual, get some clothes. François, heat some water. Andrew, we need some rags and soap."

Ambrose began to loosen the filthy clothes, which were so well fitted to his form that he suspected they had been worn for months. The yellow skin was caked with dust which did little to camouflage the large sores on the body. His flesh hung from the bones.

Andrew returned with rags, warm water, soap, and some salve. "It appears that our friend has been traveling for months," he said.

"Yes. I wonder how he made it this far," Ambrose replied.

"He almost didn't."

Ambrose gave a rag to each monk, and they began the task of cleaning the half dead man. Pasqual brought in a robe, and after laying it near the warm stove, he went to help the others.

Silently, they worked on the body, cleaning the debris that had coagulated in the sores, removing the grey film, and wrapping the wounds after each one had been covered with salve. His head was filled with lice. The lye soap was strong enough to kill them, but to prevent the possibility of infestation, they shaved his hair, letting it fall onto the floor.

"Andrew, burn his clothes and everything in his bag that looks suspect," Ambrose commanded. "François, make sure you and Charles clean this area of the kitchen very well."

The monks were so engrossed in their work, that they failed to hear the bells calling them to meditation. It was rare that anyone missed the evening gathering. Tristan had, once or twice, when a few of his lambs had strayed too far, and occasionally, one of the brothers would succumb to ill health. Each absence was noticed, for it changed the energy in the chapel. On this evening, with four of the monks missing, the remaining twelve found it difficult to meditate. Instead, they were hard pressed to solve the mystery.

This was not unusual for them. They were all so connected to one another that, in a sense, they shared the same consciousness. There was a deep love and respect among them, born of a sense of a unified family. Rarely was there any disparity between the monks.

The gentle tinkle of the bell, which signified the end of the

[20]

evening prayers, had barely sounded, when the brothers rose and hurried from the chapel. They walked as a group, with Etienne running behind them, down the halls toward the kitchen. The sudden entrance of twelve men into the kitchen startled the others who were just completing their arduous task. The small crowd surrounded the man, still unconscious, lying on the table. Etienne, riddled with curiosity, found his little bench that Brother James had made for him and pulled it over to the others. Positioning it between Andrew and Ambrose, he climbed up and leaned against the table.

He stared at the man who, in the wake of all the activity, stirred. Hesitantly, he opened his eyes, and when he was able to focus them, it was Etienne whom he first saw. The child gingerly extended his arm and touched the Oriental eyes gently with his fingers. He then withdrew his hand and touched his own. "My eyes," he said. Etienne had spent almost three years memorizing every detail of the brothers' faces, assuming his was the same. In the fall, he had been allowed to sit near the pool in the inner courtyard, and he had been surprised to see his own reflection revealing a flatter face and eyes that turned upward.

It didn't register with him that he was different. What did strike him was the similarity between this man and himself. He reached over again and touched the man's face. The man smiled weakly and ceremoniously bowed his head, before losing consciousness. Everyone watched, fascinated.

"Let's get him to a bed, Brothers, and leave the kitchen to François and Charles," Ambrose spoke quietly.

Dinner was late that evening, and the air was heavy with unspoken questions. Ambrose felt a sense of disquiet over how much he should reveal to the others. His final decision was to remain silent for a while longer.

Aloud, he said, "I am well aware of your curiosity, but it will go unsated for the time being. This is purely for the protection of the child."

"Ambrose, you know we never speak outside of these walls," Tristan said.

"Brother, I trust each one of you implicitly," Ambrose

responded. "I do not want Etienne to deduce anything unusual. He's an exceptional being and highly sensitive to your thoughts and feelings."

"Of course, it shall be as you wish," Tristan conceded, and the others nodded in agreement.

* * *

When François and Charles entered the kitchen in the morning, the stranger was there, sitting next to Etienne's bed. The brothers looked at one another and then back at the man, whose eyes were closed.

"His appearance certainly has improved since last night," François whispered.

"Let's offer him some food," Charles replied. "He looks half starved."

They carried the wood in from a storage shed outside and placed it into the belly of a large stove. Within minutes, a fire was burning, sending its heat throughout the spacious room.

François brought in some grains, cheese and goat's milk, while Charles drew some water from the well. Traditionally, they traded tasks every morning without ever discussing it. While the water was heating, Charles began the preparations for baking bread, for on this day, as on every Wednesday and Saturday, thirty loaves of french bread were turned out of the warm ovens.

Eventually, the smell of hot cereal filled the kitchen. François put some in a bowl, added some bread and cheese, and carried it over to the stranger. After laying it on the floor in front of him, he gently tapped his shoulder to arouse him. When the man opened his eyes, François pointed to the food. The stranger looked at it without moving, and then he picked up the bowl and cradled it in his slender hands.

"In spite of his appearance, he has a patrician aura about him," François mused to himself. He turned away from the man and walked back to resume his chores.

"My name is Chen Ken," the man said quietly.

Both François and Charles spun around and faced him. "You speak French?" they asked in unison.

"Only little. I study your friend Etienne. He teach me."

Speaking was difficult for him, as he was still very weak. He gracefully placed a piece of bread, soaked in milk, into his mouth and savored its presence on his palate before swallowing it.

"I tell you more later. Now, I appreciate food and gain strength." He lowered his head and became fully absorbed in his eating.

When he had finished, he placed the bowl on the floor and turned toward Etienne who had awakened. From his crib, he had been observing this latest addition to the monastery, quietly studying every feature including the bald head and long mustache. When Chen turned to look at him, Etienne expressed a delicate smile.

"How are you, little one?" Chen asked.

"Fine," he replied shyly.

"What they call you here?"

"Etienne." The child was unused to Chen's rustic French.

He had been in the presence of those who spoke the language impeccably, but the quiet gentleness of the man allowed him the freedom to respond. He recognized a similarity between the two of them, although he was too young to place it.

Chen looked up to see Ambrose walking toward him. With a sense of renewed strength he stood up, awkwardly leaning on the bed for support. When his eyes met Ambrose's, he put the palms of his hands together and bowed.

"You Ambrose," he stated.

"How do you know this?" Ambrose asked, taken aback.

"By your friend Etienne's description. He say you tall with grey hair and beard, and you have very kind face. He say I would know you by energy you carry. I know all of you, for Etienne have great love inside for all his brothers. Often he spoke of you, who he call Ambrose. No?"

Mixed feelings arose within Ambrose. "And who might you be?"

"I am here to assist T'ien Li grow to manhood."

"Who sent you?"

"I not feel well. Perhaps we seat?" Chen replied.

"Can you walk a short distance?" Ambrose asked, apprehensive over what Chen might disclose regarding himself and Etienne's father.

"I try, with great persistence."

Ambrose leaned down to hug Etienne who jumped into his arms. The smile on the child's face was so big that his eyes were pressed shut. "Good day, little one. Did you sleep with the angels?"

"Yes. Yes, Ambrose! I sleep with angels!" he answered gleefully.

Chen watched the interaction, his inscrutable face revealing nothing. He waited patiently until Ambrose beckoned him to follow. Seeing Chen's painfully laborious movement, he stepped back to assist him. Slowly they made their way to the library.

Ambrose motioned the visitor to sit on one of the large chairs, but Chen indicated a preference for the rug. When he was settled in a cross legged position, with his spine erect, he nodded to Ambrose.

"Please tell me the circumstances which brought you here." Ambrose spoke very slowly, enunciating each syllable.

"I scholar like Etienne," he began hesitatingly. Chen was not a man of many words, even in his native dialect. "I also monk. T'ien Li's mother trust me with her life. Her heart broken after she send child away, for she worry about his safety."

"I see in way of things that T'ien Li safe and happy. But she insist I come. 'If I knew you with him, Chen, my burden lift,' she say. I watch her grow pale and thin. Not right for woman in her position. I do not judge her action that make baby. But she have many people to care for. She has responsibility that she neglect. I need to change this course she on."

"I take action for her sake, for sake of her people. I go to her and give my decision. She show joy for first time in months. She give me silks and other treasures to insure my passage. I came by Silk Road. I came by sea. Long journey. Twice I attacked by men who see value in what I carry."

"I left to die twice. Twice I helped by kind people. Good man put me on coach to come here. I give him last of my jade. Driver unhappy with long journey. I sick, but he do not stop for five days. This is my story."

The barrage of words, Ambrose would come to realize, were the lengthiest Chen would ever speak. He had been trained in silence to view the physical world with detachment and to see beyond it into the supersensible worlds. Chen knew that he would never return to China without T'ien Li, and he was prepared to remain at the monastery until it was time for the child to go back.

Ambrose looked at him thoughtfully. It was apparent that Chen would be another addition to the Abbey, and there would be little choice involved. Chen had already made that decision, and Ambrose could hardly ignore the man's sense of purpose. He, himself, did not know where Etienne's future lay, or whether they were pawns in a grander scheme of things; however, the brothers could not deny the child a more balanced upbringing, whereby his native traditions would be merged with theirs.

"What are your plans for Etienne?" Ambrose asked, wondering about this unexpected turn of events for himself and the monastery.

"No plans necessary. I serve T'ien Li," was the reply.

"Very well. I'll arrange to put you in the room closest to the kitchen. This summer we shall move Etienne into his own room." Ambrose spoke clearly so that Chen was sure to understand him.

"Very well," Chen replied.

"And now I have work to do, my friend. You are welcome to remain in this room; however, you may wish to be shown around the Abbey.

"T'ien Li show me." He stood and bowed to Ambrose, and then he turned and slowly walked out of the library.

[25]

Chapter Four

It was summertime at the Abbey. The monastery was surrounded by lush green forests filled with wildlife. The vineyard was brimming with juicy purple grapes, and the sheep hungrily grazed the soft grasses. Etienne was eight and a half. He and Chen were in the Abbey courtyard.

Chen was more formidable looking than ever to the child, who had first laid eyes on him in his pitiful post travel condition. Five years of abbey life had fleshed out the small man whose muscular compactness was belied by the robes he wore. His hair had grown back around the sides of his head, but his pate was smooth and brown. His summer coloring, acquired from hours in the bright sunlight, intensified the fierceness of his piercing gaze.

Etienne knew exactly where he stood with the other monks, whereas, with Chen, there was always an uncertainty. He was never able to extract privileges from Chen the way he could from Ambrose, although there was no doubt of Chen's devotion to the child.

Everyone loved the Chinese scholar-monk who surrendered himself entirely to the brothers and Etienne. He served them all tirelessly and had become a shining example of devotion among his European peers.

Ambrose was standing in one of the corridor doorways, looking into the courtyard where Chen was instructing the boy. He observed how resolutely diligent the child was in learning everything he was taught. At eight, he was developing an aura of grace and dignity. No longer was he the funny looking child whose hair always smelled of François' olive oil.

His bone structure was refined, quite like that of his father's. Ambrose remembered Etienne, the father, and his exquisite hands deftly fingering the lyre which had been put into storage after his departure. "I must bring out that instrument," Ambrose thought to himself. "Perhaps Etienne has his father's gift of music."

Etienne's flawless skin was not as yellow as it had been when he had arrived at the Abbey. In fact, Chen was more purely Chinese, whereas Etienne had an element of the French olive coloring. It was his face that betrayed his heritage. His eyes were large and dark and slanted elegantly upwards. There was no argument concerning his beauty.

"Certainly not the traditional concept of good looks," Ambrose mused, "but in another ten years, he could cause quite a stir in the French Courts!"

How he loved to watch Etienne! His blue eyes softened at the sight of him, and his heart opened to the warmth of the love that filled it.

"Now T'ien Li," Chen was saying, "concentrate with eyes closed and tell me each movement you make while walking in my direction. What you thought. What you saw."

"I began walking toward you with my right foot. One of my arms, my left one, was placed against my belt," Etienne replied. "At first, I thought about the beginning of my lesson, and then that thought was replaced by the sight of you. On the way, I stopped and bent to pick up this leaf with my right hand."

"You were watching me, and I remember noticing, as I always do, how your whole attention was fixed on my movement. That is all," he concluded.

"Did you also think about taking swim in courtyard pool to give relief to heat? Did you not admire beauty around you?"

"Yes, I did! How do you know these things, Chen? Do you always see into people's minds?" Chen always surprised him, sometimes unnervingly so.

"I do not read minds unnecessarily. Yours, I know like the lily that grows behind my back in water. You must observe your thoughts! Your actions! Begin with Self. Know the Self and you know the world. No need to travel anywhere. All right here." Chen tapped Etienne's heart. "Now, sit and clear mind for short while."

Etienne sat obediently, his legs crossed, his back erect, and began to empty his mind. When thoughts raced through, he watched them, as Chen had taught; however, he did not hold onto any one in particular. Whenever he did, Chen tapped Etienne lightly on the head as an indicator to free the thought.

[27]

At first, this frightened Etienne, but he grew accustomed to Chen's teaching methods, and he was eventually able to sit, empty of mind, for at least fifteen minutes. Although Chen was a stern teacher, he never exhausted his pupil. Etienne always looked forward to the day's lessons. At the appropriate time, Chen rubbed his hands together, and they would open their eyes.

"Good lesson today, T'ien Li. Now go to Ambrose who waits in doorway behind me."

Etienne looked to see Ambrose standing there smiling at him. He looked back at his teacher and recalled that Chen had never turned around.

"How did you know he was there?"

"I feel his energy. Now go."

Etienne made a formal bow and ran through the courtyard into Ambrose's arms. "Hello, Ambrose!" he exclaimed.

"Tristan needs you in the fields today," Ambrose said, hugging him. "Would you like to help him?"

"Oh yes! Can I go now?"

"Of course. No running in the Abbey, Etienne!" Ambrose watched him until he rounded the corner, and then he listened for the doors to open before walking outside to sit with Chen.

"May I join you, Chen?" he asked quietly.

"Always, Ambrose. I never ask you if I may stay in Abbey. I tell you I stay. I expect same from you. Timidity not necessary."

Chen's French had not perfected itself over the years. His verbs were still largely spoken in the present tense, while only his vocabulary had expanded. "What your desire?"

"What have you heard from Etienne's mother?" he asked.

"She want to come see her son for herself."

"Will she?" Ambrose held his breath, waiting for Chen's response.

"T'ien Li's mother, noble soul. She do what she please. She just wait for opening in time, then she slip through."

"But travel is still so dangerous. And the distance..." Ambrose doubted she would ever attempt such a journey.

"That woman have strength of ten tigers. I saw her weak once. After her son left."

[28]

"Will she want to bring him back?" Ambrose tried not to admit his attachment to Etienne, even to himself; however, Chen knew the depths of his love for the boy.

"We see. Wait and see."

Ambrose stood and left the courtyard, re-entering the hallway. Time would certainly give him all of the answers, that he knew Chen already had. He felt a deep respect for the man whose simple sagacity was displayed with such humility. Chen kept his knowledge to himself, never undermining anyone at the monastery.

His presence among the brothers was a quiet example of awareness without glory, and although their principle beliefs differed, their knowledge of the Truth was the same. Yes, Chen's unfettered wisdom was a welcome aspect of Divine Grace.

Ambrose made his way into the library to pick up his mail. Among the letters was one from the Abbot at St. Benoit Abbey requesting Brothers Ambrose and Andrew for tea the following afternoon. The letter piqued Ambrose's curiosity. Audiences with the Abbot were rare, for he spent an inordinate amount of time in Paris. Moreover, it was not the time for him to receive his annual gift of wines and wool.

"Oh, well," Ambrose said to himself, putting the letter aside, "tomorrow will bring answers to all of my questions."

* * *

The monks were seated for breakfast when Ambrose brought up the subject of the Abbot. "Andrew and I have been requested for tea today at St. Benoit."

"That's unusual. What in heaven's name does he want?" Tristan asked.

"We don't know," Andrew replied. "Has anyone heard anything in the village? James, you were there a few days ago. François? Charles?"

The men shook their heads in unison, and James answered for all of them. "The villagers pay no attention to us, Andrew. We blend in with the scenery."

"Yes, Etienne and I saw hardly anyone when we went for kitchen supplies. Perhaps it's nothing to be concerned about, Ambrose," François added.

"Well," Ambrose concluded, "I just prefer to be forewarned in dealing with outsiders. You know of the unrest in Paris. We can never tell when the tides will turn."

He looked around at his brothers who nodded in agreement. Chen, who was sitting next to Etienne, was silent. There was a slight smile on his face, and yet it was more a smile of resignation than one of happiness, for Ambrose recognized the hint of sorrow that had briefly passed through his eyes.

Unknowingly, Chen had given Ambrose insight. From where the soul speaks its unquestionable wisdom, before it becomes transformed by the will of the personality, he knew that this meeting would have unpleasant overtones. "Oh well," Ambrose thought to himself, "at least I am not going into this blinded by my ideals."

Aloud, he said, "Etienne, I'm moving your lessons back one hour. There are a few matters that need my attention. Have you studied your English history sufficiently, so that I might test you?"

"Yes, Father," Etienne replied obediently.

"Very well. You may take the extra time to choose your own activity. Incidentally," he paused, "I have taken the lyre out of storage and placed it into the empty room next to the library. Be careful with it, as it's very fragile."

Andrew and Tristan smiled, knowing the veracity of this statement. The lyre was a relic that had somehow surfaced at the Abbey. Brother James, in addition to his carpentry skills, had been able to pull from himself another talent, for it was he who had restored the instrument and had prepared it for Etienne's father. Ambrose had returned it to James the day before for a tuning, and now it was waiting for the child's small fingers to become the heartbeat that would bring it to life.

Etienne was thrilled with the opportunity to have yet another activity for himself. His innate curiosity was unceasingly diverse, and it was not enough that he voluntarily helped all of the brothers in their jobs. Ultimately, he would refine himself to choose a single focus, but at this point in his young life, he was encouraged to explore all facets of experience.

"May I take it into the courtyard, Ambrose?" he asked.

"Not yet. Learn to create music with it first. When your fingers make it sing, it will become yours, and you may do with it as you please."

"All right. Excuse me, please." He stood up from his seat, collected his dishes, and carried them into the kitchen.

"Apart from his face, I'd say that Etienne mirrors his father," Tristan said to the others.

"T'ien Li only himself. He his own individual," Chen softly interjected.

"Yes, of course, Chen! You are absolutely right!" Tristan laughed.

One by one, the brothers excused themselves and left the dining room, leaving an array of dishes in the kitchen for Charles and François to clean. Each monk went to perform his chores, beginning the day with a full stomach and peace of mind.

All but Ambrose. The elder brother carried within him a growing sense of disquiet over the forthcoming meeting Abbot Martin de Fleury had petitioned. Occasionally, when he and Etienne had been in the village, they had seen a few of the Benedictine monks purchasing supplies. Ambrose had recognized a face or two from the yearly visits with the Abbot, which were often tedious, but which insured his silence regarding the Abbey in the Forest. St. Benoit Abbey would be hard pressed to acquire finer wool than what they received from the brothers.

With a variety of office work to do, Ambrose was kept occupied for the next several hours. Somehow, the more practical aspects of running the monastery had been left to him, and it was an area in which he was not only fully qualified, but one which he loved. He was deeply engrossed in the budget, when Andrew interrupted his train of thought to remind him of the time.

"Shall we feed the hungry wolves, Brother?" Andrew asked, his slender face revealing a sardonic expression.

"Is it time?" Ambrose replied, standing. His body was stiff from holding the same position for so long.

[31]

"The carriage is waiting outside the gates."

"Let me freshen up a little, Andrew." Ambrose stifled a yawn. "I'll join you in a few minutes."

He left the library to change his clothes, and it was not long before he and Andrew climbed into the carriage. They were surprised to see Chen seated inside.

"Chen, what are you doing here?" Ambrose exclaimed.

"I need fresh air. Long for ride through countryside," Chen replied laconically.

Both of the men knew Chen had another purpose, but they could see nothing in his face that revealed what it might be. Andrew signaled to Brother Gerard to leave, and the men rode in silence, each one immersed in his own thoughts.

The distance was not great, and soon the little town loomed on the horizon, beyond the trees which were becoming less dense. Unlike the Abbey in the Forest, which was a secluded walk from the water, St. Benoit was built right on the Loire River. Dominating the entire village was the Abbey church, an austere piece of Romanesque architecture which had been built in the seventh century.

It had, over the years, become a great learning center in spite of having suffered the ravaging effects of wars. However, those times were past, and the present Abbot, with his political connections, made certain that the Abbey flourished nicely.

The brothers from the Abbey in the Forest had little desire to turn their monastery into the full scale operation that Abbot de Fleury ran, for the element of privacy, which they all cherished, would be completely lost amidst the circus like atmosphere. Ambrose wondered how much time Abbot de Fleury had for contemplation.

The carriage pulled up to the Abbot's plush quarters and came to a full stop. Chen watched as Ambrose and Andrew alighted. The cobblestone felt uneven under the monks' feet, yet it was solid after the bumpy ride.

"Chen," Andrew said, "we do not know how long we shall be. I hope your errands will occupy some time."

"No worry," Chen replied. "I be here."

[32]

He waved them off and watched, concealed by the inside of the carriage, as they walked up the stone steps and sounded the knocker on the large door. After the door had opened to receive them and then closed behind them, Chen tapped against the driver's wall. "Pull into shade, Gerard. We wait there for our friends."

Inside the house, Ambrose could smell the odors coming from the kitchen as they were led past it into a small, elegantly appointed library.

"His Grace will be with you shortly," the doorman said. He bowed and left the room.

The brothers examined their surroundings while they waited for the Abbot. In front of them were two large french windows which opened onto balconies that overlooked the streets. Lush, burgundy velvet drapes in thick folds framed them, while panels of very fine white lace covered each door. There was a relatively small library, - both men noticed the recently published and extremely controversial *Encyclopedia.* Other books, apparently favored by the French Court, filled the shelves, which were set back into ornately carved walls.

Four large chairs, which faced each other in front of the windows, dominated the room. Their massive legs and feet supported burgundy and cream tapestried seats and backs. The arm rests could easily hold the weight of a man. "A man of normal size would be swallowed by these chairs," Ambrose thought, "but certainly not the Abbot!"

The only other piece of furniture in the room was an oversized oak table, which was empty except for silver goblets and crystal decanters of sherry, wine, and port, for guests' consumption. The entire floor was covered with an exquisite Aubusson carpet, a status symbol with Sagliere's insignia woven into one corner. The little town of Aubusson had received its claim to fame with her master weavers and visiting artists working together to turn out functional masterpieces.

In the hallway, the sound of footsteps drew closer. Brothers Andrew and Ambrose turned to greet Abbot de Fleury as he huffed his way into the room. "Your Grace," Ambrose said bowing to kiss

[33]

the Abbot's fat hand that was extended for such a gesture.

"Brother Ambrose," the Abbot replied, withdrawing his hand to give Andrew equal time for homage. "Brother Andrew. Please, shall we sit?"

The brothers parted to allow the Abbot ample space to walk between them so that he might appoint their seats. In the last year, he had gained enough extra weight to give him the appearance of waddling.

"Ambrose, you and Andrew may sit across from me, if you will." Before seating himself, he walked over to one of the windows and, from behind the drape, pulled on a thick cord. "I'll have Maurice bring us some refreshments."

When the Abbot lowered himself into his seat, the brothers heard the huge chair creak under his weight. He positioned himself in the chair so that his hands clasped the balls at the end of each arm. On each hand, jeweled rings squeezed his pudgy fingers. The rubies matched the color of his robes.

From out of nowhere, a small man appeared. "Your Grace?" he said, bowing.

"Maurice, please bring us some tea and pastries, if you will. Brothers, sherry?" He accepted their refusals and turned to Maurice. "I'll have some before you leave for the refreshments."

Maurice poured a goblet of sherry for the Abbot and brought it to him. He then left the room as soundlessly as he had entered. His Grace closed his eyes and inhaled the fragrance of the sherry before putting the goblet up to his rosebud lips. Dabbing his mouth with a small napkin, he held the goblet on his lap and looked at the monks a long moment, before speaking.

"And how are things in your neck of the woods, my friends?"

"Quiet, as usual, Your Grace," Ambrose replied, not wanting to say any more than necessary.

"Your wines have developed quite a reputation. There are many who wish to know the source," the Abbot continued.

Andrew was cognizant of some kind of cat and mouse game in progress, with the Abbot positioning himself as the feline. He knew Ambrose felt similarly, for upon glancing at his friend, he saw Ambrose's jaw muscle tightening up under his grey beard.

The Abbot spent an inordinate amount of time in Paris. His older brother was the famous Cardinal de Fleury who had begun his career as a tutor to King Louis XV, and who later became the First Minister. The Abbot was thrilled to have the doors to the French Courts so widely opened to him, and he had used the many privileges afforded him to his best advantage.

"As you know, Your Grace," Ambrose responded, "our continued existence is due to our anonymity. We do not have the resources that St. Benoit Abbey enjoys."

"And your wool, Brother Ambrose..." the Abbot had not heard a word Ambrose had said. "The Parisians would pay dearly for garments made from such wool. It's a pity you haven't considered expanding your business."

"We have more than enough already, Your Grace." Andrew spoke calmly. "With what we send out to you and to the King, there is barely enough for our own consumption."

"You are probably right," the Abbot remarked. "How many acres of vineyards have you?"

"Sixty, when we go into full production next year," Ambrose answered.

"And sheep? How many?"

"Around two hundred." Ambrose deliberately underestimated Tristan's flock, for he did not want to whet the Abbot's appetite.

"Well, I see that while we have expanded ourselves here, you have deliberately kept your building down in favor of the land."

"We have needed to be self sustaining, Your Grace." Ambrose smiled at the Abbot.

His Grace said nothing for a moment, while he contemplated what had been said. The rattling of china on a tray interrupted his reverie, and he looked up to see Maurice enter with the tea.

"Well! Enough said! Let us enjoy these exquisite pastries, fresh from our kitchen, and then move on to finer topics." The Abbot's right hand was freed, as he passed his empty goblet to Maurice, and with his left hand, he took a plump éclair filled with crème fraîche and covered with chocolate.

Ambrose and Andrew each took a small tea cake and some

warm tea, thanking Maurice as he served them. The thought crossed both of their minds that with delicacies such as these coming from their own kitchen, the brothers might all resemble Abbot de Fleury.

"You have recently been in Paris, Your Grace?" Andrew asked, trying to divert the Abbot's attention from the Abbey in the Forest.

"Ah yes!" The Abbot smiled. "Paris! The City of Light! How I enjoy my excursions there! Of course, you know they are still talking about the Americans and their battle for independence. Lafayette is quite the hero." He admired his éclair before continuing. "It must be disconcerting for the British to have their colonies break away, but Britain always has been at her best on sea. She fares more clumsily when her troops are on land."

"Nonetheless, she's a hard one to defeat in any battle," Andrew said wryly, remembering the struggles France and England had been involved in for centuries.

"Everyone wants power, does he not?" the Abbot asked, daintily patting his lips with his napkin. "I'll admit to you, that our participation in the Americans' struggle for independence has just about killed our finances. But such are the gains and losses of warfare."

"Your Grace surely knows that as long as there is such value placed on material things, then power will always be associated with possession, and wars will always be fought over rights of possession," Ambrose replied.

"And, Your Grace," Andrew added, "The Church has been notorious for being in the thick of things when it comes to assuring herself of her own power!"

Abbot de Fleury considered that this might be an attack upon himself, for his trips to Paris had always ensured the influence of his Abbey. They were known all over France, were they not? And the Benedictine order here was turning away potential priests until the extra buildings had been completed. "What is it that keeps these men happy?" the Abbot mused to himself, alluding to the brothers. "Do they not know that a church like this is a good life in terms of security?"

He knew that he was no formidable challenge for these scholars, and in the interests of his own power, he wisely altered the course of the conversation back in his favor.

"Ambrose. . ." He prepared himself, for this was what lay behind his invitation to tea. To draw out the suspense, he blew into his tea cup and then took a lengthy swallow. "I hear you have some strange bedfellows at the Abbey. Orientals, it is said. A boy and an older man. Are you taking in refugees now?"

"They were guided to be with us, Your Grace," Ambrose responded. "In fact, they came at separate times. That they are both Chinese has no correlation whatsoever."

"Who are the parents of the child?"

"I am not at liberty to say, and none of the other brothers, with the exception of Andrew, knows."

"Why are you so secretive about this little affair?" Abbot de Fleury's curiosity was more than piqued. It was ravenous.

"We didn't want any attention drawn to the child, so that he could be raised with a sense of family."

"Nonetheless, you understand my interest. There are charities around that are more than willing to take in orphans. Why should you?"

"Your Grace," Andrew interrupted, "there is really no great mystery to all of this. Perhaps your mind is drawing assumptions too easily. There are other monasteries that have taken in an occasional child."

"From China? Come, come, Brother, I was not born yesterday! Buddhists in a Catholic monastery? And this older one. I have seen him with the child. It's almost as if he is guarding him. Others from the village have remarked that he is very strange."

"Yes," Ambrose smiled to lighten the energy, "Chen is somewhat idiosyncratic, but we have learned to love him. We also have fully accepted him as one of us."

"Ambrose, the Chinese are Buddhists! He cannot be one of you!"

"Your Grace, you have been apprised of our openness to all philosophies in terms of our scholastic needs. It is only to our advantage to learn more about China and her people."

"Yes, yes, most certainly. Did you not have a Chinese scholar at one time?"

"We did, and he is no longer with us," Andrew answered, hoping to give Ambrose time to think.

"Well, I see. What is this child's name?"

"We have called him Etienne." Ambrose chose not to give the Abbot the child's birth name.

"Wasn't that your friend's name? The Chinese scholar?" The Abbot paused, his fingers tapping his mouth. "Now I seem to remember. I met him many years ago."

"I believe you did," Ambrose replied, wanting the conversation to end.

"Seems he actually went to China or something. . ." He was hoping Ambrose would complete the sentence; however, Ambrose ignored his remark and sipped his tea.

"I don't suppose there is a connection between the two?" the Abbot queried.

"None whatsoever, Your Grace." Ambrose stood, and Maurice appeared to take his cup and saucer. "And now, we must be going. We have already taken up enough of your time."

"Yes." Andrew followed suit, not allowing the Abbot to speak. "It was most kind of you to invite us for tea, Your Grace."

The Abbot, surprised at the change in the conversation, passed his cup to Maurice and pushed himself out of his chair. Without him in it to reduce its stature, the chair, once again, looked huge.

"Well," he wiped his brow, "I would be interested in meeting these additions to your flock, although they are hardly new. The boy has been there about nine years, has he not?"

"He has." Ambrose took Andrew's elbow and guided him out the door with the Abbot waddling behind them. In the hallway, they faced each other for the good-byes, the brothers bending to kiss a bejeweled hand.

"We need to communicate more often. The bourgeoisie are becoming a restless group in both Paris and the environs. They feel the nobility and the Church have persisted in not recognizing their power. We clergy must band together, you know. I don't like what this portends. Not at all."

"As you wish it, Your Grace," Ambrose said, as he and Andrew took leave of him.

They found their way to the front door by themselves, for Abbot de Fleury had engaged Maurice into bringing him some more pastries. It felt good to step out into the fresh air, and as Andrew closed the door, they heard the sound of wheels turning on the cobblestone street. Within moments, their carriage was in front of them, Chen opening the door.

Ambrose and Andrew seated themselves, and Gerard turned the coach back toward the forests. When the noise of the streets had given way to the muted sounds of earth beneath them, Chen spoke.

"Termites. They hungry for rotting wood."

Ambrose realized there was no need to recount the conversation.

Chapter Five

"Tristan, who is that man who keeps watching us?" Etienne asked.

"What do you mean, little friend?"

"In the last few weeks, I've noticed a man come out of the forest when he thinks we aren't looking." He continued. "When I've run across the field to speak with him, he disappears behind the trees."

"Stay near me, Etienne," Tristan commanded. "I don't know who he might be, but until I do, I'd prefer you to be close."

"Yes, Tristan."

In the last few weeks, Etienne had spent an inordinate amount of time with Tristan, helping him with the sheep. It was that time of year when large clumps of fleece were removed from the animals and placed in bags to be given to Pasqual.

Etienne loved "making the sheep thin" as he phrased it, for they looked so plump that their little legs seemed barely able to carry them. After he and Tristan had laboriously clipped them down, their bodies seemed more proportionately able to fit their legs. Etienne would bury his hands in the thick wool coats that would separate as his fingers wiggled down to touch the backs of the animals.

"I can't imagine Tristan, the miracle of making the fur of an animal into my robe. And this very fur grows back again and again!"

"That's why I love working with them, Etienne," Tristan replied. "They are such gentle little creatures who seem to have been placed upon the earth solely for our comfort. They are happy just to be grazing all day."

"I think I would not be happy with such a thing," Etienne decided. "My stomach would grow tired, and my mind would grow weak."

"Well then, I guess that we are lucky that you are you, and that they are they!" Tristan smiled at his helper. "Now, let's walk back to the Abbey. It's been a long day, and I want to spend time in the courtyard."

Tristan found Ambrose seated by the pool, staring at a lily which had opened to receive the sun's rays. Etienne had gone to the kitchen to finagle a piece of fresh bread from Charles. The tantalizing smell coming from the ovens had met them on the way into the building.

"Ambrose."

"Tristan." Ambrose looked up at the young man. "Sit down and join me."

"Etienne claims to have seen someone watching us from the forests," he said quietly.

"What else did he say?" Ambrose was interested.

"Apparently this has been going on for a few weeks. The few times Etienne has approached him, he has run back into the forest."

"I see." Ambrose was quiet.

"What do you think?"

"Well Tristan, he can be watching one of two things, either the animals or Etienne." The older man spoke with conviction. "In the event that it is the latter, I would prefer that we keep the child closer to the Abbey."

"I agree with you. Has it something to do with your meeting with the Abbot?"

"He's been unusually quiet lately," Ambrose agreed, "and his silence arouses my suspicion. He was too inquisitive to let the matter drop."

"They say he's losing some of his popularity in Paris," Tristan added. "There is greater focus on other matters that may involve dramatic changes for everyone."

"I can only pray that we remain uninvolved with all political issues. Our purpose is solely to protect the philosophies of man, to explore them, and to expand our own. It is not to force change." Ambrose seemed somewhat saddened. Intuitively, he was aware of a massive shift taking place on a socio-political level. Men like de Fleury would grasp at anything for self-preservation.

"Ambrose, what is it that de Fleury suspects?"

"He implied there is some surreptitious behavior on our part, since we have Chen and Etienne with us. His suspicions are that we are harboring some secret that might fill his coffers, were he to get involved."

"Did he draw any conclusions about Etienne's origins?" Tristan was hoping for the chance to clear the mystery that had brought Etienne to them.

"Possibly," Ambrose answered. "He recollected that we had a brother here by that name who had, coincidentally, left for China. That's about all, as far as I can determine; however, we cannot underestimate the powers of his scheming mind."

Ambrose looked down at the lily again. Tristan remembered his thoughts of twelve years' past when a homely little baby had come to live with them. Since then, Ambrose's hair and beard had become almost totally white, adding an arresting appearance to his face with those uncommonly blue eyes.

The child had changed everyone's life; however, it was Ambrose who had been most affected by the gift Fate had bestowed upon them. He had been transformed by a new maturity which expressed itself in a loving absorption. When it came to burdens, the brothers would turn to Ambrose to relieve them, for he assumed others' troubles with a beneficent ease.

His sorrow had become a worldly one, lifting itself from the personal to the impersonal. A small boy and his devoted Chen had somehow given birth to an inner understanding of mankind on a soul level. That sense of separation, that invisible barrier Ambrose had created to protect himself, had been replaced with an openness and loving trust.

"Do you think we should do anything?" Tristan asked.

"No, let us wait." Ambrose looked him directly in the eye. "Tristan, don't let your curiosity burn you."

"There's no need to worry about that." Tristan stood up, feeling slightly rebuffed. After all, he had brought Ambrose the news. "I take leave of you, Brother. My sheep need tending."

He turned and left Ambrose to his thoughts in the courtyard. Passing through the kitchen, he grabbed a crust of bread, while Charles' back was turned, and slipped out the door. Charles and François had a running battle with the brothers over such antics, for after years of Wednesdays and Saturdays, their bread was still irresistible.

The late afternoon had stirred up a small breeze which moved the intense heat, making it more bearable. Tristan noticed that the sun was slanting through the forests in the distance, and he hoped the sheep weren't scattered too widely to be accounted for. In the summers, the meditation and dinners were pushed back to accommodate those of the brothers who had to attend to the outdoor activities. With the vineyards proliferating at an abnormal rate, half the monks were in the fields. Even James had put his carpentry aside for rainy days to help. The harvest date would arrive in no time, and they all anticipated an excellent crop.

Pasqual and Chen would help with the sheep. Everyone loved to be outdoors, and only Etienne complained about hunger. Hence, François would give him afternoon treats of fruit and a small cake, to sustain him until dinner.

Tristan rolled up his sleeves as he walked. The monastery was situated on approximately two hundred acres, and he never doubted that it was a valuable piece of land. The beauty was incomparable, with the primary colors being green and blue. The tree trunks and monastery walls added contrasting colors of grey and brown, and the sheep put splashes of white wherever they went. It was a pastoral paradise if there ever were one!

He passed the vineyards and saw that the monks were in the process of watering the grapes. The cool liquid running through the furrows looked inviting enough to remind Tristan that a quick swim in the Loire was in order, after he counted his sheep. The water would refresh him after the intense heat of the day.

One by one, Tristan accounted for his animal children, as he spotted them grazing in small clusters. In spite of the large number he had amassed over the years, he could almost distinguish each one. A sixth sense told him when one might have strayed too far from the others. Consequently, he rarely lost an animal with the exception of two weak ones who were felled by a hungry wolf a few winters back. The weather had been cold, and the wolf was way out of his territory. It had frightened the other sheep enough to induce them to move closer to the monastery for protection.

[43]

The last few were grazing a little too close to the forest. Tristan felt more comfortable with them next to the rest of the herd, and he walked up the hill to coax them back. About ten meters from the trees, he saw something move. His attention arrested, he quietly moved forward. As he approached the trees, a man quickly stepped out and faced him squarely. Although Tristan had suspected it was a person, he had to squelch his surprise over the sudden confrontation.

He had seen this person before, but he couldn't quite place him. His face was indistinguishable, with the exception of a raspberry colored birthmark on the left side. It was partially obscured by a relatively new beard, which was unevenly poking through his skin. Short dark hair framed a lean face that had, perhaps, had a little too much ale in its lifetime.

"May I help you, my friend" Tristan asked cordially.

"Just looking at your land," he growled.

Tristan turned, his eyes sweeping the panorama. "It's beautiful, isn't it?"

"Who's the boy?" The stranger didn't waste much time getting to the point.

"One of us," Tristan replied. "He came to us when he was a baby."

"What's his story?"

"I don't know what you mean." Tristan was unnervingly calm.

"Who are his parents?" The man was persistent.

"My friend, that's a question none of us can answer, not even the boy."

"What about the older one who looks like him?"

"They came separately. Years apart. There's no connection at all."

"Are you sure?" the man sneered. "I know of a coach driver who was paid handsomely to bring the older one specifically to your abbey."

"Friend, you are wasting your time," Tristan concluded. "Over the years, people come to stay at the Abbey. Even I found it some nineteen years ago."

Tristan stopped to think how amazing it was, the swift passing of time. "And now, I must tend to my flock. Good day to you." He bowed and turned back to the care of his sheep.

The strays had rejoined the others, and Tristan decided that it was now the best time for his cooling dip. He walked quickly down to the river, which ran adjacent to the monastery grounds. Leaving his robe and his sandals in the tall grass, he lowered himself into the gentle current. Tristan had come to this spot for years. In the winters, when it was too cold to swim, he would sit on the banks and watch pieces of debris flowing with the current. During his earliest years at the Abbey, when he was troubled about his past, it was here that he would come. He would make small wooden boats and set them to sail, often wondering how far down the river they went.

Now, as he dried himself with his robe, he was tempted to make yet another little vessel, for within him, a faint premonition whispered its message, not speaking loudly enough for him to clearly understand. Glancing at the setting sun, Tristan realized that it was almost time for the evening meditation, so he forgot his whim and left the serenity of the riverside for the inner peace that would fill him in the Abbey.

At the rear entrance, he saw Chen sitting calmly and staring at him as he approached. Tristan knew that Chen saw into his soul, and that there was little he could hide from him.

"We in for trouble. So we are." The diminutive man spoke quietly, his eyes never leaving Tristan's face.

"What can we do, Chen?" he asked.

"Evil winds blow from heart beat of country. Fool puts on extra robe. Wise man know he can't hide the self."

For years, Chen's metaphors had puzzled Tristan who often had trouble finding meaning in their simplicity. As he opened to the teacher, he began to see the infinite beauty in his self-expression, and the meat of his words gave him food for thought.

"Come, Tristan. Let mind relax in silence." Chen rose and held the door for Tristan. Together, they walked into the small chapel where the other monks were waiting. Chen loyally followed the routines of the Abbey, for his gratitude over their hospitality had never ceased.

[45]

* * *

"Ambrose," Etienne was standing with the library door partially open. "Can I talk with you?"

"My child, of course!" Ambrose looked up from his reading to see the timidity in Etienne's face. "Come in."

Etienne entered the cozy room. Sunlight was filtering through the windows, putting splashes of yellow on the burgundy carpet. The room was naturally warm with its mahogany walls filled with books on three sides. The wall facing the west was all windows, so that Ambrose had full views of the vineyards, the hills, and the forest in the distance.

Thick gold brocade drapes bordered the windows, and although they were cleaned once a year, Etienne never remembered them being closed. They were more of a decorative frame than anything else. On either side of the heavy oak doors, there were more books.

All of the monks were free to use the library at any time, although it was considered "Ambrose's room." There were several comfortable chairs nestled against the shelves, and Ambrose's chair was always pulled up to the sixteenth century table that had been hand carved and rescued from a monastery in Orleans, before it had been destroyed by war. The table was large enough to seat six people; however, it was often covered with Ambrose's books, his mail, and Etienne's homework. On the wall opposite the table, there was a fireplace. In the winters, a constant fire burned in the hearth to staid off the cold. As a baby, Etienne would be mesmerized by the warm flames.

How Etienne loved the library! The very energy of the books soothed him, and in times of distress, he would lie on the plush carpet, reading one of the many volumes. A few were about China which he had also read; however, Etienne considered himself French above all. He knew that he had come from China, but he never inquired about it, for he trusted that, when the time was right, his background would be revealed to him. Chen gave him lessons on the philosophy and the language of China, and that was enough for him.

[46]

He walked into the room and pulled his chair over next to Ambrose. Etienne had always felt welcomed by this gentle man whose solicitous care had nurtured him from infancy. Ambrose never aged to Etienne. He always looked the same, just as Chen did.

Ambrose reached out and ruffled Etienne's thick dark hair which hung like a little cap around his face. "My dear boy, what seems to be troubling you this afternoon?"

"I am needing to know about love, Ambrose."

"Oh?" Ambrose was trying to remember when the child had ever seen a girl, and although it was common for marriages to occur between young men and women at the age of fifteen, he hardly thought that, at twelve, Etienne had entered puberty.

"Ambrose, I love you, and I love Chen, and I don't know whom I should love the most. I do not have this trouble with the other brothers, for I see them as the same. But you two are special to me." He looked at Ambrose who remained silently interested in his words. The sun streamed through the window behind him onto his white hair, giving the appearance of a halo.

Etienne continued. "Chen does not express his love for me in the way that you do, but I know it is there. I feel you are both my fathers, and I am afraid to love one of you more."

Ambrose suppressed a smile. He waited until he was sure Etienne had finished, and then he spoke. "Etienne, it's just your mind that is having this problem and not your heart. Your heart loves everyone the same, while your mind attempts to create special differences between us."

"Love does not discriminate, the mind does. The part of you that feels love, that expresses it, is the Divine within you, and that Divinity loves everyone in the same way. To speak otherwise would imply that some people are favored by God and others are not, or that some people deserve more love than others. The truth is that we all need love equally."

"Even Brother Gerard who sends me away from the stables?"

"Even Brother Gerard," Ambrose answered. "Some people have difficulty receiving love, Etienne, that's all."

"So I should love everyone as I love you?" Etienne didn't quite understand this.

"Etienne, the heart does not rationalize. It can only speak of love." He continued: "It is always the mind that separates, that puts up invisible barriers against the outflow from the center of your being. God speaks quietly, and one must train oneself to listen to His voice."

"But Ambrose, in the Old Testament, God did favor men," Etienne argued.

"The Old Testament was written by men who believed in a retributive God, Etienne. In the New Testament, a different quality is added to God, for with the birth and teachings of Christ, He became a merciful Deity."

"The revenge aspect was dropped, for as Christ pointed out so clearly, man brought troubles upon himself, and he was, therefore, through the quality of mercy, capable of redeeming himself. Hope was offered to all of mankind."

"Even Chen and others like him who may not be Christian?"

"Everyone, Etienne. The Divine Mind does not distinguish. God is an impersonal God made personal through the creative process. Besides, Chen's teachings are not dissimilar. They are merely through another perspective."

"But Chen says to know the Self, Ambrose." Etienne was confused. "He says that is what is important."

"It is, my son," Ambrose assured him, "for if one knows the Self, one also knows God and the workings of the universe. In knowing God, one becomes God. Our truths are not different. Only the words."

"Anyway," Ambrose concluded, "Chen and I do not want you to distinguish us from the others. We all feel like your father, for each of us has taken part in your upbringing."

"You and Chen have spent the most time with me, Ambrose."

"Such is our role, Etienne, but it does not preclude the others. After all, who fills your stomach when you are hungry? Who makes your clothes? Who made your finely crafted bed? Who teaches you about the animals in the forests, about the grapes? Each one of us has a part to play in your life tapestry."

"Oh Ambrose," Etienne jumped from his chair and went to hug his friend. "You always make everything fit. I'm so lucky that I have

[48]

so many different fathers!"

"Soon, we'll be your brothers, my little friend." Ambrose smiled at Etienne knowing well the formality that would grow between them in time. Eventually Chen would replace Ambrose as Etienne's main teacher, for Chen would have to align the boy with his own cultural philosophy.

"It will be just as hard for me to watch the boy become the man as it was for me when his father left," Ambrose thought sadly. Aloud, he said, "Now, Etienne, pick a book from the shelves, and we can read together before the sun goes down."

* * *

Far across the hill, Tristan could see the dark outline of a carriage coming toward the monastery. With the trees having shed all of their leaves, it was easy to distinguish objects at a greater distance. Tristan put down his book and stood up to watch it wind its way in and out of the forest. Apparently, the driver knew the area well, for the horses were moving at a generous speed.

He was curious, for it was not often that travelers came the way of the Abbey in the Forest, and when one did, it was with the erratic movements indicative of one having lost his way. He could see two black horses pulling the coach. As his eyes focused, he saw that the horses had been worked hard, for their coats were shining from lather.

For a moment, the carriage would be obscured from his sight as it passed in front of the Abbey. He could get a better look when it passed out on the other side. Tristan waited, but the horses did not come back into view. Moreover, the noise of hooves stamping the ground had stopped.

"So," he thought to himself, "we have visitors!"

He sat back down again and resumed his reading, his robe adding another brown to the earth which had assumed the drab colors of winter. There would be time at lunch to hear about the visitors. It was, most likely, nothing of importance.

In the Abbey, the brothers heard the sounds of the ringing bells that announced visitors on the other side of the gates.

"Mon Dieu! Such impatience!" Charles said irritably as he rushed from the kitchen in order to quiet the noise. He stuffed his white towel in his belt and walked out the front door.

"I'm coming!" he shouted over the noise of the clanging.

Charles slid the iron bolt back and threw his body weight behind his hands as he pushed open the heavy portals. Through the crack, he could see a man jumping back to avoid being hit. Behind him was the carriage Charles recognized as belonging to the Abbot. The snug fitting maroon and white uniform on the lackey confirmed his suspicion. On the shiny black door of the coach was the elaborate insignia of the St. Benoit Abbey stenciled in gold.

"May I help you, Brother?" Charles asked politely. He noticed the coachman sizing him up, for the man had never met one of the monks from the Abbey in the Forest.

"I have a personal request from His Grace that Brother Ambrose is to accompany me along with the child, and his servant, back to St. Benoit." The lackey's voice was a little airy, belying his nervousness. He had grown accustomed, over the years, to the opulence of St. Benoit Abbey. The mystery surrounding this monastic order made him a little uncomfortable.

"Do you know the reason for this request?" Charles was mystified. He remembered that Ambrose had not personally delivered the wines and the wool in the fall, as was his custom. Instead, he had sent Brothers James and Gerard. Perhaps the Abbot had felt slighted.

"No, Brother, I do not," he replied politely. "I was just told to carry out my orders, although there was some commotion at the Abbey this morning. Something about a special visitor."

"Very well then," Charles gestured toward the gates, "come into the Abbey with me. François will give you some food and drink, while I get Brother Ambrose."

The lackey tied the horses and then followed Charles across the courtyard and through the front doors. The foyer was quite large, with halls coming into it from two sides. He noted how clean and simple everything was. There were no ostentatious displays of wealth. The wall tapestries were woven in muted browns and reds depicting various scenes in which Christ was the main figure.

Outside the kitchen doors was a large oak table with no carving at all on the legs or the skirt. Sitting on the top was a bowl with some flowers in it. The lackey looked up to see the source of light which brightened the otherwise dark space. Part of the ceiling had been removed to allow the sunlight to come through.

"It must get cold in here in the winter," he said.

"We have a cover that keeps out the elements," Charles answered. "Autumn is fickle; however, we leave it open as long as possible. Through here, please."

He pushed open a door to reveal a large and spotless kitchen. Next to the stove, the lackey noticed some bread and cheese. Another monk walked over to greet him.

"I'm Brother François," he said, extending his hand. "Charles and I are the chefs here at the Abbey."

"If you don't mind my saying so," the coachman timidly put forth, "you're a lot thinner than our cooks."

"We keep busy here," Charles said, smiling. "Brother, will you give this man some refreshments while I find Ambrose?"

Seeing the lackey well tended under François' solicitous care, Charles left the kitchen and went to the library. As he opened the door, he saw that Chen was already with Ambrose, standing in front of the table on the soft rug. Both men turned to look at Charles.

"We ready," Chen said quietly. His face was expressionless.

"You know?" Charles asked.

"Yes, Brother, we know." Ambrose stood up and took off his reading glasses. He was still vain enough not to want people to identify him with the weak eyes that had been troubling him for years. Early in the summer, Chen had approached him in the courtyard and had presented him with the pair he was now wearing. "Blindness is folly," he had said, bowing deeply.

"I am curious Brother," Charles looked at Ambrose. "Isn't it time you tell us about Etienne?"

"It is time," Ambrose answered softly. "When we return, we shall talk. Where is he now?"

"He in his room, watching light change in window," Chen replied.

[51]

"Shall we notify him and be on our way?" Ambrose walked toward the doors, and the others followed.

Etienne heard the noise of the approaching coach long before it stopped at the Abbey. For the last hour, he had been absorbed in watching the light change in his room as the morning sun matured. Chen had given him this exercise as a method to increase his awareness. However, the intrusion of the beating hooves on the soft earth was distracting to him.

Etienne rarely heard traffic coming toward the monastery. When Brother Gerard departed for the town, his return went almost without notice, as it was the completion of an energy pattern. Visitors were so rare, that Etienne was always excited at the prospect.

This was no exception, and ultimately his twelve year old curiosity provoked him into quickly jumping up to look out of his window which overlooked the front entrance. He saw Charles greet a driver who was formally dressed, and looking a little awkward, and then they both walked toward the front door.

Settling back into his sitting position, Etienne knew that he would be told, in time, what was happening. The brothers had never kept anything from him in the past, except his own beginnings, and the story of Chen's arrival. In fact, he had always thought it was strange that, in the whole town, he and Chen were the only ones who resembled each other physically. That they should both live in the same place never occurred to him as being unusual, any more than having so many fathers who were becoming brothers as he grew older.

Etienne regained his sense of focus, and once more concentrated on the light patterning itself on the grey walls of his small cell. This was his sanctuary, and he loved it. It was bare except for a simple bed, a small brown rug for his feet on the cold mornings, and an armoire that was very fragile, in accordance with its age. The odd book would be lying next to his bed, and when he was younger, he would stick pictures on his wall. Now he was content with the barren look, for his window framed the most beautiful picture of all - that of the sky with it's changing scenery when viewed from his bed, or the entrance to the Abbey and the

[52]

forests beyond when he stood on his toes and peeked out. Soon, he hoped, he would not have to stretch to look through the window.

There was a light tap on his door. Etienne was surprised to be disturbed, for his time was not yet over; however, when it sounded again, he went to receive the visitor. His face registered bewilderment at the sight of Ambrose.

"Etienne, you, Chen, and I are going into town now. Wash up quickly and meet us at the front entrance." Ambrose spoke hurriedly. Etienne was not used to seeing him so disconcerted.

"Yes, Ambrose!" He went to the armoire to pull out his wash rag and towel and went to clean himself.

While waiting for Etienne, Ambrose went to talk with the driver who had filled himself on François' fine bread. "We'll take our own carriage. This will save you the return trip."

"Very well," the driver agreed. He had no desire to travel through the woods in the evening. "I will wait for you outside." He turned to François to thank him for the food, and then he left the way he had entered.

Gradually, the little entourage assembled. Brother Gerard was not thrilled to redress the horses, for they had already been into town once that day. The others waited patiently for him to emerge from the stables, and when he finally did, the horses and the coach looked as fresh as ever.

Gerard tended to the horses with as much devotion as Tristan gave to his sheep. He was a strange little man. What he lacked in stature, he made up in circumference. None of the brothers could fathom how Gerard maintained his excessive weight on the Abbey food which was so well balanced.

The truth was that Brother Gerard had a proclivity for the rich pastries that came from one of the patisseries in the village. Madame Denton was privy to this secret, as she greeted him thrice weekly on his village runs. She always packed a few extra éclairs, free of charge, as part of an agreement that Gerard would pray for her son who was an angry young man, prone to speaking strongly for social reform. She was optimistically noting slight changes in his behavior in the years since Gerard had been giving his blessings.

The pastries were his only sin. Gerard was a kind man given to a disposition that did not favor him socially. His overwhelming temerity was carefully obscured by a gruff demeanor. Only the horses saw the real Gerard, the horses and Chen, although Chen had no need to spend time with him to see who he was.

He had always felt awkward around the child, mostly because of his own youth that had been spent in one stable after another caring for the horses of the wealthy bourgeoisie. He had been overworked, underpaid, and never given the time to mingle with his peers. He was now a taciturn little man, most comfortable in the silence of his stables. Gerard truly looked like the archetypical monk with a fringe of dark hair around the sides of his head, his dark eyes, and his rotund belly held in check by his rope-like belt.

He saw the group waiting for him outside the gates, and as a matter of formality, he straightened himself on the seat and pulled the horses to attention. His eyes were focused ahead on the others; however, his mind was on the unfinished éclair lying in its box.

Chen, Etienne, and Ambrose climbed into the carriage. Charles closed the door once they had settled.

"Whatever the reason, I know you'll fare well, Brothers!" he said. He raised his hand and waved. "All right, Gerard." The horses started up, and behind them, the Abbot's carriage followed at a safe distance.

From the far hills, Tristan looked up from his book and saw two coaches returning in the direction from which the first one had come. He recognized the first carriage as the one belonging to the Abbey, for he saw Gerard's familiar form urging the horses forward. Puzzled, he stood up and dusted himself off before putting the book into the pocket of his robe. Giving a final glance toward his sheep, he began the walk back to the monastery.

Chapter Six

Etienne was surprised by the silence in the carriage. Both Chen and Ambrose seemed immersed in their own thoughts, although it was Ambrose who appeared to be brooding over something. Not one to intrude, he moved closer to the window and looked out at the barren terrain. What a difference from the lush green of summer! To Etienne, in the winter, the exterior of the monastery looked almost foreboding. It was definitely more comfortable in the summer when the verdant countryside softened the stark walls.

· He went into the village whenever it was allowed. Gerard was reluctant to have Etienne sit up front, and so he would nestle in the carriage waiting patiently to step down onto the cobblestone streets.

St. Benoit-sur-Loire was a picturesque little town. It was well protected, with its perfect setting along the banks of the Loire River. The inhabitants were not used to strangers who did not resemble the typical Frenchman. Hence, Etienne had grown used to the stares and the whispers.

This had occurred more often when he was younger, or perhaps he was more sensitive to it then. He would walk closely behind the security of Ambrose's robe, trying to ignore any attention that was directed at him. There was a period during which he had refused to go into town at all; however, Chen had a talk with him, and he reluctantly agreed to try it one more time. He had been assured that the problem was not with him. It was with others who perceived him to be different.

"No worry," Chen had said. "Broccoli does not laugh at cauliflower, nor horse at lamb. You here to teach others way of acceptance. Hold head high!"

Eventually Etienne ignored the stares, for the shopkeepers were always eager to see the serious child with almond eyes. There would be an extra roll placed in with the flour, or a surreptitious pat

[55]

on the head. With a child in their midst, the elusive brothers from the Abbey in the Forest somehow seemed more approachable.

Now, nearing the age of thirteen, Etienne loved the excitement of the lively town in contrast to his peaceful existence at the Abbey. He certainly had no desire to live away from the monks; however, a visit to St. Benoit was like an extra dessert on Sundays from François. Often Chen came along, and while Etienne carried out errands, Chen followed him at a short distance, keeping his watchful eye on everything.

Etienne's curiosity over this unexpected journey was bubbling up inside of him. It was everything he could do to keep from asking questions, yet, out of respect, he felt it better to refrain from doing so, until one of his elders broke the silence.

"T'ien Li, today you begin journey to manhood." Chen spoke so softly that Etienne hardly heard him over the sounds of the coach. "You must speak from inner wisdom, and not be caught by element of surprise."

Etienne looked at Chen, hoping to hear words that would inform him more fully; however, he had always been accustomed to Chen speaking as little as possible so that he, himself, must arrive at the meaning. Chen's way of communicating differed from the other monks, yet Etienne, being part Chinese, had little difficulty in hearing what he had said. He had been trained to listen not only to the words, but also the body language, the eyes, and the voice inflection. Chen had taught him that behind the words was the whole being putting them forth.

"I hope not to disappoint you, Chen," Etienne replied solemnly.

The carriage moved quickly through the forests. Soon they would enter the clearing which bordered the outskirts of town. Poking his head out of the window, Etienne could see signs of life ahead, dominated by the large church whose pointed spires sliced into the blue sky. He sat back again and looked at Ambrose who seemed sad. Their eyes met, and Ambrose smiled at him.

Behind his smile, Ambrose felt a heavy knot in the pit of his stomach. Throughout the journey, he had questioned his judgement concerning his secrecy related to Etienne's background.

[56]

Dark Places, Light Places

He wondered if it would have effected the outcome of the drama that was rapidly unfolding. Memories of the last thirteen years flashed through his mind.

Ambrose neither denied nor took for granted the love he felt for Etienne. A small part of him had wondered about the prospect of having a family; however, when he was younger, Ambrose never felt an attraction toward women in the way that his friends had. That women were drawn to his good looks and gentle demeanor went without saying, but anytime the possibility of intimacy developed, Ambrose had diverted it into friendship.

By the time he was twenty, he feared that he was incapable of love. This had made him despondent, for all of his friends had taken wives, and he soon grew tired of their incessant persuasion for him to do the same. He had been looking for an easy way out of his predicament, when he encountered a Brother Theodore who came to Nantes, Ambrose's hometown, to meet with the Abbot of one of the churches.

Brother Theodore had asked to share a table with him at a crowded café where there was little room for an extra person. They spent the afternoon talking as the crowds thinned out and then grew thick again. Theodore told him about the Abbey in the Forest and the brothers who shared it with him. There was something special about Theodore that Ambrose had never felt about other priests. Where it was the normal custom for priests to surrender to God with an attitude of servility, Theodore presented a different type of surrender, to the inner self, rather than to an external source. Ambrose knew Theodore would never humble himself to bishops or abbots, for he would demonstrate an equal respect for the individual that was not differentiated by sex, caste, or profession.

Long after Theodore had departed the café, Ambrose sat, staring into the dense smoke that hung heavily in the room. His ears were deafened to the noise of the patrons, which had been exaggerated by the consumption of too much wine, for Ambrose was lost in his introspection. When he left the café late that evening, he had made a decision.

Nonetheless, he spent three more years in Nantes, hoping that he would feel a love for someone with whom he might begin a

[57]

family, as would any normal man. One night, Theodore came to him in a dream. "It is time, Ambrose," was all he had said. The next day, Ambrose began to settle his business affairs. He bid a few of his closest friends farewell and quietly left Nantes for St. Benoit-sur-Loire.

Exactly two weeks from the dream, Ambrose pulled up outside the gates of the Abbey. When they closed behind him they shut out the secular world, along with all its expectations, forever.

Ambrose studied with Theodore for ten years, before the older man succumbed to a bout of pneumonia and left his body, in the midst of a bitter winter storm. Since Ambrose had been the closest to Brother Theodore, he stepped into his place with an ease that was supported by the other monks. He never questioned the choice he had made, for he did not have the desires of other men.

And then years later, when Etienne's father came into his life, Ambrose began to understand his own nature. As he grew closer to Etienne, he experienced feelings, the likes of which were entirely alien to him. Even his brothers noticed an unusual sense of disquiet about Ambrose.

Finally, he confronted Etienne with his feelings. The pressure from years of never having expressed love was released, and Ambrose poured out everything in an emotional outburst. Etienne listened quietly, neither rejecting his friend nor appearing surprised. When Ambrose finished, Etienne took him into his arms and embraced him. They held each other until Ambrose was calm.

"Ambrose, this isn't right, this attraction between us," Etienne had said.

Nonetheless, each ignored the inner warnings, and they pursued a quiet relationship that attracted little suspicion among the other monks. For a few years, the physical contact amounted to gentle touches and an occasional surreptitious embrace. Finally, one weekend they went to Paris to examine, and possibly buy, rare books on China for which Etienne had waited patiently. When they checked into their hotel, they registered for a single room. No one in Paris would indicate any surprise over two men being together, for nothing shocked the jaded Parisians.

Their tryst was beautiful, in spite of Ambrose's awkwardness over his first sexual encounter with anyone, much less another man. They put behind them all their responsibilities and spent the entire weekend together in the little room that was tucked into the attic of the hotel. They left it only to eat and to purchase the books which had, in fact, been the rare find Etienne had anticipated.

When they returned to the monastery, the nature of their relationship was somewhat altered by the sanctity of the place, and guilt crept in to overshadow the joy. They came together a few times in their cells late at night, but ultimately, neither of them could handle their feelings of having violated the purity of the Abbey. Etienne began to withdraw from Ambrose, and although he felt intense love for him, he carefully camouflaged it beneath his scholarly facade.

After that, nothing was ever the same. A natural frustration grew between them, until it was irreparable. It was Etienne who spared them both prolonged anguish by leaving for China. His decision was made following a heated argument between them, and within a week, he had departed.

Ambrose was devastated. He had even considered leaving the Abbey; however, the loving support from the other brothers encouraged him through the darkness. The small child, the progeny of one whom he had loved so dearly, was an ironic gift to Ambrose. Through the nurturing of Etienne, he was able to experience a sense of family, and over the years, he had learned to forgive himself.

And now Ambrose faced an ending to his role as a father to this beautiful child. He sighed deeply and looked out of the window in time to see the carriage stop in front of the Abbot's house.

"We're here," he said. Mustering a smile, he descended from the carriage into the bright light of the town.

Chen and Etienne followed him. While Etienne ran to pat the horses, Chen whispered to Ambrose. "Don't let feelings alter course of day. Stay in center, Ambrose. I have faith in you."

Ambrose looked at Chen. Immediately his gloom lifted, for Chen was right. Any energy he carried into the meeting would contribute to the effect of the outcome. "Let us dance to the Abbot's music," Ambrose replied. "Perhaps we can sing a tune of our own."

[59]

"That right, my friend." Chen smiled a toothless grin.

The three monks climbed up the steps and announced their arrival by ringing the bell.

* * *

The doorman guided Chen, Ambrose, and Etienne down the halls and well past the small library, where Ambrose had spent his last visit, to a room whose entrance was blocked by two large doors that exuded ominous overtones to what might lay behind them.

"Excuse me, please, while I announce your presence to His Grace," the doorman said. Without further ado, he slipped through one of the doors, shutting it firmly to prevent the small group from having visual access. A few moments passed before his return, which was signified by both of the doors being opened into a large room.

Time stopped for Ambrose, as he looked over Etienne's head into the large, lavishly appointed chamber. Heavy crystal chandeliers hung from a ceiling that had been painted with cherubs and maidens cavorting by the water. On the walls were rows upon rows of books. The rich brown floor was covered with three oriental carpets, into which were woven geometric designs in blues, whites, and burgundies. Tables were randomly placed, - tables that supported shiny brass candelabras, thick books, and crystal decanters of wine.

There was ample seating for twenty people, but Ambrose saw only two others seated opposite them, silhouetted against a window that covered the entire wall. He immediately recognized the grotesquely large figure of the Abbot; however, it was the diminutive form on the Abbot's right that made his heart leap into his throat.

"Brother Ambrose!" Abbot de Fleury pushed himself out of his chair. "How nice of you to come so quickly!"

He tottered toward Ambrose with his fat hand lifted in the air. Ambrose had barely leaned forward when the Abbot turned away and faced Etienne.

[60]

"And you must be T'ien Li! I have been hearing about you!" Etienne's eyes opened in surprise at the use of his birth name. However, His Grace did not notice, for his interest was diverted by Chen's imposing presence.

"Brother Chen, I presume?" Chen, ignoring the outstretched hand, bowed slightly to the Abbot and stood up, his intense eyes looking through the heavy man, whose jowls dropped slightly over Chen's lack of servility.

With an eloquent gesture, the Abbot turned to his fourth guest, the mysterious stranger who sat so quietly while waiting for the greetings to end. "May I present to you, and indeed I am humbled to entertain such a personage, the Ch'ien Lung Empress of China!" He stepped back to offer a hand of assistance as she stood to greet the three men in brown robes.

She could not help but notice the contrast between the Abbot's elegant robes and the comfortable garments that the visitors wore. Her gaze fell upon Etienne.

"My son, T'ien Li!" she exclaimed proudly. "I have waited many long years for this moment!" The Empress refrained from touching her son, who was nonplused.

Her perfect French amazed Etienne, whose astonishment inhibited any reaction. He had never considered having a mother, much less the exquisite woman who stood before him. He clasped his hands together and bowed, unable to speak.

"And you, Chen, my faithful friend. I can never hope to thank you for this moment." She smiled a perfect smile of white teeth framed by red lips.

Chen returned the smile and bowed. The Abbot sniffed into his silk handkerchief, when he saw the display of reverence Chen offered to this woman from another world. Certainly she was excessively wealthy, but he didn't see where it would be of help to the little monk.

Ambrose regained his composure in time to greet Etienne's mother. "It is indeed an honor and a surprise to meet you, Empress." Taking her small white hand, he bowed and lightly kissed it.

Ambrose understood why Etienne's father had succumbed to

the pleasures this woman might offer. She was exotically beautiful with porcelain skin and perfectly proportioned features. Her thick dark hair was pulled into a chignon that rested on the back of her head. Her nails were lacquered a bright red, and the color contrasted sharply with the pale yellow silk which covered her from neck to foot. Ambrose thought that he, too, might have fallen for this woman, in spite of the death sentence such an act incurred.

"Why don't we seat ourselves. T'ien Li, please sit beside your mother. Brothers Ambrose and Chen, you may sit next to me." The Abbot was more than happy to get off his feet, which were becoming increasingly reluctant to carry his weight.

Maurice entered the room to offer the customary tea and pastries, and after everyone had been served, he left them to the privacy of their conversation.

"Ambrose," Abbot de Fleury began, "the Empress indicated surprise over the placement of her son. Apparently she was unaware that your monastery was so small, for she directed her driver here, assuming to find T'ien Li at St. Benoit. Have you mislead her in any way?"

"Absolutely not, Your Grace," Ambrose answered. "I was under the impression that arrangements had been made with full knowledge on both sides. Is that not true, Your Highness?" He turned to the Empress.

"Perhaps so, Ambrose," she spoke softly. "Now that I have seen St. Benoit Abbey, I confess that it is more what I had in mind for T'ien Li, although I am certain he has been tended to most graciously by you." She looked at her son and smiled. She hadn't expected him to be so beautiful, considering his father was Occidental; however, his features were purely Oriental with a European refinement. No one would ever suspect that he wasn't fully Chinese.

"Chen, he has been well tutored, has he not?" Her eyes did not leave T'ien Li.

"He receive best of both worlds, my Empress."

"Then my fears are assuaged, for Chen would surely never exaggerate."

"Your Highness," Abbot de Fleury interjected. "Why do you not take your son into the enclosed courtyard? It is warm there, and you may converse with him privately."

"Yes, of course." As she moved, Ambrose stood to assist her.

"Etienne," he said, "go with your mother, and share your story with her."

Etienne eyed both Chen and Ambrose, searching for answers in faces that revealed nothing. He did as he was told, and they left the room together.

Ambrose watched them until the door had been closed before directing his gaze back to the Abbot. "When did she arrive, Your Grace?" he asked.

"Last night," he replied. "Of course, she was looking for you; however, I encouraged her to stay here, as travel at night can be dangerous. Besides, over the last few years, I've been burning with a curiosity that seems to have been sated."

"Was she in good spirits when she arrived?"

"She was fatigued, but willing to talk. Her French, as you have heard, is impeccable. Your friend must have taught her well."

"He was a scholar," Ambrose replied. "That he spoke flawlessly goes without saying."

"I must inform you," the Abbot said with assurance, "that I have offered the St. Benoit Abbey as a refuge for her son should she wish him to stay here. I doubt she will refuse me, once she has seen your abbey."

"That is indeed generous of you, Your Grace," Ambrose countered, "but he is quite happy where he is."

"Apparently his happiness makes little difference, Ambrose. She sent him off into the world at two weeks to save her own life. I can't imagine her actions would be any different now, unless she has suffered unbearable remorse over her decision."

"Nonetheless, Your Grace, it would be disconcerting to the child to be removed from the only family he has known." Ambrose had never considered the possibility of Etienne moving to St. Benoit. So, there were three options!

"He would certainly create a sensation at Versailles," Abbot de

Fleury smiled to himself. He was already planning T'ien Li's entrance into French society. "Imagine! The son of the Empress of China! Illegitimate at that! You know the Parisians and their love of scandal!"

The Abbot looked over at Chen. "Brother Chen, what do you think of all of this? Are you usually so taciturn?"

"T'ien Li has made choice. Nothing to think."

"How can you say that, my friend?" The Abbot was flustered over Chen's self-possessed calm.

He was accustomed to people being a little nervous in his presence; however, the monks from the Abbey in the Forest had never displayed this timidity, now that he recalled. Only Brother Ambrose seemed a trifle unsettled during this visit and the last one, but the Abbot sensed it had to do with his paternal feelings for the child.

"So, you think he has made a choice, do you?"

"Choice made at conception. Birth only beginning sequence of events effected by choice."

"And this scenario is one of those, I suppose?" Abbot de Fleury shook his head in disbelief.

"You are correct," Chen nodded. "We have no power in T'ien Li's game."

"Well," the Abbot huffed, "we shall see!"

He looked down to retrieve a small piece of pastry that had fallen into the folds of his robes. He was thinking that the Chinese were a very strange people, possessed by an indominatable will. However, he wasn't going to waste his energy on arguments like this, when there was another pastry to finish.

"Your Grace," Ambrose said gently, "we must consider the happiness of the child and not ourselves. I shall abide by his choice, as we all must. There can be no attachment to the fruits of our labor. The pleasure is in the sowing, in the weeding, in the watering."

"Yes Ambrose. Forgive my selfishness." The Abbot appeared to be humbled. There were always opportunities presenting themselves to him. Life had never ceased to be abundant with potential, and if one possibility expired, another would come his way. He put an éclair up to his fat pink lips.

* * *

In the small, perfectly manicured courtyard, Etienne was silent while his mother talked. He was still in a state of shock over the fact that, after years of ignorance regarding his background, he was now confronted with this dignified woman who was the Empress of China, and who, moreover, claimed to be his mother.

A small part of him wished the meeting had never occurred, for it was bound to create change in his simple life. He had never experienced the feeling of insecurity, and at this moment, it took hold of him. The very foundation of his own identity had been shattered, leaving a chasm of darkness.

Etienne had never been one to possess an overdeveloped sense of ego, or this latest news would have given him an immeasurable amount of pride that would have healed the invisible wounds inflicted by the ridicule he had endured over the years from the villagers, as a result of his difference. He was more concerned about his illegitimacy, which conflicted with his romantic childhood dreams surrounding his birth.

"T'ien Li, you aren't listening to me."

"Forgive me, Your Highness," he replied humbly, "I am trying to absorb your presence in my life. I do not know what it means to me."

"My beloved child, my presence has always been near you. Your father taught me about his Christ, and I have prayed to Him as well as to the Buddha, asking them to carry my love to you." She put an exquisite finger against his soft cheek, and when she withdrew it, the long red nail tickled his skin.

"Why have you waited until now to show yourself to me, or to write?" Etienne could not understand her neglect.

"You do not know the difficulty involved in coming to France, T'ien Li. Life does not always take the course we wish it to." She spoke softly. "Why could you have not come through my husband? Why is my only child the progeny of a man whom I loved briefly, and who lost his life as a result of his liaison with me? Do you think I have enjoyed the years without you to amuse me in my aging, without you at my side to love? How I envy Ambrose and Chen, their position in your life!"

"Will you explain to me what happened, Your Highness?" Etienne looked at her.

This was the first woman with whom he had ever conversed, with the exception of his exchanges with the merchants' wives. Her beauty made him uncomfortable, for it presented a barrier to his perspective of her as a mother.

"Very well." She guided him to a small bench where they both sat.

Etienne was oblivious to the bright orange carp swimming in the small pool. Nor did he hear the canaries singing in the trees above him. The courtyard had a glass roof that permitted the birds' freedom. They sang throughout the day, but on this day, their songs went unappreciated by the guests below them.

"Your father traveled to Peking some fifteen years ago. He was a Chinese scholar and a former Jesuit priest. He came to Peking with the hopes of expanding his knowledge of China, for although Europeans have some information on my country, it is, for the most part, quite basic. This man, your father, had a brilliant wit and an insatiable thirst for learning."

"As Occidentals are very rare in China, news of his presence reached me fairly soon after his arrival in Peking. I sent him an invitation that he might present himself at Court, and I decided that, if I liked him, I would employ him to teach me French and the ways of the Western world."

"He was fascinating to me and very handsome, in a strange way, for I was unaccustomed to the physiognomy of the West. I was a willing student who learned French rapidly. At the same time, I taught him our language."

"My husband was gone for months at a time, settling skirmishes in different parts of his empire, - Nepal, Tibet, Mongolia. Therefore, it was not surprising for me to become involved with the man who was in my presence on a daily basis. We were two lonely people. The one whom he loved was in France; my husband was married to his army."

"Ultimately, I conceived a child. You. I was panic stricken, for this was a crime punishable by death, and there was no one to whom I could turn. I managed to conceal my pregnancy from everyone, even my husband, until my fifth month."

"The Emperor unexpectedly returned from a battle and invited me to join him in viewing his armies. Naturally, this meant a lengthy journey by horseback. I became very ill about two weeks into the journey, and the court physician was rushed in to assist me. It was no longer possible to conceal my condition, for further travel would have resulted in my death."

"My husband was called into my tent where he was apprised of the situation. I knew that he would kill me, and I was prepared to die. However, he sent the physician away and knelt down at my bedside, demanding that I tell him everything."

"After my health had improved, we returned to Peking. Etienne was ordered into the Emperor's chambers where he confessed to his part in the affair. He was immediately arrested and executed. My husband was not quite so lenient with me. I would have preferred Etienne's sentence to the one I received."

"I was to give birth to you and to send you back to France, to the home of your father. None were to be made aware of my condition, save the court physician and my handservant. For the duration of my pregnancy, I was confined to a small cottage north of Peking. You were taken from me almost immediately after your birth. I had no time to send appropriate clothing with you, or any of the things I would have liked you to have."

"But you did send along a small gold Buddha and a jade rosary," Etienne interrupted.

"Yes," she sighed. "Yes, I did. I had forgotten all about that. Do you still have them?"

"Yes, Your Highness. Ambrose always kept them next to me when we studied in the library. On my twelfth birthday, he gave them to me. They now sit under my pillow."

"I was afraid they might have been stolen." She sounded sad.

"It all happened so hurriedly, that I packed what little I could into a small bag. The rosary was Etienne's, a gift from me. He slipped it to me on the way to his execution. 'For our son,' he said. Those were his last words to me."

"Did you know where I was to be sent?" Etienne was softening to this lovely woman whose voice pulled at his heartstrings.

"Yes," she replied. "I arranged your passage, everything. I did not trust my husband entirely, so I allowed small pieces of misinformation to reach him. Only Chen knew of your destination. I paid dearly for your safe passage, and I was never certain that you were alive, until Chen agreed to visit you. You see, Chen would never have gone to France without knowing of your safety."

"Chen knows much of what we do not," Etienne agreed.

"I was spared my life, T'ien Li, but I lost yours. I have never forgiven myself for this."

"Has your husband forgiven you, Mother?" The word sounded strange to his ears.

"Long ago. He is now older and wiser, and he no longer spends much time away from me. We never had a child together, and he is now willing to recognize you as his son. He wishes you to succeed him when he abdicates the throne."

"And when will that be?"

"I do not know, my son." She shook her head. "I assume he has several years ahead of him."

"Why have you come, Mother?" Etienne was puzzled. "Travel is not pleasant, and the distance is great. What is your purpose?"

"I wish to convince you to return to China with me. I want you to succeed the Ch'ien Lung Emperor, as is your right."

Etienne leaped to his feet. He clasped his hands against his heart and stared at his mother, the Empress. Chen's words in the coach came back to him. 'Speak from inner wisdom. Do not be caught by element of surprise,' he had said. However, Etienne felt himself incapable of making such a decision. His training had not prepared him for this and he was too young to direct the course of his life.

"Mother," he spoke solemnly, "let us return to the others where I might have time to think."

[68]

He offered his hand, and they left the courtyard, their arms linked together. Strangers no longer, they made their way back to the others.

When the doors opened, the three men turned to look at the Empress and her son. Ambrose stood and helped her to her chair. The Abbot smiled benignly, while Chen wisely observed mother and son.

During their absence, Ambrose and the Abbot had come to an amicable place, which helped to alleviate some of the discomfort the former had felt in the last few years. Ambrose had quietly resigned himself to Etienne's possible departure, for he realized that sooner or later Etienne would inevitably leave the Abbey. Most likely the life of an ascetic was not his destiny, in the light of his royal heritage.

"My friends," Abbot de Fleury began, "afternoon is upon us, and soon it will be time to partake of the evening meal. Will you be my guests?"

"Your Grace, it is most kind of you, but we must return to the Abbey," Ambrose replied. "Perhaps Etienne wishes to stay with his mother for the night, if you would accommodate him. We can send Brother Gerard for him in the morning."

Ambrose looked over at the boy who seemed smaller to him, with the weight of the burden he carried. Their eyes met, and a message of fathomless love and acceptance passed between them. The child looked at Chen for support. He stood beside his mother, and the resemblance between the two was uncanny. No one would ever doubt their relationship.

"Yes, yes. Of course! We can keep the child!" The Abbot wiped his mouth and pushed himself out of his chair with renewed gusto. He was improvising his strategy in anticipation of Etienne choosing to live at St. Benoit Abbey. A second chance had offered itself prematurely, and he must be ready.

"May I have Maurice show you out, Brothers?"

"Your Grace, we are quite capable on our own." Ambrose smiled. "We shall send a carriage back tomorrow around noon. He turned back to Etienne. "My son," he said, and bowed.

Etienne left his mother's side to embrace Ambrose. He bowed

[69]

to Chen who would not have permitted such a display of affection. The two monks walked out together, leaving Etienne alone with the Abbot and the Empress.

* * *

It was dark when Gerard pulled the horses to a stop in front of the Abbey gates. After two strenuous trips into town and back, he reminded himself to give his pets an extra portion of oats, for they had earned it. They were eager to get back to the stable, and Gerard had to hold them in place while Chen and Ambrose stepped out of the carriage.

"I'll be a little late for supper, Brothers," Gerard said gruffly. "The horses need a good rubdown."

"We'll see to it that Charles keeps your food warm, Gerard," Ambrose answered him. "And thank you."

"Will you be needing the carriage in the morning?"

"Yes," Ambrose paused, thinking of an appropriate time. "I believe we'll go in for Etienne right after lunch."

"All right, Brother." Gerard turned to give the horses the signal to move; however, they had anticipated his actions and galloped off in advance of his gesture, forcing Gerard to right his balance.

The men opened the gates and stepped behind the cloistered walls. They entered the foyer, without speaking, and walked into the chapel where the others had gathered for meditation. Unnoticed, Ambrose and Chen slid onto the benches, and opened themselves to being received by the sea of silence.

The little flame on the altar flickered noiselessly as the air, created by their movement, fanned it. Shadows momentarily danced on the wall before they lost their life, once again, to the stillness. The light barely outlined the motionless figures united in silence on the One Most High.

The tinkling of the bell brought them back into the individual state. The monks rose simultaneously, bowed toward the cross, and then walked in single file out of the chapel. They were barely in the hall before they turned to Ambrose and Chen with questioning faces.

"Tell us what has happened, Ambrose." Tristan spoke for the rest. "Where is Etienne?"

"Why don't we discuss it at dinner, Tristan," Ambrose responded. "Surely it can wait another half an hour?"

He had wanted to wash himself after the ride into town, and he was well aware that as the night grew colder, so did the water. Ambrose took leave of the others and went to his room to get a clean robe and some soap. The chill of the water on his body revitalized him, carrying away the fatigue that had hung over him, since he and Chen had departed from the Abbot's quarters. Ambrose placed his face against the cool rag and surrendered himself to the sensation of a good scrub.

By the time everyone had convened for dinner, Ambrose felt refreshed. He was keenly aware of Etienne's absence, a rarity in the past thirteen years, unless the child had been ill. François and Charles served soup and bread, and after the grace, all eyes were on Ambrose.

He smiled at the brothers' curiosity and at the irony of it, for in their assumably detached state, curiosity was not an energy that was encouraged. However, when it came to each other, the bonding between them precluded a sense of detachment. The feelings of love were accompanied by a genuine concern.

"Ambrose! You've kept us in the dark for twelve years!" Tristan exclaimed. "Please, enlighten our inquisitive minds!"

"You've been very patient, my Brothers," Ambrose began. "I haven't meant to delude you in any way, as my silence was solely for the protection of Etienne."

"The story is not any more grand than anyone else's, for we each have a past that is of interest to someone. As you know, his father was our Brother Etienne who left for China around fifteen and a half years ago. His journey led him to Peking where he was received at court by the Empress of China."

"She took a liking to him and he was hired to tutor her in French and European history. He was a long way from home, and her husband was gone most of the time effecting changes with his

[71]

armies. What happened is not uncommon. The Empress found herself with child, the result of her union with Etienne."

"Her husband was made aware of her condition, sometime in the middle of her pregnancy. Etienne was executed. The Empress was ferreted away to a secluded estate until the child was born. It was at this point that I received correspondence from her beseeching me to take the child. You know the rest."

"What does this have to do with the Abbot?" James asked.

"Etienne's mother has come to France, with the hopes of convincing her son to return with her to China. She thought the St. Benoit Abbey might be ours; hence, she stopped there en route. The Abbot couldn't resist a good piece of gossip and invited her to stay. Etienne is with her now."

"What does this mean for us, Ambrose?" Pasqual asked.

"I don't know. It's really Etienne's decision, and I can't make assumptions on his behalf."

"Chen," François interrupted, "tell us what the outcome will be."

"When you not attached to outcome, knowledge will follow," Chen said.

"Chen, how can you ignore our curiosity?" Tristan implored.

"It take great fortitude. You have noisy minds." Chen baited his friends. "Answer here, not in head," he said, tapping his heart.

"I think he will be back here among us," Andrew said. "Etienne's time in France is not yet over."

"You very wise, Andrew, very wise. You have no fear and can see with clarity," Chen complimented the silent brother.

Ambrose looked over at Andrew, his closest friend over the years since the departure of Etienne's father. How little he actually knew the quiet man! He had been so involved in the upbringing of the child, that he had often taken Andrew's constant support for granted. It was Andrew who always sensed Ambrose's moods and who acted as a buffer for him. It was Andrew whose comfortable silence absorbed others' energy, transforming disquiet into peace. Andrew the devoted one, the one who surrendered his personality to the service of Self. Naturally he would be filled with a quiet knowing of the way things are to be, for Andrew was the Occidental

[72]

counterpart to Chen.

"Then we can afford to be optimistic," Ambrose concluded. "My Brothers, I admit that I feel a burden has been lifted from me, from all of us."

"This calls for a dessert!" François said, standing with a flourish. "Fresh apple tart!"

James stood also. "Brothers, tonight I shall sing for you in the library to celebrate new beginnings."

Everyone looked at James. No one had ever heard him sing without the accompaniment of the others. They were all aware that he could repair a lyre, so he must have some familiarity with music.

"Well, I wouldn't miss this for anything, James!" Tristan said gleefully.

"Yes," Ambrose added. "If your debut is to be this evening, let it be for us!"

François came back into the dining hall with his tart made from the apples that Gerard had spontaneously purchased in town. The latter had entered the dinner late, after his horses had been put to bed, and the gaiety in the room had even produced a smile from the grim little monk.

After the last of the dessert had been eaten, and the kitchen had been cleaned, everyone gathered in the library to hear Brother James. To some, it was like old times, before the responsibility of the child. To all, it was the lifting of a cloud that had hung over them for some time. The mystery of Etienne's past had been revealed. That the information was open was particularly appealing to Ambrose, for he had disliked the attention the secrecy had created.

"James, sing to us." Tristan commanded gently. "Let us hear this fresh voice."

James stood in front of the small gathering. He looked at all of his brothers and then at Chen who was seated on the rug, his legs crossed under him. Briefly, he closed his eyes to calm himself, for he could feel his body trembling, as it had done years ago. When he was fully prepared, he opened his mouth to allow the sounds of devotion to come forth into the comfort of the room. The notes he sang were clear and bright, and his voice released its power as he relaxed. It opened its force upon the receptive crowd, so that all were touched by the magic. The mellifluous resonance touched the heart of each man, all of whom were entranced by the beauty.

His songs evoked memories of innocence and purity and then wove those memories into the wisdom of Divine Love. Within each soul was a secret sorrow longing to be purged in the light of forgiveness, and as James sang, these sorrows arose from the dark caverns of exile into the illumination of understanding. He was tireless. An hour passed during which the entire group had entered into a holy state of exaltation.

When he finished, the ensuing silence went unheard, for the music was still within the ears, within the heart. Gerard looked transfixed, for within him the pain of a loveless childhood was being healed. Tristan was crying. Ambrose had his head in his hands, and even Chen had eyes that were filled.

"Oh Chen," James thought. "Even you have your own pain. Is it your homeland that calls you from this alien place, or is it your responsibility to your beloved T'ien Li and the knowledge of what is to come?"

Aloud, he said, "I thank you, my friends, for letting me share my gift with you."

"James, why have we never had this pleasure before?" Andrew's voice was filled with awe.

"I left singing behind many years ago, Andrew," he replied. "As a child, I was forced to perform for people. There was so much attention on the power of my voice that I became lost to that identity. I left my family and my singing in the past when I entered these walls. It is here that I have learned the truth about myself, about who I really am, and in knowing that truth, I can share my gift again."

"It was truly a holy experience for us all, James," Tristan acknowledged. "Will you sing for us again?"

"Perhaps, but I cannot promise, for I still have apprehension about the power the voice wields over the audience."

"Then, if it would make you more comfortable, James, we'll let you choose the times you might wish to sing for us."

"I accept, Ambrose."

Ambrose got up from his chair and turned to the others. "I'm

[74]

exhausted, Brothers. It's been an interminably long day. Good night to each of you."

Slowly, the gathering dispersed, each monk going to his individual cell. Darkness fell over the Abbey in the Forest, and outside, the sky was without the benefit of moonlight.

In his room, Chen sat and looked through his window to the stars beyond.

* * *

At the Abbot's residence, Etienne sat in his room looking at the same night sky. He was thinking about his brothers and wondering if they had been told the truth about his parents. The celebration of the reunion with his mother had exhausted him. He was not used to being around such commotion, and the rich food had made his stomach ache.

Etienne hardly thought he could sleep, for his nerves were overriding his fatigue. He recounted the hours that had flown by in the presence of the regal woman whose feminine energy had made him feel awkward. He was so accustomed to being in the presence of men and their modes of expression, that he had been taken aback several times when his mother had touched him, or had straightened his hair, and especially when she had cried upon their parting so that each could partake of much needed sleep.

His feelings of inadequacy surfaced, for he had not been trained in the ways of women. If he had, he might have been more successful in meeting her needs, or he might even have been more receptive to her. It occurred to Etienne that he was totally ignorant about one half of the world's population. If his mother had been a commoner, the reality would have been accepted with a greater degree of ease. But an empress?

She had all but ignored everyone at the fine dinner the Abbot had hosted, in order to focus all of her attention on her beloved son. The Abbot had been perturbed, for there had been no opportunity to speak on behalf of St. Benoit Abbey as a potential home for Etienne. The boy had sensed the Abbot's desires and had not given

[75]

fuel to any discussion that might flame them. He had remained quiet throughout the meal of roast venison, boiled potatoes and baby peas, listening to his mother's voice as she told him about China.

He hardly remembered the names of the dinner guests, - a Countess de Grasse and her husband and a visiting bishop. Everyone had been made pale by comparison to the Empress, his beautiful Empress, his mother.

Etienne sighed deeply and pushed his head further into his pillow. The morning would soon be dawning, and he felt the heaviness of a decision weighing his heart. He knew that his choice would invariably hurt someone. He closed his eyes against the argument of his mind and lay still.

Back at the monastery, Chen was still gazing out of his window, long after Etienne's mind had grown quiet and his breathing had become rhythmical.

* * *

In her large room, the Empress sat in the comfort of her bed staring at a small candle. Her heart was laden with a deep sorrow, that had been repressed over the years as a protective measure. Her life had to go on, for she could not neglect her people. It was through her fierce determination that she had arrived in France at all, for she had spent years subtly working on her husband to receive his support for the journey. Her saving grace had been her barren years with him. He began to realize that an illegitimate son was better than no son at all, and ultimately he decided that his wife should go to France to convince her son to return to China.

He doubted the boy would succumb to his mother's desires and had told her so. She was beginning to think that he was right. T'ien Li was Chinese by birth, but his mannerisms were very French. Chen had exerted considerable influence over him, but even Chen had adapted to the life she had begged him to experience for her sake.

She was beginning to perceive her trip as pure folly. What right had she to come into T'ien Li's existence unannounced and to

[76]

demand that he leave behind everything that was familiar to him to assume a role that held no meaning in his heart?

For the first time, she stopped thinking about her own needs and considered those of her son. It was best for him to remain where he was, until he was old enough to be capable of making a decision based upon his inner wisdom. It was apparent that he was very happy in France, and it would break her heart were he to choose to come with her out of a sense of duty, only to become miserable in a new reality. His beautiful countenance deserved to be radiant with joy.

She knew she must return to China knowing her mission had been fulfilled. A connection had been made, and in the years ahead, they would correspond with one another. Their relationship would develop, as a matter of course.

The Empress felt a new lightness in her heart. A certain clarity had overtaken her, changing her perception. For the first time in years, a sense of calm had been restored in the one unresolved area of her life, that of her son. She did not know what had come over her in the late hours of the night in this strange part of the world. Perhaps Etienne's Christ had given her the peace that passeth understanding.

She felt hungry for the first time in days and regretted having picked at her dinner; however, the morning would arrive shortly, and knowing the Abbot, there would be no lack of food.

She reminded herself to apologize to the Abbot for her preoccupation with her son, to the exclusion of the other guests. The Empress turned toward the bedside table and blew the candle which had almost burned itself out. She settled into her satin sheets and closed her eyes.

Before the dawning of the new day, Chen lay back on his bed to catch a few hours' sleep. He felt at peace.

Chapter Seven

Etienne was looking out of his window, onto the street below, when he heard a light tapping on his door. He sighed deeply and went to receive his early morning visitor. The child was not unhappy to see his mother standing before him, looking beautiful in a gown of purple silk brocade. Her hair had not yet been placed into its rather austere bun, and it fell over her shoulders and down her back in a thick dark mass. She was smiling at her son who, at thirteen, was as tall as she.

"Good morning, T'ien Li. I hope your sleep has refreshed you."

"Come in, Mother. Etienne stood back and gestured for her to enter. Her presence awakened his memory of her from the day before and did not make his decision any easier.

She glided to the window and delicately pushed aside a lace curtain to give her a clearer view of the street. "My room overlooks the monastery. At least you have a livelier view." The Empress Qu'an Li looked across the room at her son, who appeared so very vulnerable to her. "He's torn over this decision I have forced upon him," she thought. "It's best for me to relieve his anxiety."

Aloud, she said, "T'ien Li, come here." She held out her perfectly shaped hands to receive her son.

Etienne noticed the nails were clear, revealing little half moons at the cuticle. He took her hands in his own and marveled at their softness. Their eyes met, and the son felt the strength offered him by his mother.

"T'ien Li," she began, "I have been most selfish. I cannot let you make a decision when you are not ready for it. It is not time for you to leave your family. They have loved you and have cared for you unselfishly, and it is evident that your home is with them at this time in your life."

"Are you happy about this, Mother?" Etienne felt relief flood his heart.

"I'm happier than I ever thought I would be," she replied, smiling at him. "Wherever you are, wherever I am, we shall always
[78]

be mother and son. The bonding is not diminished by distance."

"There is a reason for your sojourn here, and for that reason you must stay," she continued. "We can communicate freely through the mails, albeit they are slow. We are blessed that we do not have a language barrier. You can now describe your life to me in the fullest detail, and I shall understand."

"Thank you, Mother," Etienne whispered. "Maybe someday, I shall see the land of my birth."

"Perhaps you will, my son. Now, let us see what the Abbot's staff has prepared for breakfast this morning."

* * *

Andrew approached Ambrose shortly after the morning prayers had ended. He observed that his brother was looking more tired than usual. "I don't suppose the events in the last few days have helped," he thought. Aloud he said, "Ambrose, I'm coming with you into town."

The elder monk turned to look at Andrew. "Why thank you, Brother. I'd enjoy the company."

"I remember accompanying you some thirteen years ago on a similar mission, except this time, there's no cloak and dagger aspect to it." Andrew smiled at his friend. "Do you think Chen will want to come also?"

"I've already spoken with him. He feels it is best that he remain here."

"Doesn't he want to spend time with the Empress?" Andrew thought the two would have needed to share words.

"I do believe the Empress will come to our abbey, for she will most assuredly wish to examine her son's home," Ambrose replied. "Chen has decided to prepare a room for her."

"Ironical, isn't it, Ambrose, an empress at this humble place."

"Not only an empress, Andrew, a very beautiful woman." Ambrose patted his friend on the back "Our brothers will have a rare opportunity to see beauty, poise, grace, and dignity within one of the feminine gender."

"Brother, do you think a few of us will wish to renounce our

[79]

vows?" Andrew laughed to himself over the possibility of such an occurrence.

"We couldn't afford it," Ambrose countered. "Our vineyards need too much work."

They had stopped in the foyer to finish their talk. Andrew walked over to the flowers to insure the bowl had been filled with water. Farther down the hall, there was a slight commotion. Ambrose looked to see Pasqual and Chen engaged in a heated discussion.

"But this is impossible!" Pasqual was saying. "Those blankets are for the King of France. You cannot expect me to give them to you!"

"Not for me, Pasqual. For Empress of China. She come for visit. She sleep on special blankets."

"And how do you know she will stay?"

"Chen know this for certain." He stopped to face Pasqual, drawing himself into a regal position, which immediately intimidated his opponent into one of acquiescence.

"Very well, Chen. Just this once." Pasqual relented. "Does Her Highness wish a pillow to support her head?"

"Yes. Yes. She fragile flower with iron stem."

"Have you solved your dilemma, Brothers?" Ambrose interrupted.

"Dilemma solved before confrontation," Chen replied. "Nonetheless, we find it necessary to engage in follow up of words."

Pasqual did not quite understand what Chen had said; however, intuition bade him to be silent, and instead of responding, he turned to Ambrose. "Are you leaving to collect Etienne from the Abbot's house?"

"Yes," Ambrose answered. "Shortly."

"Best that it's shortly, Ambrose, lest the child begin to resemble His Grace in stature." Pasqual couldn't resist the slight barb.

"Pasqual!" Andrew exclaimed. "This is not the French Court!"

"It will be with an empress in residence," the feisty monk retorted.

All of the brothers, including Pasqual, smiled at this last

remark, for it could very well be that the truth was spoken. Andrew looked over at Ambrose, both of them imagining the repercussions should the news spread that the Empress of China was staying at the Abbey in the Forest. The King himself would most likely wish to pay his respects, although he rarely left Versailles. However, his ministers were not without designing minds, and it would be highly probable that they would swarm the Abbey, catapulting it into the light of notoriety.

"Brothers, there's work for me in the library," Ambrose said, interrupting the gaiety and stepping away from the group, "and not enough time."

The small cluster disbanded. Pasqual rushed back to his workshop to ferret away some of his woolens, for there was no telling what Her Highness might wish to abscond with, upon her departure. Andrew decided to join Tristan in the fields, and Chen went to find Brother James to convince him to make a comfortable bed from some of his extra lumber. He had all intentions that the Empress Qu'an Li would be well received at the Abbey in the Forest.

* * *

"And so, my son, what have you decided to do with yourself, now that your mother has arrived?" The Abbot wiped some gravy off his chin with a large white napkin.

"But I shall remain here, Your Grace!" Etienne replied. "There is no other decision for me to make."

"Here? At St. Benoit Abbey!?" His Grace could hardly believe his good fortune.

"No, Your Grace, at the Abbey in the Forest."

"Surely, Your Highness," the Abbot turned toward his exalted guest, "you will change your mind upon visiting the place. You are going to see for yourself the milieu in which T'ien Li dwells, are you not?"

"But of course, Your Grace." The Empress' eyes held a hint of challenge in them. "I have not traveled such distances without entertaining the notion. In fact," she looked at her son, "I am hoping

[81]

to stay with you for a few days, T'ien Li, if they will have me."

"If this is your desire, Mother, certainly Chen is already aware of it, and arrangements have been made."

"Yes, Chen was always the master at prediction. No secrets were ever safe from him. I think my husband would have fared much more brilliantly in battle had Chen been his chief advisor!"

"Ah! Such a treat!" the Abbot gasped.

Both Etienne and his mother stopped talking, for they politely wished to include the Abbot in the conversation, when he had indicated such an interest. However, the Abbot's eyes were on the dessert which had been carried into the room by Maurice, and which was being presented to him for his approval. They were to be served small meringues shaped like swans with long graceful necks. On the back of each swan was a round ball of ice cream, held in place by curved wings. A thick chocolate sauce rolled down the rich cream and on to the plate.

"Mother, do not expect this kind of food at the Abbey," Etienne whispered. "We eat very simply."

"Why would I expect otherwise, my son?" she smiled. "It is no different than the monasteries in China." Leaning forward, she spoke very quietly. "St. Benoit is an exception to the rule, I should think."

When the last of the dessert had been eaten, and His Grace was able to concentrate on matters at hand, he spoke to Qu'an Li. "Your Highness, it is with sadness that I see you take the child back to the Abbey in the Forest, when we have a perfectly suitable program for him; however, I am happy to abide by your decisions, and I consider them just, in the light of his past history with the brothers. Should you have a change of sentiments, we would always be ready to receive him."

"You are most kind, Your Grace," the Empress replied, and your hospitality has exceeded the normal limits. For this, we are grateful."

In the distance, they could hear a commotion at the front door. Etienne stood, as the visitors were most likely from the Abbey, and he was eager to see them.

"Excuse me, Your Grace." He walked over to kiss the Abbot's

hand and then went back to assist his mother. "Mother, are your valises out of your room?"

"Please!" Abbot de Fleury interjected. "One of my servants will bring them. Maurice, please assist me."

Maurice went to pull the Abbot from his chair, while Etienne and Qu'an Li walked down the hall to greet Ambrose and Andrew, whose brown robes were a welcome sight. For the first time Etienne, with a new maturity, did not hug Ambrose. Rather, he bowed to the monks. Within his heart, Ambrose felt a twinge. His son was growing up rapidly.

The Abbot waddled down the hall to see his guests depart safely. He rather liked the visits from the brothers of the Abbey in the Forest, for they were an entertaining group of men with their humble ways. He bid adieu to the Empress and her son and watched them get into the carriage, whose top had been loaded with her luggage. Abbot de Fleury did not shut his door until the carriage was out of his sight. He was lost in thought. T'ien Li's presence in his life would some day mean a tidy sum of money to him. . . . .

* * *

The ride to the Abbey in the Forest was not as comfortable as her previous experiences in carriages; however, Qu'an Li paid little attention. She was beginning to have a clearer understanding of the difference in resources between her son's abbey and St. Benoit. The terrain was a little rougher, the carriage was a little older, and instead of noticing her discomfort, she chose to look outside at the Loire Valley. She imagined the exquisite colors the scenery would offer in the spring and summer.

As the coach wended its way more deeply into the forest, she felt herself truly relax for the first time in three months. Her son was with her, and she was forsaking the noises of ships and villages for the seclusion of a monastery in the woods. She felt a healing balm spread across her soul.

She had liked Ambrose the moment she had met him; however, she had never doubted that she would like the man whom T'ien Li's father had loved so deeply. She wondered if this were the person for whom Etienne had expressed long soulful sighs, when he had thought no one was listening. Andrew was likeable enough. A handsome man with a very serious nature. Something about him reminded her of Chen.

And Gerard. Well, Gerard was finding it difficult to be agreeable, which the Empress interpreted as temerity on his part. And there were thirteen others, although T'ien Li had spoken mostly of seven or eight who seemed to have had a greater influence upon him.

The ride was, thankfully, not a long one. Qu'an Li was happily surprised to have arrived at the front gates as quickly as they had. She was ushered out of the carriage by Ambrose, while her son ran ahead to pull the cord. François, looking rather flustered, came out to receive them.

"Your Highness," he said, bowing deeply. White flour was on his sleeves, and his apron had been tucked into the back of his belt.

Behind François came the others, who had been waiting impatiently for the sight of Etienne's mother. They were monks first. Thusly, they behaved with dignity. However, they were also men, and each of them appreciated her beauty. Etienne felt a surge of pride, rush through him.

Qu'an Li immediately felt comfortable with the denizens of the small monastery. There was no display of pomposity, as she had witnessed at St. Benoit. After introductions, the monks disappeared to their respective quarters, and her son and Ambrose proceeded to give her a tour of the Abbey.

"How long has this abbey existed, Ambrose?" Qu'an Li asked.

"About one hundred years. It's been deliberately kept small, for we have no desire to accommodate many monks. There have never been more than twenty of us here at one time."

"Have you always been self-supporting?"

"As you know, we have a vineyard which turns out the best of wines, and we have a substantial herd of sheep whose wool is highly valued by those who know it," Ambrose replied. "Other than these two means of income, much of our sustenance comes from the legacies of our brothers and their families. We always

[84]

manage to get by, Your Highness. You, yourself, have been most generous. With your funding, we have added a new variety of grape to our vineyards, and we have extended the tillable land to sixty acres.

"So, essentially your income goes back into the land, your food, and necessary supplies. I see that you do not fill your monastery with art." Qu'an Li was impressed with the simplicity of the Abbey.

"Your Highness," Ambrose responded, "we have one weakness, and that is for rare books. Our library is quite extensive. Most of us have a love of knowledge that necessitates philosophical exploration through the written word, in addition to our inner experiences. Come, let us show you."

"Mother, the library is my favorite room," Etienne said happily.

The three walked down the long hall and through the doors into the impressive room. The Empress was surprised, for this room had more to offer than those she had seen at St. Benoit Abbey. It wasn't just the rows upon rows of books; it was the feel of the place. Qu'an Li could have been in her favorite room in the Great Palace, for it was infused with the same sense of love and comfort.

"Ambrose would put me on the table when I was little," Etienne said. "I still remember sitting there and listening to him reading to me, while my Buddha and my rosary lay at my side."

"Yes, Your Highness," Ambrose smiled at Etienne. "Even at the age of two, your son had a special interest in learning. You may freely come here while you are with us. This is everyone's room, although I seem to make the greatest use of it.

He put his arms around Etienne's shoulders. "Why don't you show your mother to her room, Etienne. It's the last one in the south hall."

"Yes, Ambrose." He turned to the Empress and took her arm. "Come, Mother. You may want to rest while we meditate."

"T'ien Li, I wish to do as you. Therefore, I ask for no special privileges. When you join with the others, I shall also. We do not have long together, and I want to absorb your life, entirely."

"Very well, Mother, meditation is in one hour."

It was so unusual, seeing the figure of a woman walk down the

[85]

Abbey halls, her fragrant scent lingering in the cool air. When they came to the room that had been arranged for her stay, Etienne opened the door to allow them entrance.

He was surprised to see the comfort that had been given to the little cell. One beautifully handcrafted bed had been covered in soft, white woolen blankets. On top of the small dresser was a vase with some flowers. Chen had seen that the room was equipped with a bowl and a pitcher of water for her bath, should she wish the privacy to refresh herself. On the floor was a small blue and burgundy oriental carpet that must have been pulled from storage, for Etienne could not remember having seen it before.

"Your family has been very resourceful, T'ien Li. This room is most comfortable."

"I'll leave you now, Mother, and I shall return before the evening meditation."

He leaned down and kissed her hand before turning into down the hall. Only after he had rounded the corner did he hear the metallic sound of the latch, as the door closed.

Qu'an Li settled into the comfort of her room, lying on the soft blankets and hoping to rest for a few minutes. She felt wonderfully free in the minute space, after years of overseeing the immense responsibilities related to her life in the Great Palace. There was such a protective atmosphere at the Abbey, and it was clear to her why the monks preferred it to the hapless confusion of the outside world. The thought of pushing her son into a lifestyle that was diametrically opposed to everything he had learned so far, seemed repugnant to her. "It's best that he make a conscious choice from the vantage point of maturity," she thought.

Her mind was too active for her to relax, and so she went over to the washbowl. After pouring water into it, she lifted a serviette that had been lying next to the bowl, and placed the cool wet linen against her face. The back of her eyes ached from fatigue, and the cold water squelched the pain.

Etienne's light knock at the door reminded her of time's swift passing. Together, they walked to the small chapel, where the other brothers were convening. She had often meditated in the Great Palace, for one of the monks would join her in this practice.

[86]

Originally, it had been Chen, and then a variety of them would take turns coming into her chambers, thrice weekly, in the afternoons.

The experience had always been pleasant for Qu'an Li; however, this time, there was an entirely different sensation. There was a living energy around these men that had been created by their bonding. To the Empress, it was almost a separate entity that filled the room with its light, its warmth. She immersed herself in the myriad of sensations that overcame her, for Qu'an Li was able to totally surrender herself to new experiences.

Within her was an awakening to the energy of Christ, which gave her an understanding of the heart of the man who had fathered her son. She and Etienne, during their brief liason, had differed in that one area. She had, at times, found his faith in absolution through the force of love quite childlike, and now this presence in the chapel was feeding her with an appreciation of this faith.

The area surrounding her heart was feeling a pressure, as though further expansion were inhibited by the bones in her chest. She breathed slowly and rhythmically to dislodge the energy mass within her, focusing her gaze on the flame that burned steadily on the altar. And then she forgot everything as her own consciousness merged with the Infinite.

Qu'an Li did not want to leave the chapel for dinner. She wished to remain forever in that one moment of Grace, where nothing existed for her but timelessness; however, Etienne's presence awakened her to her duty toward him. They did not speak on the way to the dining hall, for she wanted to stay in the memory of the previous hour.

She was as inconspicuous as an empress could be at the dinner, for this was the first time Qu'an Li was able to observe the entire family to whom she had sent her son, thirteen years before. She saw that the group was well balanced, in that some were scholars, some were more devotional in nature, and others had a more earthy quality. This gave her son a diverse group of individuals from whom he could learn. She was wondering how well Chen had adapted to the surroundings, when François came running into the room with Charles on his heels.

[87]

"Your Highness," Charles stammered, "we regret to inform you that, for the first time in my fourteen years as a cook, I have burned the bread!"

"He has burned the bread!" François repeated excitedly.

"But this makes no difference to me!" the Empress exclaimed.

"Your Highness, our bread is the specialty of the house!" François whined. "When all else fails, it is the bread that maintains our reputation as chefs, and today, we have lost even that!"

Qu'an Li noticed that the apron, that had been hanging from François' belt when they were introduced, was still in the same place. She felt that perhaps the burned bread somehow related to her presence, although she would never voice such thoughts. She looked across at Chen who lifted the corners of his mouth in a slight smile. This confirmed her suspicions.

"Brothers," she replied, "I have eaten to excess at Abbot de Fleury's residence, and the burnt bread is just a reminder for me to go lightly. Make no matter of this, for I shall be able to taste your fine bread before I leave."

This only mildly pleased the disconcerted monks, whose brows were knitted together in frustration. They bowed simultaneously and disappeared into the kitchen to bring out the soup and cheese. Qu'an Li barely touched her food, as she was indeed engorged from the last two days.

She was happy to leave the table at the end of the meal and to return to her room for the night. Etienne had sensed her fatigue and did not offer conversation as he walked with her. Her head was barely upon the small pillow, before she lost herself to sleep.

In the morning, Etienne went out with Tristan to help with the sheep, allowing his mother to tend to her own affairs. He needed to talk with someone, and he felt a little ashamed to discuss things of this nature with Ambrose, whom he idolized. Tristan was more human to him and, therefore, more receptive.

They walked in silence at first, several meters apart, to move the sheep out closer to the forests. Etienne no longer felt fear over accompanying Tristan to the forests, for the shadow man hadn't appeared for some time. He could concentrate fully on the woolly little animals and the familiar, if a trifle colorless, environs.

[88]

When all of the animals had been coerced into the right spot, Etienne walked over to Tristan and sat next to the slender, studious man. Tristan always had a book with him, that came out of his robes at the first sign of a brief respite from his work. He had sensed that Etienne needed to speak with him, and so he kept his copy of Voltaire's *Age of Louis XIV* in his pocket.

"What seems to be troubling you, my friend?" he asked, as Etienne approached him.

"Tristan, I don't know how to discuss this. It's all so new to me."

"Has it something to do with your mother?"

"Yes."

"Well, let's seat ourselves and discuss it, shall we?" Tristan gracefully lowered himself to the ground and patted the dry grass next to him.

Etienne settled and began to talk. "It's about me too," he stammered.

"Etienne," Tristan aided him, "does it have something to do with the nature of your birth?"

"Why, yes, Tristan. I am what they call a bastard, am I not?"

"You could say that," Tristan replied diplomatically, "but you do have royal parentage, Etienne, and there are many children born without the protection of wedlock."

"But Tristan, does it change who I am? At times I wish I never knew the reality, so that I could imagine what I pleased."

"Etienne, you are who you are because of your parents, and also in spite of them. It both affects and does not affect your destiny."

"You sound like Chen," Etienne replied.

"Well, it's true," Tristan countered. "It is very simple. Nothing matters, and everything matters. Simplicity and complexity are partners, my friend."

"Did you know my father?"

"Yes. He was a wonderful man, very bright and driven by his scholarly ideals."

"Mother said he loved someone here, but I haven't seen any woman attractive enough to take him from his vows."

Etienne's statement confirmed a suspicion Tristan had long

held; however, he would never reveal it to anyone, most of all to the boy. "If he did love someone, Etienne, he kept it from all of us."

"Tristan, I'll always feel guilty about my parentage. I'm angry with the man who fathered me and sad that he was executed. Can you understand that?"

"Etienne, don't take refuge from the world because of self-pity!" Tristan spoke vehemently. "There are many bastards, some of them high born, most of them not. It's really nothing."

"How can you be certain of this? Surely you are speaking thusly to make me feel better."

"I, too, am a bastard, Etienne, and I have allowed this to isolate me from everything. You might call me a prisoner of my own making."

"Do you know who your parents are?" Etienne felt relieved to know there was another such as he.

"Yes, Etienne. My father was King Louis XV, and my mother was a beautiful chamber maid with whom he dallied. My mother was banished from the Court when her pregnancy was revealed. The King never helped her, and her life, which for years had been very exciting, became miserable. She lost her beauty and aged rapidly into an embittered woman. I was to blame for her fall from grace, and she never forgave me. It was easy to dislike King Louis!"

"Did you ever see your father?" Etienne asked.

"Once, when I was eighteen," Tristan went on with his story. "Mother was taken ill with pneumonia shortly after my seventeenth year. She was too weak, and I was forced to care for her. She never recovered. Within a year, she had died, a little more than skin and bones. Right before her death, she told me who my father was, and then she begged my forgiveness for all of her years of bitterness. She died an unhappy, remorseful woman."

"I went to Court with the hopes of meeting my father. Mother had told me about the extravagance at Versailles, but I was unprepared for the wealth. It was then that I understood her anger, for it would have been very difficult to be banished from the proximity of such a pampered lifestyle, even though she was just a chamber maid."

"By some twist of fate, I found myself in the company of His

Highness. I was leaving Versailles, after finding it impossible to gain an audience with him, when his coach overtook me. Roads outside of Versailles are notoriously bad, and the left front wheel of the King's coach fell into a large pothole. Naturally, it was incapacitated, and I took advantage of this incident by assisting the coachman in repairing the wheel."

"The King found favor with me and came over to personally thank me. It was then that I mentioned that my mother had been in his service many years before. He paused to recall, and then all he said was, 'Oh her. I dismissed her for her immorality.' He then gave me a long look from head to toe and turned to get into the carriage. As the entourage pulled away, he leaned out of the window and called out to me. 'You didn't turn out half so badly!' I stood there, mouth agape, and watched them ride off."

"What did you do then, Tristan?" Etienne asked, spellbound, forgetting his own troubles in the light of Tristan's story.

"I was heartbroken, Etienne. For years, I had endured my mother's anger. I had done everything in my power to please her, - work, study, cook, - and she was never satisfied. She would spend the few livres I earned selfishly, leaving us hungry, but giving herself new ribbons or gloves. And then I received the final rejection from my father, who, I had hoped, would have been honorable about the whole affair."

"I left Paris, knowing my life there was over," Tristan said sadly. "I didn't have the courage to establish myself. I was quite talented; however, I turned my back on everything and came here."

"Do you ever regret it, Tristan?

"Oh, Etienne, that's a difficult question to answer. I have been very happy here, but I have never forgiven myself, my cowardice. I would not want you to choose the same course."

"You mean, by staying on here?"

"If you stay here, Etienne, it must only be because the Abbey in the Forest offers you the freedom to pursue your greatest desires as an individual, not because you have fears about yourself in relation to the world. Do you understand me?"

"I think so."

"I have learned, Etienne, that with the strength of one's will,

[91]

one can transcend any barriers that have been created."

"Ambrose told me that is how I survived on the ship that brought me to France, my strength of will." Etienne remembered a conversation he had had with Ambrose years before.

"It is true, my little friend." Tristan reached out and ruffled up his dark hair. "When we first saw you, you weren't much to look at. None of us could believe that you were still alive."

"I think François and Charles worked hard to fatten me up." Etienne smiled over the memory.

"That they did. Anytime you were awake, they offered you food. We used to tease you about looking like Abbot de Fleury, for at one time, you were all belly."

Etienne laughed. His conversation with Tristan had made him feel much better, and he certainly considered himself luckier than Tristan had been. At least his mother had seen to it that he had a good home, and what was more important, she had never stopped loving him. Within his heart was sympathy for the path Tristan had walked. How much different than his own!

"Tristan, why do you think you fared differently than I?" Etienne asked. "We both started in the same place, and yet you were deprived of all that I received."

"There is no path that is better than another, Etienne. Each soul requires a different set of conditions for its development and thus chooses them accordingly."

"You chose to have your mother hate you?"

"When one looks at the overview, Etienne, my mother's feelings toward me were unimportant. I could have ended up in the French Court, living the life of a dissipate. Because of my background, I was driven to find peace of mind. It's a precious commodity, and I consider myself blessed."

"I do not think I would want my child to fare in such a way," Etienne replied.

"Your beginnings were not much better, my son. Do you feel bad about them?"

"I don't remember them, Tristan. Besides, I am happy here."

"That is correct. Our memories are quite wonderful. In time, most of us remember the light, and not the darkness."

"Thank you, Tristan. You have helped me, and I shan't have ill feelings toward my mother at all."

"You can be thankful you have a mother like you do, Etienne. She is very beautiful, and she has endured much because of her love for you."

Etienne looked down toward the Abbey. He could see two figures walking along the road that stopped at the front gates, and upon closer scrutiny, he saw that it was his mother and Chen. He thought of how happy Chen must be to speak fluently in his native tongue. Over the years, Etienne's command of the language had improved; however, he doubted he would ever speak as perfectly as Chen.

Far beneath them, Chen and Qu'an Li were engaged in a discussion regarding the future of her son. Time was growing short for her, and necessary arrangements were being made in advance of her departure.

"I am more than satisfied with T'ien Li's progress, Chen Ken," she was saying to the attentive monk. "You have displayed exemplary discipline in raising him."

"I am part of a group, Your Highness, doing no more than my share." Chen was thrilled to excuse himself from the awkwardness of French and to replace it with his familiar dialect.

"I see that he speaks my language almost as fluently as he does French, although he does speak it with a strong accent."

"Yes, this is so. It's a matter of the ear being attuned more to one language than to the other."

"Chen, what do you think about T'ien Li's future. Will he ever return to Peking?"

"That decision has not been made, Your Highness. He has options."

"In regard to the monastery?"

"The Abbey, yes . . . and in the world as well."

"Chen, the Emperor, if he lives, will abdicate after his sixth decade. This is in thirteen years. There is no son to succeed him."

"And the possibilities?"

"He has a few trusted favorites. One of them could be made minister and carry out his duties."

"What is your desire?"

"That T'ien Li return and assume the role of Emperor."

"Perhaps, Your Highness, this might not be possible."

"Why not?"

"He will be too Occidental for his people. There would be revolts which he could not control without a military background."

"And so, my dreams of a reunion in China have no substance."

"They have substance, but your son would find conflict between his upbringing and his role as an emperor. It will make no sense to him."

"That grieves my heart, Chen. I feel my years of planning to see my child have been in vain. My vision of a reunion with him has kept me alive over the years."

"There is more to life than your child, Your Highness."

"I shall have to find it," she replied wistfully.

"Speak with Ambrose. He may have an answer for you."

"And you, Chen, my faithful friend, have you none of your wisdom for me?"

"Your heart does not search for that, my Empress," Chen said softly. "Your heart wishes to fill the void created by the loss of your son. It seeks an ever present, more soothing love."

Qu'an Li's eyes filled with tears. "Yes," she replied, "I have always wanted to know a deeper level of love than I have experienced. It does not come through another person, except in a transitory way, and yet, I have been inadequate in finding the source."

Chen knew the Empress wished to be held, to yield to another's strength and to forget her own weaknesses; however, due to his immense respect for her, and to his own nature, he could never respond in such a way. She sighed deeply and wiped the tears from her porcelain skin with a silk handkerchief.

"Forgive me, my Empress, for not being able to express what you need." Chen's eyes were filled with devotion for this woman. Had he ever claimed to have felt a personal love, it would have been for her.

"Chen, you have given me more than you will ever credit yourself for." She took his arm. "Shall we walk back to the Abbey?"

[94]

* * *

In the short week Qu'an Li was at the Abbey, she learned to love the simple life it offered. She arose at four-thirty in the morning and retired at nine in the evening. Her eagerness to live as her son greatly pleased Etienne. Each day she took part in one of his activities, so that she could fully understand his life.

She worked in the vineyards, cutting back the vines for their spring growth. She fed the horses with Gerard, tended the sheep with Tristan, watched James turn a piece of lumber into a dresser, used the loom under Pasqual's watchful eye, and helped Charles and François prepare a meal. Wherever she spent her time, she left behind happy men who had enjoyed the sense of importance she seemed to instill within each of them. The kitchen turned out another fine supply of bread, and even Gerard managed to be affable.

Her favorite times were those spent in the library, either alone or with Ambrose and Andrew. The latter was very shy and often silent; however, the Empress sensed it was Andrew who would replace Ambrose upon his death. His sensitivity seemed to preclude physical strength, and although frail, Andrew possessed a resiliant inner core.

Foremost in her thoughts was the memory of her conversation with Chen in regard to his advice that she should speak with Ambrose. She did not know how to approach him in a comfortable way, and thus, she waited patiently for the right timing. She was more than happy to peruse the books, the likes of which she had never before seen. Many of them acquainted her with the histories of France and England. Some had been written by the popular French philosophers of the day, such as Diderot, Rousseau, Montesquieu, and Voltaire.

Qu'an Li began to see the world through a perspective that was not the tunnel vision of the Chinese Empire. She was an intelligent woman who had been bound by the laws of her own country, where women were not considered to have any equality with men. That she was the Empress gave her a certain advantage, and that her husband held an unusual respect for her, enhanced her status;

however, it had required a dogged determination on her part, over the years, to establish her individual freedom which she had, of late, begun to enjoy.

Yet within, she felt herself to be a prisoner. It was in times of silence that her inner wisdom spoke of freedom, from a perspective that was not external. Occasionally, she called a Jesuit into the Palace to give her lessons. At other times, it was the Buddhist monks who came. What she sought she never found, for the Jesuits were a scholarly group, and the monks, in their silent ways, kept referring her to the self. Moreover, they all found it difficult to explain the intangible aspects of love and freedom.

At the Abbey in the Forest, Qu'an Li felt a door opening for her. There was some fear about passing through it, for the possibility existed that she might not wish to return to her old ways. She was not one to resist change, unless it had potential for momentous repercussions. Finally, after three days of reading, she decided it was time to speak with Ambrose. After a delicious breakfast of hot cereal, which warmed everyone on the chilly autumnal morning, she approached him and asked if he would spend some time with her.

"Your Highness, it would be my pleasure," Ambrose responded. "Where shall we talk, the library?"

"Yes, Ambrose, the library suits me perfectly."

Ambrose was more than happy to spend time with the woman who had captured the heart of the man he had loved. In Qu'an Li's presence, he was renewed with memories of Etienne. The Empress was the last one to have spent any time with him. To Ambrose, she was a fascinating woman, who exhibited far more depth than the women of his memory.

They left the dining hall together, passing through the kitchen, so she could thank a humbled François and Charles for the meal, as was her custom. In the foyer, Ambrose stopped to pluck a red flower from the bowl on the table. He offered it to Qu'an Li.

"For you," he said. "It would look lovely in your hair."

"Where do they come from, Ambrose? They are beautiful." She was feeling both embarrassed and complimented, for her beauty had never received much attention.

[96]

"Gerard finds them in town for us at different places. His sensitivity expresses itself in unusual ways," Ambrose replied.

The hallway was chilly, and Qu'an Li looked forward to entering the warmth of the library, where a small fire would be burning in the hearth. Her hands were cold, and she was impatient to hold them over the heat. After they entered the room, she walked directly over to the fire while Ambrose pulled two chairs across the carpet. Qu'an Li's back was to him. She felt awkward about phrasing her question correctly.

"Your Highness." He offered her a chair.

"Thank you, Ambrose."

"Now, what is it that is giving you such discomfort?" he asked.

"You can see this?" She thought she had masked herself well.

"Ever since your second day," he replied. "Something happened to you in the chapel."

"Yes, Brother, and I do not know where to begin with my question, for I am sure it will lead to many others."

"Where you begin is of no importance," Ambrose suggested. "What matters is how you feel at the end."

"I feel a sorrow here," she said, pointing to her heart. "I am sure it has little to do with T'ien Li, although that pain is also within me. It is a sense of loss, of unfulfillment, that supersedes my gender or my position in life." She looked at him to see if he were following her train of thought.

"Please continue," he said.

"On my first evening here, I felt a sensation in the meditation that was completely new to me. I cannot define it accurately; however, the thought occurred to me that the energy might be similar to the one about which T'ien Li's father spoke so reverently. It awakened something within me, Ambrose, for I felt the grace of purification accompanied by a strong feeling of loneliness."

"Do you know what the loneliness is about?" he asked, appreciating her ability to speak so clearly.

"I've thought about this, Ambrose, and it can only be a greater thirst for that same experience. For a moment, I was fully absorbed by that magnificent oasis of love in the desert of life, and then I found myself in the desert once again."

"That is not unusual, Your Highness," Ambrose replied. "We are always thirsty, and at times, we must experience drought."

"What you are saying then, is that this source of love, of absolution, is depleted?"

"No, Your Highness. It is omnipresent; however, man in his feeble attempts to absorb more, often blocks his supply."

"You also experience the loneliness, Ambrose?"

"Qu'an Li, if I may call you this," Ambrose paused until she nodded, "no one is excluded from the frustration of being human. There are times when I feel the Great Peace, and there are times when I do not, although the latter are fewer and farther between. In the times of unrest, I am learning how to be peaceful."

"Why is it now more balanced for you?"

"Partially because of my age, my acceptance of who I am, and of the way things are. In our youth, we are hungry for everything, and we reject what we have as being incomplete. At some point, one learns that one has it all."

"Ambrose, what is this source of love?" Qu'an Li was confused.

"It is all within you Qu'an Li, everything. There is nothing beyond the perimeters of your own physical self that can help you more than that which you already possess. We are complete within ourselves. Within us is perfection!"

"Is this perfection the Self?"

"This is the Self, with a pronounced 'S'. In the West, we refer to it as the Indwelling Presence, or the Christ who dwells upon the throne of the heart."

"What is the difference, Ambrose, between your Christ and Buddhism?"

"Is not all Truth the same, Qu'an Li?" Ambrose replied, smiling. "And is it not man who, through his concept of duality, creates distortion in the truth? Buddhism, in its purest form, is the study of the mind, while Christianity refers to the heart."

"However, there must be a synthesis of mind and heart to beget the eternal wisdom. Knowledge of the Self allows this union to occur and to transform one, that he might truly serve mankind."

"So, your Christ is the path of love?" Qu'an Li nodded her head thoughtfully.

[98]

"Forgiveness and mercy, as well."

"Why, then, is there such a moral issue attached to Christianity that Buddhists do not have. Why is there such persecution?" Qu'an Li could not conceive how love and war came from the same source.

"There are many reasons for this, Your Highness," Ambrose replied. "Firstly, one is dealing with a great power in Christ. Within the belief systems of mankind is the erroneous concept that this power will either diminish, or that it is not accessible to all. Consequently, a few have tried to harness it for themselves. The Church has been notorious for this, telling people that, without its sanction, there can be no absolution."

"What you are saying is blasphemy, Ambrose, if I understand the nature of your churches," Qu'an Li interrupted.

"This is true, Your Highness. This is why we keep ourselves secluded from the world."

"But the Abbot de Fleury . . ?"

"The Abbot is always a sensitive area, for he could report us at any time. However, we are of no threat to him, and we keep him supplied with our wines and our woolens."

"Is this not bribery?" the Empress smiled.

"I would suspect so, although we never refer to it as such." Ambrose returned her smile.

"Please, Ambrose, continue."

"Yes." Ambrose stopped to collect his thoughts. "As I was saying, man has always believed in the nature of power as coming from an external source, - the might makes right theory, an aphorism of the British. Along comes an exalted being who spoke in opposition to this. He told men that the power was within them, and they could use it to attain their individual freedom. He also said the pathway was narrow, for in order to tread it, we must release our concepts of everything! Our perspective must become formless, in order to be reformed."

"It is a difficult path to renounce security for the nature of the formless, for the intangible," the Empress added.

"Precisely, Your Highness. And rather than go the totality, most run to the Church. Christ was not about morality. Christ was about love and responsibility. To know love, to receive it from the inexhaustible source, the individual man must be responsible for every thought, word, and action. This is the nature of discipline."

"Which brings us to Buddhism, the path to knowing the Self."

"At the Council of Nicea, in the fifth century," Ambrose continued, "much of what Christ said that would give power to the individual was deleted from the Bible, by those who would prefer to keep the power for themselves."

"Our Buddha did not create such a sensation, Ambrose. Why?"

"Because your Buddha did not claim to be the son of God. Nor did he claim that all were sons and daughters of God. Buddha trod the wheel of rebirth to perfect himself. Christ was already perfect. Their messages are not dissimilar, Your Highness, for with your Buddha, the role of the individual is emphasized."

"Then, why is there such discomfort around love?"

"That, Qu'an Li, is the most trying aspect, for wherever love is, it shines brightly, illuminating all that is not love. When one comes face to face with love, everything within one that is impure, rises to his awareness. I feel that many of the trials on the Inner Path, are those brought about by our need to understand the nature of love and to express it. Love is creative. It needs to express itself."

"Then, my feelings of loneliness are," Qu'an Li touched her heart, "spaces that need to be filled with love."

"Yes," Ambrose acknowledged. "Those feelings are the quiet voice of the Indwelling Presence calling you closer. There is nothing wrong with loneliness, or anger, or any of our emotions, for they teach us about ourselves and about each other. Most of us discover who we are through the discovery of who we are not."

"Have you known this love, Ambrose?"

"I have known it," he replied softly.

"And have you known the love of another person." Qu'an Li knew she was being too personal; however, it was consistent with her nature to step out of her traditional character.

"Yes, Your Highness, I have."

She knew Ambrose would speak no further, a fact which she accepted.

"I have felt touched by love, with T'ien Li's father. For my husband, I feel companionship, but with T'ien Li, my heart

[100]

blossoms." Qu'an Li smiled radiantly, her whole face coming to life.

"Then you are more fortunate than most, Empress," Ambrose said.

The two sat in the comfort of silence, staring at the dying fire. Within herself, Qu'an Li experienced a blending of two energies giving birth to a balanced harmony. Her travels had not been in vain, for she would return to Peking with tremendous insight. She would neither forsake her background, nor embrace Christianity; however, deep within her being, a tiny seed had germinated, the progeny of the two philosophies that would ultimately bring her into wholeness.

She watched as Ambrose stood up to add another log to the fire, his brown robe contrasting with his white hair. "He is a handsome man," she thought. "I wonder what took him from a family life, for a man like Ambrose would look good with a woman at his side."

Qu'an Li immediately severed the continuation of such thoughts, for these were the ways of the West. She had never entertained ideas that might delve into another's privacy, until she met T'ien Li's father. Etienne had questioned everything, and he had consistently demonstrated an innate curiosity about human nature.

Through his teaching, she was able to perceive beyond the masks the Chinese presented to one another. He had told her that the eyes were the windows of the soul. Shortly after that, she began to understand her husband and lost all fear of his aggressive manner, for she knew this was expected of him. He was both the proud warrior and the wise man, and his true identity was obscured by the projection of his subjects, who exalted him.

With the absence of her servility, he had begun to regard her with a new respect. What had evolved was a friendship that surprised them both, as she became free to demonstrate her strength, he his weaknesses. He had gradually lost interest in his concubines, although the Empress was certain this was, in part, the result of age, and after many years of marriage, he had begun to develop a living relationship with his wife.

Many changes took place, but to Qu'an Li, the most noticeable change had been his agreement to her journey. At Marseilles, her ship awaited her. On board was its staff, as well as those who had been ordered to accompany her inland. However, Qu'an Li had sent them back to the ship, once they had arrived at St. Benoit Abbey, with instructions to return in one week's time.

Qu'an Li did not wish to leave her son behind for the tedious journey back to Peking; however, her time was drawing to a close, and it was best not to prolong the advent of decisions that had already been made. She had no idea when she and T'ien Li would meet again, or if the occurrence were even a probability, and yet, she could return to her world with an inner sense of rightness about his life and her own.

Ambrose heard the bell ringing and stood. "Your Highness, shall we join the others for lunch?"

"Thank you, Ambrose," she replied, "but I am not hungry, and I wish to spend some more time in contemplation. Please go without me."

Ambrose left the room, and Qu'an Li stood to move around. She walked over to the large window and looked out across the land that had been colored in the grey and brown tones of winter. She saw Chen walking slowly toward the Abbey with T'ien Li at his side. For a moment, Qu'an Li's heart flooded with the pain of a mother who has lost her child. Not wanting to hold on to it, she released the feeling. An uneasy peace settled in the vacuum left by the passing of emotion. Qu'an Li sighed deeply, and returned to the fire and her chair, which was still warm from the heat of her body.

* * *

That evening at dinner, the Empress spoke to the monks and told them of her plans. "My friends," she said, "I shall take leave of you in the morning."

Etienne's face blanched, and he looked up from his soup as his mother finished her brief message. He did not want her to leave so quickly, in spite of his conflict over her presence. Part of him wished to resume life as it had been prior to her arrival; however, that part was in conflict with the rest of him that did not want doors that had

[102]

been opened to be closed so quickly.

"Mother," he asked, "so soon?"

"It is time I return to my people, T'ien Li." She smiled devotedly at him. "I am content with how you live, and I realize the safety of this home for you."

Turning to the others, she said, "There is a peacefulness here, that is rare. I shall never forget you or your generosity." When she finished, she looked down at her food and began to eat.

An awkwardness pervaded the room following her brief statement. In the short time she had been with the monks, she had added an ineffable light to their existence.

"What time would you like the carriage to be ready, Your Highness?" Gerard asked.

"Shortly after breakfast, Gerard, thank you."

"Would you care to hear some songs this evening, Empress?" James queried shyly.

"Why yes!" Qu'an Li was surprised at the invitation. "I did not know you sang, Brother James."

"It's a well kept secret," he replied, the corners of his mouth turning into a wry smile.

The brothers were delighted with another opportunity to listen to James giving his magical quality to song. "Shall we hear you in the chapel?" Ambrose suggested.

A festive atmosphere came over the group as they concluded their meal. Only Etienne had difficulty throwing himself into the change of energy. His mind was still on the words his mother had uttered to announce her imminent departure. He looked across the table at Chen whose omniscient eyes pierced his with a silent message. Etienne straightened his back and joined the others in their gaiety.

The chapel was aglow with light, as the candles, long unused in the candelabras, were given life. An unusual warmth permeated the large room, for the silence that was usually contained within the stone walls had been replaced with an electric vivacity. The monks filled the pews, whispering to one another. Qu'an Li, Chen, and Etienne sat together with Ambrose in the front. James stood at the altar, waiting to give life to his voice.

Qu'an Li was spellbound. It was often, that in the dark of the Great Palace, she would listen to the melodic song of the nightingale, while everyone else was hushed in sleep. The birdsong broke through the stillness, contrasting sharply with it, and silence and song danced together in the night air. James' voice created a similar effect.

She could feel the choreography of sound and silence, lissome partners echoing each other in the yellow glow of the chapel . Together, they glided upward to the pinnacled roof and flowed downward, liquid gold, pouring itself freely through the air, trembling as it caressed their bodies.

She closed her eyes to the sights and absorbed only the sound. Beside her, Etienne watched her exquisite profile, as she might look in sleep, or even death, for she had surrendered her living self to the voice, in order to give it more life.

James watched the reaction of his audience, each member taking his own voyage. He filled his lungs with air and let it float out into the chapel, a tableau of sound being presented to the ears. He always felt a slight regret that he could not share in the union of bliss, for in creating the sound, he separated himself from it. From the wellspring of his soul came the healing waters. He could feel them bubbling up, each note carrying its message which only the listener could interpret. How he wanted to sit and share with his friends!

Since the brothers had become aware of his special gift, they had looked at him differently. He was a healer through his voice, and they perceived him to be unique among them. For the first time in years, James was reminded of his isolation as a youth, when he had fiercly wanted to be like other children. However, he knew the monks would gladly embrace his uniqueness, in the light that the talent of one benefited them all. His work was his woodcarving, his gift was his voice, and neither was more important than the other.

He noticed tears on the Empress' flawless skin. Etienne's face reflected the sorrow that she masked so well, and James understood the nature of the bonding that had tied the mother and the son so irrevocably together. When he had finished, he quietly walked over to his seat and joined the others in their stillness. Qu'an Li

[104]

looked at her child and pulled him closer to her. The Empress, her son, and the brothers sat quietly, their hearts woven together in a pattern of beauty.

Etienne and Qu'an Li sat in her room that evening and talked, while the stars twinkled in the night sky. There was no time for them but the moment, to which they clung with a fierce tenacity. When Etienne had trouble keeping his eyes open, Qu'an Li bade him good night.

"T'ien Li," she whispered, her voice cradling him, "your bed is waiting for you. Go, while your eyes can still see."

Qu'an Li sat through the night, allowing her thoughts to drift aimlessly. When the light of the sun, still far in the East, began to blanket the stars, she felt at peace about her departure. She got up and washed herself, and choosing a pale lavender silk gown, she dressed while the others were still sleeping.

When her valises had been arranged neatly beside the bed, Qu'an Li covered herself with a warm blanket and walked down the hall to the front door. Noiselessly, she let herself out and moved around to the rear of the Abbey.

The sheep were nestled together by the back wall, and paid no attention to her as she passed them. She could feel the warmth in the air from their body mass. There was no indication of animal life stirring, for the morning was still birthing. However, ahead of her, near the vineyard, she saw the lone figure of a man. Recognizing the familiar silhouette of Chen, she walked over to him.

"You are as a tranquil pond, Empress," he said.

"That I am, Chen," she replied.

They walked the perimeter of the Abbey land together, neither feeling the need to speak. Instead, they concentrated on the rhythm of nature awakening to a new day.

The others were at breakfast when Chen and Qu'an Li arrived. Hot porridge was waiting for them. Etienne smiled broadly at his mother and Chen, for he, too, had accepted the inevitable.

For the last time, Qu'an Li passed through the kitchen to thank the chefs for their meal. Charles had carefully wrapped a package, which he carried out to the waiting carriage.

"Some warm bread for Your Highness," he said. "There is

enough here for you to share with those who are meeting you in St. Benoit."

"Thank you, Charles." She smiled regally at the short man, whose eyes were level with her own.

When she stepped into the daylight, she saw Andrew, Ambrose, and the others, gathered to bid her farewell. Ambrose offered her his arm to guide her into the carriage. He noticed that Gerard had done a magnificent job of cleaning it, for it shone as never before.

"Your Highness!" Pasqual stepped forward with his arms wrapped around a thick, white blanket. Giving it to her, he said, shyly, "For you, in the event you become cold at sea." Chen observed that it was one of his prized blankets.

"Thank you, Pasqual. I shall always think of the Abbey in the Forest when I use this!" She turned to the others and bowed her head deferentially. "Brothers," she said, placing her hands together in front of her heart.

Ambrose waited for her to take his arm, as she turned her back to the small group. Chen and Etienne were standing outside the gates next to the coach.

"Ambrose," Qu'an Li said quietly, "you are aware of my gratefulness?"

"I am, Your Highness," he replied humbly.

"Then I needn't speak further, rather, I shall send you some funds to utilize as you please. I do not know whether we shall meet again, but we can now write openly."

"I'll have Etienne write to you regularly, " Ambrose offered. "I am sorry that you are leaving us so soon."

"It is best for us all." She stopped in front of her son and Chen. To each, she bowed gracefully.

"Good-bye, my son," she said formally. "Be a gentle warrior." To Chen, she said nothing, for their communion was wordless.

Ambrose helped her into the carriage, assuring himself that she was comfortably situated. As he was about to leave, she placed her small hand on his arm.

"It was you," she said softly.

Ambrose looked at her, his eyes questioning.

[106]

"You and T'ien Li's father are so much alike!"

He did not respond, but the sorrow in his eyes was answer enough for her. The carriage door closed, and Gerard gestured for the horses to move on. From the window, the Empress of China saw Chen, T'ien Li, and Ambrose standing together, watching her disappear into the thick forests. It was then that she allowed herself the luxury of tears, which were pushed out by deep, heart wrenching sobs. In the front, Gerard was oblivious to her crying, for the noise of the horses' hooves, and the wheels of the carriage, gave her the freedom to lose herself in sorrow.

Standing between Ambrose and Chen, as the carriage carried his mother away, Etienne repressed any emotions and remained stoical. It was the first time he could remember having encountered a sense of loss.

Because of her visit, he had been given a new identity. He was no longer the young one, who lived with the brothers of the Abbey in the Forest. He was the son of the Empress of China. This explained so much to him, not the least of which was the reason for his unusual features, in a world of olive skinned people with pronounced noses and eyes.

Within the child, a new dignity was growing. Knowledge of his heritage was beginning to separate him from Ambrose, establishing more of a connection with Chen. He feared that he might distance himself from his brothers, which would also create a sense of isolation from the rest of the world.

Etienne could feel Ambrose's arm on his shoulder giving him strength. For a brief moment, he felt very lucky to be surrounded by people like Ambrose, Chen, and the others, as he remembered the richness of his childhood. He had seen the children of St. Benoit-sur-Loire, many of them working in the fields from dawn to dusk, and few of them receiving any education or privileges. He had been gifted, considering the alternatives, and the realization of this was growing strongly within him.

When they could no longer see the coach, the three turned back through the gates of the Abbey. The other brothers had already left, and there was a ghostly emptiness to the courtyard.

Chapter Eight

She came to him in the dead of night, when he had surrendered himself to the dream world. Through the mists of the subconscious, a shadow figure approached, never coming closely enough that he could discern her features. It was a woman whose long silk gowns rustled, like the leaves of summer dancing in the wind. She was small, yet voluptuous, and she made no attempt to fully pierce the veil of his consciousness. She tarried in his dream only long enough for him to cry out, "Who are you?", and then she was gone, back into the nether worlds. . . .

Etienne awakened with a sense of disquiet. He could not dispel the feeling that hung over him. Slipping his robe over his naked body, he moved quickly about his small cell to shake off the early morning chill. His sandals were by the bed as always, and he slipped into them as he opened the door.

It was often that Etienne left the Abbey walls in the early morning to climb the hills and to watch the sun come up over the river. In the summers, the light would disperse the mists that hung heavily over the verdant lands. To Etienne, there was a sense of anticipation with each sunrise. It represented creation and new beginnings; whereas the setting sun always evoked feelings of nostalgia, for it became a time of retrospection and of hazy memories. It was with the sunsets that his mother would come into his thoughts, as the golden ball of fire was sinking behind the trees, the pink sky turning to dusk.

Over the past three years, they had corresponded regularly. She wrote long letters, telling him of her life in Peking, while his replies were shorter, although nonetheless not lacking in love. It took months for a letter to arrive, as ships from Macau were few and far between, and it was not unusual for him to receive two or three at once.

At sixteen, Etienne was an extremely well disciplined youth. He had far surpassed his peers in the realms of general knowledge, he played the lyre fairly well, and his philosophy was transforming itself, from one of concepts and form, into one of a more freeflowing nature.

With Chen, Etienne had learned to free the mind from its tendency to structure. He had become acutely aware of even the most innocuous of thoughts, for he, as their creator, had given them life. Etienne was becoming like an empty vessel. His eyes had become more clear, and his very presence made people notice him. It was not the Oriental features which caused the stares, rather it was a more intangible aspect of grace.

Physically, he was as beautiful as his mother. His skin was flawless, his teeth were healthy and white, and his hair was thick and dark. The brothers were very proud of Etienne. He was considered a very special being among them, and there was a slight reverence given him, the nature of which was usually reserved for Chen.

Chen had proven himself to be a diligent taskmaster where Etienne was concerned. He demanded perfection from him and got it, for it was unlike Chen to let anything pass his scrupulous attention. Etienne absolutely loved Chen. He felt similarly toward Ambrose; however, Ambrose had been more of a father-teacher to him, whereas Chen had always been a role model for his own refinement.

Ambrose felt a growing distance between himself and Etienne, although he knew it was normal for a boy to break away from his parents in his youth. Shortly after his mother's departure, a new reserve had come over him, and Ambrose had seen in Etienne the first budding of manhood. Ambrose was in his sixties and was not as attached to the boy as he had once been. He gave Etienne all the personal freedom he could want. Slowly, their man-child relationship had evolved into one of mutual respect between adults, and they were both happy with the fruits of it.

On this particular morning, from his position on a tree stump at the edge of the forest, Etienne could see the beginning of a summer storm forming in one ominous looking cloud, that was slowly moving in from the south. Soon, it would obscure the rising sun, and the rains would inevitably follow. The vineyards and the sheep would be happy, for the water would initiate new growth.

The previous summer had witnessed a drought that had nearly destroyed all of their grapes. The brothers had been very lucky, when August heralded in two weeks of much needed rain to balance the earlier devastation caused by nature's miserliness.

As the sun peeked over the hills through the grey mist, Etienne remembered his dream. He knew the woman held some significance for him, but he couldn't fathom why. This was the third time she had visited him, and not once had she fully revealed herself. In the dreams, he would feel a certain presence, and then she would appear. He decided to speak with Andrew about her. Andrew was most similar to Chen, yet he was more tangibly human. Etienne had often gone to Andrew with problems of a personal nature, and Andrew's guidance had never served him incorrectly.

Etienne jumped off the stump and began the walk down to the Abbey. From the position of the sun, he could tell it was time to join the others in the chapel for the morning meditation. The dew drops, clinging to the blades of grass, fell onto his feet as he made his path back.

Andrew was sitting by the inner courtyard pond when Etienne found him, later in the morning. "Good morning, Andrew!"

"Hello, Brother," Andrew replied. "How might I help you?"

"I need your guidance with a dream," Etienne spoke with hesitation, trying to collect his thoughts.

"Yes?"

"A woman, three times, has come to me, yet she does not reveal herself. I sense some importance, but I cannot grasp the meaning, and it disturbs me."

"Perhaps, it is not time for you to know her, Etienne," Andrew answered.

"What does she represent, Andrew?" Etienne looked into Andrew's dark eyes. He was aware of how gracefully Andrew had aged, for his hair was still dark, and his skin was smooth. Most noticeable were his eyes, which still reflected the light of youth.

"It could be something impersonal, like the liberty of France from her repression, or it might represent someone who will come into your life."

[110]

"But Andrew, I am a monk. There will be no woman in my life!" Etienne spoke vehemently, trying to overcome the guilt he felt over periodic desires he had nurtured in relation to the outside world.

"Have you truly decided that this is your path, Etienne?" Andrew spoke very softly. "Is this where you wish to spend the rest of your life?"

"I think so," Etienne answered honestly, "although I do wonder what Paris might be like."

"Paris is reflecting volatile signs of change, Etienne, as is all of France. I imagine that city would be a little fast for you."

"You think there will be a revolution, do you not?" Etienne asked.

"That I do, my son. That I do." Andrew sighed. "It's inevitable."

Andrew spoke with wisdom born of a keen observance. It was clear to him that Paris was quickly becoming a barometer for change. No longer was the King in favor, and his wife, Marie Antoinette, had long ago disappointed a once adoring public with her ostentatious displays of bad taste. In fact, the trend was to speak ill of the monarchy, rather than to extol its virtues. Those favorites who had been banished from Court, such as Turgot and Necker, were enjoying a new popularity, as admirers traveled to their residences in exile to hear them expound upon their views.

There were too many extremes involved to maintain any sort of balance. The Church had too much power, as did the nobility. Both of these factions were in the minority, when compared to the rising middle class, the maligned bourgeoisie, who resented their lack of influence and the arrogant disdain they endured from the nobles. This class included the wealthy merchants and trades people, who were growing increasingly embittered over not being recognized. Finally, there were too many poor, and no attention given to them, as everyone's focus was on Versailles and the coveted status enjoyed by those of the French Court.

The prisons were filled with innocents who had been unjustly incarcerated and left forgotten, particularly by the King, whose power could release them. Instead, he chose to neglect the prisoners, in favor of the royal hunt. Consequently, there were those who would never again see the light of day, or their families, for they would not receive a fair trial that would grant them their freedom, either to life outside the prison walls, or to death.

"Yes," Andrew said aloud, more to himself, "the changes are even being felt here."

"Andrew, I want to see Paris before it's too late! I want to visit all of the places I have read about!" Etienne impulsively blurted out his feelings.

"Well, perhaps you can go with us in the fall, when we bring our wines to the King. It could be a birthday present to you, Etienne." He smiled lovingly at the young man, whose eyes radiated joy over the prospect.

The brothers had always recognized his birthday, a tradition that, Etienne suspected, would soon come to an end. He would be seventeen in the late autumn, and it was time to leave behind childhood tradition in favor of his emerging manhood.

"Thank you, Andrew!" Etienne was ecstatic. "You'll talk with Ambrose, will you not?"

"Of course, little Emperor," Andrew concluded the discussion.

Satisfied, Etienne left the courtyard to begin his meditation with Chen. There was more work to be done before the day's end, for James had requested his help in hauling some felled trees back to the workshop.

Etienne spent the next hour at Chen's feet, his eyes closed, his mind still active. He focused on his breath to calm him; however, Chen had noticed a restlessness, resulting from his conversation with Andrew.

"The fish swim noisily in the pond," Chen said, referring to Etienne's thoughts.

Etienne looked at his teacher who was only too aware of his inability to meditate quietly. They now spoke only in their native dialect.

"What is it that incites them?" Chen asked.

"I may go to Paris this autumn with Ambrose and Andrew," Etienne replied, happy to share his secret with Chen, "but no one is to know of this until it is certain."

"And the reason?" Chen inquired.

"I want to visit Paris before the Revolution, which Andrew thinks is inevitable."

"Know your path, T'ien Li."

Chen's face revealed nothing; however, his eyes bore right through Etienne. He turned away to avoid his teacher's penetrating gaze and to remove the unease that was growing within.

* * *

The summer passed almost without incident. The rains came to feed the earth, and the heat was not oppressive. Etienne thought about his impending trip to Paris and wondered if it would ever become a reality. He was reminded of it one night, when in his sleep, he experienced a chilling dream.

Faces came to him, haunted, starving faces of men and women. Gaunt faces, with eyes that held vacant expressions. They stared at Etienne as he slept, and the chills which moved up his body, awakened him. Brushing the sweat from his forehead, Etienne walked over to get a drink of water from the pitcher.

He allowed some of the cold liquid to run down his warm body, and onto the stone floor. The contrast of the cold against his hot skin awakened him with a shock. His sudden intake of breath blocked out the faces, and they left him to return to their subconscious origins.

Etienne knew he would not sleep, and so he sat on his bed to contemplate the nature of his dream. Perhaps it had something to do with the prison Andrew had mentioned a few months earlier.

A few days later, Etienne accompanied Gerard into town to purchase some items for Ambrose and François. He loved the rides more than ever, and after his mother had left, Gerard had not been as reluctant to allow him to sit in the front of the carriage. Etienne had long ago learned of Gerard's unrequited passion for pastries, when he had accidentally stepped on a box containing the precious delectables that had been lying at Gerard's feet. Gerard had been upset all the way back to the monastery, putting the child into a state of humiliation. The next time they were in town, Etienne secretly bought two of the biggest éclairs and presented them to Gerard as an apology. The two became fast friends, accomplices in the negligible crime of keeping Gerard's weight over a healthy limit.

On this day, Pasqual and Etienne sat together inside the coach, singing the songs Pasqual had taught him years before. Pasqual was proud that Etienne had picked up the Spanish in the same flawless way that he had learned French.

"In the Basque Country," Pasqual said, "they would cry to hear you sing like that, Etienne."

"Do you miss your people, Pasqual?"

"Never!" he replied. "We all share the same blood, and there is the belief that we are always together in spite of distances. No Etienne, my life at the monastery has been more than I could have hoped for myself."

"What would you have done that might have been different?" Etienne was curious about the feisty monk.

"Married. Had ten children, and spent the rest of my days as a goatherd, with never enough money to feed my family." Pasqual sighed. "No, that is not a life I would have chosen for myself, and yet I would have fallen into it."

"Why?"

"Because everyone does," Pasqual replied. "And I never saw a woman with whom I would wish to suffer, much less have ten children!"

"Pasqual!" Etienne laughed. "You can be so jaded!"

"That's the French side, you know!" Pasqual leaned out of the coach window. "We are here Etienne, and there is Abbot de Fleury."

Gerard stopped the carriage and jumped down to tie the horses to a post. Etienne and Pasqual were no sooner out the door, when they saw the portly monk rushing off to the patisserie.

"It's a good thing for him that he has the horses to exercise." Pasqual clicked his tongue against the roof of his mouth, as he watched Gerard disappear into the bakery. "He'd be second to one in girth size, and that one could only be. . ."

"Your Grace!" Etienne called out to stifle Pasqual's last words.

"T'ien Li!" The Abbot said, extending his hand for Etienne's kiss. "And how do you do, these days?"

"Most excellently, Your Grace."

"My, my," the Abbot shook his head, jowls swinging from left to right, "you are looking wonderful! You have matured quite gracefully under the tutelage of your Brothers, T'ien Li."

"You are most kind, Your Grace,"Etienne replied. "You do remember Pasqual, do you not?" He turned to Pasqual who was inwardly blanching over the possibility of one heinous remark, that could have set back the relationship between the Abbot and the brothers.

He took the Abbot's hands, grimacing as his lips touched the black hairs on his fat white fingers. "Your Grace. You are looking healthy, these days."

"It's the fine food, Pasqual, the fine food." The Abbot smiled over the memory of his breakfast. "And what brings you into town today?"

"Only odds and ends," Etienne answered, knowing the Abbot's intent to keep abreast of everything related to the brothers. They were all cautious not to arouse any suspicion when shopping in St. Benoit, for many of the shopkeepers were on the Abbot's payroll. "Ambrose needs some bookkeeping supplies."

"Well, good day to you!" The Abbot waved them off and waddled over to the small park where he had spotted the Compte de Grasse and his wife.

Pasqual and Etienne separated, agreeing to meet within the hour at the printers' for their last errand. The shop had been mysteriously closed for the last few months, and the monastery needed some supplies from the proprietors, an affable man of extended girth, and his equally friendly wife. When Etienne was a child, it was she who would give him her old pens and paper scraps to entertain himself back at the monastery. He looked forward to seeing them again.

In the meantime, he walked around the village, picking out a few kitchen supplies and watching the children playing. They were not dressed well, and there was a squalor about them. They also did not appear as happy as he had remembered. He contemplated the differences and then decided that his previous observations were based on his youthful insight and not on reality at all.

They no longer stared at Etienne as before, for he had become a common sight in the little town. A few of the girls would stop their conversation as he passed, but this was to take in his exotic beauty. Etienne had long since grown oblivious to others' reactions to him, and the girls' appreciative stares went unnoticed. Across the cobblestone street, Etienne saw Gerard waving good bye to Madame Denton, as he left the patisserie, the customary small pink box in his hands.

Etienne looked more closely at Madame Denton, and he noticed that she had aged rapidly in the last year, for her hair had lost the strength of its auburn color to a washed out grey. She had lost weight as well. Etienne attributed this to the fact that her oldest son, the one for whom Gerard had been praying, had mysteriously disappeared. He had been somewhat of a vociferous dissident, freely offering his opinions on the burdens of taxation placed on the bourgeoisie. Etienne hoped his disappearance was not the result of his politics.

The day was warm, and the sun was hot. Etienne stopped at the Café d'Albert and ordered a café au lait, one of the few indulgences which he thoroughly enjoyed. He sat at one of the tables and watched the traffic. It felt good to relax and to absorb the feel of village life. His youthful desires were indicating a preference for more activity than that which the Abbey offered, but these inclinations weren't strong enough to provoke him to any action.

Etienne looked at the sun overhead and saw that it was time to meet Pasqual at the printers'. He swallowed the last of his coffee and stood up to leave, his table quickly assumed by another patron at the crowded café. The coffee had revitalized Etienne, and he hurried outside.

Ahead, he saw Pasqual waiting for him at the front door, a small package under his arm. When he reached the foot of the steps, Pasqual opened the door and walked in, Etienne swiftly on his heels. A small bell over the doorway tinkled to announce their arrival. They went to the desk to await Monsieur LeBois, who was shutting down his press in the back room.

[116]

From another room, they heard Madame LeBois' movements, as she closed a heavy drawer. Both approached the visitors at the same time. Etienne and Pasqual first saw Madame LeBois, whose tired face greeted them with a weak smile, but their attention was immediately riveted upon her husband who hardly resembled the stout man they had once known. It was all Etienne could do to refrain from gasping, for in front of him was a face similar to those he had seen in his dreams! Monsieur LeBois' cheeks were carved into deep hollows, making his eyes protrude obnoxiously around his large nose. His once thick hair had thinned down to nothing, and his skin had a sickly yellow pallor to it.

"Monsieur LeBois!" Etienne could not help himself. "What has happened to you?"

His wife moved protectively toward her husband. "Hello, Etienne," she said. "What can we do for you today?"

Etienne composed himself, and reached into the pocket of his robe for the list of supplies. "We need some stationery, the lighter parchment, some pens, and some black ink," he replied. "Oh! Also envelopes and sealing wax." His face felt warm from embarassment.

The small woman nodded and left the room while her husband stayed behind. He looked at Etienne, light coming into his expressionless eyes for the first time. "It's good to see you again, Brothers," he said, his voice barely rising above a hoarse whisper.

Pasqual reached across the counter to take the man's hand. "Bad times, my friend?"

"Prison," he replied. "The Bastille."

"Why?" Etienne asked, horrified by the sound of that name.

"That I cannot answer." His eyes watered from the strain of his voice as he spoke. "It was never made clear to me. I was simply taken away one night. A lettre de cachet, explaining little."

"How did you get out?" Pasqual asked quietly.

"Through the Abbot's influence." He answered stoically, but Etienne detected a slight movement in his eyes. "I agreed to print a certain book he wishes to be published, and to refrain from printing anything slanderous about the King and Queen in my newspaper."

[117]

"Was this a good bargain or a compromise?" Pasqual suspected the Abbot's nefarious intentions behind the whole affair.

"It released me from that vermin infested hell hole," he answered quietly.

He winked at Etienne and then limped toward the printing room. "Good day, Brothers," he whispered, as he disappeared behind the curtain.

Madame LeBois returned with Etienne's order. He paid her and then, without hesitating, gave her two hundred additional livres. Her eyes widened, but she said nothing.

"For all the years you were generous with me, Madame," he whispered.

He helped her wrap the items and then left the shop with Pasqual. Etienne was silent all the way back to the carriage where Gerard was patiently waiting, a look of complacency on his face. The ribbon on the pink box at his side had been retied, for it lacked the perfection originally given to it by Madame Denton's agile fingers.

Seeing their arms laden with packages, Gerard ran to assist them. He held the packages, while the brothers stepped into the carriage. When they had settled, he passed them into their outstretched arms and then shut the door, slapping it as a final gesture.

Gerard untied the horses, and with a little grunt, he heaved his compact body up onto the seat. The horses, knowing they were homeward bound, were only too happy to respond to his commands.

Inside the carriage, Etienne was silent. Pasqual knew he was disturbed, but he respected his privacy and left him to his thoughts. Eventually, Etienne looked up at his brother. "Pasqual, what's a lettre de cachet?"

"It's a rather unpleasant circumstance, my friend," Pasqual began. "There is quite a number of these secret letters, all of which have been signed by the King. They are essentially blank pieces of paper that give the bearer carte blanche to fill them in as he wishes. With the King's signature at the bottom, they are considered completely valid and are not to be questioned.

[118]

"Usually a name is filled in," he continued, "with a crime attached to it. No matter that the crime never occurred, or that the alleged criminal is innocent. He, or she, is hauled off to prison without chance of redressing the issue, and left to his ignominious fate. Often, families are unaware what has happened to a particular member, for once incarcerated, he is lucky to be heard from again."

"Is this what happened to Madame Denton's son?" Etienne asked.

"More than likely," Pasqual replied. "This is not the time to upset the wrong people."

"What happens to them in prison?"

"They are left to the best of their survival instincts. At one time, the Bastille was not considered to be such an awful place. Even Voltaire spent some time there. But I am told that it is now worse than all of the other prisons combined." Pasqual went on, "Many die, for few will see a trial. The King is too busy with his pleasures and does not wish to sully his reputation by signing death warrants."

"How does one acquire a lettre de cachet, Pasqual?" Etienne was both fascinated and horrified by what he was hearing.

"The King's ministers dispense them freely, often to the highest bidder, I have heard. The prisons are horribly overcrowded, with innocents living amidst hardened criminals, innocents whose only crime was to be in the right place at the wrong time!"

"But this is unjust!" Etienne cried out.

"Justice is no longer relevant, Etienne, not in these times. It is 1787, and the days of a country united under her King are history."

Etienne remembered the differences he had noticed in the town. "So," he thought, "what happens in Paris affects all of us." Aloud, he said, "Pasqual, did you enjoy Paris?"

"Yes, Etienne, but that was many years ago, when the King and Queen were still in favor. I wouldn't place myself there now for anything!"

Etienne looked out at the passing countryside, feeling undisturbed about the conversation. He still wanted to see Paris, and he was determined to go with Ambrose in November.

As they approached the portion of the road that paralleled the river in front of the Abbey, Etienne pulled the cord to signal Gerard to stop. He had been watching the sunlight reflecting off the moving waters, and he couldn't resist the chance to swim.

"Pasqual, I'll return to the Abbey in time for the meditation. Will you give the packages to Ambrose?"

"But of course, my friend!" Pasqual agreed.

Etienne waved them off and walked down to the banks of the river. The summer heat was at its most intense, and the water looked exceptionally inviting. Sliding his robe over his head, he threw it on the grass and dove into the cool, clear river. The current rolled across his naked body, washing away the perspiration and the uneasy feelings he had acquired from his trip into town. The water glistened on his tanned skin as his muscular arms guided him to the far shore. Clinging to the long grass, he pulled himself up the steep bank, turned to survey the scenery, and dove back into the refreshing river. Lying on his back, Etienne looked at the vast expanse of sky overhead.

He could see that before the evening was over, there would be a storm to cool the temperature. This aspect of summer was one of Etienne's favorites, the seasonal thundershowers, whose approach would increase the electricity in the air, building tension in the trees, and in the animals, until its release from the skies would cleanse the land.

Etienne dried himself with his robe before putting it back on, and then walked toward the Abbey, whose grey stone walls he could see in the distance. His hair, still wet from the swim, clung to his head, and his long, dark eyelashes had tiny drops of water on them that ran down the sides of his face.

He thought no more about the day's events until late in the night when he could not sleep. The memory of Monsieur LeBois haunted him. That man could be so inhumane to his brothers astounded Etienne, whose only experiences had been with the lighter side of mankind.

When he lay down and shut his eyes, images came to him, flooding his mind. They were the faces he had seen a few nights earlier. He vainly tried to transform them; however, they were insistent upon occupying his inner vision. Without warning, the

[120]

faces began to scatter, and in his mind's eye, he could perceive that presence, that special presence which always preceded his angel of the night.

The rustling of silk introduced itself, and as the shadows parted, her now familiar figure walked toward him with quiet assurance. Again she stopped, and Etienne strained to see her face. He did not know if it were another dream, or if he were awake; however, he surrendered himself to the reality of her presence.

"I come first, Etienne," she whispered enigmatically into his dreams.

She fell into the darkness of his unconsciousness, and the night passed without his knowing.

Chapter Nine

Ambrose was seated in the library at his table. He had just received a letter from the Empress, and its contents disturbed him. The correspondence coincided with a conversation Andrew had with him a few days before, about the possibility of Etienne going with them to Paris in a month's time. Ambrose had told Andrew that he would consider it, but he would need some time to think about his answer. He was hoping to let the matter drop, so that it might resolve itself.

Now there was a long letter from Qu'an Li, urging Ambrose to take Etienne to Paris at her expense. She felt it would be an exceptional experience for him, and she had made arrangements with a wealthy woman, a Madame de Grave, for Etienne to spend some time with her. This would give Etienne an idea of the outside world, so that he could make decisions about his future from a broader base of experience.

Ambrose was concerned, for Paris was an attractive city, as well as a dangerous one with its political uncertainty. Etienne's background would not be revealed, as it might prove dangerous to his welfare, so he was to visit the city under the auspices of furthering his studies. Intuitively, Ambrose felt Etienne might succumb to the false glamor and make unwise choices concerning his future. He also had to admit to himself that he did not want to lose the closest thing to a son that he would ever know.

He knew Etienne would be thrilled with the prospects, and he could hardly prevent the boy from those experiences which all young people should share. Also, Ambrose's age was beginning to make itself known, and he knew that his time was coming to a close. In fact, he had already allowed Andrew to assume some of his responsibilities. In the untimely event of his demise, Andrew would not be inundated with unfamiliar aspects of running the monastery.

The decision for Etienne to travel with them to Paris had already been made for him. It was merely Ambrose's obligation to accept it. Sighing, he straightened himself and looked out of the windows, where he could see, in the distance, the grapes being harvested. This year, it had been necessary to approach the Abbot de Fleury to secure some help from the village, for the harvest was exceptionally abundant. Everyone at the Abbey had worked, even Gerard, who had managed to lose some of his excess weight.

The sound of someone entering the library diverted Ambrose's attention. Without looking, he knew it was Chen, who had his unique way of soundlessly floating down corridors and across rooms. Chen glided up to the table.

"Let him go, Ambrose," he said quietly.

"I will not ask you how you know about this, Brother Chen," Ambrose responded, "but in answer to your words, I find that I have no choice, and that is what concerns me."

"T'ien Li's time has come."

"To leave us?"

"To learn ways of the world."

"Ah, yes." Ambrose shook his head. "He must balance his innocence with the understanding born of experience."

"We all like the salmon, Ambrose, who swim upstream to spawn, and then to die."

"Will you go with him, Chen?"

"I too set in my ways. I stay here and wait for T'ien Li."

"He will return, then. For that, I am glad." Ambrose felt a weight lift.

"T'ien Li's heart always here, Ambrose. It is his mind that travels."

"I worry about his safety, Chen." Ambrose looked at the small man standing before him. Chen was perturbed by nothing, and yet Ambrose knew that, in many ways, Etienne's departure would be hardest on Chen.

"T'ien Li has long journey ahead. He will attain wisdom through blind choices. Same as everyone, Ambrose. Same as you. Same as me."

Ambrose stood up. He put his hands on the man's powerful shoulders. "I have never told you, Chen, how thankful I have been for your presence here. The nature of who you are has been

[123]

invaluable to all of us, and my words express inadequately what is in my heart."

"We act out same drama, Ambrose," Chen replied, smiling. "Only roles change. Characters do not. Last time, you help me. This time, we help each other. Wheels of creation turn. We jump off, only to land in same place."

"I would like to think each time is better than the one before."

"Better or worse only make difference through eye of mind. Through eye of soul, all is the same."

Ambrose nodded, resigned to the truth which Chen spoke. He reached across the table to retrieve the letter from Qu'an Li. "You might want to read this," he said.

"Your heart told me what it says. That why I come to library." Chen bowed and walked out of the room, leaving Ambrose to himself.

* * *

Etienne opened his door to the sound of an unobtrusive knock. Andrew was on the other side, smiling at him. "You are going to Paris, my son!" he said, his dark eyes twinkling.

"Oh Andrew!" Etienne, exclaimed. "How happy I am!"

Andrew walked into the room and shut the door. "May I sit down?"

"But of course!" Etienne cried excitedly. "Here, sit on the bed."

"Etienne," Andrew began, "you will be leaving in two weeks' time, and we'll need to go into town today to have you fitted for some street clothes."

"Why cannot I wear my robes?"

"Because your mother has arranged for you to remain a little longer than we shall," Andrew replied. "You are to be positioned with a family, who is to receive you as a student. We do not want your background to be known."

"Which one?"

"Either. For your own protection, Etienne, it is best that you are not introduced as the Empress of China's son, and for our

[124]

protection, we do not wish the Abbey to be known. There are those who might take advantage of our position."

"I understand, Andrew," Etienne agreed. "I have seen changes in St. Benoit over the last several months."

"Very well." Andrew stood up. "We shall leave for town immediately and take care of our business."

Etienne eagerly followed Andrew out of his room and down the halls. Gerard was already waiting with the carriage, and Pasqual was seated inside. He moved over to accommodate Etienne.

"Since I'm the Abbey seamstress, Etienne, it is only natural for me to come too." Pasqual patted the boy on his back.

"Pasqual, can we stop in to see Monsieur LeBois?"

"But of course!" Pasqual replied. "Perhaps his wife has fattened him up again!"

Etienne had never been shopping for things of a superfluous nature. He found that he was unable to choose fabrics and colors, and Pasqual helped him. Since he was to be a student, it was decided that he would dress modestly. Their choice of fashions were not ones that were considered to be all the rage in Paris. They chose suitable colors, such as burgundies, browns, and greens in a warm velvet for the chilly Parisian nights. Andrew found a fashionably functional thick wool cape; however, Pasqual made him put it back.

"I can make this easily, Andrew," he said. "Why not let Etienne be covered in a cape of our wool?"

"I would like that, Pasqual," Etienne offered. "It would keep me close to you."

The shopping took two hours, before they were completely satisfied with their selections. Etienne could barely contain his excitement over his impending adventure into the unknown, but out of respect for his brothers, he remained discrete. When the bill had been settled, and the clothing had been packaged, the three monks went out into the sunny streets, leaving behind a very happy merchant who had more than met his desired quota for the week. Business had been very slow lately, and who would have expected three ascetics in brown robes to have given him such a boost?

[125]

Outside, the autumnal breeze was blowing leaves across the cobblestones. It was one of those beautiful November days, which were increasingly few and far between, a final reprieve before the gloom of winter rains had descended upon the Loire Valley.

Gerard took the packages and offered to watch them while the others went to Café D'Albert for refreshments. This time the café was not as crowded, and they found a table immediately. Etienne loved the feel of the warm cup in his hands almost as much as he loved the coffee.

"Well, my friend," Pasqual said to him, "soon you'll be leaving us for a new life."

"I'll be back, Pasqual." Etienne placed his cup on the small marble table. "The Abbey will always be my home, and I couldn't think of leaving it permanently."

"We want you to be careful, Etienne." Andrew looked at him fondly. "There's not one among us who does not love you as his own son."

"Do not worry, Andrew," he replied. "I have no fear about my trip; therefore, you should not. Be at peace that I am well guided, and well protected."

"In spite of our protection, young one, we often guide ourselves into the wrong places." Pasqual supported Andrew's concern.

"Thank you both for your solicitude, Brothers." Etienne was well aware of their feelings for him, and understood their concern.

He finished his coffee, and standing, he placed his cup on the table. "Pasqual, Andrew, I am going to inquire after Monsieur LeBois. I will meet you back at the carriage."

They nodded, and Etienne left them to their thoughts in the small café. After its warmth, the afternoon chill slapped him with its cold fingers. Folding his arms across his chest for warmth, he hurried along the quiet street to the printers'. Most of the locals seemed to have taken refuge in warmer shelters, for he passed few people along the way.

Etienne pushed open the gate and walked up to the front door of the shop. He saw that the curtains, which were usually opened to the street's activities, were tightly drawn. Taking the four steps, two at a time, Etienne approached the door and reached for the handle. Ostentatiously draped around the knocker was a large black bow, screaming out its death notice to all who saw. Etienne's hand froze on the handle, as the message sank into him. With shoulders drooping, he retreated down the steps and out into the street.

He said nothing on the ride home. Pasqual and Andrew were aware that he was disturbed, but as usual, they waited for him to reveal the nature of his turmoil. As the carriage pulled up to the Abbey, Etienne looked over at Pasqual and caught his attention.

"He's dead, Pasqual."

"LeBois?"

"Yes."

"Another victim of the ill winds that blow down from Paris," Andrew said quietly.

Etienne felt chills moving under his robes and up his body. He knew there was something waiting for him in Paris, something that both tantalized his curiosity and terrified him! He could not define the feeling, for it was blocked by his excitement.

* * *

There was a fire in the library to stave off the cold, as gusts of wind blew against the large windows. Seated comfortably on the rug were Etienne and all of the brothers who had been his parents, and his friends, for the last seventeen years. The evening had begun in celebration of his birthday and of his impending departure the following morning.

However, revelry had been overcome by nostalgia, and there was a quiet sadness in the cozy room. Each monk was remembering the past years through his unique perspective. Perhaps only Ambrose and Chen had come to terms with the wheel of destiny that was throwing Etienne, in its inexorable way, into the realm of the senses.

Chen accepted everything as a matter of course, for the laws of nature governed mankind with their relentless trials. Etienne was all purity and innocence, and the time was at hand to test these

[127]

qualities, to mold them into the quality of virtue. It was inconceivable that he not play roulette with options that would offer themselves, temptations that would spiral him upward into bliss, or downward into the chasm of despair. Only Etienne could choose his destiny. He had been given all of the tools over the years, and his handling of them would now be tested.

Ambrose had not been well lately. It was increasingly difficult for him to arouse himself in the mornings, and he was feeling the pull from the other side. He began to have visionary flashes, windows of light that enabled him an ephemeral glance into the future. What he had seen had not been pleasant. He had known for years that he would have to release Etienne to the world, and he had been preparing himself for the inevitable occasion when they would part. In some ways, his experience with Etienne's father, years before, had softened the blows of the son's departure, for Ambrose was well acquainted with the feelings of loss surrounding a loved one. He was aware that this time would not be any easier; however, he had learned the acceptance of the way things are to be.

Ambrose had a strong feeling that in the next few months, he would be counseling some of the brothers who were experiencing their own sorrow over Etienne's extended absence. He foresaw Tristan's reaction and suspected that Etienne was the only family he had known. Tristan had never revealed to him anything related to his past, and Ambrose's curiosity about it had died years ago. What he did know was that after his initial fear over his sheep, Tristan had taken the child into his own protective custody and had guided him through the years in his own inimitable way.

Ambrose looked around the room at the men who had been with him for so many years. Not one face was beaming with the light that had shone earlier in the evening. Ambrose recounted the day he and Andrew had stepped out of the carriage with the scrawny baby, and the group of men who had been so eager to see the new member of their family. Now everyone, with the exception of Andrew, had grey in his hair. Even Chen's long mustache and beard were as white as his own, although the skin atop Chen's head was as smooth as ever. The world had stopped for them all, and now it must turn again.

[128]

The elder monk stood and looked at his brothers. "Night is fully upon us, my friends. Perhaps, now is the time to retire, before melancholia overtakes us."

The room came to life, everyone agreeing with Ambrose's suggestion. Goodnights were offered, and Ambrose watched them file through the doors into the cold halls. Chen waited until the last of them had left before falling into line.

Only Etienne stayed behind, as he needed to speak with Ambrose. When the doors had closed and the footsteps had died, he turned from the fire and looked up at the man who had always been there for him.

"I cannot call you father," he began, "but that is what you have been to me, Ambrose. Forgive me for moving away from you in the last few years, but I needed to discover who I was, and it is difficult when one feels such closeness to someone."

"Etienne, I have always known of your love for me. There is no need for an apology."

"Have you accepted my leaving?"

"I have, my son."

The two men, one fair and the other dark, looked at one another, and then, as though he were still a child, Etienne ran into the arms of the man who had loved him since he first laid eyes on him. They embraced each other wordlessly, the sounds of the fire crackling in the background, and then Etienne turned from Ambrose and left the room, tears running down his smooth cheeks.

He did not sleep well that night, for his mind was restless with memories that extended as far back in his life as he could remember. His hands were holding the gold Buddha and the rosary that had spent years beneath his pillow, emerging whenever Etienne needed their comfort. He was relieved when the sky became lighter, for he had reason to be awake. Quietly, Etienne washed himself and cleared the room of the last of his belongings to be placed in his valise.

He picked up the bag and opened his door, taking one last look at the small cubicle that had been his sanctuary for the last seventeen years. Satisfied, Etienne left the room and walked down to the chapel, dropping his bag in the foyer on the way.

[129]

Breakfast was anticlimactic, for all the farewells had been dispensed with the previous night. Throughout the meal, there was a quiet peace that had settled on the monks, as if a familiar routine had been established and Etienne had already left. Etienne felt, in some way, that only his physical vehicle remained, for the energy of the Abbey had already closed him out. This did not bother him, as his heart had been in Paris for a week.

Solemnly, the little group gathered outside the front gates to await Gerard and the carriage. Tristan walked next to Etienne and laid his arm around his shoulders. "Remember what I said." He held Etienne to him. "Don't hold back on yourself for anything."

Etienne put his head on Tristan's shoulder. "Watch the sheep for me. I'll be back to help you."

Tristan looked at the boy, and all of the wisdom in him spoke in contradiction to Etienne's statement. He knew Etienne would return, but he was also aware that the young man's path would take him far from the Abbey in the Forest. His heart was heavy with the sorrow born of loss for the first person whom he had ever truly loved. Etienne had been the delightful little brother, as well as the child whom he would never have.

From behind, Pasqual nudged them. "This is for you, as a reminder of your beginnings, Etienne." He held up a well worn miniature robe. "This was the first piece of clothing that I ever made for you, and here is the latest." From behind his back, he pulled out a finely woven woolen cape that would certainly belie Etienne's modest background.

"Oh Pasqual!" he exclaimed. "This is beautiful!"

"You will be the rage in Paris, my son!" Pasqual agreed with pride in his voice.

"And don't forget these!" Charles and François lunged forward with a small package. "Rice cakes for your sweet tooth."

Etienne was overwhelmed with gratitude and love. He looked around for one last time at his family, and suddenly feeling homesick, his eyes searched out Chen for strength. He had been standing apart from the others, when Etienne's gaze found him. Chen placed his hands together in front of his breast and bowed deeply, to acknowledge the child on his journey. When he straightened and

[130]

again faced Etienne, their eyes locked - Chen transmitting his silent message, "I'll wait for you."

Etienne stepped into the carriage followed by Andrew and Ambrose. Gerard closed the door firmly behind them and secured the latch. He jumped on the step to look through the window at the travellers.

"We're ready, Gerard," Ambrose said.

Gerard stepped down and then positioned himself on his seat. With a wave to the brothers who were huddled together in the cold wind, he cracked the whip for the horses to move. The carriage lurched forward, transporting its valuable cargo north to Paris.

Long after the dust had settled, and the coach had been swallowed by the grey forests, Chen stood at the front gate staring after them. The others had taken refuge from the cold; however, Chen was oblivious to the November winds which gusted around his small frame. His face was void of any expression except for a distant look that spoke of nothing; yet, resting on his beard were large tears that had left a path, as they rolled down his face.

Chapter Ten

"Paris! At last!" Etienne was mesmerized by the sights confronting him. Never had he seen so much activity, so many people, such tall buildings!

The journey had been an arduous one, for the roads outside Paris were notoriously poor and extremely dangerous. It had taken them, at times, hours to go relatively short distances. The four travelers from the monastery avoided encounters with strangers whom they passed, for most of them looked as though they might cause trouble.

They spent one night at an inn which Ambrose had frequented over the years, and which had always been considered a safe retreat from the day's journey. However, Gerard opted to remain with the carriage and the horses, while the others slept inside. Etienne could not help but notice the hostility among the guests, whose feelings were fueled by mistrust. Even Ambrose remarked about the quality of service, and how it had deteriorated over the years. He assumed that the proprietor was having difficulties, as was everyone else.

That they had arrived in Paris safely was a blessing. Ambrose was not nearly as concerned with the return trip, for they would not be carrying any cargo, and they would have little to offer anyone.

When they began to pass familiar sights, Ambrose pulled the cord signaling Gerard to slow down. Opening the little window at the front of the carriage, he leaned forward. "Rue Jacob, Gerard. Across the river from the Louvre." He waited for Gerard to indicate that he had understood, and then he sat back in his seat.

"Is this where I'll be staying, Ambrose?" Etienne asked.

"Yes, my son," Ambrose replied. "She was expecting you yesterday, and we had better leave you now. You'll be staying at the Hotel de Grave, Etienne. The owner has assigned you a small suite of rooms, which you may have entirely to yourself. You will be expected to dine with your hostess, but Madame de Grave will explain all of this to you."

The carriage wended its way through the busy streets, people recklessly dashing in front, impatient for it to pass. From his window, Etienne observed everything with a growing excitement. The streets were muddy, although it hadn't rained for a few days, and trash was everywhere. However, none seemed to mind as they walked amidst the mess. Etienne noticed that some people managed to avoid getting dirty, while others could not help it. Women were wearing low shoes, and he saw their white ankles each time they lifted their skirts to step over something lying in their path.

There weren't just French in Paris. For the first time, Etienne saw people with dark skin walking abreast of each other. Children played, hawkers shouted their wares. Hardly a soul noticed the exotic almond eyed man watching them as he drove by.

Gerard knocked on the carriage. "We're here, Brothers." He stopped in front of a tall building jammed in among several others. To the side of the front door was a large sign that read Hotel de Grave. Etienne looked at Andrew and Ambrose, suddenly feeling awkward in his street clothes. That they seemed so comfortable in their brown robes only seemed to accentuate his growing feeling of disorientation. For one brief moment, all of him wished to return to the security of the Abbey.

"We've said our good-byes, Etienne." Andrew smiled sadly. "Let us make it easy for all of us."

Etienne composed himself and lifted his valise. "You'll be staying in Paris tonight, also?" he asked.

"No," Andrew answered. "We'll deliver our wines and begin our return journey. There are things at the Abbey that need our attention."

Andrew did not mention his growing concern over Ambrose, who had not taken the journey as easily as he had in the past. Nor did he voice his sentiments about their reluctance to stay in Paris, separated from Etienne. Both of them wished to resume their normal lives as soon as possible, to override their sense of loss.

"Oh." Etienne had hoped to see them one more time. He squeezed the handle of his bag to alleviate some of his discomfort. "I don't know what to say."

[133]

"Write to us, Etienne," Ambrose whispered.

Behind them, there was a commotion. "Move on!" someone yelled out. "You're blocking the street!" Etienne reached out of the window to undo the latch, and then he pushed open the door. He took a firm hold of his valise and jumped to the ground, landing in a small puddle. Dirty water splashed up around his stockings, leaving circular grey blotches on the pristine white.

Gerard urged the horses forward, and Etienne ran to the front of the coach. "Gerard!" he called out. "Good-bye!"

The taciturn monk looked at him, his dark eyes drooping in his round face. He mustered a tired smile. "There's an excellent patisserie near here, my friend. Have an éclair on me!" Gerard pulled a small piece of silver from his pocket, kissed it, and threw it at Etienne who caught the coin with his free hand. They smiled at one another, and then Gerard directed his attention to the traffic.

Etienne watched the coach move slowly through the narrow street. With a sudden burst of energy, he ran up to it, ignoring the trash in his path. He banged on the door and jumped on the running board. "I love you both!" he cried to the somber faces inside. Andrew reached out to clasp Etienne's arm.

"Etienne. . !"

The carriage jolted to the side and lurched forward, and Etienne was thrown back onto the street. A group of children ran by, laughing at him, their noise blocking out Andrew's words. Resignedly, he placed his valise on the ground, pressed his hands together in front of his heart, and watched the retreating carriage. Andrew waved and quickly withdrew.

Etienne's valise seemed heavy to him, as fatigue began to overwhelm his excitement. Slowly, he walked to the large gate and rang the bell. He waited patiently until the door was opened by a small, plump woman wearing a long dress and an apron.

"I am Etienne D'Aubrey," he spoke to her, smiling shyly. His flawless French surprised her, for the few Orientals she had known had trouble with the language.

"Please enter, Monsieur" she said, stepping aside to give him a better view of the large courtyard, with a small fountain at its center.

[134]

The weight of the door made a clanking noise as it was emphatically closed. "I am Felice," she said. "Please follow me."

Etienne was guided across the courtyard to the center of the building, where there was another entrance at the top of several stairs. Felice opened the door, and they stepped into a roomy, but modestly appointed, foyer. Etienne noticed the simple tapestries on the walls which added color to the room with its white marble floors.

"This way, please." Felice gestured to a doorway that opened into the hall. "Leave your valise here. Frederick will see that it's placed in your room."

Etienne obeyed and walked into the dark hallway, whose only light came from candles. Felice stopped and tapped lightly on a door. Behind it, a clear voice said, "Come in."

Felice pushed it open and bade Etienne to pass in front of her. He gingerly did as he was told, not wanting to brush up against her plump form in the narrow doorway, and walked into a room that was filled with light from the windows that faced the courtyard.

An older woman was seated in a chair by the largest of the windows, and Etienne suspected that she had watched him come through the front gates with Felice. She was dressed in a burgundy gown with white lace covering the bodice. Slender arms extended beyond the puffed sleeves, and her tapered fingers were wrapped around a white rose. She looked up at Etienne as he approached her.

"An excellent vantage point, I daresay!" she said, referring to the window. "In this way, I can determine the nature of my guest, before he does me." Her voice was husky, and it resonated in the large room with a warm clarity. She held out her hand. "You must be Etienne."

Etienne placed it in his own and bent to place his lips on her soft skin. "And you must be Madame de Grave," he replied, fully feeling the awkward youth.

"That I am. Please take a chair and bring it close, so that I can see you clearly." She pointed to a tapestried chair that had been placed against the wall. "Felice, bring Monsieur d'Aubrey some tea and biscuits."

"And you, Madame?"

[135]

"Just tea, thank you." Her lucid eyes watched Etienne, as he carefully lifted the chair and brought it across the room. She noticed the dirt on his stockings. "You must learn the tricks of the Parisians when out walking!"

Etienne looked down, embarrassed by the image he presented. His shoes seemed out of place on feet that had only known sandals. Beneath his left foot, woven into the carpet, was the face of a young woman, mocking him with her laughter. He saw that she, too, needed some changes, as her blue gown had been worn down over the years by passing feet. He placed the chair on the floor and sat facing Madame de Grave.

"This is my drawing room, my salon," she said. "It is here that I favor my guests. One door down is the library, which you will find quite extensively filled with books not unfamiliar to you, I should think. You may have full privileges in my house while you are here; however, you must have my approval before bringing in guests. This will be for your own protection."

"Yes, Madame."

"Your suite is on the third floor, directly above mine. There is a staircase that connects the two, and there is also an exit on the outside wall of the building. These are for emergencies only, and their existence is not to be revealed to anyone."

"Is there a reason for this secrecy, Madame?"

"Etienne," she replied solemnly, "when your excitement subsides, and you see Paris through the eyes of wisdom, you will become aware of an unseen element that is growing more visible each day. This element is fear. The King has become all but impotent in the eyes of those who favor drastic changes."

"People are taking sides," she continued, "for they are beginning to worry about their futures. Le Duc D'Orleans has been exiled. Necker, who is presently in exile, is pushing for a constitutional monarchy, which the King violently opposes; however, it's becoming more evident that this is the only way out of the country's financial ruin."

"And what do you feel, Madame?"

"I feel the King will not live out the century, and that France will be in ruins, but these are my views, and they do not go beyond this room."

"Why do you entrust them with me?"

"Because, Etienne, I know who you are." She paused to look at her rose, gently rubbing a petal between her thumb and her forefinger. "I know of your history."

"I was under the impression that I was to be camouflaged as a student."

"You are." Madame's sharp eyes looked directly into his face. "Nonetheless, I would not have accepted you here without all of the pertinent information."

"Why?"

"To protect myself," she said simply.

They were interrupted by Felice, who entered the room carrying a silver tray in her hands.

"Ah! Tea!" Madame exclaimed. "Put it on the table, Felice. Etienne, would you do the honors?" Felice waited until Etienne nodded before leaving them alone, to the privacy of their conversation.

Etienne walked over to the tea service. "Sugar? Cream?" he asked, pouring the hot tea into the blue and gold porcelain cups.

"Both, thank you."

He carried the steaming tea back to their chairs. "There you are," he said, presenting it to her.

"Thank you, Etienne." She put the tea to her lips, sipped some, and then commenced speaking. "Breakfast is at eight o'clock sharp, lunch is at two, and dinner is at eight. I often have guests in the evening. You are always welcome to join us; however, as our schedule is quite flexible, you are also free to engage in your own activities. I do have tea in here in the afternoons, usually alone, but I would like you to save that time to talk with me, please."

"That would be nice." Etienne liked this woman who possessed a certain fire that was previously unknown to him.

"During the days, you may explore the city, study, and do whatever is necessary to fulfill your education. It will be very easy for you to catch wind of the sentiments, for Paris is filled with gossip. If you like, you can be my eyes and ears in the city." She smiled at Etienne.

"But Madame," he interrupted, "surely you can accompany me!"

"That I cannot do, my friend, for while my sight and sense of hearing are good, my legs are useless."

"I do not understand," Etienne stammered.

"My dear Etienne, I cannot walk, a fact that has been painfully evident since I was a small child."

"What happened?" For a moment, Etienne was concerned that he might be prying.

"A careless governess dropped me down a flight of stairs. The high fever that ensued from a massive head injury left me crippled."

"I am sorry Madame."

"Why?" she asked. "I have never regretted my position in life, for even crippled, I am far luckier than most. You will have much to learn about sympathy, Etienne. Paris is filled with lost souls whose plight will pull at your heart. It is a good test for one who wishes to transcend the realm of emotions and to see things as they are," she said perceptively.

Etienne gave no reply, for he was beginning to feel the effects of the last few days. Not even the tea could lift the lethargy that was spreading across his body. Madame de Grave looked at him and smiled knowingly.

"Etienne, I think it is time for you to rest." She leaned over the arm of her chair and picked a small bell up from the floor. Its sonorous notes filled the room, bouncing off the high ceilings. Within seconds, the door opened and Felice hurried in. She took the empty teacups and placed them on the tray.

"Felice, please show Etienne to his room." Madame de Grave spoke with a gentle authority. "Perhaps he might like a bath."

"Frederick is heating the water, Madame."

"Very well." Looking at Etienne, she said, "I doubt we'll see you until morning. Enjoy your evening."

He bowed and then turned to follow Felice.

"Etienne," Madame called.

He stopped and turned on the rich carpet. "Yes, Madame?"

"If you wish to be known as a student, you must drop the habits of a monk."

Etienne looked baffled.

"You needn't hold your hands in prayer when you bow." She laughed aloud, a rich throaty laugh, her earrings dancing with the movement. "We have much to teach you, that I can see!"

Etienne returned her smile and followed Felice out of the room. They walked back toward the foyer, to the staircase which was in a room adjacent to the entrance hall. Etienne's legs were barely able to carry him up the two flights. He was thankful when Felice stopped and turned down a hallway.

"Here are your rooms," she said, opening the door before him. "Your clothes have been unpacked, and Frederick should be pouring your bath."

Etienne walked into a large room that held a sofa, a desk, four chairs, and a table. In the corner, next to one of the windows, was a chaise longue. The carpet was a cream colored tapestry, and the furniture was covered in pale green silk. Beyond the windows was another building. Although this was hardly the pastoral view from his abbey cell, the room was far lovelier.

Felice gestured him to a short hallway which lead to a smaller room that held a bed, an armoire, a chaise, and another desk and chair. On one wall was a floor to ceiling mirror that reflected the canopied bed. He saw a man deftly moving about in the bathroom. The man turned and bowed.

"Monsieur D'Aubrey, I am Frederick, and your bath is prepared." He walked past Etienne and Felice and quietly left the room.

"Monsieur," Felice added, "the fireplace in the living room is prepared. Pull the bell cord when you wish me to light it." She pointed to a velvet rope which hung from the ceiling.

"Thank you, Felice." Etienne remembered the library at the Abbey, and the warm fires he had shared over the years.

"Will there be anything else?"

"No, that will be all."

Felice curtsied and left the room. Etienne had to restrain

[139]

himself from bowing and, after hearing the door close, he explored his quarters. There was indeed a fireplace with a large mirror above it. Everything in the suite was cream, green, and gold. Etienne wondered if he could ever accustom himself to the luxury.

He walked into the bathroom and saw the tub filled with water. Only once in his life had he taken a bath, and that was at the Abbot de Fleury's house on the night of the fateful encounter with his mother. Etienne carefully removed his clothes and laid them on the chaise. It felt wonderful to be out of his shoes, which felt uncomfortably tight. Peeling off his stockings, he threw them into the tub and then stepped into the warm water.

The heat worked itself through to his bones and relaxed him immediately. Etienne lay motionless for half of an hour before washing himself and his stockings. When he removed his towel from the rack, his body was red from the heat of the water. He gave himself a swift rubdown and replaced the towel, before walking into the bedroom.

Etienne picked up the gold Buddha and the jade rosary, that had been placed on the desk, and put them under his pillow. His bed covers had already been turned down in anticipation of his retiring early. Etienne climbed onto the firm bed and laid against the soft pillows. He was asleep before he had time to reflect on the day.

* * *

He awakened to the sounds of someone moving about his quarters; however, he had no desire to leave the warm comfort of his bed. Instead, Etienne laid back and stared at the canopy which stretched across the four posters over his head. He had slept soundly, without any dreams to awaken him, and his body was finally feeling refreshed after three days of nervous exhaustion.

He heard the door close quietly, and it was then that he stepped down onto the thick carpet and walked into the other room. Someone had lit the fire, and the warmth was beginning to push the chill out of the air. The curtains were opened, and Etienne couldn't remember whether they had been drawn the night before. He looked out of the window and up to the grey sky.

[140]

The clock on the mantelpiece read six-thirty. It was rare that Etienne had slept this late, and he hurried to dress in something warmer so that he could meditate. The wool cape came to mind, for that was the closest thing to his familiar brown robe. Etienne ran to the armoire and slipped it off its hanger. It felt good to place the soft wool against his nakedness. He went into the living room and sat on the carpet in front of the fire.

Two stories below, the servants were warming the rooms for breakfast. The cooks were preparing the batter for hot muffins, and cutting the side of pork into thick strips of bacon. The eggs had been delivered, and the kitchen was humming as usual, although the memory of a good night's rest had not been entirely left behind.

Felice was in Madame de Grave's suite preparing her toilette. Madame arose promptly at six each morning. She was not disturbed until six-thirty, for it was the rule that she spent the first thirty minutes of her waking time in prayer and contemplation. Felice would enter her bed chambers and light the fire, so that her mistress would find the rooms suitably warm for her to dress.

At seven forty-five each day, Frederick knocked lightly on the door and walked in to carry Madame downstairs to the dining room. He always found her sitting at her desk, taking care of correspondence, the room smelling pleasantly of perfume and powder. He waited patiently while she heated the wax and sealed her mail.

Thus, when Etienne found his way into the dining room on his first morning in Paris, he found his hostess already seated at the head of the long, carved mahogany table. Two large candelabras dominated the space which had been prepared with place settings for two. Between the candelabras was a large vase of flowers reaching up to the massive chandelier, which hung precariously over the expensive table.

"Good morning, Etienne." Madame de Grave was elegantly attired. "You appear to have slept well."

"Yes Madame, thank you."

"Please be seated."

Etienne walked over to his chair, behind which Frederick was standing. The servant pulled it out, pushing it beneath him as he sat.

At his right was a small boutonniere with a pin sticking through its stem. Etienne lifted the rose and smelled it before placing it against his collar.

"Is this suitable?" he asked.

"Whatever you wish, Etienne."

The warm breakfast was so filling, that Etienne doubted he would eat again until the evening. He made a mental note to himself to watch his diet, as his stomach was unaccustomed to such rich foods. Frederick and Felice seemed to appear out of nowhere to exchange empty plates for filled ones.

"And what are your plans today, Etienne?" Madame inquired.

"I should like to see Paris!" he replied, excitement raising the timbre of his voice.

"Take care not to get lost," Madame advised him. "The streets of Paris wind and twist, and then change names. You may find yourself a good distance from your starting point, if you become too interested in your surroundings!"

"In St. Benoit, we had crowded forests that surrounded our abbey." Etienne put down his fork to describe the memory. "Even as a small child, I learned to find my way through the thickets by noticing the markings on the trees."

"Then this will not be much different for you, for Paris is like one of your forests, although with more activity."

Madame de Grave had rarely left the city for excursions into the countryside. Travel often proved painful for her, and ultimately, she had learned to be happy in her home. She imported her adventures in the forms of colorful guests who considered it an honor to be invited to this woman's salon.

Over the years, she had entertained and been entertained by the likes of Voltaire, Cardinal de Fleury, Necker, and other notables. The latest philosophies had been argued until the early hours of the morning, her guests often stepping into the streets in time to greet the pre-dawn smell of freshly baked bread.

However, of late, Madame de Grave's philosophies had taken a more esoteric turn, and she had grown bored with mundane conversations. She concluded that philosophers, kings' ministers, and politicians were all the same, for their entire focus was on the problems of the finite rather than on the beauty of the infinite. They perceived the world through its dilemmas, rarely with optimistic conclusions, for in the solution of one problem, another one would be unearthed.

Gradually, the number of her invitations had declined, although her home was still open to an eclectic assortment of visitors. She was a powerful woman, whose subtle influence came in the form of carefully thought out suggestions that were opportunely slipped into the conversations. On one auspicious occasion, Louis XV had warily come into her house to discuss certain problems he had been having with his ministers.

She had never met Louis XVI, although she knew him well, partly through hearsay, partly through the rising sentiments in Paris, and mostly through her intuitive perception. What she did see, however, was the dwindling of his power and the ultimate destruction of the monarchy.

Madame de Grave was more than happy to take in Etienne as a houseguest, especially after her research had revealed his interesting background. She had a few friends in high places who were able to ferret out information about the boy. Madame de Grave had carefully instructed her friends to avoid the Abbot de Fleury when inquiring about Etienne. She was fully aware of the Abbot's pro-monarchy sentiments and his willingness to send those, whose views might prove to his detriment, to places unknown. He had sneaked in under the coattails of his brother Cardinal de Fleury, and the Abbot, with his sarcastic wit and his fondness for fine food, had established himself easily among the denizens of the French Court. It was only in recent years that he was becoming more feared than liked.

One day, fate played into her hands, when the Abbot had gone to speak with the Compte de Grasse and his wife in the park in St. Benoit, following an encounter with Etienne, who had come into town. It was all very simple from then on, for the information had been received and transmitted with complete safety to all involved. The Compte and his wife had even the good fortune of having met the Empress during her brief visit.

She could see now, after meeting the boy, that he was special.

[143]

He possessed beauty, poise, innocence, discipline, and a degree of wisdom which, she suspected, would become highly developed. She could not foresee how he would fit into French society, given his upbringing, but she anticipated that his time in Paris would awaken him to another side of life, to a far harsher reality than he had ever known.

She looked up at Etienne and noticed a light around him. "You are watched over by the angels, Etienne," she said. "Do you know this?"

"I became aware of this when I was old enough to hear about my flight from China," Etienne replied. "I have never felt unloved, for I have always had many people to care for me."

"Did you miss having a mother?"

"Only after I met her. She came to the Abbey when I was thirteen. She was the most beautiful woman I had ever seen. My brothers felt this as well."

"So that explains his looks," Madame thought to herself. "And I seem to remember having met his father years ago while he was in Paris. A handsome man, and very brilliant, but an anathema to the Jesuit order here!"

Etienne continued: "We often write, and I always feel she is with me. Her visit gave me a deeper understanding of my life."

"Were you surprised to meet her?"

"Absolutely! I was both enchanted, and terrified that my life might change. I felt as though I had lost all control. However, she was more than satisfied with my situation and merely wanted to see the child she had reluctantly and painfully sent away."

"Might you go to China someday, Etienne?"

"That, I cannot say. Mother hopes that I will succeed her husband when he abdicates the throne, but I do not know if I am adequately prepared for such an undertaking."

"Is anyone?" Madame de Grave asked. "King Louis and Marie felt that they were such children when they were forced upon the throne. With death often knocking at their door, monarchs find themselves in a position of responsibility shockingly early, with little time for preparation." She sighed, placing her teacup in its saucer. "Is anyone really prepared for the destiny he has created for himself? The ability to err and to try again is certainly a privilege, Etienne. Those assigned to leadership roles don't often have this opportunity."

She rang the little bell to the left of her place setting. When Felice appeared, she looked at Etienne. "Finished?" He nodded, and she turned to Felice. "Please call Frederick to take me into the library."

"Yes, Madame." Felice quietly returned to the kitchen.

"Shall we meet for tea this afternoon, Etienne, around four o'clock?"

"I would like that, Madame," he said honestly. "I would like to feel a sense of family on my first time away from home."

"Then it's agreed upon!" She smiled and laid her napkin upon the table, as Frederick arrived to wheel her into the library. "I shall see you at four."

Etienne accompanied her to the library doors and bent to kiss her hand before departing.

"Watch those puddles!" she gaily called out to him, as he turned the corner into the foyer.

Frederick pushed Madame de Grave over to the windows. She pulled a lace curtain aside and watched Etienne cross the courtyard to the outer entrance. After he opened the gate, he looked over his shoulder to the library windows and waved to her.

"Frederick," she let the curtain fall back into place, "I am ready to prepare my dinner guest list for the week."

"Yes, Madame," he replied.

* * *

Etienne's senses were bombarded with an electric energy the moment he left the peaceful domain that Madame de Grave had created for herself and stepped beyond its doors. Although the day was still in its youth, it seemed as if all of Paris had been up for hours.

The streets were crawling with activity, - women carrying long loaves of french bread, children skipping over puddles, students like himself with stacks of books, men on horseback, carriages! Etienne's ears were not accustomed to such cacophonous noise, and initially, the sounds offended them.

He headed in the direction of the Seine, which cut through the city without concern for the bridges that were needed to cross it. Across the river, he could see the Louvre, stunningly grandiose beneath the grey sky. Without paying attention to his destination, Etienne started to walk, hoping to absorb everything that he might have missed in his short lifetime. He was careful to avoid the traffic as he crossed the streets, for he did not possess the bravura of the locals.

The smells were almost as distinctive as the sights. Coffee, breads, horses, perfume...On various corners, were vendors selling foodstuffs such as crepes or hot sausage. He could not resist spending a few sous on some roasted chestnuts whose delightful taste reminded him of the Abbey. He and Tristan had often gathered chestnuts from the trees at the edge of the forests and then brought them back to François and Charles, who roasted them over the hot stove. The odor worked its way through the Abbey, and inevitably, several of the brothers found themselves driven to distraction by the special feast which awaited them.

The weather was cool and overcast, typical of late November. Etienne was glad he was wearing Pasqual's cape, for it kept the cold from penetrating his clothes. He leaned against the wall of a tall building and popped a warm chestnut into his mouth. In front of him, there was a slight traffic jam, as two carriages, having decided to travel down the narrow road at the same time, locked their wheels. The drivers were impatiently trying to guide the horses, and a small crowd had gathered to watch their predicament.

Etienne noticed the varied styles of clothing between the more affluent citizens in their velvets and silks, and the poorer classes in their muslins and woolens. Out of the corner of his eye, he saw two women walking toward the curious onlookers. He turned to look at them and saw that they were about the same age as he, and obviously from an aristocratic background. Their hair was tied up on their heads in the latest fashion with rows of ringlets hanging down around the nape of their necks. Their cloaks were a rich

[146]

velvet, and long silk skirts peeked out beneath them.

That they were sisters was obvious, for their resemblance was striking; however, the older one, although not as pretty, had an arresting face. It spoke to Etienne of refinement born of grace, and intelligence born of wisdom. Both of them carried beaded bags in their gloved hands. The young ladies paused to consider the safety of crossing the street in front of the carriages. It seemed that the vehicles were inexorably held together, and their passage would be without incident.

The elder sister gestured to her sibling and stepped down into the gutter. She had not taken more than a few steps when Etienne heard the noise of the carriage closest to him scrape against the other. He stuffed his chestnuts in the pocket of his cape and ran across the uneven pavement, just as the carriage lurched forward, freed by the strength of the horses whose hooves resounded on the cobblestones. Without stopping to address her, Etienne grabbed the woman by the shoulders and quickly pulled her toward him, backing away from the animals who would have innocently trampled her. He held her briefly, not removing his hands until she had steadied herself. The carriage passed, and when the noise had died away she looked up at him, her face reflecting her astonishment and gratitude.

"Thank you!" she said, placing her gloved hands against her heart. "I did not imagine they would come apart that easily!"

Her sister ran across to her. "Marie! Are you all right?"

"Yes, Claire," she replied, her voice trembling. "I'm more shaken than anything else."

"Come, let us remove ourselves from the street," Etienne suggested, feeling immensely protective, as he guided Marie and her sister safely to the other side.

"How can I ever thank you?" She looked at Etienne, her blue eyes reflecting her sincerity.

"It isn't necessary, Mademoiselle," Etienne answered, feeling awkward.

"My father would not agree with you. At the least, come and have coffee with us. The Café de la Régence is nearby," she implored, invitingly.

[147]

"Very well," Etienne nodded. "One coffee in exchange for services rendered. My name is Etienne D'Aubrey." He bowed, remembering to keep his hands at his sides.

The women flanked Etienne and slipped their arms through his. Behind him, his cape tapped the back of his legs as he walked. He held his forearms in front of him, as he had noticed more gallant men doing, hoping he was acting with propriety. A million fears crossed his mind, the greatest of which related to his conversational abilities; however, he dispelled all thoughts and allowed events to take their own course.

"Up this street." Marie pointed to their right, and the threesome turned toward the café.

It was an elegant place, filled with the upper classes, for Etienne saw none of the poor he had seen earlier, and certainly no students. They found a small table with three chairs. Etienne stood while the ladies seated themselves, and then he sat between them. When the waiter had taken their order, Marie turned to Etienne.

"You are not from Paris?" He noticed that her transluscent skin contrasted favorably with her dark hair and blue eyes.

"No, I am not." Etienne replied, feeling an unfamiliar yet exhilarating nervousness.

"I have noticed that your command of the language is exceptional. Why is this so?" Marie removed her gloves, revealing small, perfectly shaped hands.

"I was raised in France, in a small town south of here."

"Where?"

"St. Benoit-sur-Loire."

"Oh, that is a lovely little place!" she exclaimed. "But certainly, they do not have good schools?"

"I was schooled in a monastery," Etienne replied.

"St. Benoit, no doubt, under the Abbot de Fleury."

It was more of an answer than a question, and Etienne did not bother to correct her. He did not want to make any allusions to the Abbey in the Forest. It was a harmless assumption, and none would be the wiser.

"Are your parents in St. Benoit?" Marie felt an unusual curiosity about the extraordinary looking man who sat at her side.

"No," Etienne replied honestly. "My father is dead, and my mother is in China."

"So, you have come to Paris to further your studies!" Marie smiled, and her entire face lit up, giving her a powerful radiance.

"Yes, for an indefinite period." Etienne desperately wanted to take the attention from him. "Tell me, Mademoiselle, do you live here?"

Claire entered the conversation, her perky face alive with the excitement offered by a day in the city. "We have three homes," she explained. "One in Paris, one at Versailles, and one in the country west of Paris. Marie spends most of her time here, while I prefer the country. Papa is an advisor to the King."

"I see," said Etienne, inwardly amused by Claire's exuberance. Turning to Marie, he asked, "What is it that occupies your time in Paris?" He wanted to know more about this magnetic woman.

"I, too, study, and I spend a few days a week at houses of charity caring for the poor."

"I have observed that there are many poor in your fair city."

"There are many more in the charity houses," she answered, bitterly. "The contrast between the wealthy and the poor is a source of shame for the French."

"Marie," Etienne said her name softly. "There will always be rich and poor, as will there always be war and peace. The fault does not lie in any one area with any one class of people."

"You are perhaps right," she resignedly acknowledged. "However, I feel an oppressive social responsibility toward them."

The waiter arrived at their table, carrying one hot chocolate and two café au laits. Marie took some money from her purse and paid him, giving him an extra sou for a tip. They said nothing while they lifted their steaming cups, paying careful attention not to burn their lips. Marie blew into her coffee to cool it down, before gingerly sipping it.

"Where are you staying while you are in our city?" she asked, placing her cup back in its saucer. Etienne noticed that her slender hands bore no jewelry.

"On Rue Jacob at a Madame de Grave's." He felt safe in revealing this to her.

[149]

"Oh?" Her eyebrows raised, but she said nothing.

"Do you have any family here?" Claire asked politely.

"No I do not. My family is in St. Benoit." It felt good for him to say this, for the reminder alleviated a slight homesickness he was experiencing.

"We have four other sisters and two brothers," Claire offered. "I am the second to the youngest, and Marie is in the middle."

The conversation that ensued was quite superfluous to Etienne, although he sensed a greater depth in Marie. He assumed that it was her sense of propriety that kept their interaction at a mundane level. Eventually, he grew fatigued by the vibrational change and he decided that it was in his best interests to retreat to Madame de Grave's. It required discipline to take leave of his attractive companions, although, he felt their paths might cross again.

"I must leave now mademoiselles. Will you be safe here, by yourselves?" Etienne stood, not knowing how to conclude things gracefully. Just when he felt discomfort rising, he spotted a flower vendor passing through the room, carrying red roses. Without thinking, Etienne signaled to the man and pulled out two of the prettiest flowers. He settled the price, paying him what he asked, and then, turning to Marie and Claire, presented one red rose to each.

"Thank you for your company," he said, honestly.

He saw red creep up Marie's neck and into her face. It was Claire who expressed herself freely. "Oh! Aren't we lucky!" she gleefully cried. "A red rose from an exotic stranger!"

Etienne bowed to them and took his leave, suddenly experiencing embarrassment over his spontaneous bravura. Without pausing, he stepped out of the café, gathered his bearings, and headed home.

It wasn't until he stopped to wait for Felice to let him through the gate that he realized he did not know Marie's last name. A twinge of anxiety pierced his heart, before he came to his senses. He knew nothing about women, in spite of the fact that most men his age were already married.

Etienne checked the time, on his way to his room, and saw that he had a good hour before tea. He left his shoes at the door, threw

[150]

his cape on the bed, and went to wash himself. His face and hands felt dirty from the street. Refreshed, he walked into the living room to meditate. An hour of silence. An hour's reprieve from the bustle of city life.

* * *

"Tell me Etienne, what were your first impressions of Paris?" Madame de Grave was dressed in a high necked rich blue gown, absent of any decoration except for a diamond brooch pinned at her throat.

She looked elegant to Etienne. Age had been kind to her, for the years had added a certain polish to her looks, which may have seemed somewhat harsh in her youth. Her most salient feature was her eyes which were a deep green and which took in everything.

"There are many contrasts, Madame," Etienne began. "In St. Benoit, everything was fairly homogeneous with a few exceptions, and I grew up with a perspective that viewed things accordingly. Here in Paris, this perspective is distorted, for I never suspected such diversity existed." He poured the tea that Felice had left for them and brought her a cup. This time Etienne's socks were white, for he had carefully observed and emulated those who walked the streets with an acquired dexterity.

"Do you like our city?"

"I think Paris is a little much for one like myself from a small town, especially after I have been instructed in the simple way of life." He paused to sip his tea, an herbal blend from England. "I think that in the future, my forays into the city must have a purpose to them. Otherwise, I prefer to remain here."

"Well!" She smiled at the young man. "I had a feeling you might express those sentiments. My library is well equipped. You can spend hours there. And we can arrange theatre visits for you, if you like."

"That would be preferable, Madame." He was honestly relieved over his decision.

[151]

"You see," Madame's eyes twinkled, "I have not missed all that much by being confined to the chair! Nor have you with your monastic upbringing!"

"Madame," Etienne paused, feeling his face flush. "I do think I will need some instructions regarding women. I have never been in their presence, and I do not know what actions are appropriate."

"Just be yourself, Etienne. Women adore trinkets, compliments and attention, but they also love honesty. If you feign otherwise they sense it, and with all the folly of today, women appreciate a man who presents himself as he is."

"I do not know what will be expected of me."

"Were you not raised to act intuitively?" Madame waited until he nodded. "Then, this is no different. Let things happen spontaneously."

She could tell he had encountered one of the feminine gender; however, since she was not one to pry for information, she let the matter drop. "What philosophers have you studied, Etienne?"

"Rousseau, Voltaire, Plato, Lao Tsu, Socrates, and the like," he answered. "It was not so much to interpret them as to see the singular thread of truth that weaves through all thought, and then to glean my own wisdom from it."

"You were given independence at your monastery, were you not?"

"Oh yes, Madame! God was kind in placing me there."

They finished their tea, and he placed the cups back on the silver tray.

"We have a few guests for dinner this evening, Etienne. Please be prompt."

Sensing a dismissal, Etienne bowed and left the room. There were still three hours until dinner, and not wanting to go to his suite, he decided to take a walk. The dark would enshroud him, leaving him alone to his thoughts. He ran upstairs to get his cape, and then he slipped unnoticed out of the front door. He felt in his trouser pocket for the key Felice had left in his room, so that he could unlock the gate upon his return.

Nightfall had almost completely descended, and the city still hummed with people going home at the end of a long day. Their

[152]

tired faces, expressing little joy, made his memory of Marie more vivid. There were none whose visage projected the serenity of his brothers, and Etienne questioned the validity of a world without peace. He passed men sitting in doorways, or up against buildings, and he knew these jealously guarded spaces were their homes for the night.

The opulence in which he was living seemed almost repugnant to him, but he could not envision himself enduring the plight of the homeless or the poor, whose futures ended in a miserable death. For all the years he had been warm and loved, Etienne gave silent thanks. His heart was flooded with gratitude over the path his life had taken.

Ahead of him a man stumbled and fell. Etienne ran to help him back to his feet, but there was too much wine in his belly and too little will. He pulled him out of the stream of traffic and laid him against the protection of a staircase. Etienne walked until the disconcerting vision of the poor had dimmed, and taking a look at his surroundings, he knew he had left them behind. He glanced up the promenade, the Palais Royal, where it appeared that the most fashionable had braved the November chill to see and to be seen.

Etienne was fascinated by their exquisite dress. He wondered if Claire and Marie lived nearby, for their own beauty would blend nicely into the environment in which he found himself. People nodded their heads in greeting, and Etienne reciprocated the gesture. These inhabitants of the city were unafraid to look one another in the eye, as if their wealth afforded them a certain freedom. In the distance, he heard the bells of a cathedral ringing the hour, and he turned in the direction of Madame de Grave's.

He was beginning to regret his excitement over coming to Paris, in the light of the reality. The back of his head ached from the chaos of the city, and it felt good to draw the cold air into his lungs. He approached the Seine and crossed over the Pont Royal. The street lamps had been dimly lit. Dark shadows passed him, faces no longer visible.

As he was nearing Rue Jacob, he passed a figure whose hand reached out and grabbed Etienne by the shoulder. His heart dropped in fear, and stopping, he looked at his assailant.

[153]

"Have you any sous?" the man asked.

"No, I do not my friend," Etienne replied, remembering he had spent the last of them for the roses. His right hand felt the unfinished bag of chestnuts in his cape pocket. "I do have these," he said, handing them to the faceless man.

The man took them and hurried off into the shadows, leaving Etienne somewhat shaken and in a hurry to be within the safety of Madame de Grave's. He found the street which would take him to Rue Jacob, and his key was turning in the lock to the entrance gate in time for supper.

* * *

Etienne's headache had increased to the point that he could no longer concentrate on the interesting conversation between Madame de Grave, the Assistant Minister of Finance, and his wife. Employing a modest diplomacy, he excused himself from the dinner table and retired to his bed chambers. He laid upon the chaise in the living room and watched the fire burning itself into glowing coals.

The quiet colors in the room soothed his pounding head, and he surrendered completely to the semi-conscious state, where one's thoughts guide themselves through the corridors of the mind, never staying long enough to be caught and clothed by conscious awareness.

Pictures of his life flashed before him, like the sunlight dancing on the rippling waters of the Loire River. He saw the faces of his brothers, the Abbey, the townspeople of St. Benoit. And then Chen appeared, wise Chen with the all seeing eye, whose image froze in the vast space of Etienne's inner sight. Etienne felt Chen's energy fill his head, replacing the darkness with light, and then there was nothing.

He sat up on the chaise, freed from the pain. The fire had almost completely consumed itself, and Etienne got up to bring it back to life. Above his head, the chimes of the clock rang out eleven times.

[154]

He stretched his body and sat on the carpet in front of the fire to recall the dinner conversation, for he felt it was important that he understood the politics of the nation.

The Assistant Minister, a Monsieur Jean Brigaud, had been greatly troubled by events that had culminated in the exile of the Duc d'Orleans. His wife, a plain woman with a lovely voice, sat solicitously as her husband elaborated about his fears for the monarchy. The King had been good to them, and the financial and social remuneration received from his position had far surpassed any dreams the young Jean may have had. He had been hoping for the resignation of Loménie de Brienne, the First Minister, for it would most assuredly enhance his own status.

Madame Brigaud was in full agreement with her husband on everything, and her round face had become flushed with anger when Madame de Grave casually mentioned that, perhaps a constitutional monarchy might be the saving grace of the country. She expressed a sharp intake of breath and had looked quickly at her husband to determine the extent of his reaction.

"But this is impossible, Madame!" He looked apoplectic. "France has always existed under a king, and she always will! How can we have otherwise, without a revolution?"

"Perhaps a revolution will precipitate the change," Madame de Grave suggested. "You have just enlightened me on the events of the past week regarding the despicable badinage that has occurred between parliament and the King, and from my perspective, when parliament begins to wield its power, the King's loss is not far behind." She touched one of her earrings with a tapered finger.

"They must be made to understand that the King's power overrides all else. It is quite simple," Jean Brigaud countered.

"Monsieur Brigaud," Madame drew herself into an erect position in her chair, "when parliament and the King battle over the millions needed to overcome our financial deficit, and the King must resort to the exile of le Duc, as well as signing lettres de cachets against his most vehement opponents in order to get his way, then it is inevitable that someone, or many, will move to impede him!"

"I cannot believe your sentiments have changed so drastically, Madame!" Jean Brigaud had exclaimed.

[155]

"My sentiments are irrelevant. I favor that which will promote the good of France and all of her citizens. It would pain me to see the process of evolution halted by megalomania." Madame was conscious of Jean's bulging eyes, "Do not misinterpret me, Jean. I have always favored the King. He gives France a certain dignity befitting her aristocratic nature; however, I also see the need for change."

Etienne had been a silent witness to the accumulation of tension in the room, and with his head pounding, there was little he could say to offer a release for the unpleasant energy. Finally, he had no choice but to excuse himself, for feelings of nausea were beginning to accompany the headache.

"Madame," he had said quietly, "if I may be excused to tend to a throbbing head, I would appreciate it."

"But of course, Etienne." She gestured for Felice. "Felice, please bring some spirits of ammonia up to Monsieur D'Aubrey's room."

"Yes, Madame." Felice curtsied and left the dining hall.

"Monsieur and Madame Brigaud," Etienne bowed to the guests, "It is to my disadvantage that I cannot hear the end of this fascinating conversation. Madame de Grave will have to reveal the outcome to me."

He kissed Madame's hand and left the room, his eyes watering from the pain. There was a small silence, until the vacuum created by his exit had been filled, and then Monsieur Brigaud jumped at the opportunity to repartée with his hostess once again. He had been inwardly pleased to see the young man leave, for there was something about Etienne that made him uncomfortable. He never did trust the Orientals, and this one had the poise of an emperor. Moreover, Madame de Grave's attention was consistently diverted from the conversation, as she had kept herself attuned to her young guest.

Etienne stretched out on the carpet and stared at the ceiling. He saw, on the mantelpiece, the unopened bottle of ammonia that Felice had brought him along with explicit instructions on how to use it. Too tired to follow her orders, he had placed the medicine next to the clock. Now, in the absence of pain, he felt a sense of revitalization that had been provoked by his sudden healing. His eyes, now clear, studied the cherubs that had been painted on the ceiling.

There was an unobtrusive tap at the door, and Etienne roused himself to open it. Frederick stood on the other side.

"Madame wishes you to visit her in her suite, provided you are feeling better," he said.

"Well, yes...yes I shall." Etienne went to step into his shoes and put on his jacket.

"There's no need for that, Monsieur D'Aubrey." Frederick walked across the carpet to a panel on the wall that backed up to his bedroom. "Here, use this passage."

Etienne looked down a steep staircase. He had completely forgotten Madame's advice, on his first day, about a secret exit.

"Knock lightly at the bottom, and she will bid you enter." Frederick noiselessly left the room.

Etienne cautiously descended the dark stairwell, until he saw light outlining what was obviously a door. He paused on the landing and tapped loudly enough for Madame to hear him.

"Enter," she called out, and Etienne opened the door and stepped into a large room.

It was not decorated differently from his own, although blue dominated the colors, and it had an elegantly lived in aura. The walls had sconces on them, little cherubs with their arms uplifted to carry their lights. A large chandelier hung from the center of the ceiling, lighting the entire room and giving a romantic glow to the blues and creams. Madame de Grave, dressed in her silk robe, was seated on a chaise longue, her legs covered by a quilt.

"How do you like the secret entrance?" she asked.

"Whatever was it for?" Etienne slid the panel back into place.

"The original owner had it installed at the request of his mistress who was also the governess to his children. Her bed chamber was the suite you now occupy. While the unsuspecting wife slept, her husband would steal away into his lover's bed, only to return in the mornings claiming insomnia."

"How did he build the staircase?"

"When his wife and children went to the country, he hastily installed it. From this side, the door looks exactly like a wall panel."

"Did the wife ever discover her husband's infidelity?" Etienne was fascinated by the subterfuge.

"Eventually." Madame de Grave smoothed the satin coverlet. "These things happen. The governess was tactfully dismissed, and the family moved permanently into the country where the pious wife was certain her husband would not get into any more trouble."

Etienne smiled at the short flights of fancy people embark upon, only to land abruptly. He sat down on a large needlepoint chair next to his hostess.

"I had a feeling you would be awake," she said. "Headaches incapacitate one, and then when they have finally run their course, one can suddenly be revitalized! Besides, I assumed you might be interested in how the evening fared."

"I apologize for leaving you in the heat of battle, but I had no alternative," Etienne offered.

"No need for apologies." Madame shook her head. "Jean Brigaud is an obligatory guest, on my part."

"Then he is not a friend of yours?"

"You might say that his presence in my house is a necessary evil," she replied. "He's very close to the King, and he never fails to give me invaluable information. He's a clear barometer for me to read, regarding Louis' concept of his position."

"And what have you deduced, Madame?"

"That the King is feeling the strains of his own impotence, and that he is doing a poor job of camouflaging it."

Madame's grey hair, which was normally piled on top of her head fell loosely around her shoulders. Etienne thought about his mother, and he wondered if her own dark hair were peppered with grey.

"Were you able to convince Monsieur Brigaud that you were not in opposition to the monarchy."

"I think he is suspicious of me, but then he is of everyone; however, I did smoothe his ruffled feathers by giving laudits to his skills." Madame removed one of her earrings and began to play with it absentmindedly.

"His wife was very quiet," Etienne remarked, unable to remember her face.

[158]

"She usually is, but I know she rather enjoys the cat and mouse game her husband and I play," Madame chuckled. "I do believe she enjoys seeing him provoked, so that she can tend to his needs on the ride home."

"And you also enjoy yourself, Madame by keeping a check and balance on pomposity!" Etienne liked this woman, and he was beginning to feel comfortable in her presence. He realized that, as he adapted to his new environment, his sense of alienation would be diffused.

"My dear young man! What else is a woman like myself to do for pleasure?" Her green eyes twinkled.

They both heard the knock on the door, and Felice entered the room, followed by Frederick. Etienne, cued by their entrance, stood up to leave. He bent down to lift Madame's hand from the quilt.

"Good night, Madame."

"Good night, my son," she replied. "Take the secret staircase. The halls will be cold at this time of night."

Etienne walked over and opened the panel. He stepped inside onto the landing and closed the door behind him, not moving until his eyes had become accustomed to the dark.

His rooms were still warm from the fire which had all but died in the hearth. The bed had been turned down, and bath water poured for him. Etienne slid into the warm tub and lay back with his eyes closed.

Chapter Eleven

Etienne was in the library reading. It was seven-thirty, and soon the dinner guests would arrive. He had been in Paris for two weeks, and some of the disorientation had worn off, leaving him more comfortable in his surroundings. He had deliberately stayed close to home, rather than choosing to fend off another headache caused by the noise and dirt of the city.

Madame de Grave had proven an excellent companion for Etienne. She was filled with an exuberance that fired him, and her witty aphorisms introduced him to yet another aspect of her rich personality. He was quite charmed by her and thankful that fate had drawn them together. Often, they would expound upon each other's philosophies, and Etienne found himself opening up to a woman for the first time since his mother. He had never talked so much, as silence had been a way of life, and his long held fears about not being able to communicate with women were losing their power over him.

Madame's self confinement did little to keep her from knowing about life in Paris. Her dinner guests brought in the latest ideas, and they were diverse enough to give an expansive base from which she could draw her own opinion and through which she could focus on the pulse of the city. She empathized with Etienne's preference for staying relatively secluded, although she knew this would change in time. He was too curious to protect himself for long.

Etienne heard the doorbell ringing to announce the arrival of the guests. He straightened his jacket and ran his fingers through his hair, hoping it would grow quickly as its length was, to him, obviously indicative of a monastic background. He did not realize that his physical beauty was so stunning that few gave notice to his hair.

The candles in the room had been lit, dispelling all shadows with their warm glow. The burgundy aubusson, and the rich oak paneling, offset the cold marble floors. Next to his suite, this was Etienne's favorite room, because of its cozy intimacy, and of the volumes of books which filled the walls. In a city of blatant contrasts, the library evoked the strongest memory of the Abbey in the Forest.

Madame de Grave would be awaiting her guests in the dining room. Etienne got up to join her, for he could hear their approach as they were guided down the hall. He walked across the room and froze as he came to the door. The only sound he heard in all the world, at that moment, was the rustling of silk that had approached him so often in his dreams! For Etienne, time stopped.

With an inner trembling that could belie his calm facade, he entered the hallway to see the face that had eluded him for so long. A man and a woman followed Felice. The three stopped in front of Etienne, who finally confronted the enigmatic figure of his dreams.

"Monsieur Etienne D'Aubrey," Felice spoke formally, "may I present to you Compte Michel de Lavernay and Mademoiselle Marie Adrienne de Chevrier."

Marie gave Etienne a brief curtsy, her eyes warning him from mentioning anything about their previous meeting. Honoring her wish, he said nothing.

"I am privileged Mademoiselle, Compte," he replied. "Shall we continue to the dining hall?"

Etienne followed the young couple, which allowed him the freedom to observe them from behind. The Count's hand was against her back, gently pushing her forward. Her head barely reached his shoulders, and for the first time, Etienne noticed her diminutive size. He had known that he and Marie would meet again; however, he had never imagined a connection between her and the woman in his dreams! A feeling of possessiveness stirred within his breast, for Etienne did not want to miss the experience of knowing her.

After the effusive greetings, Frederick seated everyone, with Etienne at Madame de Grave's right. He found himself directly across from Marie.

Madame de Grave was wisely astute. She sensed the chemistry between her houseguest and Marie almost immediately. When she had first met Etienne, Marie's image had come to her, and she had catalogued the thought. The Count had been seeing a lot of the young woman, who came from one of the wealthiest families in France, and it was rumored that a betrothal was in the offing. "Ah well," Madame thought. "Perhaps Cupid has other ideas."

"And how is your family, Marie?" she asked.

"Very well, thank you Madame," Marie replied. "Papa sends his regards."

"Hopefully, Marie will soon become a part of my family," Michel proudly added. Inwardly he wondered why he had spoken so spontaneously, when the betrothal was still a closely guarded secret.

"Congratulations to you both," Madame countered. "I say that a toast is in order. Frederick, some champagne!"

Etienne found himself lost in a void of deafness when the Count announced his intentions. He felt the wind go out of him, and upon retrospect, he uncharacteristically could not remember the first half of the evening. He endured a series of toasts for the happy couple, presenting an admirable facade.

"Are you enjoying Paris, Etienne?" A voice pierced his thoughts.

"I beg your pardon?" Etienne's mind cleared, and for him the evening began, although the meal was already half finished.

"I asked if you were enjoying Paris?" Marie repeated her question.

"I have not seen much of the city, but I have been enjoying myself here."

"Well! You must get out more!" Her eyes widened in surprise.

"Perhaps he needs a guide," Madame hinted.

"Exactly what are you doing here, Monsieur D'Aubrey?" The Count's voice intimated a slight disdain.

"Please call me Etienne," he corrected. "I am a student learning about the political situation." He was aware of this being only a half truth, but he felt it a harmless one.

"Are you part of the bourgeoisie who call themselves the Third Estate?" The Count's tone was deprecating, and Etienne could not answer him.

[162]

"Of course not!" Madame interrupted. "And if he were, Compte, it would hardly change who he is."

"Except in the eyes of society," Michel arrogantly replied, "where to be noble is to be next to God."

"Often it is the nobles who have less money than the merchants," Etienne remarked, regaining his composure, "considering the fact that many of the nobles have exhausted their funds in the maintenance of vast estates, or in purchasing titles that they might call themselves the landed gentry."

"I take it that you favor supporting the voice of the many as opposed to the wisdom of the few?" Michel snidely remarked.

"When the many cry in unison, the few will have to listen!" Etienne was surprised by his passion.

"Why, you sound like Marie!" Compte de Lavarnay was astounded. "Madame, are you harboring a houseguest who favors a constitutional monarchy?"

"Not at all, my dear Compte," Madame answered emphatically. "I have opened my house to a free thinker, whom I try not to label."

"Well, his sentiments are being spoken in too many places." The Count looked at his fiancée. "I am encouraging Marie to leave Paris for the country, where it's safer."

"Michel!" Marie interjected. "My safety is not dependent upon location."

"Our children's will be," he argued, feeling rebuffed.

"How is your work at the charity houses coming, Marie?" Madame asked, redirecting the conversation.

"They're becoming more crowded than ever, Madame," Marie answered, happy to avoid Michel's consternation. "Hotel Dieu is still the worst for deaths; however, I must confess that I find little improvement. I lost one of my favorite patients to pneumonia this week, and winter hasn't even begun."

"How nice that the poor have a place out of the streets," Etienne observed.

"Hardly a better option," Michel sniffed, "considering the germs, the filth, and the odors!"

"Michel," Marie said gently, "they are thankful for what little

[163]

we offer them."

"Yes, my pet, I suppose you are right." He reached over to take her hand.

Etienne saw a slight resistance on Marie's part. Her blue eyes flashed across at him before she lowered her gaze to her plate. Since he had been trained to read other people's energy, Etienne was ecstatic, for he knew, unequivocally, that Marie was interested in him. She would be unaware of having given herself away and would feel quite safe with her secret.

From that moment on, the evening soared for Etienne. He lost all concern for himself and blossomed, as does a morning glory after the first hint of sunlight. "I would like to visit one of your houses of charity, Mademoiselle." He decided aloud. "I want to see what is being done for the poor."

"It's an advantage to be poor in Paris," the Count huffed. "Why, even the Queen gives them money. I think their indolence is only provoked by the undue attention given them."

"Michel! How can you say that?" Marie was amazed at his words.

Michel was surprised as well, for he had never voiced his thoughts so vehemently. He couldn't imagine what had come over him, for he was behaving in a manner that was unlike himself. Having been a guest at Madame de Grave's many times before, he had often impressed himself with his innate wit and charm. He suspected that it was Etienne who had effected the change in him. There was something unusual about the man, something that Michel couldn't identify.

Madame de Grave sat back in a state of pure enjoyment, as a silent witness to the undercurrents, which rose and fell among her guests. It felt good to allow others to talk for a change, as she often wearied of hearing her own voice. She was proud that Etienne seemed to be holding his own. Compte de Lavarnay was an effete snob, whose manner often begged for a comeuppance. Neither Madame, nor Etienne, were as capable of putting this man in his place, as he, himself, was now doing. He was an unknowing victim to the energy of attraction, whose unseen authority dominated the interchange in the room.

[164]

Dessert came and went, followed by liqueurs and coffee. The evening wore on, with Michel maintaining a discreet silence for his own preservation. Eventually he grew fatigued, as did Madame de Grave. Etienne and Marie, carried away on the wings of unspoken infatuation, were charged by each other's presence. The candles had burned low in the chandelier when Michel spoke to Frederick.

"Please tell my driver to bring the carriage to the front. It is time for us to take our leave," he said, rather dourly.

Felice stood behind Madame to pull her wheelchair out from the table. "I'll push her, Felice," Etienne offered, standing.

He took hold of the handles of the wheelchair to maneuver Madame de Grave in the direction of the foyer. Felice left to get the wraps for Michel and Marie. The dinner group moved down the hallway, concluding their conversation before parting company.

In the foyer, the Count bent to kiss Madame's hand. He bowed formally to Etienne. "I'm certain we shall see each other again."

"Yes, we shall," Etienne replied, aware only of Marie's presence.

"Etienne," Marie stepped forward and offered her hand which he raised to his lips, while looking boldly into her eyes.

He said nothing, for words would have been superfluous; however, he felt her press something into the palm of his hand, the very gesture making his face burn. As Marie turned toward Madame, he placed his hand behind his back, stealthily slipping the momento into his side pocket.

Etienne stood behind Madame de Grave, holding her chair tightly as Marie and Michel left. When the door had been closed he released his grip, letting the circulation flow through his fingers.

"Well, Etienne," Madame asked with a directness, "what did you think of her?"

"She is beautiful," he replied honestly, "but I have never been with a woman, and I would have no idea what to do, Madame."

"Then it's time to learn." Madame was smiling at him. "Now, it's late. Come, let us go to bed."

Alone in his room, Etienne reached into his pocket and pulled out the gift. It was a small white handkerchief with the initials M.A. de C. finely embroidered in one corner. Etienne lifted it to his

[165]

face and inhaled her fragrance.

He lost all sense of time and fell into bliss, his heart loudly beating the rhythm of her name. When at last he crawled into bed, the handkerchief was placed under the pillow with his other treasures.

* * *

The weather grew cold and wet as Christmas approached. It made Etienne all the more comfortable to spend most of his time in the library reading. The sensations he experienced, following his encounter with Marie, threw him into a state of imbalance. After years of discipline, he found it hard to meditate, and his home at the Abbey seemed very far away.

It required tremendous effort on his part to rein in the feelings that had galloped off in all directions. In the light of all that he was experiencing was a sense of guilt over his desire for a woman, when his patterning had been one of celibacy. A part of him feared that he would sever all ties with the Abbey, were he to fall victim to his ardor. Without guidance, his ignorance of women and the ways of the world would possibly lead him into a personal debacle.

Gradually, Etienne recovered from the effects of Cupid's relentless arrow, and during the weeks of silence following the dinner, he regained his composure. Christmas and the New Year came and went without event. Assumedly, Marie was with her family, while Madame and Etienne quietly celebrated the holidays at home.

Etienne heard Felice's muslin dress brush along the floor, as she came down the hallway. She stopped at the library, and upon finding him inside, walked in.

"Monsieur D'Aubrey," she spoke quietly to muffle her intrusion. "There is a message for you."

She held out a small silver tray upon which lay an envelope. Etienne took the letter, feeling himself trembling.

"I'm to wait here for your reply." Felice backed away, giving him enough privacy to read the note.

[166]

He broke the seal and pulled out a small white card. The penmanship was feminine and small.

The pleasure of your company is requested this afternoon at two o'clock. Please give your response to your servants that they might alert my livery man. A carriage will arrive promptly at the above time.

Marie

Etienne reread the note. "Please convey my delight in accepting Mademoiselle's invitation, Felice."

Felice curtsied and left the room. Etienne placed the card against his nose, smelling the familiar fragrance. He lost all memory of the peace that had filled him only recently, as anticipation flooded his being. For the rest of the morning, he had difficulty concentrating on his reading. Time dragged, and since Madame de Grave was busy with her correspondence, he had no one with whom he could talk.

Finally, the bell sounded, announcing the arrival of the coach. Etienne barely missed bumping into Felice, who was coming for him, as he ran down the hall.

"Felice, please tell Madame that I will be spending the afternoon with Mademoiselle de Chevrier, and that I will not be in for tea."

"Yes sir."

Etienne crossed the courtyard and paused at the front gate to gather his composure, before stepping outside to greet the carriage. The coachman jumped down to assist him into the elegant vehicle, and Etienne could smell Marie's subtle perfume as the door opened.

"Good afternoon, Etienne." The soft voice from the dark spoke.

"Mademoiselle!" His hand reached for hers. "How nice to see you again!"

He sat across from her, drinking in her beauty, while the carriage moved forward. Unable to speak, he awkwardly waited for her to initiate the conversation.

"I thought you might like to come with me to the Hotel Dieu

today," she began. "You did indicate an interest in my charity work."

"Why, yes!" he responded happily. "Thank you for remembering me!"

She was dressed very simply in a blue wool dress and black boots. Her hair was pulled back from her oval face in an attractive way which accentuated her large eyes. The more Etienne looked at her, the more beautiful she became. Infatuation enhanced his appreciation.

"Etienne," she looked earnestly at him, "I wanted to see you sooner, but I felt it would be unwise."

"The Compte?"

"Yes. It was best to let the evening grow dim in his memory, for I do not want any trouble."

"Then what do you want from me, Marie?" His boldness surfaced unconsciously. "Surely you are aware of my attraction for you?"

"At the moment, I can only ask to know you better," she replied. "Is this enough of an answer for you?"

"It will suffice, although the man in me desires more."

"Are you really studying in Paris?"

"Yes and no." He attempted diplomacy with his answer. "I am not on an official program. I am merely rounding out my studies."

"Any particular area?"

"I have an extensive philosophical background, although I feel philosophy is not real until one lives it. Wisdom is an energy that is born within one's self."

"As opposed to mere intellectualism?"

"Yes," he answered. "The study of philosophy feeds the mind, whereas life experience feeds the soul. I was filled with intellectual concepts that needed to be absorbed by my whole being. How can I know myself through another's pen?"

"I agree with you, Etienne, however I sometimes think our positions in life, our inhibitions, all prevent us from knowing ourselves. Sometimes, responsibilities force us to work on other things."

"Yes, Marie, but I need to experience who I am by interacting with other people. I have this freedom right now, and so I choose to go into the world, so that the world can come into me."

"What is behind this sense of purpose?" she asked.

"Learning the nature of balance, perhaps?"

"I've never met anyone more seemingly balanced Etienne, than yourself, and perhaps Madame de Grave."

"Indeed Madame de Grave," he agreed, "and with regard to myself, well, it is easy to maintain balance without temptation. Wisdom and virtue are qualities engendered by experience, are they not?"

"And what is to be your temptation, Etienne?" Marie smiled coyly at him.

"Which apple am I to be offered from the Garden of Eden?" he asked, and then thinking for a moment, replied, "That remains to be seen."

The carriage pulled to a stop, ending their conversation. The door was opened, and the coachman reached in to help Marie and Etienne to the ground.

"Here we are." Marie looked at Etienne. "The Hotel Dieu."

She put her arm through his, and they walked up the steps and into the large, grey building. Etienne was shocked by what he saw. The rooms were filled with forlorn people, most of them needing a bath. Women, children, young and old watched them, through the eyes of despair. Babies cried, and some beds were crowded with three or four occupants each.

"We will be working in the wing with the very ill, Etienne," Marie was saying. "It won't be pleasant for you, the first time. We wash them and feed them."

She was right. Many of the sick were close to death. They needed cleaning, and they had trouble swallowing the porridge that was spoon-fed to them. Etienne complied with the orders he was given and moved among the infirm with his inimitable grace, his gentle nature offering them a brief reprieve from their fate.

The light of his being fell upon the hopeless and the dying, and his presence fed them more than the meager portion of porridge, for

[169]

Etienne was a transmitter of the divine radiance which emanated from him. Throughout the afternoon, he and Marie exchanged meaningful glances.

The energy of their attraction lit the room with a soft warmth, projecting a tranquility among the ill. The children were in awe of the quiet stranger, who had such an unusual face.

"Etienne, come here, please," Marie called out from across the room, "Help me!"

Etienne rushed over to assist an emaciated young woman whose lungs were racked in a coughing spasm. Blood filled the white handkerchief she held to her mouth. Next to her, a boy of about six or seven was crying. Etienne picked up the child and held him against his breast. He began to sing the songs that Pasqual had taught him when he was little. Tears came into his eyes over the memory of his childhood, and the contrasting one this child had.

The boy stopped sobbing and clung to Etienne, who laid his cheek against his head. The mother's face was as red as her handkerchief. Finally, her coughing ceased, and Marie laid her back against the pillow. She wiped her face and hair with a damp rag while Etienne laid the thin child at her side.

"What happened to her?" he asked, not caring whether the woman heard him or not.

"A not uncommon story," Marie replied, tenderly stroking the woman's hair. "She was a governess to a prominent family in town and ended up the mistress of the husband. When the wife heard of the affair, she found herself out of work and with child."

"Needless to say," she continued, "an unwed mother will not find a decent job for herself in Paris. She used up her meager savings, and after the child was born, she worked whenever she could, cleaning hearths, washing floors. It's astonishing that the boy has lived this long. God help him should his mother die."

"What does she have?" Etienne remembered Madame's story of the mysterious passageway and the rejected governess.

"Pleurisy."

"Is there any improvement?" Etienne felt a deep sympathy for the mother and her son.

Marie shook her head. "Certainly being here is at least quite an improvement over the streets, is it not?"

It was eight o'clock when she tapped Etienne's shoulder, signaling that it was time to leave. After the noise inside the Hotel Dieu, the streets seemed unusually quiet.

"You must be hungry." Marie hesitated before stepping into the carriage, looking up at him.

"I haven't thought about it, but indeed I am," he answered her honestly.

"There's a wonderful restaurant only a short ride from here. Shall we go?"

"Can we walk instead? The air feels good." Etienne was still warm from the Hotel Dieu.

Marie spoke to the coachman and returned to Etienne's side. "He'll follow us for safety and then wait for us at the restaurant," she said.

There was a slight drizzle, which put a fine mist on their faces, as they walked along the empty streets. The brisk night was a reminder for people to find shelter; however, Etienne and Marie were still comfortably warm when they reached the small café.

The room was not crowded, and they were seated immediately. Etienne gave Marie the honors of ordering a small bottle of wine. He had never accustomed himself to alcohol and drank it sparingly, unlike the Parisians who had a bottle for every meal. The candle at their table illuminated Marie's face and gave him a chance to see her from a closer perspective.

"I think it's very magnanimous of you to engage in the work that you do, Marie. How do you keep from being disheartened?"

"Oh, one gets used to it, I suppose," she answered, thoughtfully. "Perhaps I feel more sorrow around my peers."

"Why is that?"

"I think it's how things are now. The rich are bored and the poor are angry."

"And you think that change is inevitable?" Etienne sensed she favored Madame's views.

"I do," she replied. She lifted her wine glass and slowly moved her index finger around the lip.

"Revolution?"

"Perhaps, unless drastic steps are taken to prevent it." The wine warmed the back of her throat.

Etienne sighed. "I would not want to be here during any revolution. I have already noticed a darkness descending over St. Benoit."

"I hear it's everywhere, Etienne. Like the plague, the disease of unrest is omnipresent." The candle flame flickered, putting shadows on her face.

"You are very lovely." He shyly studied her, memorizing every feature.

"And you, Monsieur, are changing the subject!" Marie set her glass down on the white tablecloth.

"I would rather leave politics and human misery for another time. Please." He reached out and touched her arm, regretting the table between them.

"You're quite right Etienne. We should enjoy ourselves while we have the time."

Marie's choice of a restaurant was a wise one. The food was excellent; however, upon retrospect, anything would have tasted good to Etienne, who dined on her presence. Her hair had a soft sheen to it, and a few loose ends hung seductively in her face. He allowed no concern for the future to enter his mind. Only the moment was alive for him.

It was late when they climbed into the carriage to go home. Etienne sat next to Marie, never touching her, unless their shoulders bumped during the rough drive. He sat in the comfort of silence, wishing the drive would last forever. Outside, the mist had become a gentle rain, rhythmically hitting the sides of the carriage.

* * *

"You're spending an inordinate amount of time with Marie, are you not?" Madame de Grave chided, her eyes twinkling.

She and Etienne were seated in the library for afternoon tea. Outside in the courtyard, the wind swirled dead leaves around and around, up against the walls of the building, and back to the cobblestones once again. The weather had turned unusually cold, and the library held its heat much better than the salon. Frederick had just added more coals to the fire, as they wished to conserve the wood they had.

Etienne rarely ate the biscuits that were served with the tea; however, today he needed the extra energy. His evenings had been active until late, and his nervous excitement had prevented sleep, until morning was well on its way. Marie had proven herself to be a committed guide to the sights of Paris. She had taken him to the best restaurants, to a street fair, and the previous night, to the theatre.

He had been able to acquaint himself with the people of Paris. It was mostly the lower classes who attended the fair, and they had made the most of the modicum of joy they received in an otherwise dismal existence. Etienne was fascinated by the casual way they related to one another, for there were no strangers at the St. Germain Fair.

Marie and Etienne were absorbed into the crowds, and immediately caught up in the excitement. They were pulled along and encouraged to play the games, to hiss the villain in the puppet show, and to buy an assortment of cheap trinkets. When they left the noisy crowds, Marie was decorated with papier maché necklaces to replace the jewelry she usually wore. On her head was a gypsy's cap. They giggled all the way back to Madame de Grave's. For the first time in his life, Etienne was laughing.

The theatre was not as enjoyable to Etienne, for there was no respect given to the performers. The audience crowded around the small stage, heckling the artists, as they tried, in vain, to speak above the din. Ultimately, Etienne requested that they leave. There was too much diffused energy, and his head had started to pound.

"The theatre still has a long way to go to establish its credibility in Paris," Marie had said. "With playwrights like Voltaire and Racine to enhance its status, there has been a gradual improvement, but it's slow."

"Are the performers well paid?"

"No," she replied, clutching a hand hold as the carriage turned a corner. "Often they are imprisoned for insubordination. They are fiercely dedicated to their profession, and occasionally a heckler will get a strong reaction from one of the actors."

"Do the King and Queen ever attend the theatre in Paris?" Etienne wanted to take her hand in his.

"Rarely. They have their own theatre at Versailles."

"I would like to see Versailles," Etienne spoke wistfully. He had heard so much about it.

"You can." Marie casually laid her hand on his leg, sending a charge through him. "I've made arrangements for us to be presented at Court in three days' time."

Yes, he had been spending an inordinate amount of time with Marie. He looked across at Madame de Grave who was waiting for his reply. A bright shawl was draped around her shoulders to keep her warm.

"I have been very fortunate, Madame," he admitted aloud. To himself, he wondered where it all would lead.

"Has the Compte returned from his trip to the country?"

"Next week."

Etienne did not want to think about the inevitable return of Michel. For the last five weeks, he had been conspicuously absent, tending to the needs of his family estate. He was originally due to return in a fortnight; however, he had had a change in plans.

"And what will you do then, my friend?" Madame's voice had a sympathetic tone to it.

"What can I do anyway, Madame?" Etienne replied sadly. "I have been trained as a monk, not as a husband. It would be impossible for me to make her happy."

"You certainly have the money to take care of her, Etienne, and I think you vastly underestimate your potential in the world."

"Perhaps it is as you say, Madame, but I feel guilty about my other commitments."

"Such as?"

"My possible return to China, my responsibilities to Chen my teacher, and my family at the Abbey." The obstacles seemed insurmountable. "I'm still too attached to forget them, and that is what I would have to do."

"Yes," she acknowledged, "I suppose it would be difficult,

after seventeen years of living in an enclosed environment, to sever one's bond."

"I do not know if I am ready, although I have thought little of my friends of late."

"You seem apologetic Etienne."

"I am," he replied, feeling disconcerted. He went over to the tray to refill his tea cup. Madame de Grave never had more than one, lest it spoil her delicate appetite.

"Etienne, my family has long departed, and I am the only one left. I have always thought the human life is predominantly a solitary one. We come together with others for but a moment on the long journey."

"Perhaps, Madame, it's my infatuation that fuels this brooding nature of mine."

"I sense that you need to think things over, Etienne. Why don't you spend the evening in your room. I'll have Felice bring your meal to you."

"That's an excellent idea! Thank you!" He handed her the tea and prepared to take his leave.

"When do you see Marie again?" Madame was reluctant to be intrusive.

"Tomorrow. We will be going to Versailles."

"To meet the King and Queen, no doubt?" Her voice revealed her interest.

"Madame!" Etienne walked over to her side. "How can I come to Paris and not see the Royal Couple!"

"Just do not expect much, my son. They usher you in and out very quickly."

He kissed the palm of her hand and laid it back in her lap. "Good night, Madame."

She watched his elegant figure leave the room without responding. There was a growing unease within her breast that foretold of ill. She had an intuitive sense about something, but it was too unpleasant to further reveal itself to her.

* * *

Marie's carriage arrived promptly at nine o'clock in the morning. Etienne was waiting in the foyer, when the bell rang. He felt infinitely better after having spent the evening in solitude. A long meditation had produced calming results, and following it, he had contemplated his relationship with Marie.

He knew that any decisions regarding their future needed to be affirmed within himself, and eventually, he agreed to follow through on his growing love for her. Etienne was well aware that events would take their own course of action, and it was his intent to be fully present and openly expressive. If he were ever to consider marriage to Marie Adrienne de Chevrier, then a clear choice must be made.

The lackey was holding the carriage door for him, and Marie was waiting inside.

"Hello, Marie!" Etienne thought he sang out the words.

"Etienne!" She gave him a radiant smile.

"You look beautiful!" Her eyes reflected the color of her blue velvet dress with its fur collar. She was wearing a matching cape and boots. Etienne felt pale by comparison.

It was twelve miles to Versailles, and the drive took them a few hours. They passed the time discussing the events of the past few days during which they had been apart. Marie related her experiences with the poor, and Etienne recounted his conversations with Madame's latest guests, a bishop and a writer.

"And could the bishop pinpoint your background?" Marie asked.

"Almost immediately." Etienne laughed aloud. "I forgot my recent training and bowed before him, as I had always done. He was afraid I had been excommunicated from the church, since I was wearing lay clothes. I assured him that it was only temporary."

Marie's face fell; however, she recovered quickly. "And the writer?"

"He was in opposition to the Church having such great wealth and argued in favor of the Church alleviating the country's wretched finances by funding large sums of money at low interest rates. Needless to say, there was a heated discussion that burned throughout the evening. I was absolutely fascinated."

[176]

"Did you offer your wisdom?" Marie smiled openly.

"No." Etienne chose his words carefully. "I felt it would have been inappropriate."

Marie sighed and looked out of the window. The sun was shining for the first time in two weeks, and it was a relief from the ubiquitous grey skies. Not even the cold weather could dampen their spirits.

"Marie," Etienne took her arm, "what's wrong?"

"I do not like to think of you leaving Paris." Her voice was breathless, belying her nervousness.

"Why should I stay, Marie?" he asked. "You're soon to be married."

"That is not definite," she replied quickly.

"Nonetheless, you will be forced to make a decision, most likely not in my favor, and then my role will be over." Etienne felt his stomach tie in a knot.

"You cannot offer me the financial security that Michel can. My father would never agree to me marrying a monk!" Her words sliced the air.

"Yes, you are right." Etienne spoke with a tone of resignation. "Were you to marry me, you would have to accept me as you know me. But I would not wish you to be reduced to a lifestyle which is not similar to the one you now have."

"So," her eyes flashed, "we are victims of social mores! Is that the answer?"

"Marie, I am willing to do whatever you wish." He kissed her hand. "This is our decision and no one else's." Yet he wondered...

The carriage came to a sudden stop, and they looked out of the windows. "My goodness!" Etienne exclaimed. "What wealth! What blatant opulence!"

Before him, the Palace of Versailles stretched across the land like a huge monolith.

"It's awe inspiring, isn't it?" She candidly admired the palace.

They stepped down from the carriage, and walked up to the entrance. Elaborately dressed uniformed footmen lined the walk. The front doors were opened by two servants in long stockings, pants and coattails. Etienne noticed that everyone's white wig was tied at the base of the neck.

Marie announced herself and her guest, and they were led down the long halls with more servants standing by each doorway. Windows framed the exquisitely manicured grounds and their fountains that had been shut off for the winter.

"Is the Royal Couple in the Viewing Hall?" Marie asked their escort.

"Yes, Mademoiselle. There are many here today to see the King and Queen, and you may not have an opportunity to speak with them." He continued walking.

Eventually, they entered a large hall that had several doors opening into it. Inside, a crowd had gathered. Seated at the end of the room was a diminutive woman with white hair piled high on her head. Her face was moderately pretty, but her most attractive feature was her vital energy. She was bedecked with elaborate jewels that weighed her down considerably.

Beside the Queen sat a heavy set, tallish man, who exuded boredom with the task of greeting his subjects. His face was not a distinguished one, Etienne noticed, for Louis would be passed by in a crowd without a second glance. A large fur was draped around his shoulders and hung down onto the floor behind him.

Marie and Etienne slowly moved forward in the line. Etienne watched those in front of him to determine the protocol employed by loyal subjects. He was not nervous, for he had been trained wisely in all areas except women. As he drew closer, he could smell the Queen's perfume, which was similar to Marie's light scent.

"Mademoiselle Marie Adrienne de Chevrier and Monsieur Etienne D'Aubrey." Their names were announced to the Royal Couple.

Marie curtsied, first to the Queen and then to the King. Etienne followed her, bowing as he had been taught by Madame de Grave. The Queen's gaze settled on him a moment longer than usual, for she found Etienne's appearance striking. She had seen Marie at Court several times with the Compte de Lavarnay, and she wondered who this new man was. She made a mental note to ask Marie the next time they were alone together.

Etienne felt the King was indeed bored with the obligation of meeting the public, and that he had a preference to be elsewhere. It helped immensely to be able to put a face to the man who was so often the topic of conversation at Madame de Grave's.

When the introductions were over, the crowd pushed them on, and they retraced their steps back to the front entrance where they were discreetly shown out.

"Is that all?" Etienne asked.

"That is all," she answered.

"Then I must admit that I found the journey infinitely more interesting than the journey's end."

"Now you know why I prefer Paris," Marie replied, taking his arm.

They climbed back into the carriage, and after they were comfortable, she pulled a large basket out from under the seat. "I brought lunch for us!"

Etienne leaned forward to look inside. "Bread, cheese, fruit, cake and fresh juice! Marie, how wonderful!"

"This will sustain us for the ride home" She took out the bread, broke off a piece and gave it to him.

They dined while the countryside passed them by. Soon, the city loomed large and grey on the horizon. Etienne broke off small pieces of cheese and put them against her lips, watching her white teeth bite into the soft morsels. A bonding that he did not understand, was growing between them. He lost his desire for food and could not help himself from focusing all of his attention on Marie, feeling himself burn with desire for her.

The coach stopped at Madame de Grave's all too soon. Had he been in unpleasant company, the ride would have been interminable; however, Etienne hated to leave Marie, for the future had not been discussed. He desperately longed to hear words of encouragement from her.

"Marie!" He boldly turned to face her before stepping out of the carriage. "Marry me! It will not be as you fear! You must trust me!"

She was stunned. Her mouth fell open in surprise. "I can't answer you now, Etienne. I need time to think."

"Then no refusal gives me a sign of hope." He was joyful. "Promise me you will let me know of your decision?"

[179]

Dark Places, Light Places

"I promise!" She blew him a kiss from the palm of her hand.

Etienne reached out and took her hand, kissing it. He kissed each one of her fingers and then the palm, before releasing it and shutting the door. In the privacy of the coach, she lay back against the seat and closed her eyes. Her heart ached for the man who had just left her side.

Chapter Twelve

"Madame!" Etienne was both ecstatic and fearful. "How am I supposed to look presentable at a ball? The closest thing to a celebration I have experienced was my birthday at the Abbey!"

"Etienne, do not worry," Madame assured him. "I've arranged for a tailor to come by this afternoon to measure you, and the rest we can take care of ourselves."

She had just confronted Etienne with the invitation that she had received the day before. A liveried horseman had delivered a gold embossed envelope addressed to Madame de Grave and Monsieur Etienne D'Aubrey requesting their presence at a ball in one week's time, given in honor of Marie Adrienne de Chevrier by her father and mother, Le Compte and Contessa Adrien Victor de Chevrier.

Madame had kept the knowledge of the invitation to herself, for she intuited Etienne's response and had needed time to arrange for the tailor. It had been a week since Etienne had heard from Marie. The silence left little room for doubt that Michel had returned from the country. Etienne did not seem visibly upset, but Madame suspected he was versed in self containment. He had been well trained by his teacher to empty his mind of troublesome thoughts.

It would take no time to acquaint him with the procedure. For that she had no concern. However, she questioned the reason behind this extravagant social event in the middle of winter. She had a sense of disquiet about the whole affair, and it was admittedly for the protection of Etienne that she worried. She had to remind herself that he was approaching manhood, although his maturity often surpassed that of his peers.

Now standing before her, his face radiated a vitality that put a glow around him. At times, Madame felt blessed to be in the presence of a soul whose inner light gave her an understanding of Divine Grace. "When he fully comes into his own," she thought, "he will amaze people. However, he must first pass through the impetuosity of youth."

"And you will come too, Madame, will you not?"

"Why, of course, Etienne. You are to be my escort," she replied with a false gaiety.

Etienne bent down to kiss her cheek. He straightened himself and quickly left the room, walking down the hall and up the staircase to his suite. Once inside, he threw himself on the chaise, his thoughts on the upcoming week.

He had missed Marie terribly, but he trusted in her final words to him. There had still been no response to his proposal. Perhaps the ball was her answer. At any rate, he would once again be able to see her, to touch her, and to hear her voice. He doubted he would endure the week with much patience.

Etienne prepared for his meditation. He needed to rid himself of the nervous euphoria over Marie's invitation. He closed his eyes and relaxed, allowing his mind to empty. For the next hour, there was nothing, and then, in the last few minutes, a vision came to Etienne which startled him. He saw Chen and Andrew bent over Ambrose, concern in their faces. Chen looked up into Etienne's mind's eye. "His time has come to leave us," he said.

Etienne opened his eyes with a start. He had known of Ambrose's failing health for some time, and he had hoped to see him again before he died. However, this was not as disturbing to him as the disapproving look on Chen's face.

Was this a warning for him? Chen had never interfered in Etienne's choices, and he had never expressed disapproval in the past. Etienne felt guilt pervade his being. He had done nothing, that he could recall, to evoke a negative reaction from anyone. However, with a determined recklessness, he blocked his memory of Chen.

"I must pilot my own ship!" he said aloud. Miles away, behind the Abbey walls, Chen nodded his head, for he had heard the words.

* * *

The carriage pulled them slowly through the streets of Paris. Etienne felt princely in his formal attire. In the last week, Madame had educated him more than sufficiently, concerning his lack of social knowledge. He was, however, glad to have the responsibility of attending to her in her wheelchair, for it would place his focus on someone other than himself.

She looked unusually elegant in a gown of cream colored silk. Diamonds had been pinned into her grey hair. Etienne thought that Madame would have made some man a proud husband, yet he wondered if she would have been quite as fascinating without her handicap to facilitate her into her own sense of self-awareness and growth.

"Here we are, Etienne," she said, relieved that the trip was over.

His heart moved into his throat, as he waited for the carriage to stop. When the door was opened, he saw an endless staircase aglow with lanterns. It climbed forever to a lavishly decorated entrance that was alive with guests milling about.

Etienne helped the driver lift Madame out of the coach, and then followed them up the steps. Elegantly dressed servants opened the doors. After Madame had been placed in her wheelchair, she passed the servants her invitation. One of them carried it to a man who called out to the crowd below: "Madame Justine de Grave and Monsieur Etienne D'Aubrey."

Etienne looked down into the throngs of people who momentarily stopped their conversations to stare at the new arrivals. He could not see Marie among the guests, so he carefully brought Madame down the stairs and into the crowd. A butler approached them with the offer of champagne. Madame lifted a crystal glass from the silver tray, while Etienne declined. He was too absorbed with the guests to concentrate on anything else. Never had he seen so many jewels reflecting the light.

He felt a hand on his back. The current that passed through him made him turn swiftly. "Marie!" he exclaimed.

She stood before him, dressed in yellow silk and diamonds. Her blue eyes sparkled, and she looked lovelier than he had ever seen her. "Etienne," she replied formally. "How kind of you and Madame to come tonight!"

Etienne saw the reason for her inhibition. Beside her, the Count stood stiffly, his face an impenetrable mask. He coldly greeted

[183]

Madame and Etienne, and then he swiftly guided Marie away to meet other guests.

"Don't worry about him," Madame whispered, reassuring Etienne.

"What am I to do, Madame?" he asked sadly.

"Enjoy yourself, Etienne! There are many beautiful women here tonight!"

She was right. The ballroom was filled with lovely women who were honored to dance with him. He did not waste his time feeling sorry for himself. Instead, he escorted Madame around the ball room, stopping to converse with her friends. She was well liked, and Etienne was immediately accepted by them.

The music played, and the wine and food flowed unceasingly. Occasionally, Etienne would leave Madame's side to dance. Marie did not return to him until much later in the evening.

"Are you satisfied with your first ball, Etienne?"

He started and then looked at her. "You have a habit of approaching me unannounced," he replied. His eyes were arrested, as always, by her exquisite beauty.

"It is the only way that I can see you," she responded, "with Michel occupied."

"I have missed you, Marie."

"And I have missed you." Her face reflected her sorrow.

"When can I see you again?" He had to fight the impulse to take her into his arms.

"Etienne. . . . ."

Her words were interrupted by the sound of a loud bell. When there was a respectful silence, someone stood up on a decorated platform. Etienne saw the man gesture to Michel to join him, and he felt Marie grow rigid at his side.

She began to move away, but Etienne took her arm. "Stay here," he spoke with a quiet authority.

She obeyed him.

The man on the dais began to speak. "Many of you know that my beloved daughter, Marie, has been in the company of Compte Michel de Lavarnay," he began. "Tonight, we wish to make it official. I am announcing the betrothal of my daughter, Marie

[184]

Adrienne de Chevrier to Compte Michel de Lavarnay! The marriage ceremony will take place in one month's time!"

Etienne blanched and then released Marie who looked at him beseechingly, before moving quickly through the crowd to the platform. He watched her stand next to Michel, who put his arms around her, while he beamed at the guests. His eyes met Etienne's, his smile momentarily freezing, before his gaze moved on to the others. Marie avoided Etienne entirely.

He was raging over her duplicity. He felt sick to his stomach and wanted to run from the disgrace. He did not notice Madame's grip on his arm to steady his trembling.

"Etienne, shall we leave?" she spoke, breaking the silence around them.

Without a word, he pushed her slowly toward the door. He cut through the crowds, walking proudly, as Chen had taught him, his head held high. Never once did he turn around for one last look at Marie, whose eyes followed his retreat, through the ball room and up the staircase, until the doors closed behind him.

"How could she do this to me?" Etienne wrapped a cover around Madame's legs to keep them warm in the crisp night air.

"Did you not know that this was inevitable, Etienne?" she asked compassionately.

"No! I asked her to marry me, Madame, and she promised a reply! I trusted her, and now, I am humiliated over the way she chose to reject me!"

"I am sorry." Madame's warm breath could be seen in the air, as the light from a street lamp shone through the window of the coach.

"She felt I was beneath her. A lowly monk!"

"There is nothing lowly about you, my son." Madame leaned forward and put her hand on his knee to comfort him.

"Why could I not tell her about myself?" he implored. "If she had but known, would it have altered the circumstances?"

"Does anything alter that which is preordained, Etienne? If your mother had known you were to be the result of her union with your father, would she have changed her actions?"

"I do not know," he replied, honestly.

"I rather doubt she would have. We will do anything for a small measure of happiness, even, as in Marie's case, choosing the wrong man for the wrong reasons. Look at all the fruits born of actions that were carried out for one moment of pleasure."

"I assume this is my lesson," Etienne spoke forlornly, "It is preordained that I am to be a monk."

"If you want a wife, then there will be one for you," Madame said softly.

"I never asked for that, Madame. I only wanted Marie."

They were so immersed in their thoughts they hardly noticed the cold in the carriage, until they had to leave it to enter the house. Frederick carried Madame into the building and up to her warm room, while Etienne followed them, continuing on to his own suite. He opened the door to the glow of hot coals casting their dim light throughout the room.

Etienne walked over to the fireplace, and, leaning on the mantelpiece with one elbow, he looked down into the embers. For the first time that he could remember, he cried.

* * *

The next few days dragged for Etienne. He was ready to leave Paris, with its noise, its filth, and its poverty. The only pleasant aspect of his visit had been Madame de Grave, whom he genuinely loved; however, he was feeling the pull of the monastery after his vision of Ambrose. He wanted to spend time with the man who was the only father he had ever known. His heart was swollen with pain for himself, for Madame de Grave in her crippled condition, and for all of the poor and downtrodden.

Etienne spent much of his time alone in his room, sorting through his feelings and trying to make decisions about his future. He had been in Paris for almost five months, and he still could not accustom himself to the change in lifestyles. Only Marie had been able to color the city with a certain magical charm, and without her, it was once again reduced to its grey overtones. He actually preferred the sanctity of Madame de Grave's, and if he were going to remain cloistered, then the Abbey was his choice.

Etienne was sitting on his bed, holding Marie's white hand-kerchief in his hand when he heard a knock at his door. "Come in!" he called out.

Frederick opened the door and entered the room. "Madame wishes to see you in her rooms, sir."

"Thank you, Frederick."

Etienne went to the door panel and pushed it aside to descend the steps. He walked into Madame's room after tapping three times on the panel. She was sitting at her desk.

"Etienne!" She was happy to see him. "I have missed you in the last few days."

"I've been regaining my clarity, Madame," he replied.

"And what does your heart tell you?"

"I have decided to return to the Abbey." He spoke with a quiet conviction.

She looked at Etienne for a long time. "I can see that you've made up your mind." Madame waited for him to sit down. "I can't say this surprises me, Etienne. You do not belong in this jaded environment with your purity."

"You have indeed been a beacon for me, Madame." He looked gratefully at her.

"And you have been a blessing to me," she spoke admiringly. "I am sure we shall meet again. When are you leaving?"

"Perhaps in a few days' time, when I can arrange passage."

"I'll send you in my carriage," she offered.

"But the money. . ."

"Your mother has more than paid for a return trip, Etienne. Do not worry."

"Thank you, Madame."

"I wanted to tell you, Etienne, that I will be going out this evening. It is rare that I do; however, this is an old friend who is now dying."

"Will you be late?"

"I'm afraid so," Madame replied. "She lives outside the city."

"I shall wait up for you."

[187]

"That isn't necessary, but it would be a pleasant surprise."

"Very well then," Etienne stood up to leave. "I'll have hot tea waiting for you." He crossed the floor, kissed her brow and left the room.

* * *

"Will you be needing anything else, sir?" Felice asked.

"No thank you, Felice. Why don't you take the evening off, until Madame returns. I am very happy here in the library, and I have no needs other than the warm fire and a good book."

Felice curtsied and left the room. Etienne's spirits had lifted considerably, since he had made the decision to return to St. Benoit. For the first time in a month, he felt at peace with himself. A terrible burden had been lifted, and the anticipation of being with his brothers, once again, soothed his shattered heart.

Without Madame de Grave, the house was unusually quiet. Etienne heard the clock ticking in the salon, next door. The richness of the library was enhanced by the fire and the candlelight, and Etienne settled back into his chair and began to read the newspapers which had been printed in the last few days. Time passed unnoticed.

At first, he thought it was the sound of the clock chiming the hour, but then he realized someone was at the front gate. He laid the papers on the floor and left his chair, for with the servants in their quarters, only he would hear the bell. Etienne walked down the hallway and into the foyer.

When he opened the door into the courtyard, he was greeted by large flakes of snow, melting when they hit the cobblestones. Etienne quickly crossed the courtyard and opened the gate. He froze when he saw Marie standing on the other side, snowflakes kissing her hair and face, where his own lips wanted to be.

"Etienne," she implored, "I must speak with you!"

[188]

He felt mortified. "Why Marie? Hasn't your silence spoken volumes?"

"Please!" She begged him.

"Very well," he said with some reluctance, "come into the house where it's warm."

Marie turned to the driver. "Antoine, please wait for me. You may sit in the carriage to keep warm."

"Yes Mademoiselle."

Marie walked in front of Etienne, her cape propped up by the voluminous skirts underneath. Etienne closed the gate and ran to catch up to her. He offered his arm, so that she would not slip and fall onto the wet pavement.

Inside the foyer, Marie wiped the snow off her arms and her hair, while Etienne spread her cape across the chair to dry.

"Let us go into the library where it is warm" he suggested, his heart pounding.

They were both silent, listening to the sounds of their footsteps on the carpet. Etienne guided Marie into the library and pulled a chair close to his own near the fire. He unlaced her boots, pulling them off her feet and laying them on the hearth. Her feet were cold, and he rubbed them gently before lifting them onto the footstool. When he was assured of her comfort, he went over and shut the doors to the room, offering them complete privacy. It would be hours before Madame would return.

"Now," he said, returning to his chair, "what is it that you feel you must tell me?"

"I did not want it to happen that way, Etienne." Her blue eyes were filled with tears.

"What did you expect, Marie? You were aware of my invitation to the ball. You knew I would be there to hear the announcement!" He did not try to conceal his anger.

"But it surprised even me!" she cried. "Michel and I had hardly discussed marriage at all, and then, upon his return from the county, he became increasingly possessive."

"Are you implying that you had no say in the matter?"

"Yes. . ! No. . !" she stammered. "Apparently he talked to my father without my knowledge."

"Surely, Marie," Etienne remarked sardonically, "you never considered the possibility of marriage to me!"

Marie looked directly at him. "I considered it," she said. "I would far prefer to spend my life with you."

"Then what is preventing you?" he demanded. "My background?"

"Yes!" she cried.

"And if I had money, Marie, would this alter your decision?"

"Yes." She looked down at her hands, feeling ashamed to admit such a thing. "Forgive me, Etienne, but this does affect my decision."

"Then what more did you wish to say?" He stood, ready to dismiss the conversation.

"I wanted to resolve things between us. They were painfully incomplete." She kept her gaze lowered, afraid to look into the clear honesty of Etienne's eyes.

"I do not need you to patronize me Marie!"

She jumped up to face him. Her hair had fallen around her face, making her more beautiful than ever. "I never intended such!" she sobbed.

Marie began to leave. Etienne reached out, pulling her back to him.

"Let me know the joy of holding you, before you walk from my life forever," His voice was hoarse with emotion.

She fell into his arms, which encircled her body, pulling her closer to him. Her face rested against the soft velvet jacket which covered his firm chest.

"Marie, Marie," Etienne said, burying his lips in her thick hair.

He moved his hands up to the back of her head and pulled out the combs that held her hair, throwing them onto the soft carpet. Still holding her to him, he moved his fingers through her hair down around her back.

Marie's hands clung to his jacket, and she looked up at his exotic face. With the sight of her lips, Etienne took her hands from his jacket and put them around his waist. Very slowly, he pulled her to him, lowering his head until his own lips caressed hers. Together they stood, their mouths gently playing with light touches. He

[190]

brushed his lips across her face, and then, holding her head with his hands, he brought his mouth firmly down on hers.

His whole body responded. Deep within his loins was an ache to bring forth the seed that would be taken by this woman and carried into the depths of her womb, to merge with its other half. Etienne placed his forehead on her shoulder, breathing deeply to control the euphoria that raced wildly through his veins.

He brought one hand up to the top of her bodice and loosened a pearl button. Slowly, he undid the second button, reaching his fingers inside to feel her soft skin.

"Stop me now, if you have fears Marie," he whispered into her ear.

"I am my desire," she replied. "I cannot say anything but yes."

She let him finish unbuttoning her bodice, her breath coming out in short gasps of excitement. Etienne slipped the dress down around her shoulders and let it slide to the floor. He lifted her petticoats and pulled them over her head. Freed from the restrictions of clothes, her body projected a voluptuous softness that glowed in the firelight.

Etienne moved the chairs from in front of the fireplace and laid her on the warm carpet. He knelt beside her as he removed his shirt and jacket, and then he undid his pants, letting them slide down his legs. She reached her arms up to take him to her.

He touched her gently, feeling her softness, running his hands around her breasts and her smooth hips. She lay beneath him, surrendering to his exploration, enjoying the sensations his touch created within her. He kissed her forehead, her mouth, her neck, her breasts. She could feel his hardness pressing against her thigh, leaving its precious fluids on her skin.

Etienne buried his face in her rounded belly, touching the inside of her navel with his tongue. He had never imagined himself with a woman this way, and he was surprised by his intimate knowledge of her body. He licked the thin line of dark hair that ran from her navel down to her pubis.

All the while, he kept returning to her full breasts, whose nipples entered his mouth at his command. His pleasure over the sucking stirred intense feeling in his pelvic area. Etienne wondered if he had been able to drink from his mother's breasts before she had sent him away. He imagined Marie's, filled with milk for their child.

His hands moved down beyond her pubis, and his fingers spread her legs apart so that he could feel that most sacred part of her. She was moist and receptive to his fingers, and she lifted herself up to push him further into her.

Etienne's erection was filled with unrequited desire. He knelt over her to kiss her eyes, her nose, her mouth. She bit him gently on his lower lip and again on his shoulder. He lowered himself onto her, and her legs opened to receive him. With one hand, she guided him into her, and then with both of her hands on his buttocks, she pulled herself against him to feel the full thrust inside of her.

Etienne was not Marie's first lover, but she had never before felt such passion. She felt humbled in his presence, and she surrendered herself to his raw sexuality. He moved inside of her with a natural grace.

She could feel all of his energy coming together in her womb, demanding her response. His thrusts were tantalizing, as he entered her and withdrew himself. She could not bear the thought of any part of him being outside of her, and she quickly moved herself up to meet him.

Etienne's hands went under her round buttocks to support her against him. He could feel all of his fluids moving through his body, ready to burst into Marie. From his waist down, Etienne felt a sensation of pleasure that slowly moved through his lower abdomen, his bowels, and toward the base of his phallus. The momentum increased and burst forth with such an explosive release that he cried out!

He pushed himself as deeply as he could into Marie. His cry triggered her own pleasure, and her consciousness dissolved in their union. She was forever connected to this man, never again to be separated by the appearance of distance. They lay together in front of the coals, Etienne still inside of her, his head buried in her neck.

"Marie, my beloved," he said, lifting himself to look into her eyes, "take my seed and carry it with you."

[192]

"Etienne, I am so sorry." Tears filled her eyes and rolled down the sides of her face.

He bent to kiss them. "I am too," he replied sadly. "I am sorry that this is to be our only union. Now that I have tasted the nectar of your soul, I am more loathe than ever to leave you."

He raised himself and leaned down to kiss her breasts, moving his mouth down to her stomach, her navel, and stopping at the hair around her pubis where he buried his face in the coarse thickness. He could smell the results of their merging.

With one hand, he opened her and placed his tongue inside, sucking her juices into his mouth. Marie groaned in bliss over the gentle tugging. She ran her long fingers through his dark hair and around his ears, outlining each curve with her nails.

Hearing her sighs of pleasure, Etienne continued, moving his fingers around her opening. Then Marie grabbed his hair fiercely, arching her body toward him. She uttered a cry and fell back onto the floor, breathing heavily with ecstasy.

Etienne entered her one last time, with a primordial desire to merge with the totality of this woman. He no longer saw her form, and in his intensity, he perceived the Goddess in all her radiant purity. The essence of all there is! His consciousness removed itself from all physical sensation, until he saw only energy. They became only energy - lights dancing together in union. There was an explosion, and Etienne fell into the silent void.

The clock chimed twelve times. Beneath him, Marie stirred. "Etienne?"

"Yes, my Beloved?" He looked at her.

"It's midnight."

Etienne awakened immediately. "Madame!" he cried. "She'll be home within the hour!"

They hurriedly began to dress, regretting the sudden ending to their tryst. Etienne picked up Marie's combs and gave them to her. When she sat to put on her boots, he kneeled and laced them, kissing each knee as he finished.

After they were fully dressed, they held each other, and then very slowly walked down to the foyer. Etienne put Marie's cape around her shoulders and pulled her under the protection of his

[193]

arm, as they left the house.

He released her to open the gates. Antoine, having heard footsteps, was standing attentively with the carriage door open. Etienne helped Marie into the coach and stepped in after her. Very carefully, he wrapped her in blankets to insure her warmth.

"I love you, Marie," he said, cupping her face in his hands and kissing her on the lips.

She reached up to place her hands on his. "And I, you."

Etienne jumped from the carriage and shut the door. He stood outside the gate until the retreating coach was only a memory, and then he walked back to the house.

The library seemed empty when Etienne returned. The memory of the past few hours flashed through his mind in vivid images. The reality of his actions was beginning to settle with him, and the ecstasy was being replaced with feelings of remorse. Marie was pledged to another, and he had violated their commitment. His years of discipline had been thrown over in one brief moment of passion! He was an ascetic, and his path was not the way of the flesh!

To avoid his growing sense of guilt, Etienne left the library to go into the kitchen. He had promised Madame some tea, and it was time that he prepare for her arrival. The spacious kitchen had been set up for the next day, and everything was spotless. Within twenty minutes, the water was prepared, and Etienne was ready to move back into the library with the refreshments.

He heard the sound of footsteps coming toward the kitchen, and he looked up to see Felice. "Monsieur," she said apologetically, "I could have done that for you."

"It wasn't necessary, Felice," he replied, "I'm preparing tea for Madame's arrival."

"Frederick is out front waiting. The carriage should be here soon." She stood, awaiting his orders.

Etienne was aware of how she and Frederick had managed to be unobtrusively present in the months he had been with Madame. They had never asserted themselves in any way.

"Felice," Etienne asked, "how long have you and Frederick

been with Madame?" Conversing with her, helped take his mind off Marie and the intensity of the last several hours.

"For fifteen years, Monsieur. We were employed by her shortly after we were married."

"Frederick is your husband?"

"Yes, Monsieur."

"You have been very good to Madame, Felice."

"And she has to us, Monsieur." Felice replied with gratitude in her voice. "We would not have lasted that first winter, cold it was. I had lost our child and almost died. Frederick could not work because he had to take care of me. One day, he left to get our meal, a loaf of bread, and a carriage passed him. Some packages that had been tied to the top fell onto the street, and Frederick ran to pick them up before the beggars got to them."

"He followed the carriage all the way to her home, he did, running and calling to the driver. When they finally stopped, Frederick was right behind them, the bread broken. Madame was so happy with his efforts, that she employed him immediately."

"Did your health improve?"

"Not for a long time," she answered, "but she took me in, just the same. We owe her so much, we do. I could never have any more children, and so she became our lives."

"So, there are some happy endings in Paris," Etienne said, with a hint of irony in his voice.

Felice smoothed back her hair with her plump hands. For the first time, Etienne noticed the gold band on her finger. "I've been so lost in my self that I have forgotten my training," he thought to himself. "Chen would have never forgiven me for not paying attention to detail."

They heard the noise of the doors opening. Etienne took the tray and carried it into the library, laying it on the table. He looked around the room to make sure everything was in order, and then he went to the foyer.

"Madame," he said, "welcome home! Frederick, I'll take her now for some tea in the library. Will an hour be too much time?" He looked at Madame who nodded her assent.

[195]

"Very well, we'll see you in one hour, Frederick." Etienne noticed the fatigue in Madame's face. "The body is tired, but the soul resists sleep," he thought.

He pushed her close to the fire and propped her feet on the same footstool Marie's had been on earlier. Before pouring her tea, he straightened her shawl around her shoulders.

"How is your friend?" he asked.

"She's doing well," Madame replied. "Better than I imagined."

"I'm sure she was happy to see you."

"And I, her." She smiled to herself. "She's a lovely woman whom I have known since my childhood. At my age, there aren't many friends left."

"What is her ailment?"

"Pleurisy."

Etienne thought about the young woman and her son at the Hotel Dieu. He briefly wondered how she was faring.

"And now, my young friend," Madame's eyes pierced Etienne's, "you seem to be feeling something. What is it you wish to share with me about your evening?"

He was startled by her astuteness. Very little eluded her sharp perception. When in her presence, the child in him longed for the experience of being nurtured, for he was closer to Madame than he would ever be to Qu'an Li, his mother.

"Marie came to me tonight," he answered, his voice barely above a whisper.

"Were you happy to see her?"

"Yes, and no." Etienne looked into her face. "Yes, because I secretly hoped to see her one last time, and no, because her visit precipitated events that may have unpleasant repercussions."

"What are you telling me, Etienne?" Madame's heart froze with the knowledge of what he would say. Deep within the recesses of her soul, she felt her response, and an image darted through the corridors of her mind too quickly for her to see it fully. In the wake of its path was darkness.

"I made love with her, Madame." Etienne did not understand his need for such openness. "I fell from Grace tonight with a woman whom I shall never again see."

[196]

"Why do you regret your actions, now that there is nothing you can do about them?"

"Because I succumbed to my lower nature." He placed his teacup in its saucer. "Madame, since I have been in Paris, I have fallen to the world. I have become its plaything. I have reacted, rather than taking action, and all of my weaknesses moved forward to taunt me."

"This is a blessing in disguise, Etienne."

"Why?"

"Because the pathway to wisdom is very narrow, and it is wrought with lessons cloaked in temptation. Do not condemn yourself, for you are incapable of judging your own progress upon the path."

"But I have been trained to watch my actions!" he argued.

"And this was in the protection of the Abbey," she replied. "It was your schooling. It gave you the foundation and the preparation for the outside world." Madame paused for a moment. "Did you not have two teachers at the Abbey? Chen and. . .?"

"Ambrose," he answered, feeling pain in his heart.

"And what would Ambrose say to you now?"

Etienne smiled at the mention of Ambrose's name. "He would tell me to love myself. I always felt that Ambrose never judged another's actions. He was fully accepting."

"Well then, my dear, you must learn from that, for I am certain his own path was painful, and that he also learned this message along the way."

Etienne looked at Madame. He went and kneeled at her side. Kissing her cheek, he said, "You are beauty and perfection, Madame, and I shall always carry you in my heart. You have been both friend and mother to me."

Madame placed her hands on his smooth face. "It is right for you to return home, where you will have time for reflection. From the clarity of your beingness, a calm will come to restore the balance."

As if coming from the ethers, Frederick appeared, indicating the hour.

"Good night, Etienne."

"Good night, Madame," he said, "and thank you."

* * *

The morning was grey and cold with a promise of rain before noon. The weather was appropriate, considering the feeling in Madame's heart, for Etienne was leaving for St. Benoit, and she was finding it difficult to mask her sorrow. In the five months he had been with her, she had grown very attached to Etienne. It was one of those rare times when life had presented her with a gift, and as she had so often been reminded, it was not hers to hold on to but to enjoy for the duration.

The carriage was waiting at the front gate, and Etienne's bag was inside, along with a small basket of food. Madame had given Etienne some money, and all that was remaining were the good-byes. Felice, Madame, and Frederick were in the salon.

"Remember, Etienne," she said "this will always be your home, and you may use it as such."

"Thank you, Madame. I do not know if I will ever be back in Paris."

"You might very well be," she said, her inner voice confirming her words. She had felt it important that Frederick and Felice know of her offer to Etienne, in the event that something unforseeable should occur.

Etienne leaned over and hugged the kind woman who had been so generous with him. "Bless you, Madame, for coming into my life."

He stood up and bowed to Frederick and Felice. "I compliment you both on your ability to make Madame's life uncomplicated, and I thank you for doing the same for me during my sojourn here."

Felice curtsied and Frederick bowed. Both of them would miss this young man who had infused the house with his special presence.

With farewells completed, Etienne turned to leave. He let himself out the front door, and crossed the courtyard. When he reached the front gate, something prompted him to turn around and look up at the salon windows. Behind the glass sat Madame,

[198]

Dark Places, Light Places

with the curtain pulled back, watching him for the last time. She kissed the palm of her hand and pressed it to the window. Etienne bowed to her, opened the gate, and closed it behind him.

Inside, Madame slowly let the curtains drop. Putting a handkerchief to her face, she lowered her head and wiped her eyes before she looked at Frederick. "Frederick," she instructed quietly, "it is time to prepare the guest list for the week."

"Yes, Madame," the butler replied.

Chapter Thirteen

It was fortunate for Etienne that the driver was eager to get to St. Benoit. The man whipped the horses incessantly, evoking immediate response to his urgency. Fearlessly, they galloped across the rough roads, over the hills and through the forests, stopping only twice for food and rest.

The lackey appeared to be taciturn, not given to much conversation other than grunts of acknowledgement. He wasn't normally this way, for Etienne had used him in Paris; however, his wife was about to have a baby, and this journey was most untimely. It was his fiercest desire to return to his home before the birth, for after three girls, he fervently hoped this one was a boy.

Etienne paid little attention to the scenery. It was grey, and it merely reflected his internal state. He could barely contain his excitement over the thought of seeing his brothers again. They had no word of his impending arrival, and he knew his return would be a pleasant surprise.

As they approached St. Benoit-sur-Loire, the landscape became more verdant. Spring was on its way, and the river was feeding the land for its summer clothing. They galloped through the town of St. Benoit, the horses' mouths foaming.

Etienne moved next to the driver, for he wanted to watch the approach through the forests. Small buds were appearing on the trees, although spring was still withholding herself. The road began to look more and more familiar, as the carriage followed the obscure path. Etienne gestured directions to the driver, so that he would not have to stop. At last, they left the forests. Etienne looked up at the hills, where the sheep were grazing. In the distance, Tristan stood to get a better view of the carriage. Etienne waved frantically, hoping that Tristan would recognize him. His efforts were not in vain, for Tristan began to run down the hill, his familiar brown robe flowing behind him.

Etienne saw the Abbey looming in the distance. "There it is!" he shouted to the driver.

[200]

The coach came to a sudden stop in front of the large gates. The horses' bellies were heaving, their necks wet. Etienne jumped down with his valise. "You'll want some food," he said to the driver, "and the horses need to be refreshed."

"I suppose so," the man growled.

From around the side of the Abbey walls, Tristan's figure appeared. "Etienne!" he shouted, running toward him.

Etienne forgot all sense of propriety and ran into his arms, the two laughing joyfully over the reunion.

"It's good to see you!" Tristan cried out.

"And it's good to be back!" Etienne seconded the opinion.

"Didn't like Paris?" Tristan pulled back and looked at his friend.

"No." Etienne quickly averted his gaze, hoping Tristan would ask no more.

They pulled the cord to alert François to open the gates, but it wasn't necessary, for with the sound of the first bell, the gates flew open, and Charles and François hurriedly came toward Etienne.

"Brother!" they cried in unison.

"Oh François! Charles!" He held them both.

"Come into the kitchen after you have settled," Charles whispered. "Rice cakes today!"

"Where is Ambrose?" Etienne asked.

"In his room," Charles replied, shaking his head sadly.

"Then I shall see him first." He turned to the driver. "Tie the horses and come with us. These men will take care of you, and Brother Gerard will tend to your horses."

They entered the foyer, as Pasqual was rounding the corner, carrying a brown robe over his left arm. "You might want this," he said, hugging Etienne.

"Like I have never wanted anything!" Etienne gratefully replied. "Is my room empty?"

"It's your room, Etienne, and no one else's!"

Etienne hurried to his room and changed. His sandals were in the armoire, waiting for him. Before he left to see Ambrose, he slipped his rosary and his Buddha under the pillow. Feeling comfortable, he walked down the hall to Ambrose's room, and taking a moment to compose himself, he tapped timidly on the oak door.

"Come in." Andrew's voice quietly called from the other side.

Etienne entered the room. From the bed, Ambrose lifted his head, joy spreading across his face. Andrew walked over to embrace Etienne. "Welcome back," he whispered.

"May I sit with him, Andrew?" he asked.

"But of course, my son," Andrew replied. "He's not doing well."

"How much longer?"

"Any time."

Andrew left the two to reacquaint themselves in private. Etienne sat on the chair beside the bed, putting his hands on Ambrose's. He was surprised to see the change in the man who had been his father. Ambrose's face was gaunt, and not even the beard could hide its weight loss. His eyes had lost their vitality, and a grey film covered them.

"Why did you come back, Etienne?" Ambrose's voice was frail.

"I did not enjoy Paris as I thought I would, Ambrose, and I knew you were sick."

"It hasn't been the same since you left. We've all missed you."

Etienne remembered how he had almost forgotten his family in the heat of his passion, and the guilt filled his heart with sorrow. His eyes watered with unshed tears.

"I don't know why you've missed me, Ambrose," he said with honest conviction. "I haven't exactly proven my loyalty to my teaching."

"Why do you say that, my son?"

"My experiences in the last five months." Etienne paused to consider his words. "I let go of everything I knew, and I fell from my center."

"A woman?"

"How did you know?"

"Etienne, I'm as fallible as you are," Ambrose replied, weakly. "I also knew that your own beauty would draw temptation to you."

"As a test?"

"No, as an experience. Your personal will did not choose for

[202]

you to become a monk; therefore, it was necessary for it to express itself, to give you insight about the path upon which you might wish to venture. Do not denounce yourself, Etienne. Whatever happened was perfectly natural."

"I do not understand."

"Did you not always wonder about the world beyond these walls?"

"Yes, I did," Etienne admitted candidly.

"Well then, you were able to feed that curiosity. Your actions are neither right nor wrong. They merely reap what is the truth for you."

"And the truth for me, Ambrose, is to be a monk."

"Perhaps."

"Ambrose," Etienne was reticent to ask such a personal question, "did something like this ever happen to you?"

"Yes it did, my son." Ambrose felt an intense relief in the admission. "Many years ago."

"And what happened?"

"I went through the same agony that I suspect you are feeling. I simultaneously hated myself and refused to let go of my attachment to the other person." Ambrose paused to regain his energy. "However, in the years subsequent to my broken vows, I wasted too much time over remorse. Your arrival in my life taught me that life goes on in spite of our actions, and that love is the impetus behind its movement - especially love of self."

"Oh Ambrose!" Etienne laid his head on the old man's chest. "How can I forgive myself and feel happy again?"

"You will free yourself from your pain, Etienne, for you are now a man. And you will forgive yourself in time. Believe me, you will!"

"I love you Father." Etienne looked into the eyes of the man for whom he felt ineffable gratitude.

"Etienne, I've waited for your return." Ambrose's eyes misted. "I knew you would be back, and now I can leave. You are where you belong, once again."

Ambrose closed his eyes. His breath trembled, and then his chest stopped its movement. Frightened, Etienne sat up.

[203]

"Ambrose?" There was no response.

"Ambrose!" He grabbed his robe and pulled him into a sitting position.

Amrose's head rolled back. Seeing there was no life, Etienne laid him back on the bed. "Oh no! Not now! Not when I need your grace, Ambrose!" He put his face into his hands and sobbed.

Years filled with memories washed over him, and he felt guilt for not having loved Ambrose enough. He wanted him to be alive again, so that he could come to him with problems, as he had done in the past. However, Etienne knew that Ambrose was right. He was a man now, and he must put aside childish ways.

He left the room and walked down to the bell pull, which was outside the chapel. His hands gripped the thick cord, and he furiously yanked it. The noise brought the monks from their respective tasks, and when they had gathered around Etienne, he spoke to them. "Ambrose has left us. Let us prepare for his burial."

* * *

The brothers' joy surrounding Etienne's return was overshadowed by the death of Ambrose. Each monk strongly felt his absence, even more than his presence which had always been unobtrusively quiet. He was buried behind the Abbey in a small plot that had been reserved for their interments. In the eighteen years Etienne had been at the monastery, this was the first death.

He suspected it would not be the last, for in looking around him, he saw that all of the monks had aged, even Chen. A few were approaching their sixties. One day, Gerard would have trouble driving the carriage into town, and Etienne wondered who would be kind enough to get him his pastries. He suspected he would acquire many responsibilities in the upcoming years, for he was the youngest and the strongest of them all.

Chen, in spite of his age, was still vital. He had mastered the knowledge of the universal life force and had used it well. Etienne,

[204]

upon seeing Chen for the first time since his arrival, had observed that his eyes shone more brightly than ever. He had encountered his teacher in the hills shortly after Ambrose's death.

Etienne had left the Abbey to walk off his sorrow. He was trying to reacclimate himself in the wake of Ambrose's passing. The hills were mostly a winter brown; however, fresh blades of grass could be seen in areas that received the most sunlight. Etienne breathed deeply, inhaling the fresh air which he had not smelled for six months. He paused at the edge of the forest, to contemplate the last several months as objectively as possible.

"What did you learn, T'ien Li, on your travels?" Chen appeared at his side.

Etienne turned quickly and bowed before his teacher. The sorrow that had been his heart's companion of late, dissipated in the light of this man's presence. Etienne straightened himself and faced Chen without speaking, allowing a spontaneous answer to come forth.

"I learned that I know nothing." His words surprised him.

"That is good," Chen replied. "for now you are ready to be filled."

Etienne offered no response.

"When the mind realizes its treachery, it is forced to surrender to the wisdom of the soul."

"So, all of my years of training were wasted?"

"No, T'ien Li," Chen answered quietly, "you have arrived at your beginning."

"I must start over?" Etienne's spirits sank.

"You now begin to brave the storm that was created by your folly."

"Chen, you make me feel guilty."

"There is no guilt, T'ien Li. You are strong enough for any challenge. Man cannot see the other side, without first climbing the mountain."

"Will I make the summit, Chen, or will I fall once more?"

"Once, maybe. Twice maybe. The focus is on the peak."

"Tell me Chen, have you avoided my mistakes?"

"We have different enemies."

Etienne wanted to embrace Chen, to express his love for him. Instead, he bowed. "Thank you, Chen."

"I see the purity of your heart, T'ien Li."

The old man bowed and left him to his thoughts. In his parting, Etienne was filled with a sense of renewed hope for the future.

* * *

It was good to be back at the monastery. In time, life returned to normal, and Etienne resumed his routine. Initially he spent the majority of his waking hours meditating in the chapel to restore his balance. Eventually, he was able to view his Parisian interlude with equilibrium, and in the seclusion of the Abbey, he was able to put Marie behind him.

Etienne assumed whatever responsibilities he was called upon to perform. In the late spring, the ewes began their birthing, and several of the lambs needed to be pulled from reluctant wombs. Tristan and Etienne worked together, hours at a time, and after all the mothers had delivered their woolly progeny, there was only one stillborn lamb. Signs of nature's rebirth were everywhere. Birds sang their song to one another in the lush green treetops. Baby grey squirrels scampered across the meadows. And the grape vines began to produce tiny berries.

Andrew settled into Ambrose's sandals with a comfortable ease. It felt good for him to sit in Ambrose's chair, for he felt that, in some way, the spirit of his friend overshadowed him with its calming energy. Everyone was happy to have Etienne back among them, especially Chen, although he would never admit it. He silently worked on his student, imparting to him the strength he would need for his immediate destiny. In Etienne's presence, he exerted more discipline than ever, refining his vision, provoking his maturity.

"Chen, I was in St. Benoit today." Etienne was sitting with his teacher at the pool in the courtyard. "In the six months, a completely different atmosphere has evolved. Everything looks the same on the outside, but it feels different."

"What do you see, T'ien Li?"

"I see anger and fear. There is great poverty."

"Why is it that you notice these qualities more than others?"

"I do not know. Perhaps because I have experienced similar feelings within myself."

"And you held onto them with your judgement?" Chen watched a fat bee land on the petal of a white lily.

"What do you mean?" Etienne was puzzled.

"Why did you not see beauty also? Why do you see one half of the picture?"

"Because, to my vision, that half is more conspicuous."

"Then your vision must correct itself to see all things without distinction."

Etienne was silent as he contemplated his reaction to Chen's words. It was true that there was an obvious change in the town. The casual friendliness had been replaced by mistrustful anxiety. Prices were higher. Merchants looked thinner, and their eyes were hungrier.

"Chen, I would be blind were I to observe without distinguishing."

"That is not true, T'ien Li." Chen looked at him. "The eye of the soul sees all things impersonally, while the mind emphasizes one thing or another. When you tell me what you see, I know whether it is the mind or the soul speaking."

"But these things I saw are evident, Chen!"

"You will find that which you seek!"

"You have also taught me to notice details." Etienne was confused.

"No more. That was to discipline the mind. Now, you must free it."

"You speak as though it imprisons me, Chen."

Chen nodded. "You will learn that it will free you, T'ien Li." He stood up and bowed to his student before leaving him to ponder the nature of his words. Etienne sat in silence, while the bee, ignoring him, left the lily and flew out of the courtyard.

[207]

* * *

Abbot Martin de Fleury's legs struggled to carry him up the entrance steps to the stately mansion of the Compte Victor Adrien de Chevrier. He had been summoned by the Count, a few days prior, for a tête à tête, the subject of which remained a mystery . However, the Abbot would never refuse an invitation from one of the richest men in France. Perhaps one of his sons wished to enter the monastery? A thin lipped servant answered his ring and bowed gracefully, before inquiring his name.

"Abbot Martin de Fleury," he said, presenting him the card upon which the summons had been written, "to see the Compte de Chevrier."

"Please enter, Sir." The servant backed away to allow the obese man to pass through the door without crushing him.

The Abbot was insulted that the Count had not directed the doorman to refer to him as 'Your Grace', a title he had pompously given himself years ago. That he was not a Bishop was of no concern to him. His abbey was wealthier than most others in France, and with its financial power, he exalted his status.

He followed the servant through the massive foyer-ballroom to one of its many doors. His heart still pounded from the long flight of stairs. Furtively looking to see that there were no observers, he pulled out a handkerchief to wipe the sweat off his brow.

In front of him, the servant swung open a pair of doors to reveal an immense salon. The room looked cold to the Abbot, even in the summer weather. Gold filigree covered the walls, an elegant contrast to the white marble floors.

"Abbot Martin de Fleury, Monsieur."

Compte de Chevrier looked up from his reading. He was seated next to a fireplace that was, in August, attempting to heat the immense room. The Count removed his reading glasses and stood to greet the Abbot.

"Your Grace," his manner was as cold as the marble floors, "thank you for coming."

"Compte, how may I be of service to you?"

"Please be seated, and then we shall talk." The Count looked around the room for a chair large enough to accommodate the Abbot. "Jacques, please bring a chair for His Grace," he said, pointing to an oversized one in the corner.

The servant struggled with the weight, as he pushed it to the fireplace. After his task was complete, he gestured for the Abbot to seat himself while he held the chair in place.

"Monsieur Le Compte, would you care for some tea and pastries?"

The Count, knowing of the Abbot's voracious appetite, nodded his head. "If you please, Jacques."

Jacques bowed and left the room, his shoes making clicking noises on the marble. The Count looked at the fire and then seated himself once again. He cleared his throat and looked at the Abbot.

"How long are you with us in Paris, Your Grace?"

"Another week's time, and then I return to St. Benoit."

"Are you staying at Versailles?"

"But, of course!" The Abbot was trying to discern the direction the conversation was taking. "I'm to officiate at the wedding there tomorrow."

"Oh? Whose?"

"The Marquis de Robles and the Contessa Octavia du Pont." The Abbot paused, remembering a rumor he had heard. "Did you not announce the betrothal of your daughter recently?"

"Yes, I did." The Count moved uncomfortably in his chair.

"Have they married yet?"

"No. They have not. This is why I have called you here, Your Grace." The Count coughed into his handkerchief. "It seems my daughter became enamored with a young man who has callously left her with child."

The Abbot looked up at the Count, shocked by his words. "Was she not able to conceal it from the prospective groom?"

"Hardly." The Count's mouth tightened. "She became sick, and we had to postpone the wedding; however, when the nature of her illness was revealed, Compte de Lavarney reneged on his betrothal."

The Abbot was confused. "What has this to do with me, Compte?"

"It seems the father of the child is one of your monks." The Count watched the Abbot for his reaction.

"One of my initiates?" The Abbot was flabbergasted. "But this is impossible! Who told you this?"

"Marie did, after much persistence on my part." The Count had been furious with his daughter for disgracing the family name. He had incessantly badgered her, until she had broken down and, exhausted, revealed the information. The Count was hoping it was enough for the Abbot. "It seems that this young man is an Oriental, from China."

"Well, Compte," the Abbot looked flushed, "I can assure you that no Orientals have crossed my.....You said China?"

"Yes." The Count waited impatiently.

"There is only one Oriental in St. Benoit, actually outside of St. Benoit. He's not one of mine, but he is a monk!" Abbot de Fleury tapped the arm of his chair thoughtfully.

"And who might he be?" Compte de Chevrier was indignant

The Abbot sensed remuneration. He looked innocently puzzled at first, and then he asked: "Why do you want his name, Compte?"

"I wish to avenge my daughter's public humiliation, Your Grace!" The Count's face grew red with anger. "I want to destroy the man who did this to her! Her reputation has been ruined!"

"Have you considered letting her marry the man?"

"A monk!?" The Count was aghast.

"He is not just a monk, Compte!" The Abbot was delighted to be in on the scandal. "He's the illegitimate son of the Empress of China!"

The Count's eyes flew open. "One bastard begetting another? Why this is an outrage!"

"How may I help you, Compte?" Abbot de Fleury's voice reflected an ingratiating intimacy.

"You can obtain a lettre de cachet from the King's minister, can you not?"

"For a small fee." The Abbot inwardly gloated.

"I will pay whatever you need to ask, Your Grace." The Count paused. "I want his name, his residence, and one lettre de cachet! No. . . make that two!"

"Two?"

"Yes. There's someone else involved," he replied mysteriously, saying nothing further.

By the time Jacques arrived with the pastries, Abbot de Fleury was considerably wealthier. He had known all along that Etienne's presence in his life would be lucrative, and with the business out of the way, he could indulge in the delicious cream puffs that Jacques was holding out to him on a silver tray.

Chapter Fourteen

They came to him in the fall, old enemies buried in the past coming to renew their acquaintance. Ragged faces. Hungry faces. Dirty faces. They filled Etienne's subconscious mind, coming to life in the dark of night, gloating at him, pointing bony fingers at his face. And then they parted, allowing a dark robed figure to enter Etienne's dream.

From a distance, the figure approached soundlessly, its black robes billowing. Grey mists surrounded it and were sucked into the vacuum of its wake. It had no face under its hood, for the skin had long ago surrendered to time. There was only the eyeless skull, filled with the vitality of death. "You are to be one of us, T'ien Li!" Its laughter resonated through Etienne's body, sending the ghastly faces fleeing in terror from the dream.

Etienne awakened to silence. He pulled the blanket firmly around his chilled body; however, he remained cold. Finally, he threw the covers off and left his bed to move about. He lit a small candle, and held his hands over its yellow flame.

It was still dark outside, and Etienne was reminded that winter was not far away. The memory of his dream had left him colder than he had ever remembered. A darkness surrounded his soul, and he could not transform it with his light.

He slipped his robe over his body, stepped into his sandals, and blew out the candle before leaving the room. The halls were unlit, and Etienne walked the familiar path to the chapel by memory. Once inside, he slowly made his way to the altar and deftly moved his fingers around until he found the matches. Within seconds, the darkness became light as the wick of the candle exploded into flame.

Etienne sat on the velvet bench behind the altar and stared at the flame, watching it dance. He felt protected by the beautiful energy of the room. At the far end of the chapel, he heard the sound of a door opening, but he could not see who the visitor was.

[212]

Chen appeared before him, his white beard illuminated by the candle. "What troubles you, Tien Li?"

"A dream, Chen. An old dream that comes back to haunt me."

"What is its source?" Chen seated himself next to his beloved student.

"I do not know, Chen. Hollow, hungry faces taunting me. I do not know what they want."

"They want your light, T'ien Li."

"I cannot give it to them, Chen, for I do not know who they are."

"Soon you will, my child." Chen stared through the candle flame.

Etienne looked at his venerable teacher. "I'm afraid to ask you what you mean by this."

"Knowledge of your future must come from your inner self, T'ien Li. Not from me."

Etienne looked at Chen for a sign that would give meaning to his words, but his face was impassive. "I feel a darkness descending on me Chen, one that I cannot escape."

"It will control you for a while, my friend, until you gain power over it." Chen's face resembled granite in the faint light of the chapel.

"May God give me strength." Etienne shivered with the memory of his dream.

It was not long before the chapel was filled with the rest of the brothers who were happy to see it infused with light. Chen and Etienne left the altar and went to sit with them. In the stillness of meditation, much of Etienne's anxiety dissipated.

The day was without sun, and rain clouds hovered closely. By noon, a relentless drizzle had brought all the monks indoors from their work. They built a fire in the library and watched the rain running down the windows, while François and Charles heated soup and bread.

Etienne was aware of Andrew sadly staring at him. "What is it, Andrew?" he asked quietly.

"Nothing, my son," the calm man replied, "just resistance to change."

Etienne felt a presentiment, but he shook it off and resumed his

[213]

reading. The sound of bells furiously ringing at the front gate intruded upon the silent camaraderie, although no one moved to answer them.

Moments later Chen entered the library. He walked over to Etienne and put his hands on his shoulders, keeping his eyes on the doors. Charles and François, looking alarmed, came hurriedly into the warm room. On their heels were two grim faced purposeful officials.

They pushed François and Charles aside and strode into the center of the room. One of them looked around and then spoke in a husky voice. "In the name of His Royal Highness, King Louis le XVI, we have come to arrest a Monsieur Etienne D'Aubrey."

Pasqual angrily jumped up from his chair. "And what might you have to prove this?"

The second official pulled a white piece of paper from his vest pocket. He held out the notice which Pasqual took from him. Pasqual read it, frowning. "What was his crime? This indicates that a certain Compte de Chevrier has ordered his arrest, an order that has been sanctioned by the King!"

"The crime does not matter," the first official retorted. "The paper itself is enough. Where is Monsieur D'Aubrey?"

"I am he." Etienne stood to face the officials, trying to quell his fear.

"You will come with us!" the first official stated authoritatively.

The officials flanked Etienne and took his arms. A deadly silence filled the room, and Etienne looked at each of his brothers. He felt he had betrayed them, and now the finger of justice pointed ominously at him.

The men pushed him out of the room and down the hall. The monks followed, running to catch a last glimpse of their beloved brother. Outside, a black carriage waited, a grim faced lackey holding the horses in the pouring rain.

He was an ugly man, who looked disdainfully at Etienne, a large raspberry birthmark on his face matching his bloodshot eyes. Etienne recalled the man as the one who had spied upon him from the woods years ago. Age had done nothing to improve his

[214]

malevolent looks.

The officials released their grip, and he turned for one last look at his brothers who were huddled together for support. Twice they had lost Etienne to the world, and all of them feared this would be their last sight of him. Chen stood off to one side, his eyes closed, his hands folded in front of his chest.

Etienne saw him, and broke into tears. Chen opened his eyes suddenly. "Let the mind free you, T'ien Li," he mouthed silently.

Etienne was pushed into the carriage and the two officials followed, slamming the door behind them. The driver whipped the horses, and the black carriage was soon swallowed by the grey mists.

The brothers remained stunned. One by one, they turned to Chen. "What is to become of him, Chen?" Tristan asked.

"Whatever he makes of himself," Chen replied sadly. His usually passive face was filled with sorrow.

"Will he survive?" Pasqual wondered aloud. "The Bastille?"

"He will dance with Death, my friends," Andrew answered, "and only God knows of the outcome."

The group slowly dispersed and the monks re-entered the Abbey.

* * *

The journey back to Paris was harrowing. There was no consideration given to the horses, the carriage or the riders, as the driver pushed the animals beyond their capacity. The officials did not speak with Etienne. He was a prisoner. Etienne averted his gaze and stared out of the small window on the side of the carriage.

His mind raced uncontrollably. What could he have done? Hours later, the answer became blatantly obvious. Marie was carrying their child. It could be nothing else, for he doubted that Michel would ever have known about their union otherwise. And now, she bore the ignominy of their actions!

This was the storm that Chen had referred to. Etienne would have to be brave as a result of his folly, for now the faces in his dreams would become the reality of his cell mates, with death

[215]

stalking them all. He felt an intense shame over having surrendered to his animal nature.

He had so enjoyed being back in the precious sanctity of the Abbey, and now he was to be thrown into the world again. Another cloister awaited him, one which was filled with disquiet and misery. Etienne wanted to cry, but his heart was too heavy. He felt death eating his soul and transforming the light into darkness.

It was raining in Paris when they arrived. The driver finally stopped the horses, and one of the officials threw open the door. "Out with you!" he said, angrily. "You'll not be treated with any reverence here. Everyone's the same!"

Etienne stepped down, and two prison guards approached him. "What have we here?" one of them sarcastically asked. "Someone to deliver the last rites?"

"A prisoner." The second official pulled out the lettre de cachet. "Etienne D'Aubrey. Throw him in with the rest!"

The officials, their job finished, released the prisoner to his fate, and the guards escorted Etienne behind the iron gates. He did not look around when he heard the ugly sound of clanging metal. Behind the stone walls, Etienne was guided through passageways and into a massive catacomb that ran beneath the streets of Paris.

Torches lit the hallways, at the end of which were long rows of iron bars. Faces looked out between the grills to watch the new prisoner. Their eyes reflected a jaded pain, as they waited for him to take his place among them. Etienne's nightmares had finally become a reality.

Chapter Fifteen

"All right, everyone step back!" the guard shouted. "Back from the gate!"

He unlocked the cell door, and pushed Etienne in, slamming it as his final statement to the prisoner. Etienne did not move as the men and women eyed him, with inscrutable faces, absorbing the energy of the new arrival and trying to determine if he were a criminal or an innocent victim.

The cells were large and dark, with a few small windows sporadically placed to let in fresh air. From where he stood, Etienne could see that there were several rooms, all running together and filled with people. There was a putrid smell at the entrance, and he suspected that it would get worse as he walked further inside.

"What's your name?" A small woman with missing teeth and matted hair stepped forward.

"Etienne," he answered, uncertainly.

"What's your crime?" Her rancid breath made him feel nauseous.

"The crime?" He paused before answering. "Loving a woman."

"Murder?"

"No."

"Good luck in getting out of here, Brother." An older man moved next to the woman. "My name is Thomas, and it's been five years since I've seen the light of day. Optimism is not encouraged here."

"Then you are lucky, Thomas, that you are still alive." Etienne wondered how the frail man had lasted so long, for his body had no flesh on it. The only sign of vitality was the fire in his eyes.

"Well, Etienne," Thomas replied, looking him over, "it does feel good to have a monk among us!"

A few others nodded their heads in agreement. The initial shock had worn off Etienne, and he proceeded to move through the group and to explore his surroundings. His eyes had accustomed themselves to the dim light, offered by torches and the windows. As he passed an opening, the fresh air was like an elixir to him. Etienne decided to stay as close to the windows as possible, to avoid the malevolent odor that reminded him of death.

Not all of the prisoners were standing. Many were too weak to move, and they lay in small heaps on the floor. Piles of hay had been thrown about as bedding. The stone walls were damp and smelled of mold. The prison was large, yet hardly built to accommodate the number of prisoners it contained.

To Etienne, his dreams had been far more frightening than the reality, for the faces around him could only evoke compassion. They were as he, victims of circumstances, and he envisioned that he, too, would resemble them shortly.

He returned to the central area and sat beneath a window. Thomas, who had been following him, sat next to Etienne as a protective measure, for the new prisoners were often harassed unless they were given approval by an older one. Thomas was held in high esteem among the inmates, for he had accepted his incarceration with a philosophical detachment.

"What do you think?" he asked Etienne.

"There will be an adjustment," Etienne replied honestly.

"Oh, it's not as bad as you might imagine, my friend. One gets used to it and the awfulness of it seems to diminish."

"Why are you here?"

"I'm a political dissident. I wasn't very popular at Court." Thomas wiped his running nose with his arm. "Curse this cold! It won't go away!" He continued. "An unhappy noble dragged me before a biased magistrate who decided that, since I spoke so favorably on behalf of the people, I should be with them. Hence, this has become my home."

"You are a family man?"

"No," Thomas coughed. "I never was a family man, although I've got a bastard or two I suspect. And you?"

"I've been a monk all my life." Etienne felt pride in speaking of his vocation. "I spent several months in Paris to get a different perspective on life, and I fell victim to my own desires."

[218]

"Ah! The fall of Adam!" Thomas smiled. "History and myth merely repeat themselves at the hands of a seductive woman and a gullible man. What happened?"

"She was engaged to another, and I left her with child."

"I assume the prospective groom came after you."

"No. The father did. The groom most likely rescinded his proposal."

"Where is she now?"

"I do not know, Thomas." Etienne shook his head. "I was unaware of anything until I was arrested. In fact, I can only assume what has happened."

"Well, well." Thomas patted him on his back. "At the least, you've grown accustomed to cell life, have you not?"

"That I have, Thomas. That I have."

"Life isn't too bad here if you see it for what it is."

"Aren't you regretting being cut off from the world?"

"But I'm not!" Thomas pushed the hair from his face. "Since I receive messages through those windows, I'm fully apprised of what is going on in Paris."

"And what is that?"

"It's been fairly quiet lately." Thomas was thrilled to have met someone who seemed to be well educated. He felt that he and Etienne would become friends. "The summer drought ruined the crops, and the harvests all over France were deficient. It is predicted that the winter will be cold, to add to our misery."

"Then the financial state of affairs is no better than when I was here last winter?"

"No change." Thomas shook his head. "The only difference is that, with no money from the crops, and with an upcoming cold spell, everyone will be miserable. The wealth must somehow extend itself to the poor. France must take care of her people!"

"How old are you, Thomas?"

"I am thirty."

Etienne was shocked. He looked as old as Ambrose, even with the darkness of the prison to conceal the lines on his face. "Is this what prison life does to one, Thomas?" he asked bluntly.

"I have no idea how I appear, and if I did, I suppose I might be

[219]

surprised, Etienne. However, I am happy to be alive, and I know I'll live to see the Revolution!" His eyes filled with a fiery purpose. "There are those who say it won't be long now."

"What will that mean for us?" Etienne felt desolately pessimistic.

"Possible freedom. I have friends who are waiting for me. My body may be weak, but my mind is active!"

Across from them, near the iron gates, a fight was in progress over a piece of bread. Etienne watched two men pummel each other, with the victor taking the spoils, and the vanquished lying, immobile, on the floor.

"Excuse me, Thomas." Etienne got up and went to see if the man were still alive. He stretched him out across the stone and examined him. There were bruises on his face and a few cuts that would heal in time, but the man was still breathing. It was a blessing that he lay unconscious.

"Soft heart, Brother?" The toothless woman stood above him. "It won't get you anywhere here. These fights go on all the time."

Etienne stood to face her. "My friend, wherever I am placed, I intend to see all men through the eyes of compassion. I would hope that my heart is open to everyone."

"Alicia's the name. Petty theft was my mistake." His softness made her only too aware of how hardened she had become.

"Etienne." He began to bow and self-consciously stopped himself.

"I know." She squinted at him. "There are actually murderers among us, Etienne, although by now we all look alike. Those with real crimes behind them aren't going to talk. The competition is over who did the least to get behind these walls." Alicia turned and spat through the spaces between her teeth. A large piece of phlegm hit the floor next to the unconscious man. "You aren't in such bad company. The worst of them have died."

Etienne remembered Monsieur LeBois and his experience at the Bastille. A shudder ran through him. Monsieur LeBois had made it outside, only to die a few months later. He left Alicia to return to the window and sat against the cold wall.

He thought of his brothers, and fervently hoped they would
[220]

understand. His mother would eventually learn of his incarceration, and it would provoke her to return to France. He hoped that he could have a letter sent to reassure her.

Etienne was certain of one thing. Unlike his last time in Paris, when he pushed all thoughts of the Abbey away, he would now hold his home dear to him. It was from these special men that he would gather the strength to nourish himself and others. His endurance depended upon their minds uniting with his own.

A clanging on the bars disturbed his reverie. Food was being thrown into the cells. Etienne was to learn that this was the highlight of the day, and that he who hesitated lost his meal. Greed overcame everyone, even Thomas, as the prisoners scrambled and fought for bits of bread and cheese, and the bad apples that rolled unceremoniously across the floor. Etienne stood outside the melée and watched in horror.

Thomas approached him. "Here," he said, offering Etienne an apple and some cheese. "You'll have to learn to be fast, Etienne, or you'll die. Hunger means death."

"Is death really so bad Thomas?"

"For me it is, friend. For you, well, that's your decision."

Etienne thanked Thomas and took the food. He still had no appetite, but he adhered to Thomas' advice and ate the apple and cheese.

The small windows grew dark, as night fell over the city. Etienne's body was chilled by the damp wall. He decided to move toward the center, where the prisoners were clustered for warmth. The smell was still nauseating, although he knew that he would grow accustomed to it. He lay down on the stone floor and tried to sleep, but there was too much noise. Prisoners were snoring, groaning, and tossing restlessly. Finally, from sheer exhaustion, Etienne lost consciousness for a few hours.

The clanging on the doors awakened him. Breakfast. Etienne was hungry, and pushing his timidity aside, he ran for some bread and cheese. It actually tasted good, as his empty stomach was thankful to receive a small gratuity. He felt the need to relieve himself, but he was embarrassed to ask. Thomas, sensing his need, pointed to the end of the cell.

[221]

"Follow the smell. When it becomes the strongest, that is where you may leave your body wastes."

Etienne followed his instructions. He was astounded at the lack of sanitation in the prison. It was no wonder that there were so many deaths! He noticed that the invalids were closer to the waste station, and he felt immense pity that they should die in such squalor. He wondered how they ate, for many of them seemed immobile.

On his return, he stopped to see if there were something he could do to help them. Most appeared to be in the pre-death state. He gently touched each one. An older woman was vomiting, and he rubbed her back while the bile came out. "Thank you," she whispered.

"Do you need anything?" he asked.

"Only death," she replied weakly.

He passed on to the next person, a young man whose body was bleeding from open sores. "Can you turn me on my side, please?" His eyes were covered with a grey film, reminding Etienne of Ambrose before he died.

He obeyed and continued, until he was satisfied that he had done all he could. He walked back to Thomas, who awaited him.

"Is there any water for bathing, Thomas?"

"Yes, Etienne. We get water and rags once a week. Most of us don't bother."

"I think the dying ones could use it."

"Be careful," Thomas warned. "It could induce pneumonia."

"I will."

"Etienne?" Thomas awkwardly turned away to wipe his nose.

"Yes?"

"Will you pray with me?"

"Of course, my friend." Etienne laid his hand on Thomas' arm. "Sit still and close your eyes. I'll rub my hands together when I have finished." He remembered Chen's gesture.

"I think I'll welcome communing with God." Thomas was openly candid. "I hope it will soften my cynicism."

They sat beneath the window while the other prisoners went about their lives. No one had ever seen Thomas so inactive, and

[222]

they wondered what the monk had done to encourage him.

Etienne freed himself from the prison into the emptiness of the universe, into the soundless, painless vacuum. He was aware of a lightness about him that dissolved all emotions, all thoughts. It was in the lightness that Chen appeared, grinning with pride for his student. "Stay free, T'ien Li! Stay free! Do not be consumed by despair!"

* * *

"The water is here, Etienne," Thomas said. He had found Etienne among the invalids, feeding a half-starved woman some cheese, which she could barely keep down.

Etienne's third day had passed, and he had yet to see some of the faces, as it was so dark in the cells. The elderly woman, whose back he had rubbed, never turned away from the wall. Etienne suspected that she lay in her own urine, and he intended to bathe her.

He followed Thomas to get the water and the rags. Knowing Etienne needed it for unselfish purposes, the guard had made sure there was enough. He had a soft heart, and there was something about Etienne which interested him. The guard doubted that a monk would have committed a heinous crime.

"Thank you, my friend," Etienne said gratefully, as he relieved the guard of his burdens.

"You're welcome, Brother." The guard left him with the water and locked the gate.

Thomas helped Etienne carry it back to the sick prisoners. A woman, who had identified herself as Victorine, joined them. When the three arrived at the station, Etienne and Thomas put the water down.

"We'll need to clean out the waste, too," Etienne suggested. "The odor is terrible. I'll do that later, so save the water. Now, let's start here."

Etienne and Victorine attended to the first of the invalids, the man with sores on his body. "We're going to to clean you, friend," Etienne whispered softly.

[223]

"I'm so cold," he replied, his teeth chattering together.

"Well, this may chill you at first, but we'll warm you when we are finished."

Victorine loosened the man's clothing while Thomas brought the water closer. He handed Etienne a damp rag, and Etienne began to dab around the sores, beginning with the man's face and very carefully moving down his body. The amount of dirt on him astonished Etienne. They continued changing rags, keeping the water clean by dipping only fresh ones into it.

Alicia found them and offered an old blanket. "He might need this after the bath," she said matter of factly. "I can get you two others, but it will cost you two lunches."

"A good bargain!" Etienne agreed, smiling. "Bring them to us!"

"Make your bargains now, while you're strong, Etienne," Thomas warned him astutely.

The three worked steadily on the infirm, until only the elderly woman remained. Etienne was conscious of her interest, although she said nothing and kept her back to them. He crawled over to her and rubbed her shoulder. "Your turn, Madame," he said gently.

He put his arms under her frail body and laid her on her back. Her arm, too weak to remain on her face, fell down at her side. Etienne began to loosen her collar, his fingers touching a pin that needed to be released. He bent closely to examine it, and saw that it was a small brooch. As he unclasped it, a memory flashed by, and he swiftly jerked his head up to look at the woman's face for the first time.

"Madame de Grave!" he cried out. "What are you doing here?" He put his arm under her head and lifted her to him.

"Fate, Etienne," she coughed.

"It is because of me, isn't it?" he demanded, remorsefully. "Oh my God! I err and so many suffer the consequences!" He buried his face against her. "I am so sorry, Madame. Can you take it in your heart to forgive me?"

"I love you, my son." She looked at him, her eyes bulging in her thin face.

"What happened? Please tell me?"

"They came to my house for information about you. I wouldn't

[224]

give it." She paused to catch her breath.

"Why did you not tell them, to save yourself?"

"Because I love you." Spittle rolled out of the side of her mouth.

"Where are Frederick and Felice?"

"They hid in the staircase. They did not want to, but I ordered them. Frederick sometimes comes to one of the windows looking for me, but I haven't seen him in a while." Her body trembled from the effort it took to speak. "I haven't been able to look for him, either."

"I'll find him, Madame," Etienne promised. "Now, let me clean you."

Thomas and Victorine, who had been listening attentively to the conversation, immediately came forth with rags and water. Diligently, they cleaned every part of her emaciated body, including the urine and feces that had dried on her.

"I did not want you to see me like this, Etienne," she whispered, a rasping sob coming from her throat.

"I see only your beauty, Madame, and nothing else," he assured her. Looking across at Thomas, he asked, "Can you get Alicia, please?"

"Certainly." Thomas went to find her and returned a short while later.

"Alicia," Etienne asked, "I wish to bargain for a fresh pallet of hay?"

"What for?"

"I want to move this woman into the central cell with me, and I want her bedded properly."

"No one here gets special treatment, friend," Alicia reminded him.

Etienne, remembering Chen's methods, stood and looked directly at her, his eyes reflecting determination. "This woman does. I would like the pallet under my window, where it will stay until we no longer need it."

Alicia was momentarily taken aback, which only increased her awe of him. Even without Thomas' protection, Etienne would have been safe with the inmates, for they were aware of his light. "It'll cost you," she said, with a begrudging tone she did not feel.

[225]

"Thank you, Alicia," he replied humbly.

Victorine finished Madame's bath and began to dry her. "Is she crippled?"

"Yes. Be careful with her legs." Etienne noticed they were like sticks, and he wondered why they hadn't broken.

They dressed Madame carefully, and when they had finished, Etienne lifted her into this arms. "I'll be right back," he said to his friends.

He walked back through the rooms to where Alicia was standing beside a large pile of hay. "Is this good enough?" she asked, revealing a toothless grin.

"God bless you, Alicia!" he sang out.

"If He had, I wouldn't be here," she retorted sardonically, embarrassed with the compliment.

Etienne laid Madame down and arranged her as comfortably as possible, before going to clean the waste area.

"I'll return shortly, my dear friend." He brushed her hair from her face. "Alicia, please watch her."

Respectfully, Alicia sat. As Etienne began to rise, Madame touched his arm. "I'm thankful you've come back to me, Etienne. It makes my last few days much easier." Her large eyes filled with tears.

Etienne leaned over and kissed her forehead. "I will watch over us until we are both free, Madame, and that's a promise!"

He nodded to Alicia and left to continue his work. Thomas and Victorine were covering the patients with blankets that had been vigorously shaken to remove the wrinkles and the dust.

"I don't know how to thank you two," he said.

"We're happy to have you here, Etienne," Victorine admitted. "Before your arrival, no one was selfless enough to care."

Thomas picked up the remaining water and rags and walked over to the waste area. He poured, while Etienne and Victorine scrubbed, and eventually, there was a slight change in both the smell and the appearance. Etienne sloshed the last of the water across the floor and put all the rags into the empty buckets.

"I'll leave these at the front gate for the guards," he decided aloud.

[226]

A path was cleared for them by the prisoners, and they returned to their area. Etienne sat next to Madame and held her hand while she slept. Thomas and Victorine joined him, while Alicia stood guard. In the few days he had been at the Bastille, Etienne had attracted a small circle of friends.

Victorine was a petite woman whose pride indicated she had come from a well born background. Etienne could not guess her age, but he imagined that she had been very beautiful before she had been thrown into the Bastille. She held no anger, and this surprised him.

"Victorine, where do you come from?" Etienne knew that there were no secrets among inmates. Privacy was not an aspect of prison life.

"Versailles was my last home, but I will not be returning, if I'm ever released from here."

"Why not?"

"Too many memories. It's time to start a fresh life."

"What happened?" Her insouciance piqued Etienne's curiousity.

"Can't you guess?"

"I wouldn't want to," he answered, honestly.

"I loved a man, but not enough to lose him to another woman, so I had him poisoned." She looked at Etienne to see if his face registered surprise, and was happy to see that there was none. "I couldn't control my guilt or my grief. Soon, guilt emerged victorious, and his fiancée had me thrown in jail."

"Why aren't you angry, Victorine?" Etienne was puzzled.

"This has become my home, Etienne. You may not understand this, but here I do not have to face my crime, and my guilt does not lord its power over me." She self-consciously put her hand up to her hair and straightened it. "At Court, every one admonished me. Here, we are all the same. There are no judgements."

"What happens when you are released?"

"I fully intend to die before then," she said adamantly.

"Oh Victorine, that makes me feel sad, to see you renounce your life!"

"When I came here," she said, ignoring his remark, "I was

pregnant. I carried his child in my womb, and I lost it. I wanted to die, and for a long time, I lay where you found your Madame. Perhaps your God had other plans for me, because I found my health improving. My only anger is with myself, over my inability to bring about my death. There is no anger for anyone else."

"We all have our stories, do we not, Etienne?" Thomas added. "I'm sure even Madame has an interesting tale to tell."

Etienne smiled and leaned over to stroke Madame's forehead. She had been listening to the conversation, and it infused her with an energy she had not felt for the month she had been inside the stone walls of the Bastille. With no one to care for her, she had become ill almost immediately. A few of the inmates who had grown tired of walking around her, moved her to the death station, thinking it was her illness that had made her too weak to walk. There she had lain, too proud to ask for help, begging for death.

She recognized Etienne's voice the first day he had rubbed her back, but she could not bring herself to face him. Madame would have preferred anything, rather than to have him see her in this humiliating position. And then his light poured over her, and she knew that he did not see her as being any different than before. Etienne saw only her beauty through the eyes of love.

Madame had known that Etienne would return to her in some way. Her soul had known the answer to that which her fear had blocked. She felt a sense of absolution knowing that she could die with him at her side.

The clanging on the bars hurt her ears. The small group around her quickly dispersed to get their meager food rations. She heard the sound of bodies hitting each other in the frenzied scuffle, and then Etienne was back at her side, urging her to eat some bread and cheese.

* * *

Etienne did not eat for three days. He gave his food to Alicia, who divided it among those who had procured the blankets and the straw pallet, and to Madame de Grave. Her health was not improving, but to pacify him, she ate.

[228]

Gradually his hunger could not be ignored, and on the fourth day, when his food belonged entirely to him, he ate ravenously, his stomach aching for more when he had finished. He realized how much energy he had exerted in caring for the other prisoners.

The man with the sores on his body died in his sleep. Victorine had come to Etienne while he was meditating, his hand in Madame's, and tapped him on the shoulder. "Etienne, will you come and pray for one of the invalids?" she politely requested.

"Who?" He opened his eyes.

"The one with the sores. I think he's dying."

He left Madame's side to follow Victorine. She was right. His breathing was becoming erratic. They kneeled on either side of him and took his hands.

"We can both pray, Victorine," he encouraged.

"I think I've forgotten." Tears came to her eyes and she turned aside to push them away before Etienne saw them.

An hour later, the man was dead. Etienne laid his hands across his body and covered him.

"I'm envious that he was able to go, and I wasn't, Etienne."

"It's not your time, Victorine." Etienne felt that she was not yet complete with life.

Thomas approached them. "I've called for the guards," he said quietly. "They'll be here shortly."

"When there's death, they come quickly." Victorine informed him. "They don't want diseases to spread."

Etienne heard the guards ordering the prisoners back from the gate. A crowd followed them to where the dead man lay, and they curiously watched as the guards threw him on a stretcher and carried him out.

"I didn't even know his name," Victorine said softly.

Already, the straw he had been sleeping on was being fought over by two women. Thomas shook his head and gestured for Etienne and Victorine to leave with him.

"It's times like this when I am forced to reconsider my own perspective about the masses. They make the nobles appear to be angels." He spoke cynically.

"There's no rank in here, Thomas," Etienne replied. "Even the

[229]

highborn leave their noble stature behind, and all become equal."

Victorine slapped Thomas' shoulder. "Look at me, Thomas! What he says is right!" She laughed aloud, and the sound was like a tinkling bell. "There's not one of us alive who does not have the capacity to fall from his status. Some have a shorter distance to fall. Others do it in a grand way!"

"We do lose sight of our goals," Thomas agreed.

"And some of us fall in order to find our goals," Etienne added, speaking for himself.

Alicia came running to them. "Etienne!" she called out. "A man's at one of the windows asking for your Madame de Grave."

"Where?" His heart lifted with excitement.

"I told him to wait while I found you!" She waved him toward her. "Come, I'll show you."

Eagerly, he followed her to one of the windows where he could see someone's legs. Alicia whistled through her fingers to get the man's attention, and he stooped to peer through the opening.

"Frederick!" Etienne exclaimed.

"How are you, Etienne?" Frederick smiled openly at the monk whose face he was genuinely surprised to see. "How is Madame?"

"I'm well, and she is asking for death," he answered, his hands reaching up to touch Frederick's.

"I'm very happy you are with her."

"How did you know?" Etienne was perplexed.

"Some of your friends came by the house to leave these with you." Frederick pushed a few blankets through the window. "They sent their love and made me promise to bring them here."

"Oh, thank you!" Etienne held Pasqual's warm blankets. "How are you and Felice?"

"We're all right." Frederick turned to look at something behind him. "I must go. Guard coming. I'll stay in touch."

He was gone before Etienne could bid him farewell.

"Who was that?" Alicia asked.

"One of Madame's devoted servants."

They walked over to where Madame lay sleeping. Etienne removed the filthy blanket that had been keeping her warm and placed one of Pasqual's blankets on her. She opened her eyes.
[230]

"A gift from the monastery, thanks to Frederick," he said, wrapping the soft wool around her.

"How is Frederick?" she asked, her voice catching.

"He appears well. He's concerned about you."

"I know he's happy to see you here."

"I think he'd prefer to see us both somewhere else."

They both smiled at Etienne's remark. "Etienne," she whispered, "if you get out of here alive, please go back to my house."

"I will, Madame."

"There's something I want you to do for me." Her voice was weak.

"Anything, Madame!"

"In my room, behind the secretary, is a safe where I keep my jewels and some money." Her breathing was labored. "Take what you need, and give the jewels to Felice and Frederick. They can get good money for them. Please tell them the house is theirs. Will you do this for me?"

"I want you to walk out of here with me, Madame." Etienne took her hand.

"You know I won't do that."

"I know," he admitted sadly.

Chapter Sixteen

A piercing scream tore through the darkness. Etienne's body shook as it abruptly pulled him from sleep into the waking state. He sat up and rubbed his eyes, feeling the dirt on his face. Next to him, Madame stirred fitfully.

Etienne stumbled to his feet and walked in the direction of the scream, where he could still hear a commotion. He saw shadows moving frantically. "What is the problem?" he whispered to a man who was holding his hand up to his mouth.

"Damn rats!" The man's pain had turned to anger. "One of them bit me."

"Serves you right for trying to hide food," the woman next to him admonished.

"Let me see your hand, friend." Etienne reached for the man's hand which had indeed been badly bitten.

A large chunk of flesh, between his thumb and his index finger, was missing. Etienne examined it carefully. "Since there's no water in here, I would suggest you try to find a rag to hold the bleeding. Put your saliva on the wound to clean it."

"This is the second time this has happened to me," the man added, filled with self-pity.

"Well, you'll learn, Patrice," the woman retorted, "or you'll die. These rats carry diseases."

"She's right," Etienne agreed. "It's best to eat all your food immediately."

"If it isn't the rats, it's other prisoners. He's a fool either way."

"You two can settle your own disputes," Etienne suggested. "I'm going back to my bed."

"Thanks," the man said in a barely audible tone.

Etienne returned to Madame de Grave's side. It was impossible for him to sleep, and he contemplated his last few months of prison life.

Time had passed quickly, once he had established a routine. He had become close to Thomas and Victorine. Alicia, in her own ineffable way, had attempted to come into the group. She was more of a loner, however, moving through all circles, while belonging to none.

It was Alicia who knew everything that was happening among the prisoners, and it was she who knew how to procure various items for Etienne. He was amazed with what she could unearth. She had been a street urchin, and prison was more of a home to her than she had ever known. Moreover, she used her street ways with the inmates, who fared poorly when confronted with her. Everyone learned, sooner or later, to let Alicia finagle her needs from them, for she was unrelentingly persistent.

Etienne was happy to be in alliance with her. She was a guardian angel to those in need, although she drove a hard bargain. She adored Etienne and maintained her tough attitude around him for her own protection.

Victorine was quiet and helpful. Her desire to nurture was fed by her solicitous concern for Etienne, Thomas, and Madame de Grave. If Alicia was the guardian angel, then Victorine was the good fairy. There was a sauciness about her that always expressed itself at the right time. It balanced the heaviness that surrounded them. She had a charming, self deprecating wit coupled with an innate wisdom.

Thomas was taken by her, although he did everything to conceal it. For a champion of the poor, and a political savant, to be enamored with a French courtesan was too much of a contradiction. However, he found her astute in political matters, and her interaction with him always gave him food for thought. Both of them were too cautious to become romantically involved.

The mere thought brought a smile to Etienne. Occasionally there were couplings, but these were more for physical release than anything else. Romance did not flourish in a place where one's body and one's innermost thoughts were his only sanctuary. There were enough fights over the rights of possession to add jealous tirades to the hostile encounters. Besides, it was hard to see beauty beyond missing teeth, matted hair and dirty bodies.

No, existence here was on a survival basis, and friendships

[233]

were often formed for that reason. Etienne, himself, had grown thin and had lost his healthy look. However, he maintained his vital glow, having focused his thoughts and energies outside the realm of his own discomfort.

Victorine had been a blessing with her absence of malice. Her behaviour had taught him that there were other ways of coping with prison life than the path of resistance. He placed his attention on his friends, especially Madame, who was now sleeping more than she was awake. Etienne was surprised that she had lasted four months, and he suspected that she remained purely through his will. He did not want her to die, for her passing would remind him of Ambrose. Each of them had been a parent figure to him.

Etienne never had the brothers far from his thoughts. Throughout the long days, he would imagine himself being schooled by Chen, or talking with Tristan, or reading in the library with Andrew. Pasqual's songs ran through his head constantly, and when Etienne ate he imagined himself being fed from the Abbey kitchen.

His connection with Chen was the most powerful. Not a day passed without some message of strength coming from him. The distance did not hinder their communication, and this gave him hope. Chen had not given up on Etienne, for he did not see his student in terms of a physical reality. Their bonding was the Divine Reflection of its own beauty, as seen through the eyes of the All Knowing Soul.

Beside him, Madame started coughing. Etienne leaned over to rub her back, to help her release phlegm from her lungs. He was concerned that she had pneumonia, for in spite of the two blankets, it was bitterly cold. Thomas had been correct with his predictions. The winter was the coldest Paris had seen in a long time, and everyone was tired of hearing the racking coughs that plagued the prisoners.

"Madame, are you all right?"

"Yes, Etienne," she lied.

From behind, Thomas tapped him on the shoulder. "Etienne, can you come here, please?"

"Yes, Thomas."

[234]

They walked to the other side of the cell. "You must release her, Etienne," he began. "She needs to die."

"I can't Thomas. She's my last contact with the outside world."

"The outside world no longer exists. Your world, Etienne, your only world is here. You still haven't accepted the reality that this is where you might spend the rest of your life." Thomas was trying to be gentle with the young man who, as a rule, was much wiser than he.

Even so, Thomas was fully aware of the dreams one harbored upon first becoming an inmate. For two years, he had deluded himself into thinking he would soon be free, and then one day, he merely accepted what might be a reality. There was a possibility that Thomas would never walk the streets of Paris again, that his body would be thrown on a stretcher like the others who had died and who had been unceremoniously burned. After this acceptance of his fate, his anger dissipated, and time had passed more quickly. The last three years had gone as swiftly as the first two, and now, with Etienne's presence, nothing mattered. He was thankful God had shown him some mercy in sending Etienne into his life.

"Thomas," Etienne replied, "I'm aware that I have been doing as you say, and I know that Madame's life is connected to me, but I fear the darkness that I will face with her death."

"Victorine and I will be with you, Brother." Thomas reassured him. "And you know Alicia will keep you busy with her peddling."

"All right, Thomas," He reluctantly agreed, "I'll encourage her to free her spirit."

"Thank you, Etienne."

"No, I'm the one who should be thanking you for bringing to my vision that which I have refused to see." Etienne walked away, determined to release his attachment to Madame, although he could not ignore the leaden feeling in his heart.

He sat down and took her hand. Raising it to his lips, he kissed it. "Good-bye, my dear, dear Madame," he whispered quietly.

Her fingers pressed his. "Thank you, Etienne."

He did not move again. He sat through the day without eating, until it grew dark, oblivious to the noise around him, listening only to her breath which grew fainter and more sporadic. Finally, it stopped. He covered her with Pasqual's blankets and waited until morning to alert the guards.

Thomas and Victorine walked on either side of Etienne as Madame was carried away, the blankets still over her.

"Be gentle with her, please," he appealed to the guards. They nodded sympathetically and left the cells.

"Are you all right, Brother?" Victorine asked him, taking his arm.

"Yes. Yes I am, Victorine."

* * *

Madame de Grave's death affected the small group for a few days. They were left to fill the empty vacuum created by her absence. Etienne kept looking for a sign of Frederick at the windows, so that he could inform him. He offered Alicia some bread and cheese in exchange for her vigil.

When she finally came to him, Alicia was bringing him different news. "There's a woman asking for you."

"What's wrong, Alicia?"

"Seems her friend, the one who was bitten by the rat, is sick." She rubbed her nose with the back of her hand and then smoothed her hair. Etienne's beauty, even in the filth of prison, made her acutely aware of her homeliness.

Etienne followed her to the sick man and examined him. He was sweating profusely, and his body was trembling from the cold.

"Bring me some rags, Alicia, and find some water, please." Etienne lifted up the man's eyelids to inspect his eyes, which had rolled back into his head. "When did he become this way?" he asked the woman.

"Several hours ago," she replied. "I thought he had an upset stomach. He's so good at grabbing the food, and he sometimes eats too much."

"It looks like this rat bite is infected." Etienne held up the swollen hand. "I think we'd better get the guard."

[236]

"They won't come for this!" she replied angrily. "Only if we're dead!"

"He will be soon." Etienne attended to the dying figure.

"Can I help, Etienne?" Thomas stood over him.

"Thomas, do people often hide food away here?"

"Yes, why?"

"Well, that rat is carrying something. I think everyone should be warned."

"It does no good, Etienne." Thomas shook his head. "Most people in here are happy to die."

Alicia brought a wet rag. "This is all I could find, and don't ask how I wet it. It's sterile!"

Thomas put his hand up to his mouth to cover his smile. Alicia's impudence amazed him at times. He watched as Etienne washed the man's hand and then wiped the sweat off his body, knowing that his efforts were in vain.

His fever continued to rise, and finally, the body succumbed to the shock. The man died quietly. "He's gone," Etienne told the woman, wishing he could have done something more.

"I knew he'd leave me, the bastard!" she lamented. "What am I going to do now?"

"The same as the rest of us, Madame." Thomas suggested. "Wait."

Frantically, she bent over and sucked the dead man's sore. "If he gets to die, then I can too." She spat the taste of urine out of her mouth.

"I'll get the guards," Etienne said, relieved to have something else to do.

He realized that Death courted them all. One by one, it claimed its victims. Etienne wondered if his time would arrive, and if it did, what his choice would be, if he had one. He was thankful for his friends and hoped they would stay together.

* * *

To everyone time was marked by Death taking its share of

prisoners out of the Bastille, or by new inmates arriving. Thomas and Victorine defined periods by the names of those who had left or arrived. No one wished to admit the number of months that passed.

Etienne's physical strength deteriorated. He was afraid to ask if his hair were turning white, as Thomas and Victorine's had, but he knew that his body was little more than skin and bones. His stomach had adjusted to its lack of food, and he no longer felt the gnawing hunger.

Frederick had come a few days after Madame had died. Alicia had kept her agreement and notified Etienne, who gave him the news.

"Frederick, she's no longer with us."

"I am so sorry to hear that, Etienne. Was she at peace?" Frederick's shoulders sagged with grief and sadness.

"She was happy." Etienne felt a stabbing guilt over the reason she had been imprisoned. "I apologize for this, Frederick."

"It's no fault of yours, Etienne," he assured him, thankful that he and Felice were safe.

"She wants you and Felice to have the house."

"We'll wait for your return, Etienne." Frederick spoke with an optimism that he did not feel.

"I'll be there." Etienne reached for his hand and clutched it. "Do you have enough money?"

"Yes. Is there anything I can do for you?"

"You can." Etienne paused. "Please send word to the Abbey, telling them that I'm safe, and ask them to inform my mother."

"Anything else?"

"Frederick, come back once in a while, please?"

He nodded. "If something is to happen, you will know."

"Thank you."

"Until later." Etienne watched Frederick's legs move away from the window.

Etienne leaned against the wall, watching the eclectic assortment of people with whom he lived and felt a growing loneliness. Not wanting to wallow in self pity, he went to find Thomas.

[238]

Frederick kept his word. Every few weeks, he came to inquire about Etienne's health. To avoid arousing suspicion, they never talked longer than a moment. It was customary for people on the street level to stop and stare down at the prisoners, but those who hesitated for any length of time often faced angry guards.

Etienne continued, with Thomas and Victorine's help, to clean and feed the dying. It was an unceasing task. He never invited personal friendships, with the exception of Thomas, Victorine, and Alicia, although Alicia maintained a discreet distance. Etienne had a love of solitude, and in spite of his proximity to so many people, he had a protective aura that few attempted to penetrate.

Everyone liked him. They respected his calming influence. His solicitous concern for others reminded them of their own selfishness. Whenever there was a problem, Etienne was called to help, with Alicia on his heels ready to bargain.

The winter was unbearably cold, and spring was a welcome relief. The sunlight and drier weather alleviated some of the dampness in the cells. Etienne was happy that his place under the window was becoming more bearable for him to sit. Outside, he heard the birds calling to one another, and he imagined himself in St. Benoit-sur-Loire.

"Etienne!" Thomas was excited.

"Yes, Thomas, my friend. What is it?"

"I have some news for you."

"We're being released," Etienne joked.

"Well, that's always a possibility." Thomas sat next to him on the floor, his eyes fired with enthusiasm.

"Tell me this exciting information." Etienne smiled at his friend, aware of the exhaustion taking over his body.

"Two days ago, the Estates General met at Versailles."

"And?"

"It was pandemonium! The members of the Third Estate were forced to wear black uniforms, while the clergy and the nobles dressed like peacocks."

"The Third Estate being the merchants and the trades people."

"Yes," Thomas agreed. "There was such disharmony, that the entire meeting was dismissed by an irate King who closed the conference hall. The Third Estate moved onto the tennis courts and declared themselves the National Assembly. They swore by oath to give the country a constitution!"

"What does this mean, Thomas?"

"The King is getting pushed against the wall." Thomas was emphatic. "My feeling is that, by this summer, everything will break."

"What about us?"

"We're likely to get a trial," Thomas optimistically offered. "It should give us a fair chance for freedom."

"Dare I hope?" Etienne's faith was dwindling.

"Etienne," Thomas looked closely at his friend, "is something wrong with you?"

"No, Thomas. I'm just feeling tired." Etienne admitted to the fatigue he had been carrying over the last few days. "It's not important."

"Could you have caught something?"

"Who knows? I just need to sit and relax a while." He turned to Thomas. "I'll join you later."

Thomas left him to his solitude, and Etienne leaned against the wall for support, releasing all thoughts and sense impressions. In his mind's eye, he saw only black spaces. Nothing came to take him away from the emptiness, until the grey mists appeared, and the robed figure approached. His white face, smiling hungrily, was momentarily visible beneath the cloak, and then he left Etienne to his emptiness.

The vision did not worry him, for he was too tired. Chen's face came to him, filled with compassion. "You must travel this part of your journey alone, T'ien Li."

Etienne did not try to fathom the meaning of Chen's words. He allowed the fatigue to cradle him, seeing nothing, hearing nothing, thinking nothing. Into the vast abyss he fell, and his consciousness was sucked into the void.

"Etienne?" A woman's voice reached him from the ethers. He felt the pressure of a hand somewhere upon his body, its weight pushing him down.

[240]

"Etienne!" Victorine hurriedly went to find Thomas, who was passionately discussing the latest political events with a new arrival, extracting from him any information that he could.

"Thomas," Victorine grabbed his arm, "come quickly! It's Etienne!"

Thomas turned away from the man. "What's the matter with him?"

"He's been sleeping for hours, and he doesn't respond to me when I call him."

"Philippe, I must go to my friend," Thomas excused himself. He immediately followed Victorine through the clusters of ragged people. They found Etienne still sleeping, oblivious to all noise. Thomas examined him.

"I don't know what can be done, Victorine," he said when he had finished. "Nothing appears to be wrong."

"Perhaps his spirit has lost the will to remain with us, Thomas," Victorine replied, feeling nausea rising from the pit of her stomach. She froze. "Thomas, I couldn't bear to lose him. He gives me faith in myself and in the hope that someday, I'll be free."

"Victorine, he won't die!" He tried to soothe her fears, ignoring his own.

"I felt that if God placed Etienne among us, it was to inspire us! He doesn't belong here, except as a light for us." She smoothed her hands across Etienne's face, tears filling her eyes.

"Let's lay him here," Thomas suggested, inwardly praying for strength.

"Who will help us with the invalids? Who will calm my restless soul?" Victorine began to shiver uncontrollably.

"Get a hold of yourself, Victorine!" Thomas pulled her to him. "I'll take care of you. Will you not trust in that?"

"I'm afraid to depend on you for anything, Thomas." His firm grip hurt her shoulders.

"Why?" Thomas felt rebuffed.

"Because, although your heart is pure, you think that I am your political enemy." Victorine's eyes filled again, this time for the unrequited love she was beginning to feel for him.

[241]

"Here in prison, Victorine, I do not differentiate between us."

"Your social consciousness does," she retorted saucily, trying to hide her vulnerability.

"Will you trust me, Victorine?" His eyes revealed the honesty of his heart, and she relented.

"I'll trust you," she agreed, quietly.

"Thank you." He smiled at her, openly acknowledging his affection. "Now, what about our friend?"

Etienne was aware of their presence, as a weary traveler sees a distant lamp glowing in a bleak storm. He could not bring himself to speak, for he could not find his voice. Instead, he opened his eyes for a brief second before succumbing to sleep. Victorine had seen his effort, and she kissed his forehead.

The days turned into the past, one by one, with Etienne having no memory of them. Thomas and Victorine treated him as though he were conscious, talking to him, trying to feed him. He did not respond. Death stalked him. They left his side only to treat those who were also yielding to death. Four prisoners died and were carried away before Etienne awakened.

As he surfaced from the chasm of darkness, he saw figures from his past - Monsieur LeBois, his mother, Madame Denton, Ambrose - all of them reaching for him, pulling him to them. He saw Tristan, standing tall and watching him carefully. Marie and Madame de Grave passed through his inner vision. Etienne did not know whom to follow, for too many directions offered themselves. He became confused and retreated further into the void. As the images became more vague, a bright light shot through the space, honing in on him, drawing him back.

Blinded into submission, Etienne let it draw him toward it. As it lured him closer, he saw that it came from within himself, that he was the source. The light fed him and gave him the strength he needed to make his choice. The way back to life was illuminated, and he followed the path, unceasingly grateful for the guidance.

"Thomas," he whispered, "are you there?"

"Yes. Yes, Etienne!" Thomas bent down to his ear. "It's time you came back to us!"

Victorine came and sat across from Thomas. With Etienne

between them, each took one of his hands to help him on his journey. Etienne finally opened his eyes to see them looking at him with love.

"Welcome back," Victorine said.

"How long have I been in the nether worlds?" His voice was useless. There was no strength to it.

"About six weeks."

"Here, Etienne." Thomas lifted his head. "Drink this." He poured water into Etienne's mouth, drop by drop, allowing it to be absorbed by the body. When Etienne had drunk enough, he laid his head back onto the straw.

"I don't think I'll be much better than I was when I was near death," he stammered.

"You're with us again, and that makes my heart sing!" Victorine assured him. "Nothing else matters!"

"I don't know what happened."

"Be still Etienne, and gather your strength."

He felt that his place was among the invalids, for he could not walk. Thomas had to help him relieve himself into a small container, and Victorine bathed him when the water came. Etienne's strength enabled him to lie still and watch, nothing more.

Occasionally, the other prisoners would approach him. Alicia made sure that he had extra nourishment. He could hear her bullying the inmates when the food was thrown into the cells, pushing them out of the way, loudly proclaiming that which was rightfully hers.

Within several days, Etienne had regained enough strength to speak. "What news have you received, Thomas?"

"Can you listen, or will I tire you?"

"I am thirsty for the words you wish to speak," Etienne said, smiling.

"The King called for another assembly of the Estates. This gesture on his part, was an acquiescence to the proponents of a constitutional monarchy."

"Was it successful?"

"No," Thomas answered. "King Louis reneged and called in his troops to protect his rights. He also dismissed Necker."

"I do not recall Necker. Who is he?"

"A Swiss banker, financially very astute, who has been an advisor to the King. The dismissal was a slap in the face to the bourgeoisie, who felt that Necker represented the Third Estate."

"What were the King's reasons?" Although he was exhausted, Etienne was fascinated with the climactic moves that were about to change the course of French history.

"He became filled with the sense of self-aggrandizement. He declared himself willing to accept bankruptcy if the Assembly did not allow him an extension of credit." Disdain filled Thomas' voice.

"And? Did they?"

"No, but the news has spread throughout the country. Everywhere, people are angry. My sources inform me that riots have begun, and the King's troops are inadequate to quell them."

"Oh Thomas! This is good news, is it not?"

"Yes, Etienne. When the masses join together, the few will be forced to comply."

"What is the date, Thomas?"

"July 13, 1789. Why?"

"I was just wondering how many months I have been here."

"Eight."

"It seems like forever." Etienne sighed, thinking how beautiful the Abbey was in summer.

"I understand your feelings, friend." Thomas replied. "Now, please eat some bread. Something is in the air, and I feel you will need your strength."

He was right. There was something in the air. It was of such intensity, that the kinetic energy gave a pricking sensation to the skin. Etienne wondered if it had been created in the prison cells or in the city.

Whatever the origin, the prisoners were aware of it. The intensity grew, waiting to be released. No one could sleep, as the night embraced them. Etienne listened to the other inmates tossing about. He went within himself, struggling to calm his nerves. With the arrival of dawn, Chen came to Etienne. "I am waiting, T'ien Li! Time is precious!"

Etienne was thankful when daylight began to filter into the cells, for he had a reason to be awake. Victorine, seeing his eyes were opened, shook him gently to get his attention.

"All night long, I had this feeling," she began. "It was similar to what I felt before I was told that I was to be sent to the Bastille, except this time, there was no heaviness."

"What might it be Victorine?"

"I sense freedom, Etienne. I question my feelings, but this is the answer they give me."

"Then they speak the truth, for your intuition never deceives you," he replied.

"How can you be sure of this?" She was skeptical.

"The intuitive self is that one part of you that speaks the Truth," he answered. "It comes from the purity of your center, and it is absolute until the mind dilutes it. Even now, you try to argue with its message."

"Yes, I do," she admitted.

"Do not color it, Victorine. Honor it."

Thomas looked up at the window. He saw his friend, recognizable by the red scarf tied around his left ankle, standing on the other side. It was unusual for him to come at this hour. Thomas jumped up, eager to hear his message.

"Raymond," he whispered out loudly, "I am here."

The man lowered himself quickly. "Today, you are a free man, Thomas." He straightened himself and disappeared.

Thomas went back to his friends.

"What was it Thomas?" Victorine was puzzled by his expression.

"Your intuition may prove to be right, Victorine."

"Whatever are you saying?" Victorine and Etienne looked at Thomas with anticipation.

"That was Raymond. I think, my friends, something is about to happen."

Etienne was silent for a moment. "This is the energy we have all been feeling, Thomas. Haven't you noticed the restlessness?"

Thomas spoke with a strong conviction. "I can only assume

that there will be some kind of prison break! Victorine, we'll have to help Etienne." He lowered his voice. "We must stay close to one another today."

Sometime before noon, the noise began. A distant roar, almost indistinguishable from the murmuring voices in the cells, could be heard beyond the windows. To Etienne and Thomas, it was the sound of the culmination of years of anger and frustration. The roar grew stronger, rising to a deafening crescendo. It was the voice of angry mobs crying out in unison as they approached the prison.

Inside the cells, prisoners gathered at the windows to watch. The retort of gunshots pierced the air. Hundreds of legs and feet marched past the windows. Etienne was carried closer to the gates.

"Just in case we need to leave hurriedly," Thomas assured him.

Alicia ran over to them, the energy of the excitement vibrating from her small frame. "What's happening?" she asked.

"What have you heard, Alicia?" Thomas knew she must have picked up some information.

"I can't believe what I've been hearing!" she replied, hesitating as she spoke.

"Just tell me!" Thomas insisted.

"It sounds like the mobs are tearing down the Bastille!" Disbelief registered in her voice. "They are screaming for our release!"

Thomas and Etienne stared at Alicia as her words registered. "My God!" Thomas exclaimed. "I can't believe it, but it's true!"

"What makes you so certain, Thomas?" Alicia was surprised that he had so readily accepted her information.

"Alicia, you've never been wrong yet, have you?" he teased.

"Well, I don't like to remember my mistakes," she admitted honestly.

"Alicia," Etienne interrupted, "please go to the windows and listen. Don't say anything. Just listen to the outside, and bring us back whatever news you can."

From where he sat, Etienne could see the crowds thickening. It was almost impossible to see the light between their legs as they moved en masse. More shots rang out amidst the angry cries. The impenetrable building was trembling from their outrage. Over his

[246]

head, he heard the thumping sounds of feet marching purposefully. They traveled the length of the cells, and came down the steps.

Victorine huddled next to Etienne. "I'm frightened," she said.

Thomas bent and put his arm protectively around her. "Stay with me." He looked over at Etienne. "Are you ready to get up? Can you walk with us?"

"I'll try, Thomas," he promised.

They positioned Etienne between them and watched the throngs tearing at the gates, screaming for the release of the prisoners. Etienne saw a man squeeze himself through the huddle, his arms waving in the air. In his hand was a large key ring. "Let me pass!" he yelled. "I've got the keys!"

A path was immediately cleared for him, while the prisoners watched in stunned disbelief. No one could accept within himself what was happening. Each was dumbfounded over the possibility of freedom.

"I've waited so long for this, I don't know how to receive it." Thomas voiced the thoughts. "Is prison any worse than the mass hysteria I see before me?"

"It's safer," Victorine added, shivering.

The gates were opened, and the crowds moved back. Slowly, one by one, the prisoners stepped outside. Each was received into the arms of a rescuer and helped up the stairs. When they were finally able to move, Thomas and Victorine walked forward with Etienne's arms around their shoulders.

He had trouble coordinating his legs, but he used his mind to control the weakness. When they entered the hall, a large man approached the trio. "Let me carry him," he offered. "You two follow closely behind."

Thomas took Victorine's hand and walked up the steps with her. "It's been almost six years, Victorine," he said wistfully. "Did you ever think you'd see Paris again?"

"Only after Etienne came to us, Thomas," she replied.

Outdoors, the July sun blinded them. A large path had been cleared for the prisoners. People were shocked to see their abject physical condition, and the anger of the mob surrendered to sadness. Occasionally, a family member was recognized, and cries of joy blended with the sorrow and the pity.

After the prisoners had been guided out, the sorrow was transformed into revenge. The hordes returned to their original intention of tearing down the Bastille, stone by stone. To them, it represented everything that was oppressive. The Bastille symbolized the monarchy and its dehumanization of the people of France. United, they were going to prove that any bastion, regardless of its strength, was no match for the change which would push them all forward.

At the end of the pathway, the man placed Etienne down on the ground, and let Thomas and Victorine take him. "Thank you, my friend," Etienne said, with gratitude.

"It was my privilege, Brother," the man replied, bowing to him.

"Where shall we go from here?" Thomas asked, looking around to gather his bearings.

"Etienne!" A voice called out. "Etienne!"

The small group turned in the direction of the voice. Frederick and Felice were pushing their way through the people.

"Frederick! Felice!" Etienne emitted a hoarse laugh.

Frederick was breathless and excited. "We've been waiting for you with the carriage."

Felice began to cry when she saw Etienne. "Do I look that bad, Felice?" he asked sadly.

"I hate to admit it, sir, but yes, you do." She wiped her eyes with her handkerchief.

"Come with us," Frederick gestured to them. "Here, I'll help carry him."

They made their way toward the carriage. "These are my friends, Frederick. Thomas and Victorine. They saved my life."

"Then they will come back to Madame's house with us," Felice ordered. "We'll pour you a bath and put fresh clothes on you."

The trio let out an exaggerated sigh of relief. Etienne was helped into the carriage by the men, and Victorine and Felice followed.

"Drive slowly," Frederick cautioned the lackey. "They aren't used to the motion."

[248]

Etienne was reminded of his rapid journey to St. Benoit-sur-Loire. "Frederick, did the driver's wife have that baby boy he wanted so badly?"

"No." Frederick smiled. "He had a fourth daughter. She's with child now, and once again his hopes are up."

"What do you think?"

"I think it had better be a boy!" Felice added her opinion. "He's becoming unbearable, and the poor woman can't have many more children!"

Thomas was oblivious to the conversation, as he was reflecting on his feelings. He had always reviled wealth, and now he was riding in a luxurious carriage toward a stately home, where he would be cared for. He knew that Victorine would feel comfortable in the surroundings, and he feared that their intimacy might suffer. In the prison, he had not been reminded of their social differences. For a moment, he wished he were back at the Bastille where life had been simpler. He realized that he loved Victorine in a way he had never felt for another, and he did not want it to end. His friendship with her had blossomed into something beautiful and pure.

Beside him, Victorine was experiencing similar sentiments. She had been given the opportunity to view a different aspect of life while in the Bastille, and it had drastically changed her rather narrow perspective. Where once her focus had been fancy balls and gossip, it was now directed toward others and their needs. Thomas had a unique strength that she hadn't noticed in other men, and she was fearful that he would join the crowds that championed the repressed. Victorine was aware that her beauty was no longer an asset, and that it was time for her to seriously consider her future. She hoped that Thomas would want to share it with her, although such a possibility had never been discussed by either of them.

Etienne, watching them, clearly read Thomas and Victorine's thoughts, for they spoke loudly. He was aware that something special had been created between them, and he hoped they would develop it further.

"Here we are," Frederick said, as the driver slowed the coach to a stop.

Etienne was helped across the familiar courtyard and up the

[249]

steps into the foyer, with Thomas and Victorine following slowly.

"Frederick," Etienne said quietly, "put Thomas and Victorine in the suite next to Madame's. I'll have her suite, if that's all right with you."

"That it is, sir," Frederick replied formally.

"I don't know if I'll remember what a bath is like," Victorine sighed.

"What time will you be wanting dinner?" Felice asked.

"Is eight o'clock agreeable with everyone?" Etienne looked at his friends, who nodded happily. "Nothing too heavy, Felice. Our food has been meager."

"Very well, sir."

Etienne felt sudden remorse over Madame's absence, as he was carried into her room. It was prepared as if she would return to it. The familiar blues and creams soothed him, and he sat on the chaise while Frederick poured his bath.

"I have something for you, sir," Frederick offered.

"Frederick, please call me Etienne," he admonished. "We are well beyond the formalities. Tell Felice to do the same."

"Yes, sir - Etienne." Frederick disappeared and returned a few minutes later with a small package. "This was left for you."

Etienne untied the string and removed the paper. Neatly folded inside was a fresh robe and a belt, and under them was a new pair of sandals. Etienne put his face in his hands and wept.

"Forgive me, Frederick," he said between sobs. "I never expected to be free again."

"Apparently, your friends did." Frederick wanted to comfort the young man. "They left this package for you at the same time they left the blankets, and I was told to keep it here."

"I am overwhelmed by the love people have shown for me." Etienne dried his eyes in the soft wool.

"Perhaps, Etienne, it's a reflection of what you give to others."

"It's a nice reflection, Frederick."

"There is one other thing you might use." Frederick walked over to Madame's armoire and opened it. "Madame always hoped she would be able to walk with this one day," he said, pulling out a cane. "Perhaps she was really saving it for you."

[250]

"Oh Frederick!" Etienne exclaimed. "It's perfect! I can teach myself to walk again without burdening anyone."

"I'm glad you like it. Now, I'm going to finish preparing your bath."

Frederick left Etienne, who lay back against the chaise. His body was unused to the nurturing feel of such comfort, and he was asleep almost as soon as he had closed his eyes.

Chapter Seventeen

It had been three days since the prisoners had arrived at Madame de Grave's. Each one of them had changed considerably. They had eaten regularly to build up strength, and aside from the residual pallor of prison life, all were filling out. Etienne was able to walk, with the help of his cane, and Thomas had cut his hair so that he would be more presentable to Victorine, whose beauty was still blatantly evident.

Etienne and Victorine were in the library talking when Thomas found them. It was agreed that he would go into the city to ferret out information, using his reliable sources. It had not taken long, and he was back within a few hours.

"It feels good to be in the safety of this house," he said, carrying a chair over to the others. "It's dangerous out there. Even those who instigated the riots are frightened."

"What did you hear, Thomas?" Victorine understood that much of his nervousness was due to his last six years in isolation. She doubted that he would be as highly visible to the public, as he had once been.

"The Assembly has convened again to draw up a constitution, and the King, in response, is gathering his troops at Versailles," he began. "Right now, as I am speaking to you, women from Les Halles are marching to Versailles to kill the King and the Queen. They are calling out for the baker, the baker's wife, and the baker's son."

"I don't understand." Etienne interjected.

"The King's financial situation is the reason behind the lack of bread on their tables," Thomas answered. "My friend, Raymond, told me that he had never seen such relentless anger."

"Are the streets safe?" Victorine was worried about Thomas walking freely through the city.

"Yes, and no," he replied. "As long as you don't represent the symbol of wealth and oppression, you can move about fairly safely;

[252]

however, the force of the rioters is incredibly powerful, and it's best to stay out of their way."

"How long do you expect this to continue?" Etienne asked. He was hoping to leave for the Abbey as soon as possible.

"Until the frenzy dies down, and the people have been placated with realistic promises. I'm told these riots are taking place all over the country."

"I must see Marie!" Etienne spoke loudly, surprising himself with the spontaneity of his words. He felt an abysmal fear surge up.

"Who?" Victorine had not heard her name mentioned before.

"Marie. The woman for whom I was imprisoned," he repeated. "I must see her!"

"Etienne, I don't think you should travel," Thomas warned. "You are still too weak."

"Thomas, I know that something is about to happen." He was deaf to their concern.

"Now?"

"Is this your intuition speaking, Etienne?" Victorine remembered their earlier conversation.

"Yes, it is."

"Then I shall ride with you." She turned to Thomas. "Get Frederick, and tell him to prepare the carriage quickly."

Victorine's sense of urgency overrode Thomas' surprise at her sudden command of the situation. He left the room, without responding, to find Frederick.

Etienne and Victorine were in the foyer when the carriage arrived at the front gate. Without assistance, Etienne walked very slowly down the stairs, holding the balustrade with his right hand and his cane with the left. His legs already felt much stronger, although it would be months before he would walk without support.

Victorine and Thomas went on ahead of him, Victorine's hands resting in the crook of Thomas' arm. Etienne smiled to himself, knowing that they had reached an agreement. They stood back to allow him to climb into the carriage, and then Thomas lifted Victorine.

Etienne called out to the driver. "The Compte de Chevrier's

[253]

residence, please." Nervously he settled back into the seat.

The drive seemed interminable. They kept the coach windows open to watch the street activity, which was unusually quiet. There was still a kinetic energy in the air. Shops were closed, and there was little sign of life. The prevailing noise was the sound of the horse drawn carriage racing across the cobblestones.

"Where is everyone?" Etienne wondered aloud.

"It's eerie, isn't it?" Thomas added.

"I feel queasy about something, Etienne, do you?" Victorine asked.

Etienne nodded. He recollected how busy Paris had been on his last visit. He remembered the promenades, where the women and the men would walk to show off their finery to each other. Even the lower classes had enjoyed them on Sundays. This wasn't the Paris he recalled.

A few blocks before Marie's house, the driver stopped the carriage and stepped down. Thomas leaned toward the window.

"What's the matter, friend?"

"Can't go much further," the lackey said, matter of factly. "There's a crowd ahead."

Thomas looked down the street. "He's right," he answered, sitting back in the carriage. "A big crowd."

"Then we shall walk," Etienne decided. "It's probably safer, anyway."

He opened the door, and the driver stood by as they descended from the carriage. "Wait for us here," Etienne requested. "If you should see us coming, drive up to meet us."

"Anything you say, sir." The lackey had a foreboding about the venture, and he wanted to be heading home.

Victorine and Thomas flanked Etienne, and they slowly made their way down the street. As they drew closer to the crowd, its noise grew louder. They seemed to be encircling something which was the focus of their anger. Arms waved in the air. At the center of the throng, someone cried out, and the rest responded in unison.

"They sound very angry," Victorine shuddered.

"I wonder at whom," Thomas added.

They reached the edge of the enraged mob and stood there,

trying to determine if it would be worth their efforts to pass. "Her house is that large one with the balconies," Etienne pointed to it.

"Shall we walk around, or through?" Thomas asked.

"I want to go through!" Etienne's stomach was churning.

"Then we shall go through, very carefully," Thomas suggested. "Let's stay together. If we are separated, meet back at the carriage as soon as possible. All right?"

"Yes." They answered in unison, fear in their eyes.

Methodically, and very slowly, they moved into and became absorbed by the group. It was difficult to avoid assuming the energy of anger, for its power was overwhelming. They gestured to one another before making any directional changes, allowing Thomas the lead. Gradually, the openness of the street was behind them. At the center of the circle, several people stood, fearfully huddled together.

"Shall we, the people, show them who has control now?!" A man shouted.

"Yes! Show them!" the crowd roared.

"How?" The man incited them further.

"By the might of our unity!" they responded hysterically.

"What can you see, Thomas?" Etienne shouted to his friend who had pushed himself ahead of them.

He craned his neck and looked over the heads. "I see a woman, a baby in a pram, a man, no. . . three other men, and another woman!" Thomas replied. "They look absolutely petrified!"

They were pushed forward by the motion of the crowd. Etienne's legs ached, and it was all he could do to remain standing. Luckily, people were so close together that his body was supported by those around him. Victorine passed in front of him toward Thomas. She felt safe, for she had lost her well bred look in prison.

People were waving sticks and stones. As Etienne came close to the inner circle, he heard the sound of a rock hitting a body. A woman screamed in fear and pain. Etienne did not care who the intended victims were. He knew they had as much right to life as anyone, and he pushed himself through to help them.

When he was freed from the pressing bodies, he lost his balance and fell forward, his cane landing beside him. Someone bent to pick

[255]

him up, and he steadied himself before looking around.

She was the first one whom he saw. Their eyes met, his filled with shock, hers frozen with fear. They lost all awareness of everyone but each other. Etienne saw the rock approaching, but he was paralyzed by his inertia. Marie saw nothing, only Etienne. When the rock hit her, she fell, her body crumpling onto the pavement. Etienne threw himself next to her to protect her.

"Marie!" he screamed above the noise of the crowd. "Why did you not come for me?"

"I couldn't," she whispered, feeling the life drain from her body. "I felt such shame. Can you ever forgive me for ruining your life?"

Etienne's eyes filled with tears. "My darling, darling Marie!" He pulled her into his arms and buried his face in her hair, no longer hearing the noise of the crowd.

"You have a son," she murmured, wincing in pain. "He looks just like you." She lifted her arm, pointing toward the pram, and then let it fall weakly at her side.

More rocks fell, pummeling their bodies with angry thuds. "Leave me Etienne! Take the child with you!" she begged, with one last gesture of strength. "Do not let us both die!"

"I want you with me Marie!" he pleaded desperately.

"In my heart, I will always be with you." She closed her eyes, her head rolling to one side.

Etienne felt as if he were being sucked into a dreadful vacuum. Dark shadows emerged, their fingers wrapping around him and pulling him back into the void. He heard nothing, saw nothing, felt nothing. The face of Death beckoned him, once again, and he welcomed its horrible offer.

He began to shake, violently, and he could not control himself. "Stop! Stop!" he cried out into the void.

"Etienne! It's me, Thomas! Come! Let us leave!" Thomas' voice entered the silence. He continued shaking Etienne, until the latter responded.

Slowly, Etienne came back into the present. He looked up at Thomas and Victorine, his face ravaged by pain. "The baby Victorine! Take the baby!"

[256]

A rock hit Etienne on the side of his face, drawing blood. He laid his head back on Marie's breast. Thomas grabbed him under his arms and pulled him away from her lifeless form.

"This is behind you Etienne!" he ordered. "Now let us think about ourselves, while we still have life!" Thomas bent over and retrieved Etienne's cane, and then he turned and pushed his friend against the violent throng toward the outside of the circle.

Etienne turned around for one last glimpse of Marie, but the mob had closed in around her. Numbed to the core, he allowed Thomas to guide him, until they were a safe distance from the riot.

Etienne recalled that he had not seen Victorine. "Thomas! The baby! Did you see Victorine take it?"

"I saw nothing, Etienne, only you." He allowed Etienne to lean against him, for his strength had given way. "Those poor souls," he added disconsolately.

"That was Marie, Thomas," Etienne sobbed, hearing nothing again but the pounding of his heart in his ears.

"I know, my dear friend. I know."

"I had a feeling that something was terribly wrong," Etienne's aching remorse reflected in his voice. "I had to see her. How awful that it was only to be present at her death!"

"Try not to think about it, Etienne." Thomas felt adolescently awkward over his inadequacy in comforting his friend.

"I had a son, Thomas. She said he looked just like me, and now he's dead too."

"We don't know that, Etienne," Thomas tried to calm him. "Perhaps someone took pity on him."

"If he looks Oriental, I doubt it." Etienne stopped walking. "Where's Victorine?"

"I hope she went back to the carriage." A wave of fear ran through Thomas, for he could only remember having been aware of Etienne falling protectively over the woman. Knowing that he must save him, he had forgotten everything else.

As they moved further from the mob, the driver spotted them, and whipped the horses. Etienne struggled to control his legs from collapsing.

"You get in first, Etienne," Thomas suggested, as he opened the

[257]

door. He quickly looked in and saw Victorine's familiar face, eliciting a sigh of relief over the sight of her. He helped Etienne up the step and turned to the driver. "Take us away from here!"

"Yes, Sir!" The driver waited to hear the latch close, before he directed the horses homeward.

Victorine had been waiting for Etienne. "I think he belongs to you," she said, smiling radiantly. "He looks just like you."

Etienne stared in wonder at the small child, a miniature of himself. "He has blue eyes!" he laughed. "A little of Marie will always live through him."

"How unusual those eyes are," Thomas added, thoughtfully studying the child.

The baby looked at his father, examining his face with serious intent. Etienne held out his arms, and he leaned forward to be held by him.

"Is this what it was all for, Thomas?" Etienne asked sadly, kissing his son's dark cap of hair. "Did my life begin and end for the birth of this baby?" He felt a desolate emptiness in his soul.

"We can never know, can we?" Thomas answered.

* * *

"I think, Etienne, it's time you tell us your story." Victorine wiped her mouth with a napkin.

They were all seated in the dining hall, and the child was asleep beside them. He had adapted easily to the change, although Etienne knew that further adjustment would be inevitable. He felt awkward with parenting, and he was thankful that Victorine was there to help him.

They could not decide on a name, and feeling that Chen had already chosen one, Etienne let the matter drop. The baby quietly accepted Etienne, and he was eternally grateful that he had arrived in time to rescue his son. The memory of Marie lying dead in the street, brought sudden chills into his heart.

Etienne drank some tea. "My story is like everyone else's, Victorine. Some of it is fascinating, and some of it is ordinary."

"Begin with the fascinating part." She smiled at him.

"My mother is the Empress of China, and my father was a monk from the Abbey that became my home, although I was born in China," he began.

"An empress!" She was astonished. "That explains so much about you, Etienne."

"Please go on," Thomas urged.

"My father went to China to study," Etienne continued, "and he became the Empress' tutor. They had an affair, and I was the result."

"And history repeats itself, does it not?" Thomas added. "What happened to your father, Etienne?"

"He was executed, and for my own safety, Mother smuggled me out of China to France."

"Has she ever seen you?" Victorine held her cup while Felice poured more tea.

"Yes," Etienne answered. "She came to visit me when I was thirteen. I was shocked. I didn't know I had a mother, for I was only accustomed to all of my fathers."

"If she came all the way from China, didn't she want you to return with her?" Thomas asked.

"She did, but she knew my destiny was at the Abbey. She sent a teacher, some time in my third year, to stay with me."

"Chen," Victorine stated.

"Yes. How did you know?"

"You spoke of him often during your long sleep," she replied. "I knew he was of great importance to you."

"Is he waiting for you at the Abbey?" Thomas asked him.

"Yes, he is." Chen's presence in Etienne's life was the one factor that kept him from wanting death.

"What will you do now, Etienne?" Victorine hated the thought of parting with him.

"I shall take my son back to Chen, and we shall return to China." He spoke decisively. "It is time for me to return to my

[259]

homeland and to my mother."

"It will be difficult for you, Etienne," Thomas said.

"Yes, Thomas, it will," Etienne agreed. "But I have learned that the soul can endure all things. I will be guided."

"We'll miss you." Thomas spoke for both of them. "Terribly!"

"And I you, but distance is not a barrier." Etienne smiled at his friends. "We've shared something very special that can always be relived with memory. You will feel it in your hearts when I am thinking of you!"

"When will you go?" Victorine suddenly felt very sad.

"Sometime in the next few days." Etienne turned toward Felice. "Will you and Frederick meet me in my room tonight, after we have finished supper?"

"Yes, sir." Felice curtsied, forgetting Etienne's desire for informalities.

Victorine carried the child up to Etienne's room, where a small crib had been prepared. His sleep had been undisturbed by the movement, and Etienne was made aware of his exhaustion from the tragic day. The baby was severing his connection with his mother while attempting to bond with the stranger who had suddenly come into his life.

"Good night, Etienne."

"Sleep well, Victorine."

He closed the door and went to sit at the desk. When Frederick and Felice arrived, he was ready for them. Felice gave him a bottle of milk. "In case the baby awakens wanting some food," she said.

"Thank you, Felice." Etienne gestured for them to sit down. "As you already know," he began, "Madame's wishes were for you to have the house."

"Yes, this is so," Frederick agreed, wondering what he wanted to say.

"Before she died, Madame told me about something else that she wanted you to have." Etienne took a box off the desk. "She felt that you could sell these to cover your living expenses." He opened the box to reveal the contents.

"Oh! My God!" Felice gasped. "Whatever will we do with these!?"

[260]

Before them was Madame's jewelry, rubies, sapphires, emeralds, diamonds, and gold. It was worth a veritable fortune. Etienne gave the box to Frederick.

"What about yourself, sir?" Felice asked.

"I was told to take what I needed," Etienne replied, "and I have."

"Are you sure it's enough?" Frederick was concerned with Etienne's generosity.

"I'm sure. I have enough for my passage home, both to the Abbey and to China. Do not worry about me, Frederick." Etienne reassured the man. "I am fine."

"What about your friends?" Felice asked.

"I'm taking care of them," he offered. "I don't know what their plans are." The baby whimpered in his sleep, and Etienne looked over at him.

"It's just a dream, sir," Felice suggested.

"Well," Etienne concluded the discussion, "Thank you for all of your help. I know you'll both be very happy."

"We will, sir! That we will!" Felice beamed at her husband. "I never thought we'd go from rags to riches. I tell you, Frederick, our luck changed the day you met Madame de Grave! Life has been a blessing since then!"

"You deserve it," Etienne said, rising, "and now I must sleep, my friends."

Frederick held out his hand for his wife to take, and they walked toward the door, the box of jewels under his arm. Before the door closed, Felice peeked in. "We've been blessed to know you, sir. Good night, now."

Etienne walked over to look at his son, covering him with a light blanket. "You are beautiful, my child," he whispered, "but I do not know if you truly belong to me, or if your destiny is elsewhere."

Etienne went to lie in the chaise, as he had every night since his return. He could not bring himself to sleep in Madame's bed, for it was enough that feelings of loneliness engulfed him whenever he entered her room. The wheelchair had been placed next to her bed, and one of her shawls was draped across it. His gaze remained on it, until he slept.

Dark Places, Light Places

* * *

"Thomas, is it quiet enough for me to leave Paris?" Etienne was feeling pressured to return to the Abbey. Something was not right, for he had not been able to attune himself to his brothers without feeling a sense of chaos.

"Oh Etienne!" Victorine cried out. "I do not want you to leave!"

"Victorine, I must go," Etienne insisted. "But I am curious about what you have decided to do."

Felice came into the salon and offered tea to the guests. In keeping with Madame's schedule they had tea each afternoon. However, Felice insisted upon pouring it, instead of Etienne. Beside them, on the floor, the baby gurgled over a few large kitchen spoons which held great fascination for him. Etienne looked at the woman in blue, woven into the carpet, whose laughing face had mocked him and his soiled stockings on his first day at Madame de Grave's. Now his son lay upon her, his little fingers picking at her smile.

"Victorine and I have decided to stay together." Thomas reached for her hand. "We have no idea where we will go, but life takes care of its own."

"Felice and Frederick will be happy to let you remain here until you find your own place, Thomas. Isn't that so, Felice?"

"That it is, sir." She smiled at Etienne and then looked over at Thomas. "The fact is that we welcome others in this big house."

"Thank you both," Thomas replied with gratitude. "It will not be for long," he assured her.

"Time is not important, sir," Felice argued.

She finished serving the refreshments and left the salon. Etienne looked over at Thomas. "Now that you've answered my second question," he began, "tell me, what has happened to the King and the Queen?"

"The country is not safe, Etienne. Everywhere, people are taking the law into their own hands, burning chateaux and churches and sowing destruction across the land." Thomas was feeling pessimistic about the immediate future.

"And the Royal Couple?" Etienne asked again.

"They were miraculously saved," he answered. "The mobs stormed Versailles, and the Queen's death was a certainty had not Lafayette taken her onto one of the balconies and publically kissed her hand."

"Did this pacify them?"

"Yes. Lafayette is a true representative of the people. If he sanctions the Queen, then they trust in his decision."

"I thought the Queen did not like Lafayette," Etienne interjected.

"She no longer does, but she's not fool enough to lose her life over sentimentality!"

"Did the King relent his position?"

"Yes," Thomas replied. "Necker is back, trying to make sense out of the financial situation. There is a rumor that the clergy's vast fortunes may be confiscated, but this is only a rumor."

"Is it safe enough for me to leave, Thomas?"

"I don't know." Thomas answered him frankly. "If you can get out of Paris, it will be with the Grace of God. I've heard no word beyond that."

"I'll have to trust, then," Etienne decided. "Chen is waiting for me, and time is short."

"I don't think you'll have a problem, Etienne" Victorine said. "You are wearing a robe, and you still look as if you came from prison. If anyone stops you, be honest with him."

"My concern is not only for me. It's for my son and the driver."

"We understand," Victorine replied, "and we'll pray for you."

"Thank you." Etienne knew Victorine spoke sincerely, for she had come to terms with God in the Bastille, and it had helped to remove many obstacles.

He looked at his friends and was aware of how different they seemed from the first time he had met them. Love had given each of them a strong sense of power and purpose.

Etienne's encounter with them had been a turning point for them all. He knew that, without Thomas and Victorine, he would have succumbed to death. It was their strength that had pulled him back through the gates.

He was more than thankful that he had not been in prison for as long as they had. He felt a healthy respect for them. Victorine was looking quite the lady with a fresh glow in her cheeks, and Thomas was blissfully proud of her. Etienne suspected that Thomas' political views would soften, and that the disparity in their lifestyles would diminish. He also knew that Victorine's once frivolous life would take on a new meaning.

Each of them would be a gentle teacher for the other, and they would find themselves treading the middle path rather than toward the extremes. The direction of Etienne's own life was not as clearly defined for him. Etienne hoped that he would make the right decision for himself and for the child.

The baby tugged at Etienne's robe. He reached down for his son. The child snuggled against him and patted Etienne's finely chiseled face with his chubby hands.

"You have a beautiful son," Victorine said, wistfully.

"Yes, he is!" Etienne was feeling an unusual sense of pride.

"Have you made any decisions for him yet?"

"No. I have not."

Victorine fiercely hoped that, one day, she would give birth to her own child. She had no qualms about spending her life with Thomas. The fact that their love had developed slowly was a blessing, for in getting to know Thomas, she never looked at him through the projections of her own desire to be with a man. Their mental relationship had deepened into an emotional and spiritual bonding which had completely fulfilled her. She intuited that life with Thomas may have its unexpected surprises, but their bonding would carry them through.

Dinner was unusually quiet, for their thoughts were on Etienne's imminent departure. Enough words had been spoken, and what remained was to heal the hearts of sadness. Even Felice had trouble keeping her eyes from watering. She knew that she would never see Etienne again.

After they had finished eating, Etienne made arrangements with Frederick to hire the carriage in the morning. The lackey had been awaiting his orders, and he was only too happy to leave well in advance of his wife's delivery. Felice gave Etienne a bottle to take to his room for the baby, and the small party retired early.

[264]

Chapter Eighteen

For the last time, Etienne departed from Madame de Grave's. Thomas and Victorine walked with him across the courtyard, Victorine's arms wrapped around the small child. Etienne paused to look at Felice and Frederick, who were standing in the doorway. He placed his cane against his legs, put his hands together at his breast, and bowed to them as a final gesture.

Overhead, the sun was shining brightly. It was a clear, warm July morning that promised more heat before the day's end. The horses looked anxious to exercise. It was a good sign. Etienne turned to embrace Thomas, while Victorine put the baby in the coach.

"Thank you, Thomas for everything," he said. "My heart is filled with sorrow that we have no more time together."

"Let's not speak of it, Etienne," Thomas replied. "I would prefer to believe what you told us about tuning into each other's hearts."

"Thomas, this is for you, to give you and Victorine a fresh start." Etienne handed him an envelope. "Don't open it until I've left, please."

Thomas looked at the envelope, knowing what was inside. "How? Why?"

"Don't ask. Just accept." They looked at each other in silence, and then they embraced one last time.

"Take care of yourselves, and of Felice and Frederick for me, please."

"We will, Etienne." Thomas had regained his composure. "Thank you."

Victorine stepped from the carriage, and Etienne held her. "Victorine," he whispered into her ear, "you will have two children, one before next summer."

She froze against him. "How do you know this, Etienne?"

"I know it," he replied. "Don't tell Thomas yet."

"If one is a boy, we'll name him after you." Pulling away from him, she whispered, "Thank you! That makes me very happy!"

"Those were long months we spent together!" Etienne smiled at the memory. "I love you both."

"Etienne," Thomas asked, "what is your Chinese name?"

"T'ien Li," he answered. "Soon, I expect that will be my only name."

He painstakingly lifted himself into the coach with Thomas' assistance. Next to the baby was a large basket of food for the journey. Etienne put the child on his lap, while Thomas shut the door.

"Bon-voyage, Etienne."

"Good-bye, my dearest friends." He waved.

Etienne did not look out of the window, as the carriage pulled away from the curb. Instead, he closed his eyes and concentrated on removing the painful heaviness from his heart.

The streets were still fairly empty, and they made good time leaving Paris. "I'll not miss you," Etienne thought.

The countryside was in its full summer regalia, dark greens against the blue skies. Etienne saw occasional smoke clouds in the distance, and he wondered whether they were from burning chateaux.

Because there had been little rain, the road was hard and travel was easier. There were no ruts to hinder the carriage. The child grew weary on his father's lap and slept. Etienne laid him on the seat and covered him with a blanket. The pressure of the seat against his fat cheek pushed his mouth open into a small circle.

The long drive gave Etienne time to contemplate. It was time to return to China, but he had no idea what was there for him. He was indecisive about fulfilling his mother's wishes to become the Emperor, for his time in Paris had expanded his awareness about the cruel reality that the world presented.

And what of Chen? Would he remain with him? Somehow, Etienne had never imagined his life without him. He felt that he still had much to learn from his teacher. Chen's ways precluded the life he would lead as an emperor and Etienne had no desire for the life of a warrior. His battles were internal.

[266]

He lay back and envisioned his life without his brothers. It would be hard, although prison had given him a feeling of independence. He imagined how his father must have felt upon entering China, and Etienne smiled at the ironies of life. He looked at the sun which was moving across the sky. Evening would be upon them soon, and he wondered if the driver would stop.

Almost as if he had read Etienne's thoughts, the lackey slowed the carriage down and came to an uncertain stop. Etienne leaned out of the window. "Is anything the matter?" he asked.

The driver had no time to answer. "Who are you, and where are you going?" a man shouted.

Etienne opened the door and stepped out of the carriage, using the cane to balance himself. When he stood firmly on the ground, he spoke to the man who had confronted them. "I am traveling to St. Benoit-sur-Loire, my home," he replied. "I live at a monastery there."

The man was flanked by a menacing looking group, who were ready to do his bidding. "What were you doing in Paris, and how did you acquire such a nice carriage, if you're a monk?"

"The carriage belongs to an old friend who has helped me." Etienne felt the lackey's nervousness. "I have recently been released from prison after eight months."

"Prison? Where?"

"The Bastille."

"Anyone else in the carriage?"

"Yes, a baby. Would you care to look?" Etienne was concerned, but he did not betray his feelings.

Two men stepped forward and went to look inside the coach. "He's right, Jacques, only a baby," one of them confirmed to the other.

"Where's its mother?" Jacques demanded.

"She's dead," Etienne answered quietly.

"All right," he said begrudgingly, "you can pass, but you'd best tie this on the front of your carriage, so that you won't be stopped again."

He gave Etienne a small tricolor flag with a bold cross running through it. Etienne tied it in full view next to the driver, and laboriously climbed back into the carriage.

"Go ahead, pass." Jacques waved them on, and the crowd dispersed. The lackey whipped the horses, relieved to be out of danger.

The rest of the trip was uneventful. The horses were given leniency, and the pace was relaxed. The baby slept in spurts, and when he was awake, he sat quietly, eating his food, or playing with Etienne. Etienne could not sleep, for his uneasiness increased as they came closer to St. Benoit.

He understood why, when they arrived in the town. Smoke was in the air, thick clouds of black smoke hanging ominously over the village. The driver stopped and requested Etienne to ride up front, as he had forgotten the directions to the Abbey. Etienne was astonished to see the town which he had remembered so vividly.

"My God! What has happened here?" he exclaimed.

"The Revolution is everywhere!" the driver answered with pride.

In front of them, only a vestige of the town remained. The church was still standing, but the Abbey, as well as Abbot de Fleury's residence, had been burned to the ground. It had ocurred recently, since wisps of smoke still curled in the air above the rubble. Several of the buildings around the village had been destroyed, and the streets were empty.

"Let's go," he urged the driver. "I don't like this."

He held the baby tightly, as the carriage picked up its momentum. The smoke had found its way into the forests, for the shafts of sunlight which filtered through the trees were mixed with grey. The acrid smell made his eyes water. On his lap, the child watched the passing scene solemnly.

Etienne was impatient. He could barely contain himself, as he waited for the forests to open to the Abbey land. Finally, he could see the clearing, and he looked up into the hills for the familiar sight of Tristan and his sheep.

There were no signs of life anywhere. Even the vineyards were empty. A numbing feeling spread through him. Slowly, he realized that the smoke was not only coming from St. Benoit, but from the Abbey as well.

[268]

The driver pulled up to the gates, and Etienne saw that they had been burned to charcoal. Behind them, the Abbey lay in ruins, desecrated by the forces of anger and hatred.

"Looks like you no longer have a home, Brother," the driver said.

"Someone must be here." Etienne's optimism seemed false

"Do you want me to wait for you?"

"No," he answered, stepping down, "I'll be all right."

The driver passed the baby to him, and then he removed Etienne's food basket from the coach. "Are you sure?" He did not like the idea of leaving Etienne alone.

"Yes," Etienne assured him. "Nothing more will happen here now."

"Well, I'll be off then" The driver resumed his seat, somewhat uncomfortably. "Good luck to you, Brother."

"Thank you" Etienne watched him turn the horses back toward the town, and then he faced the Abbey ruins.

He put his son down, and looked around the buildings. The stones had been pried apart and thrown indiscriminately around the grounds. The entrance to the Abbey was nothing more than a gaping hole. Etienne could see through the foyer and out to the pastures beyond. The chapel seemed to be partly intact, reminding him that even to angry mobs, some things were sacrosanct. He thought of the library and all of its wonderful books.

He bent down and picked up the baby, positioning the child carefully on his hip. It was difficult for him to carry his own weight much less the child. His movement was painfully laborious. Step by step, they approached the foyer and headed for the chapel. Etienne finally reached the doors and pulled one open.

Inside, the sunlight filtered through the beautiful glass windows, as though nothing had happened and time had stopped. The candelabras had been removed from the altar, and the pews were empty, with the exception of one lone figure sitting quietly.

"Chen!" Etienne called out, relieved. "I knew you would be here!"

Chen turned around and looked at his beloved pupil. He was astonished by the physical change in him. Etienne hardly

[269]

resembled the youth who had left the Abbey eight and a half months ago. His bones stood out in sharp angles, his face was lined and gaunt, and there were streaks of grey in his black hair. Etienne was almost twenty, yet he looked years older. Chen was aware that his youth had left, and it pained his heart.

He walked toward Etienne. It was then that he noticed the child for the first time. He stopped suddenly and looked at the boy, who bore an uncanny resemblance to his father. Except for the eyes, those clear, blue eyes. Chen looked back at Etienne, who waited patiently for his greeting.

"You were gone a long time, T'ien Li," he said softly. "You leave a boy and return a man."

"A lifetime, my beloved teacher." Etienne looked into Chen's glowing eyes. "I'm so happy you are alive!"

"I was with you, T'ien Li, until this." He gestured to the area around him.

"Where is my family, Chen?" Etienne feared the answer.

"Everyone is gone, T'ien Li. Some have left their bodies. Others have disappeared into the forests. Only Gerard is here with me."

"Why?"

"He waited for your return." Chen saw that Etienne was tiring. He reached out to take the baby. "Come, let us sit."

They walked slowly to the front of the chapel where it was sunnier. Chen put the child on the carpet, while he and Etienne sat on a bench.

"Who died?" He had trouble breathing, the weight of Chen's news bearing down on him.

"Almost everyone. Tristan. James. Andrew. Pasqual. They came in the night, a raging storm. Everyone suffocated in the smoke."

"How did you survive?"

"I was in the hills. In your absence, sleep often eluded me."

"And Gerard?"

"He was with the horses. They had been nervous all night, and his concern for them saved his life."

"What is happening, Chen?" Etienne felt that he could hear no more.

[270]

"It is the world of maya, T'ien Li, not the reality," Chen replied. "At the center of the illusory chaos, there is peace. When you live in the center, you see things differently." Chen paused, and Etienne pondered his words.

"Where do I go now?" Etienne put his face in his hands.

"You know the answer, T'ien Li."

"And you? Where are you going? Will you stay with me in Peking, if I choose the path my mother wishes?" In his heart he knew Chen's answer and he was afraid to hear it spoken.

"No, T'ien Li. I shall travel high into the mountains where I will make my home."

"Where?" Etienne's heart fell.

"The Anye Machin Range on the eastern edge of the Tibetan plateau. A place has already been prepared for my arrival." He paused, examining his student more closely. "I have been invited to live in a very small monastery that is nestled in the mountain range. Few go there. I will, T'ien Li."

"Chen, I will miss you." Etienne felt the heaviness of sorrow. "Can I not go with you, if I choose?"

"There is a place for you, if you choose, T'ien Li."

Etienne gave no response. There was a long journey ahead when he would have time to consider his options.

"Shall we find Gerard?" Chen stood. "A ship leaves Marseilles in two day's time. We must go now, T'ien Li, if we are to be on it."

"First, Chen, I must say good-bye to my family. Will you take my son?" Etienne watched him pick up the small child, and he noticed how his teacher had aged.

He left the chapel and walked out to the back of the Abbey where, when last he saw it, there had been only a few graves in the small cemetery. Now, the earth was freshly turned over. Etienne counted eleven new graves. His friends, his parents, his brothers! All of their love and wisdom, all of their efforts with the land and its children, culminating in the ignominy of slaughter!

"Is it God who goes awry, or is it man?" Etienne cried aloud. "Surely their end could have been more graceful, given the peace they brought to this small spot of earth!" He wiped his eyes with his free hand, while his other hand trembled around the cane. "Where

[271]

is the mercy of their beloved God that speaks for this?"

Anger pulsed through Etienne's veins, renewing his strength. He remembered all the injustices man had created through his folly, and he began to question the veracity of the unseen authority that mankind called God. Ambrose was the lucky one, Ambrose and his Brother Theodore, for they had eluded the malignant shadow that had spread across the nation. Etienne was certain that his time in France had ended.

"There is nothing here for me, anymore," he whispered."

"Hello, Etienne." A familiar voice interrupted his melancholy.

Etienne swung around, stumbling from loss of balance. Gerard rushed forward to catch him, and they embraced tearfully. "Oh Gerard! Why did this happen? Why were we spared?"

"We have more work to do, Etienne."

"Are you so sure of that, Gerard?"

"I must believe it, Etienne, or I would bring myself to my own death." Gerard steadied his young friend and looked more closely at him. "I'm glad you've finally arrived."

"I see you haven't been eating your pastries." Gerard's girth was considerably smaller.

"St. Benoit was not a safe place in the last month."

"Who did this, Gerard?" Etienne was unaccustomed to the anger that raged in him.

"The same people who razed the town, Etienne. They felt that we were connected to the St. Benoit Abbey."

"And the Abbot de Fleury? Is he still in the safety of Versailles?"

"No, Etienne. He was there when they seized his abbey."

"I don't understand. Why is it that man can be so hateful?"

Gerard began walking him toward the front of the abbey. "These people have been denied that which is their divine right."

"What is that?"

"A small measure of happiness, security and peace. When one has never experienced it, one becomes poisoned by anger." Gerard took his free arm. "We must leave. You have a ship waiting."

"Where will you go, Gerard?"

"I don't know, Etienne. I don't know."

The carriage was waiting where Gerard had left it before he

went to find Etienne. It lacked the polish it once had, but Etienne could see that it was still sturdy. Almost twenty years ago, it had carried him from the Port of Marseilles to the Abbey in the Forest, and now it was time to return to his roots. The wheel had come full circle.

Chen and the baby were inside with some food and a small bag of clothes. Gerard helped Etienne up the step and watched him seat himself before he shut the door. When Etienne was comfortable, and his cane had been placed on the floor beneath him, Chen held out his hand.

"These are yours, T'ien Li."

Etienne felt something drop into his palm, and when Chen removed his hand, he saw his familiar gold Buddha and his jade rosary. He gently placed them in the pocket of his robe and smiled. He did not look back at the Abbey, as the carriage pulled away. He reminded himself that it was only a memory and that he was to look forward toward the unwritten tomorrows.

Epilogue

By the light of the moon, he watched the small procession walk up the mountain side, their lamps swinging back and forth in synchronization with their movements. He could see that there were five in all, including a guide, a necessity, for on their own they would never have made it.

It was rare that anyone wandered into this part of the Anye Machin Range. The dangers were well known, - precipitous falls into bottomless chasms, wrathful skies bringing forth sudden storms. It was a no man's land at an altitude of twenty thousand feet. Only those beings who lived in their light bodies were able to enjoy this proximity to the heavens.

From this small place on earth, high in the mountains, those who lived in what the natives referred to as the Place of the Sun People, were able to do their work, unhindered by man. Small huts were built into the steep walls of the mountain, all of them connected to a central hall, where the thirteen who lived there met daily to make decisions regarding the world and the path history would take. From the snow covered crags, they sent out their combined forces to protect, and to manifest, that which was yet to come upon the earth.

They envisioned the necessary evil of wars and the ephemeral nature of peace weaving themselves together into the future. Their focus was on a single thread in the tapestry of civilization, one delicate thread that needed their strength of vision to ensure that it would not be broken, in spite of man's attempts to do so. Although the thirteen could not interfere in man's choice of action, they could illuminate the path of least resistance to those visionaries who lifted their sights above that of the masses; who would, through their intense efforts, their dreams and their progeny, herald in new beginnings for mankind.

He was thankful that the travelers had chosen a night when the skies were clear and the weather was bearable for the last part of the

[274]

difficult ascent. Their movement was slow, and he saw that they were extremely fatigued. Patiently, he waited, protected by the warmth of his thick furs and boots. He guided them with his thoughts, so they would not make the wrong turn as they were nearing the base of the steps.

When he could hear the sounds of their breathing in the thin air, he turned and walked back into the hut. The cold night wind blew into the room, and the small pile of cinders in the open stove glowed brightly. After picking up a bundle on the cot, he once again returned to the vantage point, just as the small group reached the top.

One of the men stepped forward to take the bundle. "Will he sleep undisturbed?" he asked.

"He will."

"The Empress wishes to know if you have changed your mind."

The leader could barely make out the face of the man to whom he spoke. He was curious to see it, for much had been said about him, and even in the moonlight, he sensed a holy presence before him. He wondered if the child he held were at all like the father who stood facing him now. To be accepted at his age, and with an illegitimate son, into the Place of the Sun People, said more about him than any of the stories that had circulated regarding his birth or his upbringing. Knowing this was one time in which his curiosity would not be sated, the leader stepped back into the group to wait for an answer.

"Please give Her Highness my deepest love and gratitude. Tell her that I am giving her the son she could never have in me. I know she will raise him well."

"Will there be anything else?" The leader was having trouble with the altitude and needed to return to the base camp.

"One thing more. Please tell the Empress that the child is to know, when he is of an age to understand, that I am watching over him, and that I will always be there to guide him when he is in need. He has only to call my name."

"Very well." the man turned to the guide. "We are ready."

Wearily, the small group retraced their path to the steps and

[275]

began to descend the steep mountainous path winding beneath them.

When they were well on their way, T'ien Li walked back to the hut. His legs were aching, and he needed to sit down. He did not leave the door open any longer than was necessary, and he went directly to the fire to add more wood.

He did not sleep that night. Instead, he watched the cinders reduce themselves to ashes, and when the morning sun moved up the mountains, he was awake to greet its brilliant light. He lifted himself from the bed and picked up his cane before leaving his room and joining the others who were awaiting him in the great hall.

THE END

DARK PLACES, LIGHT PLACES
Share the experience
of this exciting novel with
your friends and family

Also by the same author
REFLECTIONS OF CONSCIOUSNESS
The Zodiacal Journey

A compellingly beautiful perspective on a very complex subject. *Reflections of Consciousness* offers the reader a powerful insight into the dynamic of energy behind each of the twelve astrological signs, as the soul progresses around the Zodiacal wheel. Written from a viewpoint of soul understanding, this little book is for anyone who wishes to penetrate the more superficial aspects of astrology to reach the essential archetype that lies behind each sign.

ORDER FORM